FJORD LAND

M.E. Rostron

Bellingham, Washington

Publisher's Note: This is a work of fiction. Names, characters, places, and incidents are a product of the author's imagination. Locales and public names are sometimes used for atmospheric purposes. Any resemblance to actual people, living or dead, or to businesses, companies, events, institutions, or locales is completely coincidental.

Cover by Kenzie Mahoskey

Ordering Information: orders@villagebooks.com

Fjord Land/ M. E. Rostron. -- 1st ed.
ISBN 978-1-7335229-4-6

Also by M.E. Rostron

Fiction

The Kabul Conscript
Cape Decision

Nonfiction

The Roving Fitzgeralds:
The Memoirs Of Roy Madison Fitzgerald (editor)

To my wife and daughter, and in memory of the daughter and sister who was taken from us much too soon.

In his profession the truth was rarely obvious. Deception and duplicity were expected and more the rule. From his point of view this was a truer reflection of the reality of the human condition than most religious, political, or philosophical apologists provided.
—"The Kabul Conscript"

Skagway, Alaska

On a pleasant morning in early August, 2002 the immense cruise ship, *Opal Princess* disgorged a steady stream of passengers onto the Skagway dock. The ship, nine hundred fifty feet long, with a beam of over one hundred feet, and housing over four thousand passengers and crew—more than twice the swollen summer population of the tourist town itself—was visible from anywhere in town. It towered over the the well preserved gold rush community, whose tallest building, the Golden North Hotel, was a quarter the height of the vessel's two hundred foot tall gleaming white superstructure.

Some summer days during the four month tourist season, Skagway, located at the far northern end of Southeast Alaska's northern most fjord, entertained as many as four of the "Love Boats." Two of the massive vessels could just barely fit end to end at the dock that ran along the steep cliffs on the southeast side of town. One or two more could be shoehorned into the small harbor at the White Pass Railroad pier in front of the town, further to the west.

Sandwiched between the giant floating cities, adding yet more traffic in bodies and automobiles to the mix, were the Alaska Marine Highway facilities; the ferry system that connected the major communities of Southeast Alaska. Although there was plenty of depth to accommodate the thirty foot draft of the largest vessels, the huge tidal fluctuations—fifteen feet and more, presented some challenges to berthing the massive ships. Additionally, the brisk winds that often funneled down Lynn Canal, the long narrow fjord that terminated at Skagway, sometimes prevented the ships from docking. On those occasions they were forced to turn back and substitute a stop at Haines, some fifteen miles further south, or retreat all the way back to Juneau, to the disappointment of both the passengers and the owners of the dozens of gift shops lining Skagway's main thoroughfare, Broadway Street.

On this day the winds were calm, and the captain and crew, aided by the local tugboat had experienced no difficulties in maneuvering or docking. Most of the passengers were headed to the train station to board for the scenic trip up the famed White Pass, one of the two mountain passes leading to the Yukon and the historic gold rush towns in the Canadian interior. Other tourists continued on to the picturesque restored downtown, to run the gauntlet of the gift shops lining the wooden boardwalks of the eight block long business district.

The Jenkins family; Jim and his wife, Denise; Jim's sister, Tess; and their children; eight year old Jimmy Jr., and twelve year old Samantha, had previously purchased a tour package which included the train trip, and an afternoon helicopter excursion to the glacier fields in the mountains above Skagway. It was their first trip to Alaska, and first on a cruise ship. All, especially Jimmy Jr., were excited to explore the town.

"Let's stay together now, Jimmy!" his father called as the exuberant boy ran ahead along the dock, threading his way through the other disembarking passengers.

"Ah dad—you guys are too slow! I want to see those pictures on the rocks," he called, pointing at the spray painted words and images that decorated (or defaced, some said) the sheer cliffs above the dock.

"Maybe we can on the way back. We don't have time for that now—come on back now, Jimmy!" his mother insisted.

But the boy had been cooped up for too long on the tour ship, and continued on, ignoring the entreaties of his parents.

"Samantha—go get your brother and bring him back here! We've only got thirty minutes until the train leaves." her aunt Tess ordered.

It was her opinion that her younger brother and his wife were much too lenient with their son.

The girl, more obedient than her unruly brother, darted off after the boy. She caught him just as he was attempting to climb over the dock railing.

"What are you doing, Jimmy? Why do you always have to cause trouble?"

"There's something down there—I saw it, Sam! Let go of me!"

"You can't go down there. The sign says keep off. Anyway, you'll probably fall in and they'll have to get the fire department and police to rescue you."

Still, Samantha was intrigued.

"Look yourself," her brother said, pointing to one of the gaps between the thick planks of the dock.

His sister got down on her knees and peered into the shadowy darkness of the understructure. She caught her breath. Her brother was right. Something, or rather someone, was half floating in the nest of beams below.

A half hour later the police and fire department personnel had the area above the find roped off. A few curious tourists lingered with cameras at the ready, but most, including the Jenkins family had moved on to the somewhat less morbid attractions of the historic gold rush town.

In the water below the dock the Skagway chief of police, Dan Segrestein, Tim Vesti, an off-duty officer who had answered the chief's urgent request for help, and Ray Standers, the Alaska Department of Fish and Game supervisor from Haines, who was visiting Skagway on a poaching investigation, approached the body cautiously in the Fish and Game launch.

The dead man was wedged between two large beams. A rope around his neck tied off to another beam held the corpse's upper torso out of the water, so that the body moved like a grotesque marionette with the undulation of the wavelets lapping at the pilings. A sheet of cardboard, damp from exposure was pinned to the body's chest with an unusual looking knife.

Various sized letters cut from magazines were glued to the placard The message read: "TOUR SHIPS OUT OF ALASKA—LAST WARNING!" Pasted below this message was a cartoon image, also cut from a magazine, of a bundle of dynamite with a lighted fuse.

Ray tied the skiff off and let it drift away a few feet. Officer Vesti, an accomplished amateur photographer, took photos from different angles as Ray slowly pulled the boat back in hand over hand. After putting on gloves, Ray untied the rope holding the body to the beam, while the police chief and his fellow officer gingerly slid the victim aboard. The chief extracted the dead man's wallet. It was soaking wet, but his ID was laminated and legible.

"I recognize him. He was some sort of federal agent—name's Jack Dolon," the chief observed, before depositing the wallet and ID into an evidence bag."

"That's a rare and very old Tlingit knife," Ray commented, as they motored back to the small boat harbor.

"Hopefully the lab can lift some fingerprints from it," Chief Segrestein remarked.

They docked the boat and transferred the body to Skagway's only ambulance—a vehicle which doubled as the town's hearse—from which it would be transferred to a small plane and flown seventy-five miles south to the coroner in Juneau.

After the plane took off with its grisly cargo the three officers gathered at the Skagway police station to discuss the morning's discovery.

"Please, not a word to the press, or anyone else—not even your families—until I get some direction from Juneau on this," the chief urged.

"Of course," Ray responded. "That threat to the cruise ships makes this a matter for the feds."

"Yep—9-11 changed everything last year, and anything that even remotely smacks of terrorism gets immediate attention—as it should. Anyway we don't have the resources to handle this on our own, and I'd bet Juneau doesn't either. The state and feds will want your negatives, Tim, but before we send those in I'd like you to develop some prints for our own use."

"I'm on it, boss," he replied.

The officer picked up his camera case and left the office for the make-shift dark room he had set up in the furnace room at the back of the police station.

"I imagine the FBI or CIA, or some other agency will send people in to investigate in the next few days, but in the meantime I'd like to hear any ideas or obser-vations you might have before we send our reports on to Tenax," the chief continued.

Sergeant Joe Tenax was the Juneau based state trooper in charge of investigations in Skagway, Haines, and the areas north of the capitol city, and Ray Standers' boss. The "Brown Shirts," a law enforcement agency unique to Alaska, performed tasks that included wildlife regulations enforcement and regular state trooper duties.

"I have a couple of thoughts," Ray replied.

"I knew that guy a little too. I worked with him last year briefly on a case—that drug bust down in Juneau, you might recall. Charlie Jackson got mixed up in a smuggling operation trying to pay off his ex-wife. Jack Dolon was some sort of special agent working that case. He never said which federal agency he worked for —I gathered that was classified. He was pretty tight-lipped. We spent two days on the water together, and I don't think he put together more than three or four sentences."

"That's another reason the feds will waste no time getting here," Chief Segrestein observed.

"Also, whoever killed Dolon knew something about knots—maybe a fisherman or logger. That's a textbook hangman's knot around his neck, and he was tied to that beam with a nice double bowline," Ray observed.

"Anything else?" the police chief asked.

"The knife, of course. There aren't many like that around. It's a museum quality artifact, and worth a lot to the tribe, and to collectors and historians. I'll get hold of you if anything else comes to mind. I'll be in town for a couple more days at least. I got a room at the Skagway Inn this trip—damned lucky to score that as busy as it is around here this time of year."

"Well, try to stay out of trouble Ray, I've got enough problems on my hands," the chief joked as the Fish and Game officer got up to leave.

"You got it Dan. I promise to be a good boy scout and stay out of the Moe's and the Red Onion—at least while I'm on duty," he quipped, naming two of the several lively Skagway bars.

CHAPTER 1

An Intriguing Call

As David Stuckrath was enjoying his second cup of coffee on an early spring morning in Bellingham, Washington, his recently acquired cell phone rang. He did not recognize the number, but the area code was 907—Alaska. It was probably someone he knew, also with a new cell phone, as the gizmos were becoming quite popular in the north, now that there was finally limited service in some parts of the state. Juneau had been his home for the previous twenty years, so he answered.

"I'd like to speak to David Stuckrath," the masculine voice replied.

"Speaking, who is this?"

"Hey David—it's your old college dorm buddy Larry—Larry Nemous—class of '72—remember?"

"Wow, what a pleasant surprise! it's been a few years. What inspired your call, Larry?"

"Well, it's not entirely social, although I hope we can catch up on each others lives this summer. I'm calling from Sitka, and I've got a proposition for you, David."

"Alaska—I thought you had moved back to Wyoming?"

"That's a long story, best told around a campfire with drinks at hand. As you know I did go on to get my doctorate in archeology. Until this spring I had been teaching in Casper, but since last summer I've been up in Alaska doing some excavating on Kuiu Island. I've got a pretty good budget to work with, an intimidatingly large area to explore, and a real need for a historian with some local knowledge. Naturally I thought of you."

"Larry, I'm complimented, I really am, but I don't have any desire to go back up north. I left Juneau for good last year after my son was killed. Anyway, I'm not a professional historian—I just teach high school history—that is, I used to..."

"I know about your son, David, and I'm so sorry to hear of your family's tragedy. I can certainly understand why you might not want to return, but you won't have to go near Juneau if you don't want too, and I really could use your help. Beyond that, there is an intriguing historical mystery on the island that I hope to unravel, and I think you'll find it pretty compelling too. Don't be so damned modest. You're one of a handful of experts on Southeast Alaskan 18th and early 19th centuries history. I read your master's thesis on Russian boatbuilding in Yakutat—excellent sleuthing!"

"I don't know, Larry. I'm pretty comfortable here in Bellingham. Karen and I separated after my son's death, but my daughter, Cindy is living here with me. She's graduating from high school this spring, and I feel like it might be my last summer to spend much time with her before she's off to college and her own future. That means even more to me now that Marshall is gone."

"I get that, David, but do an old friend this one favor; have lunch with me next week. I'm flying down to Seattle for a few days. Let me lay out the whole situation for you before you make up your mind. I can either drive up to Bellingham, or you can come down to Seattle—or we can meet somewhere in-between if you like. Bring your daughter too! I'd love to see her."

David and his daughter, Cindy met Larry Nemous for lunch at an Everett waterfront restaurant a week later. It was Cindy who ultimately helped the archeologist persuade her father to take on the task of investigating another part of Kuiu Island, which Larry Nemous did not think he had the time or manpower to attempt. Larry described the primitive living conditions. He would have to construct a campsite, and rely on infrequent trips to the nearest town, Sitka for supplies. There was no permanent human population on Kuiu Island, an area of 758 square miles—roughly the size of Maui, and larger than Oahu or Rhodes—that harbored the world's densest population of black bears.

Cindy insisted on coming too, and suggested they take their sailboat, the Cape George Cutter, *Lethe* to Kuiu Island as more comfortable, safer living quarters. The boat would also give them more independence and access to Sitka, a small city about a hundred miles away by water from Larry's camp, on the opposite side of the adjacent Baranof Island.

Father and daughter were both experienced sailors. Cindy Stuckrath had done a fair amount of boating with her family before they moved away from Juneau. She had explored the San Juan and Gulf Islands with her father since arriving in Washington state, but she had never sailed the Inside Passage—the eight hundred mile route from Puget sound along the coast of British Columbia and Southeast Alaska. She was excited to make the voyage. David immediately realized the adventure would allow him much more time with his daughter than he would have otherwise had with the inevitable distractions of Bellingham and nearby Seattle and Vancouver.

"Won't you need someone to take photos of the sites?" Cindy asked. "I could do that for you."

"That line item is included in our budget proposal. What's your experience, Cindy?"

"My son's nick-name for her was Annie Oakley," David interrupted. "She's a hell of a shot with a camera or a gun!"

"Seriously, dad! I actually do have professional experience, besides being our school newspaper and sports photographer, I've done quite a bit of freelance work. I've never done any archeology shoots, but I'm sure I can handle it."

"Do you have some examples of your work I could see?"

Sure, and I've just started building a website you can check out too," Cindy replied.

"Well that's quite a score for our crew." The archeologist declared. "A photographer and historian package deal!"

"We won't be available until Cindy graduates," David said.

"That's good timing, actually. I won't be on site myself until the end of June My funds aren't unlimited, but I can certainly pay your expenses and a reasonable salary for at least two months. In fact, you living on your sailboat simplifies a few logistical problems and saves expenses, I would think," Larry replied. "I assume you have an inflatable or some sort of dinghy, which means I won't have to buy or rent another one for the expedition."

"So now that you've cast your line, what's that bait you said I would be so excited to rise to?" David quipped.

"As I said earlier, my crew is investigating some caves and middens in Port Malmesbury. We're primarily interested in verifying the chronology and reexamining some sites earlier archeologists identified and recorded back in the 1970s, but didn't have the time, funds, or permission to properly excavate. In 1954 a prospector found a metal plate inscribed in latin which he reported, and a rubbing was even sent to the Smithsonian. The plate seemed to date from the sixteenth century, possibly from the Francis Drake expedition of 1577-1580, but the Smithsonian told the miner it was most likely a hoax. Subsequently the plate was lost or stolen, but we now think we know which cave it came from. My team will be reexamining that in greater detail, along with our other sites—and this is where you come in, David."

"You want us to help excavate more caves, then?"

"Yes, but you'll be on your own, north of my camp in Tebenkof Bay. A few months ago I was contacted by Ray Standers, the head Fish and Game officer and biologist based in Haines. He had a report from a Juneau fisherman who was concerned about a boat he had seen anchored in Tebenkof Bay last fall. The fisherman went over to say hello, but when he got close a man he didn't recognize—definitely not any fisherman he knew—ran down to the beach and shooed him away with a shotgun. He was angered by the incident and curious, so he hung around out of sight on the other side of the ridge over in Petrof Bay until he heard the boat leave a few hours later. He went to the spot and found the tracks of the men leading up into the brush and trees inland. It seemed suspicious, so he reported it to the troopers."

"I know Ray a little. His kid and my son Marshall sometimes snowboarded together with several other boys. Ray helped investigate the death of Henry Daise, the judge who sentenced my son to prison, where he was killed. I like Ray—he's a hell of an advocate for the salmon and the environment, and not afraid to speak his mind."

"Ray decided it was worth looking into, so he investigated. He thought maybe some poaching was going on, or illegal digging in one of the old Tlingit burial caves. You will of course remember that Tebenkof Bay had a major Tlingit settlement until a small pox epidemic decimated the population in the early 1800s, and the few survivors moved away. In case Ray found any evidence of mischief, the fisherman had given him the boat registration numbers, so he could find the scalawags. What he found was far more interesting, and is the reason I wanted you up here. I remember you went on some archeology digs in college, and you've got far more knowledge of Southeast Alaskan history than I do."

"So what did he find?" Cindy prompted, impatiently.

Larry ignored her interruption but picked up the pace of his delivery.

"Ray followed a path until it appeared to end at a dense thicket. But he's an expert at tracking, and it didn't take him long to figure out the men had purposely disguised their real route. The trail leading to the thicket was just a diversion. Their actual track led to a small cave in the side of a cliff that was hidden behind some thick overgrowth. Ray saw that the floor of the cave had been recently dug up. There were old bones scattered around, and signs that the cave had been used by the Tlingit many years earlier. Ray had his camera, as he was prepared to document any animal remains if he found evidence of poaching. When his camera flash went off he saw a bright reflection at the back of the cave. This is what he found."

With a dramatic flourish Larry dropped the object on their restaurant table.

"What the hell?" David said, picking up the coin.

David's master's thesis had been on the subject of early Russian activity in Alaska, and he had taught history at the Juneau high school before resigning and moving to Washington after the death of his son. He liked to keep abreast of the latest developments in Alaskan history and archeology. David was aware of Samuel Bawlf's theory that Sir Frances Drake's expedition may have made it that far north, but no concrete evidence had surfaced that he knew of, and most historians dismissed Bawlf's arguments, though there were stories passed down by the indigenous tribes of a visit by Europeans generations before the Russians, Captain Vancouver, or the Spanish explorers arrived in the late eighteenth century. Additionally, over the years a few items salvaged from shipwrecks and dating from an earlier period had been found along the northwest coasts of Canada and Alaska.

"Ray found this on Kuiu Island? This is a sixteenth century Spanish real!"

"Specifically, it is a type 1542 one real minted some time between 1568 and 1572 in Lima, Peru. I had it checked by a professional numismatist. That was one of the reasons I came down to Seattle. I think it's possible it came from the Spanish ship that Drake captured on his voyage north along the west coast of the Americas. Somehow it ended up here, and that's the mystery I hope you can help us with."

"Incredible!" David said, reluctantly handing the silver coin back to the archeologist, who passed it over to Cindy.

"What do you think, Cindy?" Larry asked.

Cindy examined the silver coin closely, surprised at its weight.

"It looks brand new."

"I had it cleaned, but you're right, it looks newly minted. I don't think it was ever in circulation. It was most likely part of a shipment of precious metals en route to Europe to add to the coffers of the Spanish crown."

"Kuiu Island was where that cougar killed the man who murdered Marshall, wasn't it?"

The Stuckraths had agreed shortly after Marshall's death to never utter the name of their son's killer, Grant Tadlock. Tadlock had died after being mauled by a mountain lion the year before, near Gedney Harbor, a few miles southwest of Tebenkof Bay on Kuiu Island.

"Yes, it is. There are several small caves—really more like grottos, located in the same general area, according to what Ray told me," Nemous replied.

He didn't know if the death of Marshall Stuckrath's killer on Kuiu Island would influence David's decision one way or the other.

"I definitely want to go there then," Cindy said.

"This is a pretty odd coincidence, or synchronicity, or something like that. I guess our business in Alaska must be in some way unfinished," David mused, half to himself.

"Good! It will be great to have you up there—both of you!" Larry Nemous declared, a little too brightly.

After the archeologist insisted on picking up the restaurant tab they said their goodbyes in the parking lot, with plans to rendezvous in Port Malmesbury, the location of Larry Nemous' archeology base camp. There he would see to it that they got any needed supplies for their sojourn on Kuiu Island.

"You've got to call mom and invite her. She'll be on summer vacation. She should be there with us," Cindy said, as David threaded his way through the I-5 traffic on their way back to Bellingham.

"What makes you think she'll come? Do you know something I don't?"

David and his wife, Karen had separated shortly after their son was killed. David left Juneau on their sailboat, ultimately settling in Bellingham with his daughter, soon to be a freshman at the university there. Karen had sold their home in Alaska and moved to Eugene, Oregon, taking a job as an assistant to a professor at the University of Oregon. Although David had repeatedly begged her to join them in Bellingham, and had made several trips to visit her in an effort to repair their marriage, she had so far refused.

"I think I can talk her into going with us. Let me try at least."

Cindy wanted more than anything to see her parents back together. She too had tried repeatedly to persuade her mother to rejoin them.

"Don't you love dad anymore," she had asked, on her last visit a few weeks earlier.

"Of course, I will always love David. But everything is spoiled for me now—even marriage. I just can't bear the idea of living that intimately with anyone, even your dad."

"What about me? I live there too?"

"You could move down here with me, and still visit your father often—even go up and sail in the summer. I could get a bigger apartment. You could transfer to the U of O," Karen suggested.

"Dad needs me, and I've made friends in Bellingham."

"So that's it—you must have a boyfriend! Tell me about him."

"I said friends, not a boyfriend, mom. But yes, I am dating someone."

"You can't fool your old mother," Karen said. She took her daughter's face in her hands, then stepped back and studied her.

"When did you become such a ravishing beauty, Cindy? I imagine you will drive those college boys crazy."

"Dad says I look just like you did at my age, when you both met in Afghanistan, only taller."

"Really? That seems so long ago," Karen said, wistfully. "I just might have to make a trip up to Bellingham—if only to meet your boyfriend."

They did not talk again of a possible reunion that visit, and Cindy, not wanting to build up her dad's hopes, had not told him of the conversation. Some of the best times they'd ever had as a family were sailing their boat, *Lethe* on the spectacular fjords of Southeast Alaska. Karen felt sure that she could talk her mother into joining them if it involved a sailing adventure.

CHAPTER 2

Dyea

On July 23, 2002, a lateral moraine of the West Creek Glacier liquefied, causing debris to slide into a glacial lake located in front of the glacier's terminus. The debris displaced a large volume of lake water into West Creek, generating a tremendous flood that poured into the Klondike Gold Rush National Historic Park and the community of Dyea, Alaska. This flood caused extensive damage to private property, bridges and roads, and forced the immediate evacuation of Dyea residents and approximately 50 campers from nearby campgrounds. This flood event surpassed the estimated 500-year flood for West Creek, producing a peak discharge of 16,209 cubic feet per second.

Safe in his hillside cabin far from the affected area, the July 23 flood of West Creek and the Taiya River had not impacted Hiram Hatcher directly, though many of the Taiya River valley residents suffered property damage, and the valley and campgrounds had to be evacuated. Fortunately the water had gone down quickly, and most were able to return to their homes the following day.

Hiram knew all of the handful of people who, like him were year round residents of Dyea. He enjoyed winter in the small valley as much or more than the other seasons. He liked the schnapps fueled cross country skiing parties, the holiday celebrations, and the casual winter get-togethers with his neighbors. In the summer the area saw its population grow to over thirty residents and many more campers. Earlier that summer the electric company had begun work on extending power lines from Skagway to Dyea. This new convenience would inevitably bring even more people to the area, a prospect that displeased Hiram and some of the other residents.

All the residents pitched in to help their neighbors clean up after the flood. On his way back home, after a strenuous afternoon of shoveling mud and muck a few days after the disaster, Hiram encountered campers under some scraggly trees that grew close by the cliff near where the trail to his cabin began. Although they were technically trespassing, a few scattered encroachers were tolerated as long as there were no complaints by the residents while repairs were made to the park campgrounds. There were three of them; two young men and a very attractive woman, seated under a makeshift tarp awning attached to their vehicle, an early 1970s Dodge van with Washington state license plates.

"Are you thirsty?" The woman called out to him, holding out a can of beer.

It was a warm afternoon and Hiram had worked up a good sweat shoveling and raking the heavy flood deposited sludge and gravel.

"I'm not going to say no to that!"

"Pull up a stump and rest your butt—the beer is cold," one of them, a slight man with long hair tied in a pony tail offered.

The woman handed him a PBR. Hiram took a long swig from the can.

"Ah—that hits the spot—thanks! I'm Hiram, Hiram Hatcher."

"Fantastic—I love alliteration in a name! I'm Mary Murphy—so we have that in common. This is my twin brother, Simon," she said, giving the pony-tailed man a gentle punch in the shoulder.

"Actually, I'm the oldest, by almost three minutes. Liam here is the baby, by age, but not by size, as you can see. You'll find he's often a man of few words."

Liam was an imposing figure—bulky tattooed arms, bald-headed and black bearded, with the build of a habitual barbell booster. He didn't smile, or offer his hand.

"I talk plenty if I've got something to say. Some people talk too much for their own good," Liam retorted.

Hiram noticed the man's remark seemed aimed at his brother. He had the feeling he'd interrupted a family quarrel.

"Hiram hatcher, eh? H. H.—like Humbert Humbert," Simon said.

"My brother practically worships Nabokov. He's a writer, though he's never published anything."

Mary was grateful for the distraction, which was why she had called out to the stranger. It didn't hurt that he was good-looking in a rugged sort of way, and seemed amiable.

"Does your middle name start with an H too—like H. H. Holmes, the serial killer?" Liam asked, sardonically.

"Be nice Liam, I'm sure he's no monster," Mary scolded her brother. "Anyway, that wasn't Holmes' real name. Maybe you're more the Hugh Hefner or Howard Hughes type, Hiram?"

"Ha, ha–if only I had that kind of money. I'm certainly no Heinrich Himmler or Harry Houdini, and I can't write like Herman Hesse, or play the keys like Herbie Hancock—maybe more the Hubert Humphrey type—at least politically."

"Well, better Hubert Humphrey than Herbert Hoover," Simon opined.

"I saw your rig down at the campgrounds a few days before the flood. Were you here for that?" Hiram asked, thinking it best to change the subject. In his experience it was never good to talk politics or religion with strangers.

"Luckily we missed it. We were up in the Yukon. But we like it out here in Dyea. It's peaceful—too damn many tourists in the towns this time of year," Simon answered.

"But since we're visitors ourselves, we really have no right to complain," Mary corrected her brother.

"I feel the same way. Except for the weather, summer's my least favorite time of the year here," Hiram declared.

"We thought you might be coming over to give us the bum's rush. One of the locals asked us to move yesterday, so we found this spot. There aren't many places to camp this time of year, it seems," Mary observed.

"True, and with the campground shut down, even less than usual. But you should be okay for a while, as long as you pick up after yourselves and don't raise too big a ruckus. I live in a cabin above the ridge. I've got no problem with you staying here," Hiram reassured the trio.

"Do you live here year round?" Mary asked.

She really was exceptionally pretty, Hiram thought. Her thick, brown hair was cut very short, in contrast to her twin brother's long locks. She was obviously and fetchingly braless in a tight cut-off tee shirt that left her midriff bare. Her tanned, shapely legs might be those of a figure skater or a dancer, Hiram fantasized.

"I do. Winter's a great time in Dyea—just the locals and occasional Canadian visitors, and I don't mind the mostly dry cold."

"What the hell do you do all winter to keep from going crazy?" Simon asked.

"You do have to be the type that can entertain yourself. I've got my chores—woodcutting, keeping the place warm, shoveling snow, and feeding the chickens. When the snow gets deep enough I do a little cross country skiing. I go to Skagway once a week or so, and now and then up to Whitehorse for a little R & R—and I've got my art projects to keep me occupied."

Somehow, when he tried to explain the joys of living off the grid and away from town it sounded unexciting and quotidian, but Hiram enjoyed his way of life, and he was almost never bored.

"That doesn't sound so bad to me," Mary said. "We grew up on Orcas Island—you know where that is? It's about as rural as it gets in Washington state. I wouldn't trade that for the finest city apartment or condo."

"Yeah—except that's all gone now," Simon said, sullenly.

His sudden shift in mood took Hiram by surprise.

"Well fuck that anyway! I'm in the mind for something a bit stronger than beer."

Simon rummaged in the van and emerged after a few minutes with a bottle of tequila.

"I packed it so well, I couldn't remember where I put it. Anyone else want a shot?"

"Oh why not," Hiram said. "Tequila and warm afternoons were made for each other, and there aren't all that many warm days in most Alaskan summers."

The bottle made the rounds. Mary retrieved more beer from the cooler. As the booze loosened their tongues, except for Liam, who seemed to grow more taciturn with every drink, Hiram found that the siblings shared his views about the cruise ships and corporate tourism. Additionally, they seemed to harbor a special hostility towards the railroad.

"Without the railroad, they wouldn't have a tenth as many cruise ships," Simon declared.

"I don't know—a lot of people get excited about the old gold rush era buildings the park has restored, and national parks always attract a lot of tourists," Hiram argued.

"I guess you can't burn the damn place down, like what happened to most of the old Western boomtowns. I hear they've installed sprinklers in all those old buildings," Mary joked.

"Skagway has plenty of attractions for visitors even without the railroad. It was closed down for a few years in the 1980s, and there were still lots of love boats and thousands of tourists. They like watching Soapy get shot at the Days of 98 show, and they flock to all the gift shops and bars to piss away their money. I guess if Soapy Smith was around today, he'd find some way to skim his share from the tourists instead of the miners," Hiram said.

"Of course you know the railroad bosses had Soapy killed. They put Jesse Murphy up to it—blackmailed him into doing their dirty work." Mary declared.

"Well, from what I've read I agree it wasn't Reid who fired the shot that finished off Soapy, but I don't think anyone knows exactly why Jesse Murphy did it, or what happened to him after. He vanished from the historical records, and there was no serious inquiry. They made Reid a hero, though his character seems to have been at least as bad as Soapy Smith's," Hiram opined.

"Hey—who knows, maybe you guys are related to the guy who really killed Soapy—but I guess Murphy's a common enough name."

"We do know why Jesse did it, and how it all came down," Simon replied.

Liam shot him a warning look, but said nothing.

"How did you come by that special knowledge? Are you a historian, or are these tequila visions?" Hiram said, laughing. He was getting pretty drunk, and the Murphys had at least matched him drink for drink.

"Jesse Murphy was our great grandfather," Mary announced.

"She's telling the truth. We got the whole story from grandma before she died," Simon confirmed.

"Have you traveled here to set the record straight? You should talk to Hunter Clio, the local newspaper publisher, or Soapy's grandson, Jeff Smith who's writing a book about his infamous ancestor. Of course they'll need to see the proof that you really are Jesse Murphy's descendants before either of them will publish your story."

They seemed sincere, but Hiram was skeptical. He'd read a fair amount about Soapy Smith and Skagway history, but never anything about the fate of Jesse Murphy.

"We're giving our options some thought. We have Jesse's confession to grandma that he killed Soapy Smith. Jesse worked for the railroad in 1898. He was a guard on that pier the night Soapy was killed, and he had Soapy's rifle at the end. That much is documented. Whether Jesse Murphy took it upon himself to finish Soapy off, or was asked or encouraged to do it by Graves and the other railroad men depends on whether you believe he was telling the truth to our grandmother," Mary replied.

"But we do have the Orcas Island property deed. It was signed July 10, 1898—two days after Soapy was killed, by Samuel Graves, the president of the railroad and head of the vigilante group trying to get rid of Soapy and his gang. It was witnessed by a railroad lawyer. It's a transfer of sixty acres for 'services rendered,'" Simon added.

"You really are serious! You actually have an 1898 land deed from the railroad?"

Technically not from the railroad itself, but from one of the main backers," Simon explained.

Mary went to the van and retrieved two plastic bags.

"This one is the deed. Don't take it out of the bag —it's pretty fragile. The other is Jesse's confession. His son's wife, our grandmother wrote it down," Mary said.

The property deed was yellowed and the writing had faded, but the date, text and signatures were legible.

"If that document can be verified, it would convince me and a lot of other people that your ancestor was paid off for committing murder. Otherwise, why give him property so far away, and why did he leave Skagway immediately after Soapy's death, when he was employed by the railroad and could have kept on working?"

"Jesse was in no position to refuse. He'd shot a wounded, defenseless man, and might have been arrested. Frank Reid shot Soapy twice. Neither shot would have killed him, but Soapy had mortally wounded Reid. Jesse took Soapy's rifle and killed him with it after the duel was over," Mary continued.

"Jesse came up to Skagway from Washington, and sailed on the same ship with Graves. He intended to look for gold, but ended up working for the railroad. He told grandma that Graves convinced him the good mining claims in the Yukon were all taken, and he could make far better money working for a sure thing. One of the group of English railroad investors had property in the San Juan and Gulf Islands. Grandma said the arrangements were made to shut Jesse up and get him quickly out of Skagway after Soapy's death," Simon explained.

"Why do you even give a shit about any of this stuff—family honor?" Hiram asked. "I don't get it. Maybe I'm just too drunk," he added, taking another pull from the tequila bottle, which was by now nearly empty.

"Oh, it's not Jesse's reputation, or even getting the history right that we care about. It pisses us off that Reid was made a hero, when he had a pretty shady background himself, but that wouldn't have been reason enough to come up here. Don't get the idea we're living in the past," Simon replied.

"But if not to set the record straight, why come here—just to see where it all happened?"

"Maybe it's nobody's business, and maybe you've already shot your mouth off enough, Simon," Liam said, glaring at his brother.

Simon turned to Liam, started to respond, but his sister interrupted.

"Our grandmother died a few months ago. Grandpa Murphy had already drowned in a fishing accident over ten years earlier, and grandma never remarried. She and grandpa had spent their entire lives on Orcas Island, and raised our dad there. They worked hard—built a nice home, a barn, logged part of the acreage, and planted an orchard. Grandpa and dad were also commercial fishermen. They led busy lives, and were pretty well off by island standards. After grandpa died dad and mom came back to Orcas to help grandma with the property. The three of us—Simon, Liam, and myself—had moved around a lot after high school, but we always returned to the island summers to fish and work in the orchard. Naturally we expected dad and mom would inherit the property when grandma died, but that's not what happened," Mary related.

"It's complicated, but basically our great grandpa fucked up," Simon interjected.

"Jesse's wife left him for another man. He saw little of his son, our grandfather and his only child, after his wife moved off the island. He started drinking and gambling, and accumulated some serious debts. He must have felt like the railroad still owed him. He tried to blackmail them—threatening to tell the press about the railroad's role in Soapy Smith's death, and their part in cheating Soapy's wife out of her share of Soapy's money and property. The railroad ignored Jesse, and the press wasn't interested, or didn't believe him. But one of the original English railroad investors decided the publicity might hurt the bottom line. He paid off Jesse's debts, but only after forcing him to sign over the acreage as collateral and agreeing to a high interest mortgage contract," Simon continued.

"Grandpa sobered up for a few years, worked hard, and made his payments. Then he got word his ex-wife had died in a car wreck. He'd never given up hope of winning her back. He started drinking again and defaulted on his payments. Another of the big railroad stockholders lived in Victoria, B.C., and bought the property. Although Jesse eventually got clean again and offered to buy back the land, the new owner would only agree to a lease, renewable at the landowner's pleasure every ten years. The lease was renewed every time until a few months ago when the property changed hands again, and grandma got a letter informing her that the new owners were taking possession. They gave her six months to move out," Simon continued.

"Shit—that's harsh!" Hiram exclaimed.

"Harsh enough. She had a stroke and died a few weeks after she got that letter. Our parents hired a lawyer, and offered a good price for the property, which was refused. They went to court to try to make their case, but lost again—so here we are, living in this crappy old van, homeless and hopeless. Dad and mom spent every dime they had fighting to get that property back."

"Things may not be entirely hopeless," Simon disagreed. "We've still got options. The Alaska press might be interested in our story, and we could appeal directly to the railroad. Or there might be other ways to pressure the owner or the railroad to return what is rightfully ours."

As the afternoon wore on they eventually drank all the Murphy's tequila and beer. Hiram invited the siblings up to his cabin for dinner.

"I'm blasted, and hungry as hell. I've got a big pot of stew and some left over apple pie you're welcome to, up at my place."

Mary and Simon were quick to agree, and even Liam admitted he could use something to soak up the booze. They spent the rest of the afternoon and evening eating, talking, and drinking up much of Hiram's beer stash, which he kept in a sort of makeshift root cellar partially dug into the ground, just off the path that led to the chicken coop and outhouse.

"There's one more six-pack out there, if you're still thirsty," Hiram finally said, "but I'm done for the night." It was nearly midnight, and Hiram was feeling drowsy.

"Sure, why not," Simon said. "One for the road!"

"More like one for the ditch," Mary countered. "You're certainly in no shape to drive anywhere—hopefully you can still stumble down the trail to the van without falling on your faces! I'll go with you, Hiram, I could use some fresh air."

Mary held open the rough wooden door of the root cellar while Hiram retrieved the last of his beer. When he came out, without saying a word, she took the beer from him, sat it on the ground, and kissed him.

"You're full of surprises," Hiram said.

"You don't like surprises?"

"I didn't say that."

They kissed again, longer, and Mary guided Hiram's hand up under her shirt.

"How 'bout staying for breakfast," Hiram suggested, blearily.

"That sounds wonderful. Do you have room in bed for two?"

"It'll be tight, but I think we'll manage."

"We were beginning to think you got lost, or maybe eaten by a bear," Simon joked when the two returned.

Mary aimed a scowl at her brother.

"I guess it's time for us to mosey on down to the van, Liam" Simon said, after the two bothers had downed another beer each. "Thanks for your hospitality, Hiram," he added.

"Come on up in the morning. There'll be coffee in the pot. The hens are laying, and I've got a couple pounds of bacon in the cooler," Hiram offered.

The next morning Hiram suggested that Mary stay with him. "...at least while you're in Skagway."

She readily agreed. She was tired of camping, and the siblings' budget did not allow for better lodgings. Hiram was an enthusiastic lover, not without a certain rough charm, and obviously smitten.

Her brothers continued to sleep in the van, most days showing up at Hiram's cabin just before the dinner hour. Mary was close to her brothers, and liked the way Hiram welcomed them. She had long ago vowed never to marry or have children, but if not for that, she imagined she could do much worse than this maverick woodsman. Mary would not allow that she had ever been in love (teen-age infatuation did not count), but as the days went on, and their mutual lust for each other showed no signs of flagging, she admitted, but only to herself, that this might be as close to that fabled state as she had ever been.

For Hiram, there were no doubts. He had found the woman of his dreams, and lived in a constant state of what he could only characterize as a sort of excited contentment, where all his senses seemed preternaturally acute, and each day seemed filled with infinite potential. All his old routines became numinous. He delighted in showing Mary and her brothers the details of his way of life and the place where he lived; the little garden he struggled to keep up just beyond the root cellar; the daily schedule of chopping wood, feeding the chickens, and gathering eggs, and the network of old trails that led into the valley and along the mountain side.

Hiram didn't own a vehicle. The Murphy's van made life easier. Hiram didn't have to hitchhike or wait for neighbors to give him a ride to Skagway. Liam helped out splitting and stacking the cords of wood that would be needed to keep his cabin and workshop warm during the long winter. Liam relished the physical exertion, and the wood pile grew at a rapid rate.

Hiram was proud of the metal sculptures he cut and welded in the old shed. Mary could appreciate Hiram's obvious talent, but the Murphy brothers were more interested in the old mine shaft hidden beneath the building where Hiram created his art. For a few days that July and August of 2002 Hiram was happier than he had ever remembered being, but like the brief, intense northern summers, that joy and contentment would not last.

CHAPTER 3

A Portentous Encounter

Earlier that summer, on their way north to Skagway from Washington the Murphys had met Jim Lothar in Juneau when he towed their van off of the Alaska ferry after it had refused to start. Like more than one man, he had found Mary Murphy too charming to resist after she described their predicament to him. Lothar was at the ferry terminal to see a friend off, and offered to pull the Murphy's van to a Juneau repair shop, saving them the substantial expense of hiring a commercial tow truck. Luckily the problem turned out to be minor, and the repair inexpensive. In gratitude they invited Lothar to stop by their campsite outside of town for dinner and drinks.

In the course of his employment as a bartender and manager at the Moby Dick, a Juneau bar that had existed in one form or another since the 1890s gold rush era, Jim Lothar had picked up a fair amount of local historical mining lore. While they were discussing the region's gold rush history Simon revealed that the Murphy siblings were the descendants of the killer of

Soapy Smith, Jesse Murphy, and had told him about the loss of their inherited property.

Jim Lothar readily sympathized. He had reason to dislike the railroad too. As a teenager he and a friend had been caught stealing tools from the train yard. Because of his youth the railroad had not prosecuted, on condition that he spend one hundred hours clearing brush and picking up trash and construction debris along the route. It had been exhausting and dirty work. Jim still held a grudge against the company. As the Murphy's talked an idea occurred to Jim.

"I'm not surprised you were cheated," Jim said. "Maybe I can help you do something about it."

"How?—and why would you even want to help us?" Liam asked.

"I know those tracks pretty damn well. We can't make them give back your property, as that would obviously tell the railroad who they were dealing with, but we might be able to force them to pay you for your loss. Of course I would expect a token of appreciation for my help."

Mary Murphy, who was idly stirring the coals of the campfire, looked at her brother and shook her head. She had a bad feeling about the man, who had earlier revealed he had done time at the Juneau jail, and was currently on parole. He made no effort to hide his salacious scrutinization of her. But Liam and Simon had both hit it off with the friendly, loquacious ex-bartender and were intrigued. The three had come north with no specific plan. They had discussed the possibility of making their case directly to railroad officials in Skagway or Whitehorse, or perhaps bringing their situation to the attention of the local press, but they could not agree on a definite strategy.

"...a small token? Mary asked.

"When you hear my idea I think you'll agree that you'll need my help, and it involves quite a bit more effort on my part than just chaining up to your van," Lothar said, reminding them of their debt to him.

"Okay, so let's hear it," Liam said.

"Now, understand nobody will be harmed, or even put at risk. I know the White Pass route like the back of my hand. There are several places where the train could derail at slow speed without danger to the crew or passengers. It would be up to you to communicate somehow with the railroad officials."

"You're talking of sabotage and extortion! If we're found out, it's prison for all of us," Mary said, but the idea was strangely tantalizing.

"Nobody will find us out if we do it right. You just have to make sure the phone call or letter you send to the railroad is not traceable, and I'll arrange it so we have a secure way for them to get the money to us. I know something about how to do that," Lothar continued.

"I'll bet you do," Mary said, under her breath. "So what's your cut?" she asked.

"Considering my risk, and the favor I would be doing you, I should think a fifty-fifty split after expenses would be more than fair."

"We'll give you twenty-five percent," Simon countered quickly.

"I see some negotiation will be necessary. How much money do you want?" Lothar asked.

"We would need enough to buy something similar to what our family had on Orcas Island. Somewhere in Washington or Oregon—probably around five hundred thousand," Simon replied.

"If you're only willing to offer twenty-five percent for my risk, you'd better ask for a lot more than that," Lothar retorted. "I'm not in for less than a quarter of a million."

"I'm sure there's another way," Mary said. "Anyway, it's getting late, and we've got to get up early tomorrow. We have tickets on the next ferry to Skagway."

"I tell you what," Lothar said. "I'm heading up to Skagway myself in a few days. I'll work out the details. Meanwhile, you go ahead and give it some thought, and we can talk more then. How will I find you?"

"We read about a camping area out in Dyea, a few miles from Skagway. You can find us there when we're not up in the Yukon," Simon answered. "We plan to get up to Dawson City and check out that area too."

"Well, don't do anything foolish, or contact anyone from the railroad or press until we've had a chance to talk more," Lothar said, standing to go. "I really do hope to see you again, no matter what you decide," he continued, directing his lecherous gaze at Mary.

"Ugh! That man gives me the creeps," Mary said after Jim Lothar's pickup pulled out of their campsite.

"We probably won't ever see him again, but I think it's worth thinking about. I do agree we shouldn't talk to anyone from the railroad or the press yet. Let's keep our options open for now," Simon suggested.

"He seems like a somewhat fishy but likable guy, but I agree. Someone like that has little to lose and a lot to gain from a caper like this," Liam agreed.

"In for a penny, in for a pound, if it comes to that. He's not the only one who has nothing much to lose," Mary said.

CHAPTER 4

A Risky Scheme

Jim Lothar walked the few blocks up State Street from his room at the Golden North in Skagway, where two telephone booths stood by the sidewalk adjacent to an empty lot. He didn't want to take the chance that someone from the front desk might listen in on a call from his room. After a few rings Sabastos Melas, the assistant purser for the *Opal Princess* answered the phone.

"What do you want now. I already told you it's too hot to do business," the testy cruise ship's officer answered.

"I've got an idea. I don't need to come aboard. Let me stash the stuff somewhere where you can pick it up—say in the small boat harbor. We don't have to meet. But I tell you I'm almost broke. I've got to have some cash."

"It's still too dangerous. It'll have to wait until my next cruise north. I know there's another detective on board, and I can't risk it."

Melas was wise to be cautious. From his stateroom agent Jack Dolon, disguised as a crew member, listened to the purser's side of the conversation fed to him from a wireless transmitting device he had planted a few days earlier in the purser's room.

"Can't you at least give me a little cash to hold me over? I've got barely enough to pay for a room tonight, and catch the next ferry back to Juneau."

"I'm sorry Jim, you'll just have to make do somehow on your own. Now don't call me again!" Melas said, and hung up.

Lothar really was nearly out of money, and he was starting to think he would have to fence the relics some other way. He had learned it was never good to have all your eggs in one basket, but in this case his other usual source of income, drug dealing, had dried up. His old contacts avoided him, now that he was a convicted felon.

He remembered the wild plan he had suggested to the siblings he had met in Juneau weeks earlier. He recalled the woman, Mary, had been cold to the idea, but the brothers seemed genuinely intrigued. Maybe it wasn't such a crazy plan. It could work, and if it did, he wouldn't have to deal with Sabastos Melas, Craig Martes the poacher, or any like them again. He would be set for quite a while.

He placed a call to an old acquaintance in Skagway, an ex-railroad worker and explosives expert he had dealt with in the past. Jim Lothar and his sometime collaborator, Craig Martes had used dynamite in an only partially successful attempt to rob an old Tlingit burial site. Unfortunately the charge had been excessive and most of the artifacts were destroyed or damaged. Lothar offered the man twice what he wanted for dynamite and blasting caps if he would wait a few days for his money.

As Lothar walked back to the Golden North he saw Simon Murphy coming out of the grocery store. It seemed his luck had changed for the better! Simon had come to town from Dyea to check his email at the library, and pick up groceries and booze. While they sat in the van at the grocery store parking lot Jim explained the details of his plan to Simon.

"It sounds like you've got everything pretty well figured out, but it's still too risky."

"Nobody will get hurt, Simon. I know those tracks and the train schedule. I'll time the charge to go off well before the train gets there. It won't even do much damage, but it will scare the railroad into sending us the money," Lothar insisted. "It's the only way this is going to work. They've got to have a demonstration that we mean business."

"Look Jim, I've got to get back to Dyea. You said you don't leave on the ferry until tomorrow. I'll give it some thought, but I don't want to involve Mary or Liam. We've got plans to go up the road to Whitehorse tomorrow. I'll figure out a way to stay behind. You come on out to Dyea around noon and we'll talk more."

The next morning, when Mary and Hiram walked down the path from Hiram's cabin to her brothers' campsite Simon was not waiting at the van.

"What happened to Simon?" Mary asked.

"He's spent half the morning shitting his brains out in the woods," Liam answered.

After a few minutes Simon appeared, walking slightly bent over, and holding his stomach.

"Do you need to go to the clinic?" Mary asked.

"No—it will pass I'm sure. I probably just over-did it on salmon and beer yesterday, but I'd better stay here. You guys go on without me—I'll be fine. Luckily we've got plenty of toilet paper."

Mary insisted on taking Simon's temperature. After she determined he had no fever, she decided it would be okay to leave him alone. Hiram told him to go up to the cabin, where he would be more comfortable, and at least there was an outhouse.

"You drink lots of liquids—and I don't mean beer, Simon!" Mary ordered.

Simon was relieved to see them go. It was at least two hours to Whitehorse, and assuming they spent another two hours shopping and having lunch there, he didn't expect them back until late afternoon at the earliest. He should be able to go over details with Lothar and make a decision well before the others returned. Unfortunately Jim Lothar arrived at Hiram's cabin two hours late. He was carrying a large canvas duffle bag and was somewhat winded from lugging it up the trail.

"...sorry I'm late. I had some things to take care of in town. Anyway the ferry's running behind."

"Make it quick. I need you out of here before everyone gets back. I don't want my sister, brother, or Hiram to know about this if I decide to go along with it."

"I would have never found you if those girls on their horses hadn't told me where the trail was. Your directions could have been a hell of a lot better. How'd you score this place? Rentals are hard to come by this time of year in Skagway."

"Mary has a new boyfriend. It's his cabin," Simon explained. "Liam and I still sleep in the van. We don't mind—more room now with our sister here."

"I look forward to meeting the lucky fellow," Lothar replied.

"I'd rather not get him involved in this either. It's none of his business, and the less he knows the better. Why the duffle bag?"

"I've got a little problem," Lothar explained. "The word is they've got a bomb and drug sniffing dog team they're bringing in for training at the ferry terminal. I can't risk trying to take this stuff with me to Juneau. Just hide it here somewhere until I come back."

Simon took the bag and unzipped it.

"What the hell! Dynamite sticks and Tlingit relics? There's even a bentwood box in here. What are you up to anyway?"

"The dynamite is extra, left over from what I used on the tracks, in case we need a little more persuasion. For your information, some of the relics are Haida, not just Tlingit, and It's none of your business what I'm doing with those."

"It is my business if you're up to something that's likely to attract more attention to us, assuming I even agree to your plan!" Simon insisted.

"It's nothing for you to worry about. Just a little side venture. I don't want to attract attention any more than you do. Anyway, the sooner we settle our business, the sooner I get out of here."

"Wait a minute! You said this dynamite is extra? You already set charges on the tracks?"

"Yes, like I said, but not on them, underneath. They won't blow until I connect the timer, once we agree to go through with this. The extra sticks are for insurance—in case the first charge doesn't get the their attention properly. Now, why don't you shut up for a minute and listen to me."

Jim Lothar took an envelope from his coat pocket and waved it at Simon.

"All the information you need is here if you decide to go through with the plan. Once the money is wired to the first bank account, it'll pass through several more accounts electronically before the final one—you follow me?"

"Sure, I get it. The railroad wires the money to one bank, but we pick it up from another."

"That's the gist of it. Our money will be instantly redeposited in a different bank and in a different country than where the railroad first wires it. Your job is to figure a way to communicate with the railroad without them finding out who we are. I assume you've thought about that, right?"

Jim passed the envelope over to Simon.

"Pretty slick. How'd you figure it out?"

"That's a trade secret. Let's just say I have some previous experience in international transactions."

"Wow, St. Kitts in the Caribbean!" Simon exclaimed, after scanning the contents.

"We can withdraw the money there, but it would be safer to move it one more time. Panama would be good. It's an international banking center, and they don't ask too many questions. I wouldn't stay there too long either. I'd suggest some place like Ecuador or another less developed South American country."

"Why Ecuador?"

"Believe me, there are far worse places in the world. You might even decide you like it there—great climate on the coast, low cost of living, and plenty of expats around, I'm told. But whether you decide to stay in Ecuador or to settle somewhere else, once you're there I advise you to take that money out slowly. Don't withdraw it all in cash either. That attracts attention too."

"Sure, that makes sense. So what will you do?"

"I'll meet you in either St. Kitts or Panama City. I'll take a different route. I suggest you don't take your sister or brother with you to the banks. I trust you won't piss away my share before I get there. I've written down a couple of ways you can contact me."

"Okay, I'm in, then. I know my way around computers and the internet. I'll use the internet to contact the railroad. I can make it so they won't be able to trace my emails back to me. You'd better get going before Liam and Mary get back from Whitehorse," Simon insisted.

"I'll be in touch. I've got to get down to Juneau, but I'll be back in a couple of days to set the timer and get things rolling."

Jim walked quickly down the trail from the cabin. About half way down he heard Simon's siblings and Hiram talking as they climbed up the trail. He hid behind some brush and trees until they went by.

Meanwhile Simon thought about the best place to hide the duffle bag. He remembered the trapdoor under the shed Hiram had showed them that led to the long abandoned mine shaft. Hiram had remarked that it would make a great wine cellar. Simon had shut the shed door and was walking back to the cabin when Hiram, Mary, and Liam appeared, carrying bags of groceries and other essentials that could be purchased less expensively in Whitehorse.

"Hey, I was just thinking of going down to meet you. I'm feeling better—almost back to normal self again, but maybe a few pounds lighter," Simon joked.

"Is someone up here? There's a fancy new pickup parked down near our van," Mary said.

"No—probably just some hiker or tourist. Was anything missing from our campsite?" Simon asked.

Simon realized with relief that Jim Lothar had somehow avoided meeting them on the way down or at the campsite.

"Everything looked fine, but I swear that pickup looked just like the one that guy who pulled us off the ferry drove," Liam said.

"You mean Jim Lothar? Maybe he's looking for Mary. I'm pretty sure he's got the hots for her," Simon teased.

"Oh, do I have some competition, Mary?" Hiram asked.

"Knock it off, Hiram. I can see you've been hanging out with my brothers too long."

"Oh, I think You hit a nerve, Hiram. What woman could resist a man with a truck like that. It's the modern day version of the knight in shining armor—or is it shining amour."

"You fuckers are disgusting. That guy is a creep," Mary said.

"I thought he had a pretty good idea for getting back at the railroad," Liam offered.

"What idea?" Hiram asked.

"Nothing but bullshit from a professional bull-shitter," Mary said.

"Never mind that. I haven't been able to eat anything all day, and I could use a snack and a beer. Unless you want to go down the trail again and see who it is, I vote we have a cold one," Simon declared.

"Well, we don't own anything worth stealing anyway," Liam agreed.

CHAPTER 5

No Turning Back

A few days later Hiram borrowed the Murphy's van to run into Skagway, check his post office box, and take a finished sculpture to one of the gift shops. Mary and her brothers had elected to stay in Dyea. Hiram's birthday was the following day. Mary had convinced her brothers to help her clean the cabin, weed the garden, and clear out the trails to the chicken coop and outhouse in lieu of buying Hiram a present.

Since his meeting with Jim Lothar Simon had realized that he had to make his case for extorting money from the railroad to his brother and sister. It had been foolish of him to think he could keep the plan secret from them. Lothar was back in Skagway, and Simon had invited him to come to Dyea while Hiram was away. Although Mary disliked Jim Lothar, he hoped the man would leave a better impression this time. After Hiram left for town Simon told Liam and Mary about the plan, and to expect Lothar soon.

"He won't stay long, but we need to hammer out a few more details if we agree to go through with his plan," Simon explained.

"You're out of your head, Simon!" Mary exclaimed.

"Now wait a minute, Mary," Liam said. "It might work. Let's hear the man out at least."

"What—are you both smoking the same crack pipe? You're fucking crazy. Sometimes I can't believe we're even related!"

The door knocker clanging interrupted their quarrel.

"I see I timed my entrance perfectly!" Jim Lothar announced. "Another happy family get-together, it seems."

"I want no part of this hare-brained scheme. You're wasting your time," Mary snapped.

"What kind of greeting is that? I've been hard at work for our cause. The least you could do is offer me a beer if you have one."

"Sure, Jim. I think we could all use a drink. As you probably gathered, this is the first Mary and Liam have heard of our plan. I guess I should have told them earlier," Simon explained.

Lothar slumped down into one of the bean bag chairs, and gratefully accepted the cold can. He was tired, dirty, and sweaty from his earlier hike from the highway to the railroad tracks and back.

"Where's your boyfriend, Mary? I was looking forward to meeting him this visit," Lothar asked, after taking a big gulp from the beer can.

"Hiram will be back soon, and I don't think it's such a great idea for you two to meet," Mary said, testily. "He's got no business with you."

"Hey, I'm only trying to be friendly—but have it your way. I won't be long. This morning I went up to the pass and set the timer. The train will derail at slow speed tomorrow morning."

Lothar took another long swig and waited for the Murphys to react.

"Wait a minute! That wasn't our agreement! You said we would discuss this first—not that you would just go ahead and sabotage the train without telling me!"

Simon had to make a show of being outraged, but in truth he was glad Lothar had taken the initiative. He had already decided to go through with the plan on his own if necessary. Once he had the money he was sure he would be able to convince Mary and Liam to join him in Ecuador, or wherever he decided to go.

"Hey—no reason to get excited. It's all up to you now. You can take advantage of the situation, demand payment; or you can just pretend it never happened. In which case I'm happy to leave town and say no more, with no one the wiser," Lothar replied.

"But one more thing. The $250,000 we discussed earlier isn't enough, considering the risk. I want half. That's only fair. It's my idea, and I've done the dirty work of setting the charges, and figuring out the bank account routing details. Besides, whoever heard of someone demanding less than a million," Lothar insisted. "We'd be the laughing stock of all the professionals."

"I don't consider myself a professional criminal," Simon replied.

"Demanding a million is just stupid. Such a large round number in one deposit will look suspicious," Mary declared.

"Okay, then make it $900,000 or $999,999 if you want, but my take is half of whatever we get if you decide to follow through. I'm an honorable man, so a handshake will do."

"Sure, but this doesn't mean we agree, just that we'll give it some more thought," Simon dissembled.

Simon and Liam shook hands, but Mary refused. Lothar shrugged, said goodbye, and left.

"You aren't really going to go through with this, are you Simon?" Mary asked.

"Of course not, unless you and Liam agree too," Simon lied.

"I'm in. I guess it's two to one in favor," Liam said.

It was rare for him to disagree with his sister, but he was excited by the idea of having enough money to buy a new home for his family, and he liked the idea of getting back at the railroad.

"This isn't a majority rules kind of decision! We'll all go to jail if we're caught, and we will be caught!" Mary insisted.

"Not all of us. You and Hiram can continue in your Elysian love nest here in Dyea. You don't have to take part, and Hiram doesn't even have to know about it," Simon argued.

Mary decided to try another tack.

"We've always been best as a team. We're family. We make important decisions together," she appealed.

"Yeah—like when we decided to go to court to try to get our property back and ended up going bankrupt paying the lawyers off. That was a great team decision," Simon reminded his sister.

Their argument was cut short by the arrival of Hiram. The Murphy siblings said nothing to him about the visit. Hiram was somewhat surprised when Simon and Liam, who had been unusually quiet during dinner, left shortly after, without their usual after dinner beers.

The next day rumors spread in Skagway of an early morning train derailment, but there was nothing in the local news or any official confirmation from the railroad. Most who heard the gossip speculated that the railroad was not saying anything for insurance reasons, and to avoid impacting tourism.

Simon was convinced Lothar's plan would work. Without telling Mary or Liam he emailed the railroad from a library computer.

$990,000 to be delivered as follows—or expect much worse! If we find you have contacted law enforcement, you will be doubly sorry.

The missive was followed with bank deposit information.

Simon was the most knowledgable of the siblings about anything related to computers and the internet. He had majored in computer programing in college, and had become proficient at writing code, though he had dropped out before attaining a degree. Simon and another classmate had once used their access to the campus computers to change some of their grades. The university caught on, but their computer science professor was so impressed with their cleverness, if not their morals, that he interceded for them. Their only penance was spending many tedious hours helping the university librarians digitize the microfiche records.

Simon did not think the email could be traced to a particular individual, but just in case, he had acted alone, so he could honestly say his brother and sister were not involved if he was caught. He called Jim Lothar from a phone booth and told him that he didn't want his siblings to know, but the notice had been sent to the railroad.

"Then the game is on!" Lothar said. "I bet they send the money right away. They can't afford to risk an interruption in the tourist traffic. I'm headed up to Skagway again on the next ferry. I'll see you then, and I'll take that bag of goodies off your hands," he said, referring to the dynamite and Native American relics Simon had secreted away in the abandoned mineshaft under the work shed.

CHAPTER 6

An Unfortunate Altercation

Agent Jack Dolon was one of only a small number of people in Skagway with reliable wireless phone service. He could place and receive calls from nearly anywhere in the world with the satellite phone the Agency provided, and his communications were encrypted and secure. Before leaving the *Opal Princess* he called his supervisor, Richard Head in Seattle. He told his boss he didn't know when Jim Lothar and the purser would get together again, but he was sure that Sabastos Melas sensed he was being watched. If he couldn't catch the two conspirators together, he could at least get Lothar, who was in possession of contraband. They might be able to convince him to turn on his cronies with the promise of reduced charges. It would be easy to find and arrest Lothar in the small town of Skagway, Dolon explained. His shiny new pickup would be obvious, and there were only a few places where he could get a room for the night, most of them on Broadway street.

Ultimately the Agency was far more interested in apprehending Melas and his international colluders than Jim Lothar. Lothar was only one of a network of small-time crooks supplying Melas and his ring of associates with Native American relics and illegal animal parts, which were then sold to wealthy collectors in Europe and Asia.

"You've got my approval and blessing, Jack. We've certainly got enough to make it stick in court. I also agree Lothar will probably incriminate Melas if we offer him a deal. But we need to move quickly, because I'm going to have to take you off this case."

"Why, after we've put so much time and effort into it?"

"Have you heard anything about a train derailment up on White Pass?"

"Of course—it's all over town, but nobody got hurt, and minor derailments happen often enough that it's not big news. The locals say the railroad isn't talking about it because they don't want to scare the tourists."

"I can tell you that was no accident. A charge was set off that took out a small section of track just before the train arrived. For now, go ahead and pick up Lothar, but the sabotage is a much bigger concern. I'll have to take you off the Melas case to investigate that, unless I can find someone else to do it—preferably someone with local experience."

"Well, besides Conrad Slocum, who's been AWOL since he sailed into the sunset last summer, who else do we have that has worked up here?"

"Really, no one. Our agents who have been posted in Alaska have been stationed in either Anchorage or Fairbanks. You and Slocum are the only two who have worked Southeast Alaska. But thanks to your foresight last year, I think we'll be able to convince Slocum to end his overlong truancy."

"Whatever you say of course, Richard." (The two were friends, and unlike Conrad, Jack never used the diminutive.) "But there's definitely unfinished business on the *Opal Princess*. Sebastos Melas isn't the only crew member involved. I think we're only looking at the tail of the dragon."

"I can give you until tomorrow evening to round up Jim Lothar, but after that the derailment investigation will have higher priority. I'm getting a fair amount of pressure from higher up, but I promise you can get back on this case after I convince agent Slocum it would be in his best interests to return to duty in Alaska."

"By the way, congratulations on your promotion—director!"

"Thanks, but you're a week early. Carson has a few more days in the director's chair before I take over. My good fortune is yours too. The Agency's budget has multiplied. The Alaska region is going to get its own supervisor with the pay raise and perks that come with that. I've got some say on who gets the position. You've earned it, and I can't think of anyone better."

"I appreciate your confidence in me, Richard. I won't let you down," Jack replied.

It galled supervisor Head to admit that the Agency needed Conrad Slocum's skills and familiarity with Southeast Alaska, just as it had relied on his expertise and language abilities in Afghanistan during the

1970s and 80s. But since the events of 9-11 the demands on his office had grown, and he was short-staffed. Richard was ambitious. A quick solution to the threat to the railroad would be a feather in his cap. In spite of his recalcitrance, agent Slocum was one of the best he had, and agent Dolon's equal or better in Alaskan matters.

It didn't take much sleuthing for agent Dolon to figure out where to find Jim Lothar. One of his contacts, a local who drove taxi during the tourist season, had seen the new Dodge Ram pickup heading out Dyea Road. As he crossed the bridge over the Taiya River Dolon encountered one of the national park rangers driving back to Skagway. He blinked his headlights and waved the officer down. The park ranger told him he had seen a shiny new pickup truck heading out to the Dyea flats maybe a half hour earlier.

Dolon found the pickup, now somewhat less glossy from the dust of the unpaved Dyea Road, parked near the Murphy's van. He guessed the van belonged to tourists camping in the area because of the lack of space in the campgrounds. He didn't think Jim Lothar would drive out to Dyea unless it was to rendezvous with someone who was poaching, or for some other nefarious reason, and he couldn't imagine Lothar would take the ferry from Juneau just to hike and see the sights. He had to be up to something.

After searching the immediate area Dolon noticed a well-used trail that led up the flank of the mountain. He decided to investigate. As he approached the cabin he heard loud, angry conversation. He circled around to the back of the building where he could observe the group without being seen. Jim Lothar was engaged in a heated altercation with Hiram Hatcher and another man and woman. He recognized Hatcher as a man on his watch list because of his criminal record and well-known history as an eco-activist.

The woman was furious.

"Fuck you Simon! You think it's okay to involve Hiram, Liam, and myself in your risky plot without our knowledge or agreement! Now you've put us all in danger!"

"Look Mary—you three aren't involved, but now that Jim and I have set things in motion, I'm committed. This plan will work. They'll have to pay, and Jim has a foolproof way to get our money without anyone finding out who we are," Simon argued. "Then we'll be able to buy dad and mom a nice place—maybe even another property on Orcas, or one of the other islands."

"So you say. I don't trust Mr. Lothar as far as I can throw his sneaky ass! If this works without you getting caught, which I fucking doubt, he'll probably just take all the money for himself!"

"Hey—I resent that," Lothar countered. "Haven't you heard of honor among thieves? Besides, the way it's set up you might even get there before me and withdraw all the money. I'll be at your mercy!"

He thought it best to humor Mary, and that she would calm down after she had her say.

"We're not thieves. They owe us that money for taking what was rightfully ours," Mary shot back. "But this wasn't the right way to do it. We should have gone to the press, like I suggested—now we can't do that, and most likely one or all of us will end up in jail, you fucking morons!"

"All right Mary, enough is enough. Even if what you say is true, what's done is done. Now we need to make the best of it," Simon insisted.

At that moment there was a disturbance behind them, and they turned to see their brother, Liam, struggling with another man.

Earlier that day Hiram, Mary, and Simon took the van to Skagway. Liam elected to stay at the cabin, where he was helping Hiram with the wood splitting and stacking chores. For Liam the physical activity helped to relieve anxiety and stress. Mary and Simon returned to find Jim Lothar's pickup parked next to their camp. They both wondered how they would explain the man's presence to Hiram, but Mary took the initiative.

On the hike up to the cabin Mary told Hiram how they had met Jim Lothar in Juneau, and about his plan to extort money from the railroad. Simon confessed to letting the man store his contraband in the old mine entrance under the shed. Hiram told Mary not to worry. Lothar had probably only returned to retrieve his stolen goods so he could fence them. In any case, Hiram was confident he and Mary would be able to encourage the man to abandon his scheme and leave them alone.

When they arrived at the cabin things went downhill quickly. Simon admitted he had already sent a message demanding money to the railroad. Mary lashed out at her brother.

Liam hated to see his sister and brother fight. He wasn't sure who was right, but he agreed Simon shouldn't have sent the extortion message to the railroad without his siblings approval. To avoid their quarrel Liam went back into the house to put away the groceries they had picked up in town. Through the kitchen window he caught a glimpse of someone creeping through the woods towards the back of the house. Liam went into the bedroom and opened the back door to investigate. As he emerged agent Dolon swung around to confront him.

Liam had grown up sparring with his tough fisherman father, who had been a legendary scrapper before he married. His dad had told him that the number one strategy for winning a fight if it looked inevitable, was to utilize the element of surprise.

"Always hit first, without warning, and hit hard," his dad had told him. "Don't waste time with threats or arguing. Many times it's the person who throws the first punch who wins the fight."

Instinctively, before the stranger could speak or make a move to the sidearm he carried, Liam's fist shot out. Jack Dolon was himself an accomplished combatant, who had often tested his abilities against other agents in his division, and had benefitted from working with accomplished martial arts experts. But Liam's first powerful punch connected solidly with the side of Dolon's head. He was dazed, and slow to react. Even so, it took all of Liam Murphy's skill and strength to get the agent in a choke hold and drag him around the side of the house, where the others saw them.

"Give me hand someone!" Liam called out.

Dolon was quickly recovering from the blow, and though lighter by some twenty pounds, he was an even more skilled and experienced fighter than the bigger man. He kicked Liam's legs out from under him, and they both went down. Liam fell heavily on top of the agent, as the others ran towards them.

"It doesn't look like you need any help now," Simon observed.

Jack Dolon had ceased moving. He lay face down. His head was cocked at an odd angle.

"It looks to me like you killed the fucker," Lothar said, turning the man over. "...or at least knocked him out. Well I'll be damned—I know this guy! He's the asshole that arrested me last year. I think you just took out a federal agent!"

"Maybe he's just unconscious," Mary said, hopefully.

"Get out of my way. He needs help," Hiram said.

He had training in CPR, and had been a volunteer EMT in Haines. Hiram checked for a pulse, and found just the faintest trace. He administered CPR for the next twenty minutes while the others looked on, but agent Jack Dolon was passed reviving.

"I think his neck broke when you fell."

"I didn't mean to kill him!"

Liam was nearly in tears.

"It was like fighting with a tiger—I couldn't get him to stop—and he kept reaching for his gun!"

"It wasn't your fault, Liam," Mary said, hugging her brother. "We're all witnesses, and we saw him trip you. It was just an unlucky fall, but now we really are screwed."

"Maybe not," Lothar offered. "I think I have a way we could, pardon the joke, kill two birds with one stone."

Lothar was overjoyed that the agent was dead, and that someone else had done the job, accident or not. Lothar's parole terms stipulated he was not allowed to leave Juneau. If Dolon had reported his presence in Skagway he would most likely have gone back to prison to finish out his sentence. Moreover, he was aware that the agent was on to Melas and his smuggling ring.

"What the hell are you talking about, Jim? This is a disaster anyway you look at it," Hiram said.

"At the very least we should be in the van racing to the clinic now. The longer we stand around talking, the more suspicious this will seem."

"We're not taking him to the clinic, but we will take him to town—later," Lothar insisted." Just hear me out."

Ultimately Lothar convinced the Murphys and Hiram Hatcher to go along with his improvised plan. They would make it appear to the railroad and law enforcement that agent Dolon had been killed as part of the extortion plot by the same environmental terrorist or extremest group that had derailed the train. Once they were in agreement they discussed what to do after they dealt with Jack Dolon's corpse.

"Obviously, we need to get the hell out of Alaska as soon as we can," Lothar advised.

"I agree, and the sooner the better," Hiram said. "But I don't think you should fly out of Skagway," he told the Murphy siblings. "Once the body is found they'll be watching the airport, the highways, and the ferry terminal. You can take my boat to Haines or Juneau and get a plane from there."

"What about you Hiram?" Mary asked.

"Look, we'll attract too much attention together, especially since I'm a convicted felon with a history as a radical environmentalist. I'll be a prime suspect. I'll find another way out of Alaska on my own, and meet you later," he promised.

Before they left Dyea with Dolon's body the Murphy brothers packed what they needed for the trip south, and Mary sadly removed her few items of clothing from Hirams's beat-up dresser. Hiram planned to spend a few days in Skagway before leaving. At the very least he would need to withdraw his money from the bank, do something with his partially finished metal sculptures, and find some excuse to explain to George

Ripinski why he was giving up the cabin on such short notice.

"Hey—you can join us in Ecuador," Liam told Hiram, hopefully.

He knew Mary was attached to the man, perhaps even in love, though she had never admitted it to him or Simon.

"I'd travel to hell itself to be with your sister, and I've always wanted to visit South America—but first we have to get out of here before law enforcement figures out who we are."

Later, during the darkest part of the short Alaskan summer night, using a travois rigged up from a tarp and two branches, they drug the body down the trail to the van. On the drive to Skagway it occurred to Lothar that, having retrieved his duffle bag from the abandoned mine shaft under Hiram's shed, he now had the means to make his enemy, Sam Thornton, the focus of the investigation into Dolon's death.

Once in the Skagway harbor the four men loaded the corpse into the Boston Whaler that Hiram co-owned with his landlord, George Ripinski, while Mary kept a look out on shore. Without starting either outboard engine, the men quietly rowed and paddled the short distance from the small boat harbor to the cruise ship wharf.

Simon had made up a cardboard sign using cutout letters from the old magazines in the shed. Hiram, who had worked as a fisherman and and a forest fire fighter, was an expert with knots. He made sure the body would not float away as the tide came up, and added a hangman's knot to a rope around Dolon's neck for an additional touch of macabre. To the Murphy brother's and Hiram's horror, instead of pinning the cardboard to the timbers of the pier above the dead man, as they had planned, Jim Lothar took an old Tlingit knife he had stolen from Sam Thornton weeks earlier and plunged it to the hilt through the ransom note and into the unfortunate agent's chest.

"It looked like you actually enjoyed stabbing that dead man, Jim," Simon remarked, after they returned to the van.

"Let's just say I never did get on too well with Jack Dolon, and I admit I'm not sad to be rid of him."

"Do you think anyone saw us?" Liam worried.

It seemed to him that things had careened out of control. He couldn't suppress the feelings of dread, anxiety, and paranoia that had assailed him since agent Dolon's death.

"I walked around the parking lot the whole time you were gone. Nobody came or went. There was a light on in one of the sailboat cabins, but I don't think anyone was there, or if they were, I'm sure they were asleep at this hour," Mary assured her brother.

"That old Tlingit knife has been in the news, and it will incriminate the owner. That will give us a few days at least, but they'll eventually figure out it wasn't him, I'd wager," Lothar warned the others.

"It's too late to run all the way to Haines. You'd better stop at Burro Creek and catch a few hours of sleep," Hiram advised the Murphy siblings. "I heard that the caretaker is down in Juneau, so nobody will bother you."

"You've got all the bank information you need. That money will flash through several different accounts in seconds, and we'll be able to get it safely when it's convenient. The railroad will pay up now, for sure. They can't afford any interruption to their tourism money stream, which amounts to a hell of a lot more than we're asking for," Jim said.

"I'll set up several secure email accounts once we're safely away from Skagway," Simon said. "It's best we stay in touch that way."

"How about a few dollars of my share in advance?" Jim asked. "I promised to pay for the dynamite, and I'm just about flat broke. I don't want to sleep in my truck. I can't get out of here until the next ferry leaves, and I'd like to get some rest in a real bed tonight."

"Sure," Hiram volunteered. "I'll cover it, they'll need their cash for the trip south."

Hiram gave Jim Lothar all the money he had in his wallet, enough for the man to at least get a room if he could find one. Leaving the others to transfer the Murphys' belongings from the van to the Boston Whaler, Jim headed into town on foot, where he was fortunate to find a vacancy at the Golden North Hotel.

After helping Mary and her brothers load the boat, Hiram pointed out the waterproof container in the storage area under the console.

"There are charts of most of Southeast Alaska from here down to Ketchikan in that box. There's tarps, extra line, flares, and flotation jackets under the seat cushions. George and I always keep keep the fuel tanks topped off, and the two five gallon containers are full too. The fishing gear will just be in your way, so I'll take that stuff back to the van," Hiram said.

He knew the siblings had spent most of their lives in the San Juan Islands of Washington, and were experienced boaters. He wasn't worried about their safety, but he couldn't bring himself to say goodbye to Mary.

"When you get to Haines take the first flight you can to Juneau—even if you have to charter it. I'll hide the van in the woods when I'm done with it. That'll keep them guessing for a while if they do somehow connect us to this. Someone will find that body tomor-row—most likely somebody from one of the morning cruise ships, but by that time you should be on your way to Juneau, where you can catch the first available flight to Seattle. From there you've got lots of options. My main worry is that they somehow connect Jim with this, and he rats us out. I don't trust him. How are you set for money?"

"We've got enough to get us south, and credit cards if we run short on cash," Simon replied.

"What will you do?" Mary asked.

She doubted she would ever see Hiram again. There was a hollow feeling in her stomach, though she wasn't the least bit hungry.

"Don't worry about me. I'll land on my feet somewhere, and I'll find you—that is, if you want me to."

"How will you do that? None of us have cell phones, and we sure as hell don't want to involve any of our family or friends," Simon wondered.

Hiram ripped a scrap of paper from a magazine in the van and wrote down an address.

"This is a post office box in Oregon I've had for years. I used to move around a lot when I was fighting forest fires, and it was convenient to have one place to pick up my mail. When you get settled somewhere, I hope you send me a nice postcard," he said, handing the paper to Mary.

"If we don't end up in jail, I'll send you a fucking ticket, and you better get on that plane!" Mary said, struggling to hold back her tears. She put her arms around Hiram and gave him a long kiss. "I'll miss you, Hiram—take care of yourself, and don't let some floozy distract you!"

"You mean like you did?" Hiram said. But the joke felt and fell flat.

"I was more than just a distraction, wasn't I?"

"Oh, so much more, and you know it. Now you'd better get going, before I change my mind and get in that boat with you!"

It was dark at the boat slip, where one of the harbor lights had burned out. As quietly as they could, with Liam at the wheel, the Murphys idled out of the small boat harbor. Mary sat next to Simon on the midship thwart, and watched the glow of their van's headlights fade as Hiram drove away. She wondered how she could be so crazy as to sacrifice what she had for such a dangerous and far-fetched scheme. It was like a game of blackjack where she had twenty in her hand and took another card with the wild hope it would be an ace.

When he judged they were far enough away from the harbor Liam pushed the throttle forward. The boat accelerated, angling across the water towards Burro Creek, a few miles south on the other side of the fjord. In the dim light they could just make out the entrance to Nahku Bay and the Dyea inlet to the north. Mary and her brothers were silent. It was futile to attempt conversation over the sound of the onboard motor, and all three had similar melancholy thoughts. They knew there was little chance they would ever again see this spectacular land they had grown so fond of, and that held such a profound connection to both their past and future.

CHAPTER 7

Hawaii

From his table on the covered deck of the restaurant Conrad Slocum watched birds fighting over scraps of food the diners threw onto the narrow strip of lawn overlooking Honokohau harbor. The prominent signs advising patrons not to feed the birds were almost universally ignored by the patrons, both tourists and residents. Conrad noted with dismay that since his last visit to the Big Island of Hawaii the invasive house sparrows had grown noticeably in number. He disliked the birds —their abrasive screeching, and their bullying tactics, but he could not help but admire their adaptability and tenaciousness. Still, other species, including several native honeycreepers, two determined Saffron Finches, and the Mynas seemed to be holding their own in the the scramble for french fries and burger bun bits. But it was obvious to Conrad that unless something was done about the house sparrows the local avifauna and even some of the more attractive invasive species would soon be overwhelmed by the obstreperous sparrows. He imagined the vastly outnumbered Hawaiian natives must feel much the same about the Haoles, their term for the non-Hawaiians, especially the Caucasians, taking over the islands.

Conrad was not the least surprised when a man, conspicuously overdressed for the eighty-five degree midday temperature in long pants and a sports jacket, sat down without invitation across from him, and placed a black leather attache case on the table. Conrad had noticed the rented Jeep Wrangler with the three men inside tailing him earlier that day. He knew who they worked for, and he was not surprised they had found him here at last. The Agency had probably followed his movements since the day he had sailed away from Alaska a year earlier.

The man was no stranger. Supervisor Richard Head worked for the same intelligence agency Conrad had been avoiding for months, while he sailed among the tropical Pacific islands from his new home base in Hawaii.

"Hi Dick—what took you so long to find me?" Conrad asked.

The supervisor hated the diminutive, which was the reason Conrad took every opportunity to use it. The two did not enjoy a good working relationship. Although Supervisor Head was Conrad's titular overseer, Conrad enjoyed special status due to his close long-time relationship with the current director of the Agency in Washington D.C., Paul Sherman.

"Oh it wasn't hard. We could have contacted you months ago if we had wanted to," supervisor Head replied testily.

"That so? Then why today in particular?"

"We've got a little job for you. I'm sorry to say you'll have to give up your island paradise vacation, though."

"I do like this place. I'm not sure I want to go back to work."

"Of course I could order you, but I believe you will change your mind after I show you what I have in this briefcase. But it would be best if we could go somewhere a bit more private—as soon as you've finished your lunch, of course."

"I've suddenly lost my appetite. How about my boat. It's down in the harbor. Of course you knew that already."

Conrad lived aboard his beautifully restored sailboat, *Tisiphone*, a 38 foot wooden Ingrid cutter, tied stern-to in the Mediterranean fashion in the tiny harbor below the restaurant. While Conrad paid his bill the supervisor waved a signal to the other two agents waiting in the Jeep, before following Conrad down to his sailboat.

In the privacy of the boat's cabin supervisor Head retrieved a folder from his briefcase and passed it without comment to Conrad.

"As much as I hate to admit it, Dick, I am tempted," Conrad said, after scanning the documents and photos. "But what about my boat—I can't just fly out two days from now and leave it sitting here. I'll need some time to get it hauled out and safely stored or shipped to my new posting."

It was an intriguing case—not only the obvious threat to the cruise ships and the Alaska tourism industry, but the alternative possibility that someone or some group harbored other motives for agent Jack Dolon's murder. Dolon had been stationed for several years in Juneau, where he mostly aided local authorities investigating cross border drug smuggling, illegal Native American relic and fossil ivory trade, and other criminal activity that violated federal laws. Regardless of the motive for the murder, it was a puzzle begging to be solved.

Conrad, after months of voyaging in the South Pacific, had found to his surprise and dismay that he sometimes missed the very different challenges of his old employment, in spite of the fact that he had essentially gone AWOL to escape the demands of the Agency. Perhaps he had only needed this extended vacation, he mused. Maybe, after the accomplishment of his long-standing sailing dream he was ready now to go back to the only work that he had ever felt suited for. Conrad had worked for the Agency for nearly thirty years. In spite of his reservations, he could think of no other tolerable way to make a living, and his bank account was seriously depleted from his recent travels.

"There's no need to worry about your boat. We've seen to it that you get immediate priority with the harbor office. In fact, we've taken the liberty of scheduling your haul-out for tomorrow morning. It's up to you whether you want to store it, or have it shipped back—our office is authorized to cover the expense either way."

"I'm guessing the events of September 11th have resulted in a significant increase in our budget, and I seem to be reaping some of the benefits. I'm truly honored and most heartily grateful, but I'm in no particular hurry to trade this lovely island climate for the snow and ice of a Southeast Alaskan winter."

Supervisor Head waved aside Conrad's remarks and continued with his briefing.

"Then perhaps this will go the rest of the way to convincing you that cutting short your Pacific idyll and coming back to work is in your best interests," he continued, as he handed a manila envelope to Conrad.

Conrad extracted the photograph of the disembodied legs and contemplated it for a time before returning it to the envelope. The year before, on remote and unpopulated Kuiu Island in Southeast Alaska, Conrad had taken his revenge upon Grant Tadlock, the killer of his son, Marshall Stuckrath. He had wounded the man, and watched without interfering as a cougar mauled Tadlock to death. After agent Jack Dolon and Alaska Fish and Game officer Ray Standers retrieved the bodies of Grant Tadlock and the cat, agent Dolon, who envied and disliked Conrad, had taken possession of the legs. Lodged in one of the limbs was the bullet fired from Conrad's .308 rifle. Dolon had shipped the frozen legs, along with other evidence of Conrad's actions, to supervisor Richard Head.

"Oh, you can keep those photos if you want, I've got the negatives, of course. The tracking device we attached to your boat, which you easily removed, was put there for you to find. Naturally we had other methods of keeping tabs on you."

In spite of himself, Conrad felt the hairs on the back of his neck stand up. It seemed the Agency held all the cards. Every year agents were required to go to a firing range and re-certify with any firearms in their possession, whether personal or Agency issued. After sailing out into the Pacific for Hawaii Conrad had briefly considered throwing his rifle overboard. But after reconsideration, he realized the Agency had documentation for every gun he owned, including serial numbers, photos, and bullets and shells fired from each weapon. The Agency retained this information for verification of who fired in any cases where an employee injured or killed someone in the course of an investigation or arrest.

"Of course we knew all the time about your little affair with Karen Stuckrath, and a DNA test confirmed you were the father of Marshall. I wonder how your old friend David Stuckrath would react if he knew? Of course we tender our belated condolences on your son's death—but surely you don't imagine your unlawful vengeance doesn't come at steep price?"

"I assume that price is my continued fealty until the time comes when you have no further use for me?"

Conrad fought down the urge to grab his asthmatic supervisor by the throat. It would only take a few minutes to throttle the man, and an hour more to dispose of him at sea. But the other two agents waiting in the Jeep would be more challenging to deal with.

"When you put it that way, it seems overly harsh. It's not as though you were forced to accept employment as an intelligence agent all those years ago in Afghanistan. I shouldn't have to remind you that all our choices come with consequences."

"Most jobs don't require you to become an indentured servant."

"Most employers don't retain employees guilty of murder. Really, Conrad, you speak from a position of great privilege. Anyone else would be in prison for the actions you have taken. You think of this as a kind of blackmail, but looked at from another angle, you are a very lucky man. Not many who fantasize about revenge are able to carry it through without far more serious repercussions."

"If that is the price I must pay, then so be it. I don't regret my actions."

"I've only one more day on this lovely isle, and I'd like to spend it like any other tourist, lounging on the beach with a tropical drink in my hand, so I'll get to the nuts and bolts of the situation. Besides the late Jack Dolon, you are the only agent we have who has spent any significant amount of time in Southeast Alaska. With Jack gone, you're our man now. Because of the note's threat to the cruise ships this case rises to the level of terrorism, which, since the attack on the Twin Towers and Pentagon last year, has become our main focus. You'll be working with Fish and Game officer Ray Standers, and trooper Joe Tenax, as you did last year on the drug case—that is, before you abandoned everyone and sailed off into the sunset."

The previous summer Conrad had been assigned to intercept a large shipment of meth precursor chemicals from a Chinese vessel at Coronation Island, a few miles off Cape Decision at the western end of Kuiu Island. Although ordered to work with agent Dolon, Conrad had sent him on a wild goose chase, and used the investigation as cover for his own ends, revenge for the death of Marshall Stuckrath, his son as the result of a brief affair with Karen Stuckrath twenty years earlier.

Ultimately it was Jack Dolon who had arrested two of the drug smugglers. Conrad had sailed away to Hawaii after causing the death of the third smuggler, Grant Tadlock—the man who had killed Marshall Stuckrath in prison, where the freshman college student had been serving time for possession of a small amount of cocaine.

Supervisor Head reached into his briefcase again, this time pulling out a cardboard accordion file.

"Officially you're replacing Jack. This also comes with a promotion—I suppose an unusual reward for an employee going on the lamb for a year. But apparently some official way above my pay grade decided you would be more effective if your title had more heft. You're now our new 'Southeast Alaska Subregion Supervisor.' Coincidently the acronym does seem to suit you. Admittedly your staff consists of just one person, yourself, but the promotion does come with a nice bump in pay, as well as the authority to access Agency funds—up to a certain limit, without consultation with our Seattle office—that is, me. But of course you're completely responsible for any actions you take or any expense the Agency incurs because of your decisions. You will still report to me. Carson is retiring, and I'm taking over the regional directorship."

Several years previously Conrad had turned down the supervisor position, on the grounds that he was not interested in the added responsibility, or in spending his days at a desk. Even though he would still answer to Richard Head, the new position gave him far more freedom from Head's tendency to micromanage the agents under him. He guessed, correctly, that this development must be due to the influence of his old mentor, the man who had originally recruited him in Afghanistan, and who was now in charge of the Agency, Paul Sherman. Jack Dolon and supervisor Head had been close friends, and he knew this promotion, which Richard Head would have prevented had been able to, must gall.

"As you will see when you read the documentation, Jack had been investigating several persons involved in the smuggling of fossilized ivory and Native American relics, including a couple of tour ship employees and their Alaskan collaborators. We had two pawns in the game who were assisting Jack. But of course our investigation into the smuggling ring must now take a backseat to finding out who was behind Jack's murder and that threatening note pinned to him."

"...were assisting Jack?"

"Two undercover officers were on loan from the Alaska State Troopers. It seems one of them fell or was thrown off the cruse ship, *Opal Princess* north of Ketchikan in Clarence Strait. It's more than a little suspicious, obviously. A few days before his remains were found in a fisherman's net the undercover officer had told Jack that he had enough evidence to arrest two *Opal Princess* employees. Jack had planned to make the arrests when the ship docked in Juneau on its return voyage from Skagway, before he was killed."

"So we're already down a knight and a pawn—not a very auspicious start to our little chess game, it would seem."

"I know you and Jack did not get along, but he was a good man—one of our best, and the Agency would insist on investigating his death even without the national security issue. The troopers are holding one suspect, Juneau fisherman Sam Thornton. Another possible suspect, our old friend from last year's drug bust, Jim Lothar is out on parole, but hasn't been located. A third person of interest, the radical environmentalist, Hiram Hatcher has yet to be contacted or investigated. Trooper Tenax and Fish and Game officer Standers can fill you in on the rest when you get there."

"What do we know about the cruise ship crew members?"

"At this point the assistant purser of the *Opal Princess*, Sabastos Melas might be a suspect too, or perhaps one of the other crew members."

"Here are the tickets for your flights to Anchorage and Juneau," the supervisor continued, adding the documents to the collection of paperwork already on Conrad's galley table.

"You'll have to find your own way up to Skagway by plane or ferry. Of course keep records of your expenses and submit them as usual."

"Wow—it seems you have thought of everything—even first class seating."

"Regrettably there were no coach seats available on such short notice," Supervisor Head replied.

CHAPTER 8

Return To Alaska

Conrad flew from Hawaii to Anchorage and caught a connecting flight to Juneau. He was able to book passage to Skagway on a small commuter plane early the following morning. The weather was clear and warm, with a light north wind. The view as they flew over Lynn Canal—one of the longest and deepest fjords in the world, ninety miles from its northern terminus at Skagway to its junction with Chatham Strait, and nearly two thousand feet deep in places—was spectacular. The sheer sides of the mountains rose abruptly from sea level through the violets and greens of the lower elevations to the blindingly white ice-caped peaks above the tree line. The pilot of the small four passenger plane flew high enough that Conrad and the two other passengers were for a time level with the vast Juneau ice field, a fifteen hundred square mile area of over forty interconnected glaciers stretching nearly one hundred miles to the border of British Columbia.

After a brief stop at Haines to drop off one of the passengers, the plane continued on fifteen more miles to Skagway. Although Conrad had been to Skagway on previous Alaskan assignments, he never tired of the view of the the branching Taiya and Nahku inlets as the plane dropped abruptly to the runaway paralleling the Skagway river.

Skagway, only four blocks wide and twenty-four blocks long, had a year round population of less than eight hundred, which doubled during the brief tourist season. The isolated and tiny town, lost in the vast northern wilderness, received nearly a million tourists a year, almost all between mid-May and September.

Ray Standers, the local Fish and Game officer and marine biologist, was waiting for Conrad on the tarmac in the parking area at the edge of the runway.

"Well hello Conrad—good to see you again! Is that all the luggage you have?" Ray said, as he shook Slocum's hand.

"I'm traveling pretty light this trip, Ray—at least until my boat gets here on the barge."

The previous summer Conrad had met the biologist while berthed briefly in Juneau. The two men had hit it off, despite the fact that Ray had been assigned to interrogate Conrad as a possible suspect in the death of the Juneau judge, Henry Daise. Ray had come away from that investigation ambivalent about Conrad's role in the judge's demise, but convinced that Conrad had wounded Grant Tadlock and left him to be killed by a cougar on remote Kuiu Island. Ray had not disclosed his suspicions to anyone, including his boss, sergeant Joe Tenax. The biologist was not aware that Marshall Stuck-rath was Conrad's biological son, but his investigation had revealed that Conrad had been friends with David and Karen Stuckrath since the 1970s, when they had met in Afghanistan. Ray believed that Conrad had caused Tadlock's death because of his friendship with the couple.

"No boat, no problem! I've got access to boats a-plenty. I imagine you've come back to Alaska to finally take me up on that offer I made last year to take you fishing, right?"

"I wish that was all there was to it Ray, but unfortunately I'm on the clock again, and from what I understand, you're not going to have much leisure time either—at least until we find out who killed Jack Dolon."

"It's true I've been temporarily kicked off my regular beat to help you, but I've got one rule about work—I never let it interfere too much with fishing! I'm sure we can sneak away for at least a few hours while you're here. You've got to keep your sense of perspective—all work and no play makes Jack a dull boy," Ray declared.

He opened the back door of the dusty Explorer, and shoved Conrad's small suitcase and duffle bag into the cluttered space behind the seat backs.

"A certain 'Jack' is the reason I'm here, of course, though he was apparently no dull boy," Conrad observed as the two men seated themselves.

"Yeah? Well, at any rate he wasn't sharp enough to avoid the dull knife that ended his run. The coroner said the blade showed no evidence of having been honed for decades, and a lot of force must have been used to shove it into poor Jack's chest. How did you end up on this case anyway—or is that classified? And don't bullshit me—I know you're not a goddamned FBI agent."

"I suppose the less I say about that the better, Ray. But otherwise I'm pretty free to share anything I know relative to the case with you, quid pro quo of course. You already know Jack Dolon worked for the same agency I do, and he was on assignment when he was killed. Oh—and one more thing you should know: Jack Dolon didn't die from the knife wound."

"Well then how the hell did he die, and why didn't anyone tell me that?" Ray asked.

He shook his head in disgust as he started the car.

"I guess I'm on a need to know basis. Maybe I'm just supposed to be your chauffeur for this investigation, Conrad."

Ray was obviously irritated, and Conrad too wondered why the Fish and Game officer hadn't yet gotten the final report from the coroner.

"Ray, you know damn well I don't have a chance of figuring this out without your help," Conrad assured him. "At any rate it turns out Dolon's neck was broken hours before he was stabbed."

"When I discovered him there was a noose around his neck, but I could see that was done later, so I just assumed he died of the knife wound," Ray said, somewhat mollified.

"I understand it's a bad time of year for you to be taken off your regular duties on the rivers during the height of the salmon runs, so I know you're motivated. I am too, for my own reasons, so we'll push hard, if you're agreeable."

"I'm lucky I have a great crew in Haines. Most of them have worked for me for years, even the seasonal help. I hate to admit it, but they'll do fine without me breathing down their necks. I guess the longer I work the fish weirs the more salmon-like I become. I crave the seasonal routine just like they do—but at least I don't have to die at the end of summer after I spawn," Ray quipped.

Ray parked the car on Broadway Street in front of the Golden North Hotel, and accompanied Conrad as he picked up his key on the main floor and deposited his luggage in his second floor quarters.

"You were damned lucky to get a room this time of year."

"I don't think it was luck. I'm sure some tourist is very unhappy about a lost reservation or some other sort of mix-up," Conrad replied. "How do you suggest we get started?"

"Why do they even need us on this case, when you must know they've already arrested Sam Thornton down in Juneau?" Ray asked.

"I think we can agree Sam Thornton was most likely not the killer. My understanding is that you two are old friends, and I bet you're not too pleased they locked him up. Did they tell you Dolon had been working undercover most of the summer, posing as a security guard for the *Opal Princess*? My boss thinks his death is more likely to be related to that investigation than a dispute over a woman, and I'm inclined to agree."

"I'd bet my next paycheck Sam is no more responsible for that murder than I am. He's been in prison before on assault charges, but he's never been convicted—he's finished a few fights, but he never starts them. He's basically a peaceful guy—unless he's confronted or hassled. Do you have enough pull to convince the state to let him go, or at least grant bail?"

"I wish I did. All my people have is a garbled recording of agent Dolon being threatened on board the cruise ship. He was wearing a wire. It wasn't working very well, but it did pick up part of a pretty heated exchange he had with someone the day before he was killed."

"Threatened—how?" Ray asked.

"The man told Dolon that he knew he was a detective, and if he wanted to stay healthy he had better find another line of work."

"...any idea who confronted him?"

"My supervisor at the Agency tells me it was the assistant purser of the ship—Sebastos Melas—a Greek national with a pretty unsavory reputation. He's suspected of being partners in a smuggling operation with someone you will certainly remember, Jim Lothar."

The previous summer Ray and Conrad, together with Jack Dolon had been involved in the investigation which led to the arrest and conviction of Lothar, a

Juneau bartender, on charges of poaching, drug smuggling, and illegal export of protected fossilized ivory and protected animal parts.

"Jim Lothar was paroled this spring. Sergeant Tenax isn't too happy about it," Ray said.

"So besides Sam, who definitely had a beef to pick with agent Dolon, there are at least two more people who had no love for Jack; the purser and Jim Lothar. My boss also wants me to investigate the Fjord Foundation—that anti-cruise ship environmental group based in Haines—because of the note stuck to his chest, of course."

"That's crap. I know all those people. There might be couple who would pour some sugar in a bulldozer fuel tank or chain themselves to an old growth tree, but none of them are violent," Ray declared.

"Maybe so, but I'm obligated to at least interview the president of the organization. I agree they probably don't have anything to do with this, but all the local members will have to provide alibis for the time of the murder."

Conrad paused, then went on. "Something occurs to me, but since you and Sam are friends, you may not like it."

"What's that, Conrad?"

"If we can keep Sam where he is for a little longer, and keep the media focused on him as the suspect, the real killer might get overconfident or careless, and we might get lucky."

"That is a lot to ask," Ray said, shaking his head. "Sergeant Tenax would have to run it by the judge. Sam has a hot-shot lawyer who claims she has evidence that proves he didn't murder Dolon. She's insisting on bail—and she may get her way."

"*She's* a hot-shot lawyer?"

"Judge Daise's daughter, Linda. They say she's one of the best defense lawyers in the state. She moved back to Juneau and joined her dad's old firm. Sergeant Tenax, who should know, says she's as persistent as a pit bull. I doubt we can keep Sam locked up without her cooperation."

Conrad was practiced at dissembling his feelings, but even so he had to make a conscious effort to stay calm.

"I've met her, perhaps I can persuade her to help us out."

Ray looked closely at Conrad, and shook his head.

"That doesn't sound very likely. After all, she might hold you partially responsible for her father's death, since he fell out of your sailboat."

Conrad noted Ray's slight emphasis on "fell," and realized that Ray must still have some doubts about judge Daise's manner of death, although, after a brief investigation, it had been ruled an accidental drowning. In spite of their friendly rapport, Conrad knew from his previous encounter that the biologist was perhaps as an astute observer of the human animal as he was of wildlife. Conrad was reminded that there was an element of personal risk in his return to Alaska.

"I don't think so, Ray. She believes her dad's death was an accident. She made it a point to talk to me before the judge's funeral. I think I might have helped her feel better about her dad's last hours."

Conrad thought back to the reality of the judge's final horrific moments as he struggled in the water, and of pleasant fiction he had substituted to ease Linda's grief and remorse.

"Well good luck with that. Hey—what do you say to a drink? It's been a thirsty day, and who knows what gossip we might pick up from the locals after their hard day of fleecing the tourists," Ray said, glancing at his watch.

"The tour ships are getting ready to leave, so at least the bars won't be packed with souvenir hunters. I'll introduce you to a few of the more observant drunks —someone might know something helpful."

CHAPTER 9

The Red Onion

Forest Bradley Olorus Jr.—"Brad" to everyone who knew him—the long time bartender and inventory supervisor at the Red Onion Saloon, looked up from washing glasses as the two men walked in. It was that brief quiet time of the day when the cruise ship passengers were heading back to the love boats for their drinks and dinners—included at no extra cost with the tour package—but before the regulars showed up for their after work potations. Other than the four members of a visiting rock band ("The Lumberjacks," the poster on the door announced.) setting up their sound gear in front of the large picture window that faced Broadway, and an older couple seated at the far end of the bar, Ray and Conrad were the only patrons, in sharp contrast to the usual summer daytime crush, and the lively evenings.

Ray Standers was on good terms with Brad. He shared with him a love of the rugged outdoor lifestyle the area offered. The bartender lived several miles out of town, about half way between Skagway and Dyea, off the electrical grid in a log house he had constructed himself.

Brad was a black-bearded, swarthy man with a long drooping mustache, who some had remarked needed only a sombrero and bandoliers to pose as Pancho Villa's doppelgänger. The bartender was a native Texan and one-time history professor who had abandoned the security of that life years earlier, and never looked back. Brad had paid his way through graduate school bartending, and was famed for his expertise at margaritas, which were made assembly line style at the Red Onion and served out in quantity to the locals on Cinco De Mayo—the last holiday the locals enjoyed together before giving over their town each summer to the hordes of cruise ship tourists.

"Aren't you a little early Ray—I don't think I'm supposed to serve you when you're on duty," Brad chided.

"As you can plainly see, I am not wearing my regimentals," Ray said, spreading his arms wide to display his usual off-work uniform—well worn Carhartt jeans, and a Halibut jacket, the light wool coat practically de rigueur throughout Southeast Alaska.

"As a matter of fact, this highly skilled but sadly underpaid public servant has been on duty since before five AM this morning, and has certainly earned more than a token libation for his strenuous exertions on the part of the citizens. I'll start with the usual, if you please, sir."

"Are you off-duty too?" Brad asked Conrad, assuming he too was an officer, or one of Ray's several seasonal employees.

"If Ray says so," Conrad laughed. "You can serve me in good conscience."

After they got their drinks—a double shot of Irish whiskey neat and a glass of water for Conrad, tequila and a pint of Juneau craft beer for Ray—the biologist introduced Conrad as an old friend, vacationing in Alaska.

Brad was in most ways a perfect bartender. He was a good listener, discreet, who had a sixth sense for when not to ask too many questions. He was certain he had seen the trim, tall, clean-shaven man before, but couldn't remember if it was in the bar or elsewhere. He did not ask how the two men were acquainted, or what Conrad did for a living. Brad Olorus had found it best to assume all visitors to the bar were simply tourists, unless they volunteered more information. But he intuited there was something different about this man, who, unlike most tourists, gave only a passing glance to the numerous mildly risqué gold rush era prostitute photos, and the collection of antique bedpans hung from the time-tarnished shiplap walls.

The bartender had no such reservations about quizzing Ray. The biologist lived in Haines, but was a frequent visitor to Skagway, a mere fifteen miles by plane or boat, though the only road between the two towns ran hundreds of miles through the Canadian Yukon.

"I thought you were normally up the Chilkat River counting salmon this time of year, Ray. What brings you to our fair city?"

"The Juneau office wants me to unofficially check out the Dyea flood situation, and give them at least a preliminary report on the effects of that catastrophe on the fish. I told them I'd mosey on out and take a look in exchange for a few more days paid vacation."

This was partially true, and was also a good cover for his primary duty, working with Conrad to find the source of the threat to the cruise ships, and the killer of agent Jack Dolon.

The July 23 flood of West Creek and the Dyea River had been the biggest news of the summer, apart from the murder. A local and state emergency had been declared, and residents were evacuated by National Park Service personnel. The clean-up was still underway.

"They opened the trail two days after the flood, but it's messy in places. The tour guides are unhappy though—losing money every day the river tours are restricted," the bartender said.

"So I hear," Ray replied. "Still—it could have been a lot worse. At least no one was killed or injured."

Their conversation was interrupted by the band's drummer, Joe Tipoplo, who had finished setting up his drum kit and stepped up to the bar to order a drink.

"Hey—I know you! Conrad Slocum, right?" the drummer said. "What the hell are you doing up here in the middle of this god-forsaken wilderness?"

"Joe—well I'll be damned! I guess I could ask you the same thing," Conrad said, rising from his barstool to take the man's hand. "The last time I saw you, you were playing in Seattle. That must have been at least a couple of years ago."

"Our band's on a tour of Canada and Alaska—well actually just Alaska now. The Canadians wouldn't let Tom, our bass player across the border—seems he had a pot bust in his past he hadn't told us about. So we booked the rest of the summer in Skagway, Haines, and Juneau."

"I think I recognize at least a couple of the same band members," Conrad said, indicating the three men setting up sound gear.

"Yeah, it's still the same four guys; Tom, Terry, Jeff and myself. We've played together off and on since the early seventies. We're still The Lumberjacks—at least officially. For a gag we changed the band poster a couple of weekends ago to 'Assembly Of Dogs.' The owner of this fine establishment, Madame Lucy, only let us do that once," Joe said, grinning.

"Apparently a few of the God-fearing weren't too happy with that. It doesn't pay to piss off too many locals in such a small town. But hey—I'm pretty sure we've improved some since you last heard us, and this place gets crazy wild on weekends—right Brad!"

"Indeed—but it's more fun on your side of the bar. I'll be on call for a double shift," the bartender replied, somewhat peevishly.

"By the way—which one of you guys is really Jack Lumber?" Ray teased.

"If we had a dollar for every time someone asked us that, we wouldn't have to set out the tip jar," Joe replied.

"You guys really do get around. The first time I saw you was in Kabul, back in 1973, and since then I've heard you in four different states, and three countries, Conrad remarked."

"Well, we still enjoy touring periodically, though we've got a lot less tolerance for the sort of flea bag motels we used to stay in. We've upgraded to an RV, with real beds and a kitchen—luxury! As a band we hope to set the record for playing in the most obscure places. We're shooting for Siberia next; that is if Tom's pot bust doesn't rule it out."

"What's the craziest place you're ever played?" Ray asked.

"Afghanistan is definitely in the top three, but Valdez during the pipeline years was pretty wild too."

"Speaking of wild and crazy, I heard that Soapy's Wake, I mean the real one at the graveyard, not the sanitized party they had two days earlier at the Eagles Hall, was out of control this year," Ray said.

Soapy Smith was a notorious con artist who, with his gang of bunco men, virtually ruled Skagway for a time during the Yukon gold rush. He was killed in a gun fight at the peak of his influence on July 8, 1898. His headstone, along with Frank Reid's, who was also killed in the clash, was at the north end of town, past the railroad maintenance yard. The man who most likely finished off Soapy after Reid wounded him, an employee of the nascent White Pass Railroad, Jesse Murphy, was never prosecuted and left town a few days later, never to be heard of again. Instead, Frank Reid was given credit for putting an end to Soapy.

In the 1970s descendants of Soapy Smith, actors from the "Days Of '98" musical drama staged for the benefit of the tourists at the Eagle's Hall theatre each summer, and other locals initiated the ritual of drinking and toasting Soapy's memory on the anniversary of his demise. When their bladders were full many relieved themselves on Frank Reid's grave. This created enough of a scandal, especially after Frank Reid's descendants heard of the ribald ceremony, that the police had began patrolling the area on subsequent July 8th evenings. But that didn't stop the celebration. It still took place each year, but in secret when the police were so busy with the thousands of tourists they hadn't time to interfere with this now hallowed Skagway tradition.

"Indeed it was a wild wake this year!" the bartender agreed.

"Damn! I'm sorry I missed it—I was up on the Chilkat River, counting fish" Ray said.

"There were quite a few strangers there. A group of drunks showed up after someone at Moe's blabbed about the time. I liked it better when it was just the locals," Brad declared.

"Did the cops get wind of it?" Ray asked.

"I'm sure chief Dan knew about it, but it was a record six ship day—four love boats, plus the *Yorktown Clipper* and *Spirit of 98*. The cops had their hands full on the docks and downtown. There was one especially ob-noxious asshole at the cemetery who wasn't content to just drink and piss on Reid's grave. He went on a drunken rampage, ranting about Reid and the railroad. When he broke his booze bottle on one of the gravestones a couple of our local toughs threatened to kick his ass, but another guy—a pretty imposing looking character, and a woman, stopped them. The woman pulled out a can of bear spray. Luckily, the three of them beat a hasty retreat, and no one got hurt. I asked around, and someone said they're camping out in Dyea. I'm guessing they must be tourists who heard the talk at Moe's," the bartender related.

Joe knew very well who the three were, but did not comment. He had enjoyed a one night stand with the woman, Mary Murphy, and pursued her afterwards without success. He was still smarting from her rejection.

"They're probably Canadians. That's who we usually blame for any mischief," Ray said, laughing.

"Well, I hope you'll come out and hear us tonight, Conrad," Joe said, changing to a more comfortable topic. "There's a local sax player, Harry Beardsley whose going to join us on a few numbers tonight. It'll be be busy, so come early if you want a place to sit."

A group of customers entered and shoved two tables together. The bartender left to help get them settled and take their orders. The drummer left to rejoin his bandmates, who were still setting up the sound system.

"Have you thought about tomorrow, Ray?" Conrad asked.

"Well, since your boss insists we need to investigate the Fjord Foundation, we might as well head down to Haines and get that out of the way. We'd best leave early before the wind kicks up. I vote we go get the boat organized now, before we drink anymore, so it's ready to go in the morning. Then we can grab some dinner, and finish off the night back here if you're game."

Conrad agreed, and the two drove to Skagway's only grocery store, then to the Skagway boat harbor to stock the Fish and Game launch for the trip to Haines and back. Conrad wanted to view the area below the cruise ship dock where Jack Dolon's body was found, so they motored the launch's dinghy the short distance over to the wharf from the small boat harbor. Conveniently, it was one of the few August evenings with no ships in port.

"With all the daylight this time of year, it seems surprising no one reported a boat in the area the night of Dolon's murder. There must have been someone in the boat harbor or on the road to the dock. Maybe it was too late for fisherman, but perhaps teenagers out partying, or a random insomniac tourist?" Conrad speculated.

"It does seem a little odd, but maybe the person or persons was lucky, or perhaps rowed or paddled instead of motoring—and it does get pretty dark for a couple of hours—dim enough that a quiet rower might not be noticed," Ray suggested.

Conrad inspected the site closely, trying to form an idea of how the murderer set up the body, which would have been difficult, with the waves slapping up against the dock supports, and the boat gyrating in the water.

"I think there must have been two or three of them. With all the sea motion under here, it would have been a tough job for just one person."

"I have to agree," Ray said. "But if that's true, and Jim Lothar's our main suspect, who the hell helped him, and why? Jim has a few old smuggling cronies in Juneau—could have been one of them I suppose. At any rate, it seems Lothar might have already cleared out. His parole officer in Juneau told the troopers he hasn't reported in for August yet."

"I suppose that makes him even more of a suspect. I'd better catch a flight to Juneau tomorrow, and see if I can track him down. We'll have to put off the trip to Haines until I get back here."

"That's okay by me. I'll have no problem staying busy while you're gone, and now the boat's stocked up and ready to go when you get back here."

"I'd also like to talk to the Skagway police chief at some point, if just to let him know who I am, and why I'm here," Conrad said.

"Good idea. One of Dan's officers is a pretty decent photographer, and you'll want to look at his photos. They might have some you didn't see in your report."

The two men went back to the harbor and berthed the boat. After dinner at one of the Broadway restaurants they were back at the Red Onion in time to find a table before the band started their first set. They stayed until well after midnight, listening to the music, and talking with the locals during the breaks.

Ray was acquainted with the saxophone player, who managed the Skagway ferry terminal. He showed him a photo of Jim Lothar and asked if he had by chance seen the man getting off of the ferry in the days before or after the body was found under the cruise ship dock.

"He most likely would have been driving a brand new, blue Dodge Ram pickup" Ray said.

"I'd have to go back and look at the passenger manifests for the date, but I do remember noticing a pretty nice looking Dodge pickup coming off the ferry a week or so ago," Harry Beardsley replied.

He took a long pull from a can of Rainier, and continued.

"The only reason I remember, is because I've been thinking about a new pickup myself. I'm more of a Ford man, but I have to admit those Rams look pretty good too. If you come on down to the ferry terminal tomorrow we can check that out, Ray."

At each break Conrad and Ray noticed that the drummer, Joe Tipoplo hurried over to a table near the back of the room where an attractive, short-haired woman sat with two men, one with shoulder length hair, and another who sported a thick beard and shaved head.

"That must be the woman the bartender was talking about earlier," Conrad observed.

"You mean the one at Soapy's wake?" Ray asked.

"She fits the description, and so do the two men she's with. It looks like she's made quite an impression on Joe."

"Well, I'll grant that drummer has good taste in women," Ray said.

Ray, with many friends and acquaintances in Skagway, spent the evening talking to the locals and dancing to the loud rock covers the group played with more energy than finesse—the band members being for the most part at least as pixilated as the patrons. Conrad observed the scene with amusement, pacing his drink consumption. They made plans to meet for breakfast at the Sweet Tooth restaurant, which opened early, before walking down the boardwalk to their respective rooms.

CHAPTER 10

Lime River Prison

Linda Daise, the junior partner of the Juneau law firm Solon, Phrastus, and Daise was late for her first face to face meeting with her new client. It especially irked her, as it was her only appointment that afternoon, yet she still managed to arrive ten minutes after the scheduled time, due to the poor service at the Juneau restaurant a few blocks away from her downtown office. She had only recently moved back to Juneau, her childhood home, after less than a year at a busy Seattle firm. Her father, Henry Daise, a prominent Juneau judge, had died the year before. With an offer of partnership and a percentage of the firm's profits, Theodore "Theo" Phrastus, her father's close friend, had persuaded her to move back.

Her client, commercial fisherman Sam Thornton, had been arrested the day before. He stood as the guard ushered her into the interviewing area at the Lime River Correctional Center, and locked the metal door behind her. Sam was a big man, with a barrel chest and powerful arms. When the subject came up Sam would always say he was half Tlingit and half Norwegian, but his heritage was really much more complex, with Aleut, Russian, and Hawaiian genes in the mix. His dark complexion contrasted strikingly with his bright blue eyes.

"Sorry I'm late. Before we get started, Mr. Thornton, I must tell you that I am aware of the altercation between you and my father in Spruce Cove last year, just before he died. If you think I have a conflict of interest, and would rather find another attorney, or work with a different firm, I will understand," Linda opened.

The previous summer, while waiting out a storm in Spruce Cove, a small village near Ketchikan, Sam had forcefully detained Linda's father, Henry Daise, so that David Stuckrath, whose son had been killed in the Juneau prison after being sentenced for drug possession by Daise, could hold a sort of people's court on the question of the judge's moral culpability in the death of the young man.

"That doesn't bother me at all. People I trust have told me you're one of the best—and your retaining fee was reasonable," Sam replied.

"Good—then let's get straight to it," Linda replied.

They sat on the two plastic chairs provided. Linda extracted a folder from her briefcase.

"To start with; I don't care if you committed the crime or not, and you don't have to tell me one way or the other. Whatever you say is strictly between the two of us. Nothing you tell me can be introduced in the court room without your permission. How do you wish to plead?"

"I didn't do it—not guilty. But I'm not sorry he died. He was an arrogant asshole."

"Understood, but we have other issues to deal with besides the homicide itself. Because of the contents of the note found pinned to the victim, this case rises to the level of terrorism; and because of the Twin Towers and Pentagon attacks last year, there's going to be a lot of interest and attention from the press. Besides the local and state media, we're even getting calls from the major national news agencies down south. I'm sorry to say that with all the excitement and the domestic terrorism indictment there is little chance getting you out on bail—at least for the time being."

"That doesn't bother me too much, other than financially. I've stayed in worse places. I'll be missing a good part of the fishing season, but I've got a friend running my boat, so it's not a total loss."

"Let's get to what the prosecution has on you. It amounts to some circumstantial evidence, and plenty of motive. First: Although your fingerprints weren't found on the knife, the note, or the body of the victim, they can prove you were in possession of this particular knife prior to the homicide—at least as late as June. Secondly, there is the incident in Skagway, where you and the victim apparently got in some sort of scuffle."

Linda showed Sam a photo of the old Tlingit knife that had been taken when the relic had been on display at a Juneau gift shop, and a photocopy of the sales receipt with his name on it. Sam, recognizing the historical importance of the knife, had bought it two years earlier. She showed Sam the Haines newspaper article interview with him discussing the age and importance of the artifact, with the headline proclaiming Sam's intention to give the the knife to the Whale House in Klukwan, an old Tlingit village located some twenty-five miles distant from Haines on the banks of the Chilkat River.

"Yeah, but the knife was stolen from my house this summer, before Dolon was killed, along with some of my most prized Tlingit and Haida heirlooms. Someone broke in and took the knife, a bentwood box, a mask, and several other old relics that I inherited when mom died. Funny though, they didn't take any of my guns, and I've got a couple that are pretty valuable. I think they were in a hurry, and knew exactly what they wanted."

"Why haven't you said anything about this before, Mr. Thornton?"

"Sam—just call me Sam—and I hope you don't mind if I call you Linda, okay? I figured I'd have a better chance of getting my stuff back if I kept mum and did a little sleuthing myself. Mostly it seems like the cops don't put much effort into investigating native relic theft. I guess it's a pretty low priority for them."

"If we can prove the knife was stolen before the murder, we might have a chance of getting you released, or the charges dropped. Of course the prosecutor could argue you staged the burglary, I suppose. Can you provide anything that shows you were not in possession of the knife at the time Dolon was killed?"

"I did take some pictures. I'm still hoping my home insurance might cover some of my losses. Several of those relics have been in my family for two or three generations, and they're priceless to me. I just bought the knife to give to the Whale House. I didn't want it going into someone's damned private collection, or a museum down south. It belongs to the clan."

"Okay, so the photos you sent to the insurance company can be dated. I'll subpoena those, and that should convince any jury of your innocence, if we end up in court. It may even be that the prosecution will drop their case against you when they see that evidence. It's a good start—but there's still the motive—your dispute with the victim. The prosecution can call at least a dozen patrons of the Red Onion Saloon who witnessed that altercation between you and Jack Dolon."

Linda shuffled through her folder and scanned a sheaf of papers.

"According to the police report, bartender, and witness statements you and Jack Dolon were kicked out of the Red Onion and proceeded to get into fight on the boardwalk in front of the bar. Witnesses say you had Dolon on the ground before the police arrived and separated you, which apparently resulted in one of the officers getting slightly injured. So there's the resisting arrest charge too. Several witnesses report they heard you tell Dolon you would kill him. Was that just the heat of the moment, Sam, or is there more to this that I should know?"

"It's true I said that. I was drinking, but not so drunk I don't remember saying it. It was a personal matter between us," Sam replied, reluctantly.

"It may have been personal then, but it's not now. If the prosecutor can convince the jury that you had real motive to kill Dolon, they might convict you regardless of your photos, which, as I said, they could argue were staged. I can see you don't want to talk about your conflict with Dolon, and our time is nearly up. I shouldn't have to remind you what is at stake here."

"Well, it's pretty hard to keep secrets around here anyway. He was after my girlfriend. We were going through some rough times, and he wouldn't leave her alone—but I didn't kill him. If I really wanted to, I could have done it then, or some other time. Anyway, my girlfriend and I broke up afterwards. I was stupid. She was nothing but trouble," Sam said, dejectedly.

"What about an alibi? Can you remember what you were doing August ninth, around midnight?"

"Sure I can. I was out fishing, like always this time of year. My log's in the boat, and I'm good about maintaining it. My partner, Jake Terrance, was fishing with me, and I'm pretty sure a couple other fisherman saw us that day."

"So how can I get hold of your log, and talk to your partner?"

"When he's not actually fishing the openings, or offloading fish at the cannery dock he'll be in the harbor at Haines, or at one of the bars in town—shouldn't be too hard to find him."

Linda closed her briefcase and stood.

"Is there anything else you can tell me that might be helpful?"

"There is one thing, maybe. I hear through the grapevine there's a guy working with Ray Standers on this case. He's a federal agent of some kind—I don't know exactly who he works for. I met him last year in Spruce Cove. He's the man who owned the boat your father fell off of. His name's Conrad. I don't remember his last name. Maybe he and Ray can help. Ray and I are on pretty good terms, and Ray might have an idea where Jake is too."

Linda suddenly flushed and caught her breath. The previous summer she had met Conrad Slocum at her father's funeral service. They had followed up with lunch at a Juneau restaurant. Although their mutual attraction to each other was obvious to both, and they were both living in Seattle at the time, Linda had always wondered why Conrad had never contacted her, though she had made a point of giving him her card. She had even suggested they go sailing together on Conrad's boat, but had never heard from him again.

"I'm acquainted with Ray Standers. I'll talk to him. In the meantime you can always reach me if you think of anything else. Regardless, when I see you next I should have a better idea of what the prosecution intends, and with a little luck I may have you out of here on bail in a few days, though I won't promise that. Our time is up, but I'll get back to you as soon as I have more information."

"Hey one more thing, Linda. I never got the chance to say I'm sorry about your dad. I'm sorry too about the way things went down in Spruce Cove last year, but I owed David Stuckrath, and felt like I had to help him out."

"Didn't my father have you locked up a couple of times? Maybe you wanted to get even a little bit too?" Linda replied.

"Yeah, but I was in the wrong. I never held that against him. He was just doing his job, and I was a lot younger then, and drinking way too much. That enforced sobriety didn't hurt me any. It probably even helped me get my shit together."

"Sam, although we've agreed to be on a first name basis, we don't have to be friends, and you don't owe me any apologies or justifications for anything that happened between you and my father. We'll keep things professional. You're paying me to beat these charges, and I'm going to do everything in my power to get you out of here—and the sooner the better."

The door opened with a metallic click and the guard entered.

"Thanks, Linda," Sam called out as the lawyer left the room.

After the guard led him back to his cell Sam sat on his bed, thinking. He wished he hadn't said anything about Linda's father. His awkward condolences were worse than having said nothing at all. He'd made her feel bad, and hadn't meant too. He liked the woman, and he wanted her to like him. He liked the way she looked, the way she talked, the way she moved, and the way her mind worked. It wasn't even that he wanted to flirt, he realized. He wanted somehow to gain her respect and friendship, but because of the incident with her father in Spruce Cove he suspected and regretted that might not be possible.

Perhaps I was too harsh, Linda thought, as she drove from the prison back to town. It was usually best to keep client relationships strictly professional, though often friendships developed. She had read the Coast Guard report about the events in Spruce Cove, taken from an officer's conversations with the group of boaters and residents who had been forcibly detained by Sam. By all accounts it had been an intense encounter. Her father had become enraged, threatening legal action against Sam and David Stuckrath. Conrad too had been there, and she had spoken with him about it. She decided to let Sam know at her first opportunity that although she didn't approve of his bullying, she acknowledged his motivation was sincere, and she harbored no animosity towards him.

CHAPTER 11

Moe's Bar

As Conrad Slocum undressed for bed after his night at the Red Onion with Ray Standers, he was unaware that one of their persons of interest in the murder of agent Jack Dolon, Jim Lothar, was having a drink at the Golden North bar a floor below him.

The Agency and the Alaska State Troopers knew that Lothar, now on parole, had not abandoned his smuggling activities. Agent Dolon had been working undercover on the *Opal Princess* much of the summer. Another investigator had mysteriously fallen off the ship and drowned earlier in the season. Jack Dolon had recently told his and Conrad's supervisor, Richard Head that he suspected the assistant purser, Sebastos Melas was on to him. But although Lothar and the purser had reason to get rid of Dolon, there was no evidence that directly connected either of them with the dead man— at least not enough to justify an arrest warrant.

The Alaska State Troopers still considered Sam Thornton to be the main suspect, but Conrad and Ray disagreed. The troopers had shipped the corpse, knife, cardboard sign, and the ropes used to tie the dead man to the pier to the much better equipped and staffed Seattle laboratory. They hoped the more sophisticated facility would find physical evidence that might be useful in the investigation. So far the results had at least proved the knife was not the cause of death, reinforcing Conrad and Ray's doubts that the fisherman had anything to do with it, or the threat to the cruise ships.

Conrad did not let the unanswered questions about the investigation keep him from falling quickly to sleep. It was an ability he had developed from years of postings in far-flung locations. He had found that a good night's sleep led to clarity of thought the next day. He was convinced that his unconscious mind was busy making connections while slept that would become apparent soon enough.

Jim Lothar was not in a good mood, and the booze wasn't helping any. His previous lucrative relationship with Melas had disintegrated even further after agent Dolon was killed. No amount of protesting had shaken the purser's conviction that Lothar had been responsible.

"Look Sebastos—even if I did kill that asshole, why would I leave a sign on him? It doesn't make any sense," Lothar had protested when he had called the purser earlier that day.

"How should I know? Maybe you wanted to confuse the cops. I don't give a damn. I'd bet my next paycheck you stuck him, you lying bastard—and you fucked up a good thing! We could have made some real money! I'm sure they've got another undercover detective onboard, but I have no idea who it is. At least Dolon was the enemy we knew. We're done doing business for the time being," Melas had insisted. "When this blows over we'll talk again," he added, cooling down some from his tirade.

Jim Lothar was in a real bind. He'd come up from Juneau to Skagway to try again to sell the purser the valuable artifacts he'd stolen weeks earlier from Juneau fisherman, Sam Thornton, and given to Simon Murphy for safe keeping in Dyea. Earlier that summer, while Sam was out fishing, he'd had a fling with Sam's girlfriend. In the course of a drunken assignation she had made the mistake of telling Lothar about the Tlingit and Haida relics the fisherman kept in his home.

Since Jim Lothar had gotten out of prison most of his old contacts avoided him, and he relied completely on Sabastos Melas for his income. For a time, shortly after he was released on parole, he had been reduced to sleeping in his car. Fortunately a meeting with one of his old contacts at the Moby Dick bar in Juneau, where he had run a profitable side operation selling drugs while bartending before his arrest, had introduced him to Melas. The purser augmented his cruise ship wages by supplying shipmates and tourists with the inebriates they couldn't get at any of ship's bars—pot, hashish, cocaine, speed, heroin, or whatever else he could acquire. But Melas had an even more lucrative side business fencing fossilized ivory, poached animal parts, and Native American artifacts to his connections in Europe. That summer Jim Lothar had been one of his most reliable sources for the contraband.

The profits from this arrangement had set Lothar up with a nice Juneau apartment, and made the down payment on his new Dodge Ram pickup. But the loss of this income, even for a few weeks, with no savings put aside, would be catastrophic. He needed to quickly get his hands on enough money to pay his way out of Alaska to his rendezvous with Simon Murphy, before the parole officer or the troopers caught up with him. He had spent the money Hiram had given him a few days earlier, and was nearly broke again. What money he had left had been mostly spent on his room for the night, and dinner.

Lothar downed his vodka tonic, and left an uncharacteristically meager tip. Ruefully he reflected that he had even been forced by his lack of funds to resort to the bar swill, rather than his usual—Stoli, or if they had it, Belvedere—which in more affluent times he would never have adulterated with tonic water. From the Golden North he crossed to the east side of the street, heading north on the boardwalk towards his pickup, which he had parked a few blocks away from the congested downtown. He had a vague plan to hide out in Dyea until he could figure something else out. He assumed Hiram must have left Alaska by now and the cabin was probably empty.

On the corner of the alley between fourth and fifth street Moe's Frontier Bar was going strong. A group of revelers stood outside, smoking and laughing. As he walked by one of the men called his name.

"Hey Jim—what brings a man of your high character to this cradle of iniquity?"

"That's a long story, and a sad one."

"Well no sorrow is so profound that it can't be assuaged, at least temporarily, with a wee dram or two. Come on inside and join us."

"Sorry Alfalfa, but times are hard, and I've probably had enough for the night anyway."

"That doesn't sound like the old Jim Lothar I used to know—a man who would never refuse to tip a glass with an old acquaintance!"

Timothy "Alfalfa" O'Donnell was a big bear of a man, well over six feet tall, and a good eighteen stone. His bushy beard enlarged an already sizable head that seemed to rise neckless directly from his shoulders. He affected to look, dress, and even speak like a nineteenth century gold rush miner. On busy cruise ship days Alfalfa delighted the tourists by reciting Robert Service verses in his stentorian voice. He put a burly arm over Jim's shoulders and half dragged him into the noisy bar.

"I've got to tell you I'm flat broke. I've just about reached rock-bottom this time."

"I'm sorry to hear it, but I'm confident your woes are temporary, and in good time they will pass. You've paid your debt to society, and your luck will soon change! You will recall that some time ago, while dispensing potations at the Moby Dick, you extended me a line of credit with no surety but my word of honor, after a dastardly pickpocket purloined my wallet. I'm pleased to repay the favor. We'll celebrate this serendipitous encounter in style! I assure you that Skagway is a town where my credit is honored everywhere."

Alfalfa knew Jim Lothar only from his visits to Juneau, where he had been a frequent occupant of the barstools at the Moby Dick while Lothar had been manager and bartender there. Alfalfa knew of Lothar's drug smuggling conviction the year before, but was willing to give him the benefit of the doubt, now that he had served his time.

"My good man!" Alfalfa called out to the bartender. "Let's have another round for the house!" Raising his powerful voice to get above the bar hubbub, he declaimed:

"You come in good season, the table is laid;
The rich, fragrant coffee is steaming and hot;
The varied potations are there all arrayed;
The beefsteak is done, aye is done to a dot."

"That doesn't sound like Robert Service," a man at the bar remarked.

"You obviously have a good ear for poetry," O'-Donnell replied.

"Well I should hope so—I was reading Service when you were still in diapers, Alfalfa."

Miles Jameson owned the Days Of '98 show, and inhabited the role of the outlaw Soapy Smith several times a day for the tourists from the cruise ships at the

Eagles Hall theatre. He was so convincing as the notorious conman that some believed him to be Soapy's incarnation. Alfalfa and Miles were great friends, with a mutual love of Skagway and Yukon gold rush history.

"In this case you are correct. It is in fact Jack London, somewhat modified to suit the present circumstances," Alfalfa replied, pulling outwards on his trademark red suspenders and letting them snap back for effect.

"It figures. London could write a hell of a story, but his poetry is mere doggerel."

"What!—this is sacrilege—to impugn the good name of one of the greatest of our literary figures! I should call you out! Only the fact that your usual good judgement and taste has been clouded by a few too many libations prevents me from suggesting pistols at twenty yards in the middle of Broadway."

"I certainly appreciate that, Alfalfa. I've already been shot dead four times today as Soapy Smith, and I don't think I'm up to another go-round."

"...and while I'm calling you out, another thing bothers me," Jameson.

"What in the world are you talking about now?" Miles said, shaking his head.

"Well, everyone knows—at least everyone in Skagway—that Jesse Murphy finished Soapy off with Soapy's own rifle after Frank Reid wounded him, but you still end every show with with Frank and Soapy killing each other in a Wild West duel."

"That's what the tourist brochures say, and it's what the cheechakos expect," Miles replied. "Anyway, I'd have to pay more actors if I portrayed it exactly as it happened—and it's damned hard keeping even my little cast in some kind of shape for those morning shows."

"Yeah, everyone knows that's why you hire mostly Mormon actors," an eavesdropping bar patron sitting next to Miles intruded.

"...and I would appreciate if you all didn't make such a goddamned effort every summer to corrupt my young innocents," Miles pontificated.

"Ah, but they're only too willing, only too willing I'm afraid," Alfalfa intoned. "Skagway seems to have that effect on people who stay for any length of time."

While Alfalfa held forth at the bar Jim Lothar had noticed an old business associate at an adjacent table. Craig Martes was a wiry, goat-like man in his early sixties who, when not making his living as hunting guide, poached or sold animal parts to make ends meet. Lothar and Martes had worked together off and on for many years, with Lothar acting as a middle-man and Martes supplying the illicit goods.

"Craig, how are things?" Lothar asked, taking an empty seat across from the older man.

"...couldn't be better, couldn't be better! Life is good. I heard they commuted your sentence, Jim."

"I wish—just an early out for my exemplary behavior. I still have to report to that damned parole officer, and I'm not even supposed to leave Juneau without getting permission."

"So why you playin' hooky up here in Skag-town, then?"

"With the *Opal Princess* in town, I'd hoped to do some business, but that didn't work out. Seems that since that dead man was found under the dock everyone's pretty uptight. My man onboard won't even talk to me until the excitement blows over. So I'm at loose ends—can't even afford to get drunk on decent liquor. Maybe you've got something for me?"

"I'm sure you had nothing to do with that guy's sad demise, right Jim? Well, never mind—none of my business anyway."

Craig had a certain respect for Lothar, who had a reputation for violence when crossed. The look in Lothar's eye told Craig he might have overstepped. He quickly changed the subject.

"Uh...yeah...there's always ways to make some spare change, if you've got the talent and inclination. As it happens, I have a particular item that might be of some interest to your contacts."

"...that so? The usual stuff—you got it with you?"

"Nope, you'll have to come to Haines and take a look. I'm heading back there tomorrow in my skiff. You're welcome aboard, or you can wait for the ferry if you don't like the idea of getting a little salt spray on your hide. I can just about guarantee this will be worth your time. I'm not talking about bear paws or oosiks. This is different—very rare and damned odd—but I won't say more, you'll have to judge for yourself."

"...sounds interesting. What time you heading out?"

"You know me—I like to get a good start on the day—comes from so many years of hunting and trapping. Can you make it by 6:00? That's a good hour later than I'd usually leave."

"Sure, I'll be there. I guess that means only one more for the road, then. Can you spot me a drink on credit, old boy?"

"I'd be happy to, but there's no need. Alfalfa just ordered another round for the house."

Jim Lothar turned his head just in time to see the bartender ring the bell.

"How about a toast to Alfalfa! This one's on him too!" the bartender announced to loud cheering.

.

CHAPTER 12

Awkward Reunion

...for those who stand in a confessional relationship to ourselves can never love us, never truly love us. —Lawrence Durrell, "Justine"

Conrad had wanted to take a morning flight to Juneau, but no seats were available until that afternoon, and even that flight was repeatedly delayed. He'd made a four o'clock appointment with attorney Linda Daise, but it was nearly seven PM by the time his plane landed. She agreed to meet him after hours.

The year before Conrad and Linda had met at her father, judge Henry Daise's funeral. Motivated partly by mutual attraction, and partly by Linda's desire to hear more about the circumstances of her father's death, they had gone out for lunch together at a Juneau cafe after the services. This time Linda suggested one of the downtown nightclubs where lawmakers and their entourages liked to gather after hours when congress was in session. It was summer recess though, and the bar was quiet. Conrad had already taken a booth when

Linda arrived. She sat her briefcase on the table between them, unopened but still looming like a physical indication of her reticence. Conrad ordered a round of drinks and appetizers, remarking that because of all the uncertainly over flight delays he hadn't had dinner.

In spite of herself Linda had felt her heart rate increase and her face flush when Conrad called. Their phone conversation was brief and impersonal, but the sound of his voice over the poor satellite connection brought up a confusion of conflicting emotions. She wanted to ask why he had not contacted her again after their first meeting a year earlier, and regretted that she hadn't been even more obvious in encouraging him. She had made her attraction to him clear without being, she thought, overly aggressive. Some men, she knew, were repelled by that—but no, she remembered—the attraction was mutual. He had seemed to enjoy their tete-a-tete and flirtation as much as she had.

After returning to Seattle Linda had waited in vain for his call. She knew he was some sort of intelligence agent. Eventually she surmised that he had been reposted elsewhere, perhaps in a situation that prevented him from contacting her. The other possibility, that she might have been wrong in thinking the attraction was mutual, was not worth thinking about. What motive could he possibly have to fake that?

Linda knew he felt some degree of responsibility for her father's death. Besides a secret assignment, that could be the only other reason he had not contacted her again after their first meeting. But she had explained that her father, judge Daise, was a seasoned boater who had spent many years cruising and sport fishing the Alaskan fjords. She had reassured Conrad that he had no reason to feel any responsibility for her father's death. Accidents happen to even the most skilled and experienced boaters, she had reminded him.

After Conrad called a second time to tell her his plane was delayed she gave up trying to get anything done, and left work early. She took a walk through downtown Juneau, past the boat harbor, across the bridge to Douglas Island, and over to Homestead Park, before finally going back to her house for dinner.

"I'm sorry about the delays, Linda. The planes were full, and apparently there was a mechanical problem of some sort. I hope I haven't ruined your evening plans."

Linda's brisk walk, besides somewhat relieving her anxiety at the prospect of seeing Conrad again, had given her time to think more about how she felt, and how she would play her cards when she saw him again. She had felt rejected, and she acknowledged—if only to herself—that her pride had been hurt. She knew she was attractive to most men, and rejection was not a familiar feeling. She was used to being the one who declined or accepted the advances of suitors. Linda had been married for a short time in her early twenties, but had remained single since because of her reservations about the institution of marriage, not for lack of admirers. She resolved to pretend that his whereabouts and failure to contact her during the intervening year had not troubled her.

"That's okay—flight delays are more the rule than the exception here in Southeast Alaska. It's good to see you again, Mr. Slocum. You said you wanted to talk to me about Sam Thornton, so I assume you're involved in the Dolon murder investigation."

"I'd hoped we were still on a first name basis, Linda."

What a rogue. Five minutes together and he's pretending things haven't changed since our meeting a year ago.

"That's fine with me—Conrad—as long as you understand ours must be an adversarial relationship. I'm sworn to defend my client, and I'm in no way obligated to cooperate with any investigation."

Her words came out colder than she had intended. In spite of everything, the attraction remained, and could not be denied.

"Must we be adversaries? I disagree. Shouldn't we be allies? Why can't we help each other get to the truth? My goal is to discover who killed Jack Dolon, and if that is really the same person or persons who derailed the train, and left that threatening message. I also want to find the motive. Is money the only reason, or is there something more? Of course I hope to prevent whoever is behind this from killing again. In my experience figuring out the motivation usually leads to finding the culprit."

Conrad was well aware that Linda's feelings for him must be ambivalent, but he needed her help, and more urgently, he found he wanted her every bit as intensely as at their first encounter.

It seemed to Linda that Conrad was talking on two levels—or was she just reading into his words because of her reluctant attraction to him?

"Truth!" she shot back. "A commendable pursuit of course, but not my affair. I only have a responsibility to defend my client, not to help you figure out who the killer was or his or her motives. I'm legally bound to do my best to keep my client's freedom, regardless of what your investigation reveals. Tell me how cooperating with you helps Sam Thornton's situation."

"If I told you I don't believe Sam was responsible, would you be more inclined to help?"

"I might, if you were willing to say the same thing to the prosecutor and judge, and help me get Sam out on bail, where he'll have a better chance of making his case. Quid pro quo, as they say."

Linda could not help wondering if Conrad was just leading her on, hoping to get some inside information from the defense.

"It's a bit more complicated, I'm afraid. I honestly don't think Sam had anything to do with the affair, and neither does our mutual acquaintance, Ray Standers, who is my partner in this investigation. But Ray and I agree that keeping him incarcerated a while longer, and letting the press think we have the killer locked away might lead the real perpetrator to get careless, and give us a better chance of getting to the bottom of this. The threat to the cruise ships and railroad could be real. There's no way we can patrol the entire length of the railroad and closely monitor every cruise ship that comes up the inside passage to Southeast Alaska. We have to hope for some kind of break."

"I'm not convinced your idea has much merit," Linda replied.

"Why would someone go to all the effort to break into Sam's place, steal that Tlingit knife, and murder someone with it, if not to frame Sam? If we can prove Sam is telling the truth, that's an obvious conclusion that any juror will buy."

"Do you actually have another suspect, or are you asking me and the court to hold Sam in a prison cell indefinitely, while you sniff around and hope for something to pop up?"

"No, not indefinitely. I wouldn't ask if we didn't have at least one other suspect under investigation. The fact is we have at least two, and we don't want to tip them off. I'm hoping to track one of them down tomorrow morning here in Juneau, before I have to get back up to Skagway and Haines. I'm not asking for much time."

"What are we talking about here—days, weeks?"

"I think ten days should give us time enough to shake the trees and see what falls out."

"I heard you spent last year in Hawaii. When you were shaking the palms one of those coconuts must have fallen on your head. Ten days is too long. I'd be willing to talk to my client about your proposal. I could agree to four or five days, if Sam okays it. If so, I'm willing to go with you to help propose the idea to the prosecutor and judge."

"I see. It seems some parleying will be necessary. Any chance I could at least persuade you to let me buy us another round. The waitress has been hovering for quite a while."

"On that score at least you have my full cooperation!"

They both laughed, and suddenly the tension between them dissolved. Linda usually trusted her instincts, and was rarely wrong about her first impressions. This was a man she could fall in love with.

Conrad too felt the change in the atmosphere. They ordered another round, then a third and fourth. Their talk turned to lighter matters, then finally circled around to their first encounter a year earlier.

"I know what you want to ask me, and you deserve an answer. I should have at least contacted you before I was called away. In any case, I haven't been back to Seattle or Alaska in a year." (That much at least was true.) "I'm afraid this happens all too often in my line of work."

It was the response Conrad had decided to make to Linda if he ever saw her again. He'd said similar words several times to women, especially during his first years with the Agency, when he had often been reposted on short notice. But this time it was an outright lie. He had run away from both his job and this woman who seemed to offer him what he had long desired, but never found—the possibility of real, lasting love and intimacy. Conrad too was rarely wrong about his first impressions, and though he was practiced at prevarication, this fabrication was more difficult than most.

"That must make it hard on your relationships. Everyone needs to know where their lover is, and when he or she might see them again. Even soldiers get some contact with their families, and some idea of how long they might be away."

Linda tried not to sound resentful, but she couldn't help thinking he might have managed a way to let her know he would be out of touch for so long.

"But we're not lovers, so that hardly applies to us, right?" Conrad smiled disarmingly.

When he smiled that way, Linda found herself imagining him as a young, mischievous little boy.

"...so if we had been—intimate, you would have told me you were going away, and when you would be back?"

"I'm saying I can't just talk to casual acquaintances, or even friends sometimes about my work or postings. As a lawyer, you should understand that, Linda."

It occurred to Linda that their conversation had become a game of badinage only delaying what they both desired. Conrad would be leaving tomorrow, and who knew when she would see him again. Impulsively she leaned across the narrow table and kissed him firmly and quickly on the mouth, then kissed him again, much longer, letting her lips linger until she became conscious of the table edge biting into her stomach, before pulling away.

"Conrad, the next time you have to leave suddenly, I want to be the one person you do tell. Let's get out of here and over to my place before I sober up and change my mind!"

They called a cab, leaving both Conrad's rental car and Linda's Subaru in the parking lot. The cab driver smiled to see the two in the rearview mirror, cuddling and kissing like teenagers in the back seat. Lovers nearly always tipped well.

CHAPTER 13

An Unusual Discovery

While Conrad spent a frustrating morning trying to get a plane from Skagway to Juneau, Jim Lothar and Craig Martes were speeding down the fjord to Haines. Craig's boat, though an open skiff, had a console with a protective windshield which deflected much of the spray as they skimmed across the short chop at twenty-five miles an hour. The two powerful outboards were capable of pushing the skiff at more than twenty miles an hour faster in calm conditions. In his line of work Craig sometimes had need of a boat that could outrun the local law enforcement vessels.

Between the drone of the engines and the rhythmic smack of the hull on the water it was too noisy for conversation, so the men spent the trip drinking coffee from the large metal thermos Craig had brought along. Once Craig cut the engines and coasted nearly to a stop. The sharp-eyed hunter pointed out a group of white spots on the side of the mountain, just below the snow line. With binoculars Jim Lothar was able to observe a trio of mountain goats—one of the favorite targets of Craig's hunting and poaching activities.

The hunt was strictly regulated, and it was illegal to shoot the animals from the deck of a boat, but the chances of being caught were slim with a minimum of discretion.

From the Haines boat harbor the two men drove to Craig's home, perched above the main highway a few miles out of town. Craig unlocked a large metal building that served as his workshop and storage building. Inside along one wall a long work bench held an elaborate array of reloading equipment. An assortment of vicious looking snares, ranging from the small, delicate looking varmint mechanisms, to powerful wolf and bear traps hung on the wall above the bench.

Craig dialed a combination on one of his four massive gun lockers.The heavy safes contained a collection of firearms and ammunition that could have outfitted a platoon. He took a cardboard box from a shelf inside the safe. With Lothar eagerly looking on, Martes carefully unwrapped the towel covering the object within the box. It was just recognizable as a corroded and oddly shaped pistol.

"What the hell is that?" Lothar asked.

"It's a lot of cash for us both, if you can find the right buyer."

"For that rusted hunk of crap? You've gotta be kidding!"

"Well, it does need some cleaning up, but it's what savvy collectors call a puffer. It's a wheel lock pistol, probably originally from Germany. They made 'em in the 1500s, after the matchlocks, but before the flintlocks, which I'm sure you've heard of. Collectors or museums will pay a lot for these—not too many of them around," Craig continued, placing the pistol carefully back into the box.

"Well I'll be damned! Who the hell did you steal it from?"

"I didn't steal it, and I think there's more valuable booty to be found where I got this old pistol. I worked damned hard for it, and it's mine by finder's rights the way I see it. If I don't sell it I might just add it to my arsenal. It's almost two hundred and fifty years older than my oldest black powder rifle."

"So when you say valuable—what kind of money are you talking about?"

"I'm no antique expert, but I do know a little something about firearms, and I'm a bit of a collector myself. I've read that at fancy auctions like Christies these old guns can go anywhere from twenty to a hundred thousand, depending on how rare they are, the condition, and who owned them."

"At least one guy I do business with might have the connections to get a good price, but of course his cut for something like this would be high. But if it's worth what you say we could still make a pretty tidy profit. So you think there's more where you found this?"

"I'd be surprised if we found any more wheel locks. I read they were expensive and rare compared to the old match locks of that era, but I'm pretty sure there's more stuff that's just as old and maybe just as valuable where I found that. If you're interested in helping me out, and don't mind getting some dirt on your hands, we'll split fifty-fifty—after expenses, of course."

Jim Lothar was thinking that the assistant purser of the *Opal Princess*, Sabastos Melas, with his European connections, would be the perfect man to handle any such finds once Melas was willing to see him again. If not, he had successfully fenced fossilized ivory and other contraband through a contact in Whitehorse, though that was more risky than dealing with the cruise ship purser, as it involved crossing the boarder.

"I haven't had time to pick up much action since I got out of the big house, and as I said last night, my cash flow isn't so good at the moment—so I'm in. What's this about getting my hands dirty, though?"

"It's kind of a long story, but here's the bones of it. Back in the 1950s there was a prospector who found some sort of metal plate out on Kuiu Island. He thought it looked pretty old, so he took a rubbing of it and sent it off to the Smithsonian, but the plate itself somehow got lost or stolen. Some say it's evidence that Francis Drake came here in the 1570s. It always seemed like a tall tale to me, but this spring I met a man, Frank Dermit, who said he had actually seen the thing, and told me he knew the area where the prospector found it.

We dug around in a couple of caves on Kuiu Island and came up with this gun, a helmet, and some other odds and ends mixed in with some old human bones. But we had to stop digging when a fishermen showed up. Instead of playing it cool, that idiot Frank chased him off. But we saw he just went over to the next inlet, and was still hanging around. I knew all he had to do was report my boat registration to the troopers and we'd be screwed. So we hid the cave entrance with some brush, erased our trail as best we could, and left. That dumb shit took the helmet, and I took the gun."

"Then why are you asking me to help out—what about your partner, Frank Dermit?"

"He's not my partner. For one thing, he doesn't have any connections to sell the stuff—he's more the adventurer type I guess you'd say, and a real hot-head when he's drinking, which is most of the time. We didn't get on too well, and he got a pretty good bruise on his cheek and a sore jaw to show for his bad attitude. We could've spent all the time we wanted digging more treasure if Frank would have just stayed calm. I'm worried he'll get shit-faced and blab about it some night at a bar, and someone else will get there before we can, if we don't get right on it. If Fish and Game or the troopers get wind of this they'll send someone out to watch the place until the Indians and archeologists take over."

"Give me a couple of days to get organized. I've got some unfinished business to take care of, then I'm your man. "

"Okay but the sooner we get down there the better. We shouldn't be gone more than a few days. We'll take my fishing boat. It's slower than the skiff, but safer, and we'll have a place to sleep, cook our meals, and get out of the weather if it turns bad."

CHAPTER 14

Skagway And Haines

After an unusually late start, and a leisurely breakfast with Linda Daise, Conrad spent the rest of the morning trying to track down Jim Lothar in Juneau, with no success. After lunch, Linda, as she had agreed, went with him to meet with trooper Tenax, Sam Thornton's prosecuting attorney, and the judge assigned to the case to discuss keeping Sam in prison a while longer while Conrad and Ray continued their investigation of other possible suspects. They compromised on a week, after which time the judge insisted Sam must be offered bail, or freed if no more evidence was found to incriminate him. Against the district attorney's objections the judge also insisted that Sam receive some sort of financial consideration for his inconvenience if the prosecution decided to drop charges, and in the meantime he must be moved to a better cell.

Linda drove Conrad to the airport. Conrad, after promising he would call frequently, more than a little regretfully boarded a plane back to Skagway.

Early the next morning Conrad and Ray set out from the Skagway small boat harbor in the Fish and

Game launch. The sky was a clear cobalt blue. The forecast was for mid seventies with a light winds—perfect conditions for their trip down Lynn Canal, a fjord otherwise notorious for funneling ferocious northern or southern gales and building up frightening seas, with very few places to shelter between Skagway and Haines.

Two miles south of Skagway a turbulent stream, Burro Creek, plunged through the forests and down to the fjord from the ice fields above. The creek supplied water for a small private salmon hatchery operation. The complex had a dock, hydro-electric plant, the owner's large log house, a caretaker's cabin, and several more outbuildings. Ray saw the caretaker's skiff at the dock and suggested they interview him.

"How goes it, Earl?" Ray asked, as the man took their bow line.

"Been better," he said, tying off the line to one of the cleats on the small floating dock.

"Some assholes broke into the cabin when I was gone. They didn't latch the door, and a bear got inside and tore it up good. I'll be a couple of more days getting it all cleaned up."

The caretaker was middle aged, with a grizzled salt and pepper beard. He wore dirty coveralls and a Skagway Hardware baseball cap. He doffed the hat and scratched his head in a gesture that simultaneously managed to communicate greeting and puzzled dismay.

"Probably Canadians," Ray quipped.

Ray unofficially inspected the hatchery operations, and he and the caretaker talked some about the seasons's salmon return before the Fish and Game officer abruptly changed the subject.

"Say Earl—did you happen to be working here when that guy was murdered at the cruise ship dock, the night of August ninth?"

"Let me think a minute. Nope—I was in Juneau picking up supplies, but I got back early the next morning. I remember because I had to chase some strangers away."

"Strangers, eh? What can you tell us about them?"

"When I got back George Ripinski's boat was tied to the dock, but he wasn't here, or Hiram either. I guess either he or Hiram Hatcher, George's fishing partner, must have rented the boat out to the strangers—something they do sometimes. There were three of them camping out by the old ruins—two men and a woman—off the trail past the waterfall. They said they had been fishing, but it got late, and the water was rough, so they decided to stay put for the night. I told them it was private property, and they had to go. They didn't put up much of a fuss—it looked like they were already packing to go when I got to their camp anyway. But I could tell they weren't too happy about being seen here, or given the bum's rush."

"What kind of boat is it, Earl?" Ray asked.

"It's a pretty nice Boston Whaler—one of the seventeen footers—older but in good shape. It's got two newer Yamaha outboards—a ninety horse, and a trolling motor. George and Hiram own it together I gather. I got a pretty good look at the boat, as I was irritated that I had to move it to properly dock mine. It seemed like they were pretty well outfitted for a camping trip, but I didn't see any fishing poles. Maybe they were looking to poach a goat or bear. I figured they must have come from down south, or Canada."

Earlier in the conversation Conrad had pulled out a small notebook and begun writing in it.

"Did you watch them leave? Did they say where they were headed?" Conrad interjected.

"So, it's pretty obvious you two are investigating that murder, eh?" Earl answered. "I guess I should have gone in right after it happened and talked to the Skagway police, but it didn't occur to me there was any connection until now."

"There probably isn't," Conrad said. "We're just trying to be thorough."

"Well, to answer your question; I didn't ask where they were from or where they were bound. They took off at a pretty good clip heading south."

"We'll need their descriptions and any other details you can remember, of course. I don't suppose you got any of their names?" Conrad queried.

"I didn't ask them, and they didn't introduce themselves. One of the guys was a pretty tough looking character—over six feet and more than two hundred pounds for sure, and built like a football lineman. He had a bushy beard and a shaved head—oh, and tattoos on his arms. The other guy was smaller—just average sized, about like me, but with long, really long light brown hair—past his shoulders, tied back in a pony tail. He seemed to be the one in charge, and did all the talking. The woman was nice looking—pretty curvy. Her hair was cut short. They were all pretty young—early to mid-thirties, I'd say. The big guy didn't say a word, but the way he glared at me made me pretty nervous. I was glad to see them go."

The men said their goodbyes. Ray started the engine and Earl gave them a shove away from the dock. On the way south Ray picked up the pace some, and they soon arrived at the Haines harbor.

They were met there by Justin Cook, president of the Fjord Foundation, a local nonprofit environmental organization. Justin was tall and thin, with intense periwinkle blue eyes and a halo of curly hair above an open, friendly face. He had a soft-spoken easygoing manner that revealed nothing of the steely determination with which he pursued perceived polluters and other bad operators in the region. Under his able leadership the well-funded group had earned both the the respect and enmity of the mining, logging, and cruising industries.

Justin and Ray were on the friendliest of terms. Both believed strongly that the salmon and wildlife must be protected from the rapacious designs of corporate interests. Justin had labored summers for over two decades as a commercial gill net fisherman. Over the years he had worked all the fisheries in Southeast Alaska from Ketchikan to Haines. He had run unsuccessfully for state representative twice, both times being narrowly defeated by candidates who were far more accommodating to the mining and cruise ship concerns.

The three men walked up the dock to the parking lot, where one of Ray's employees waited to drive them to the Fish and Game headquarters.

"You don't have any objection to being recorded, do you?" Ray asked Justin after they arrived at the Fish & Game office.

"Of course not, Ray. The Fjord Foundation has nothing to hide, and no one in the organization has any connection whatsoever with that man's death, or those threats. But with all the rumors flying around, I'd love to get a little positive press about now. I hope you'll make it known that we're cooperating with the troopers on the investigation."

"Thanks, Justin. Our bosses want us to look under every rock, and I need to cover my ass—especially since the Anchorage office has given me shit for years about being a paid up member of the foundation. I finally told them that I donate to Sea Shepherd and Green Peace too, and if they didn't like it they could speak to my lawyer. That called their bluff pretty well," Ray laughed.

"Coffee anyone? Sorry I've got no cream, just this powdered crap." Ray said when they had seated themselves.

After he filled their cups Ray brought out a small cassette recorder and placed it on the table. The three men stated their names and ages. Ray noted the date and time, and began the interview, mostly reading from a list of questions he and Conrad had agreed to previously, with Conrad occasionally interrupting to clarify a point. Ray first asked Justin for the names of all the executive officers of the foundation, and the major financial donors.

"I thought you would need that, so here's a current list of all our members, officers, and sponsors," Justin said, taking an envelope from his jacket pocket and laying it on the table.

"I know most of these local people, and a couple of the out-of-staters," Ray said, after scanning the list briefly.

"What about these two Washington State donors from Seattle and Bellingham; Frank Carlson, and David Stuckrath? Is that the same David Stuckrath who used to teach high school in Juneau?"

"Yeah—you know him too?" Justin replied. "Oops—sorry—I know I'm supposed to be answering the questions, not asking them! Carlson's an old college friend. David Stuckrath has been a contributor for years. You probably remember he taught in Juneau, but moved south after his son was killed—uh, for the record." Justin added.

The conversation released a torrent of memories. Conrad had a fleeting but intense evocation of scattering his share of his son's ashes the previous year on the waters off Cape Decision, Kuiu Island as he sailed out into the Pacific at the beginning of his voyage to Hawaii and beyond. With an effort he shook off the vision and refocused on the task at hand.

"Mr. Cook, we appreciate your cooperation with this investigation, and the information you provide will help us to eliminate your members and contributors as suspects. I'm actually more interested in the names people who, for whatever reason, have been refused membership. I also note from your bylaws that the officers can blackball any member or contributor from running for office who they believe might compromise or endanger your organization's reputation. Have you actually prevented anyone from running for office who was a member? Have you ever kicked anyone out of the foundation?"

"We've had to reject or dismiss a few people over the years—mostly for misrepresenting us to the press, or other similar objections—but only a handful. I could get their names from the minutes I suppose."

"Have you ever failed to seat an elected officer for any reason?"

Justin looked uncomfortable, and hesitated before answering.

"There was one particularly bad incident about three years ago. The man was popular with the board, a very vocal advocate for the foundation, and one of our bigger individual donors—Hiram Hatcher. We found out he had been convicted of tree-spiking back in the 1980s, down in Oregon. We just couldn't keep him as a member, let alone as an officer. It caused a big stink, and we lost some donors over it, but I still think it was the right decision."

"How did he take it?" Conrad pressed.

"Not very well at first. He made some vaguely threatening remarks—nothing specific, but it made me damned uncomfortable. He said 'we would regret it'— even talked about legal action. At the time I could tell he was barely containing his anger. I remember he slammed his fist down hard on the table at one point. But in the end he got himself under control. Fortunately nothing further came of it. I understand he has a cabin in Dyea now, and lives off the grid pretty much as a hermit."

"Besides his past, was there anything else about Mr. Hatcher that made you or the other officers uncomfortable?" Conrad continued.

"One of our foundation members, who lived near Hiram, and considered himself a friend, told me that after Hiram had a few drinks in him, he would start complaining about how ineffective the Fjord Foundation was—said we should be blocking those cruise ships with fishing boats and nets, or scuttling them before they got to Alaska. He said that was the only way to stop them, anything else was just a waste of time and money."

"He threatened to scuttle a cruise ship? I hadn't heard that, though I knew he was one of the more radical members," Ray said.

"As I understand it, he didn't threaten to do anything himself. He said that's what should be done. I thought it was just drunk talk. We decided it was in everyone's best interest to keep things quiet. At the time, we had a major publicity campaign going, and the officers thought the dustup with Hatcher could hurt the foundation. If Hiram turns out to be responsible for that man's death, I'll wish I had reported him. At the time we didn't know about his other felony, and thought he was just venting his anger."

"What was his other conviction for?" Conrad asked.

"Assault—a bar fight with a logger a couple of years before he was busted for tree-spiking. Apparently Hiram was even tougher than the logger, who the bar owner convinced to press charges. The logger called him a 'god-damned hippie tree-hugger,' and Hatcher knocked the man right off the barstool, and proceeded to kick the crap out him before the patrons broke things up. The logger was badly hurt—and ended up in the hospital with a concussion."

"It sounds like we need to pay Hiram a visit," Ray Standers said. "If you don't have any more questions Conrad, I say we call it a day and get something to eat."

"I agree—especially about eating," Conrad replied.

Ray switched off the tape recorder, and he and Conrad thanked Justin for his cooperation.

CHAPTER 15

Bears And Eagles

As Ray and Conrad walked back to the small boat harbor after their lunch at a popular Haines restaurant and health food store, one of Ray's seasonal employees pulled along side of them with an urgent message for the biologist.

"I'm sorry Conrad, there's a problem out at the Chilkoot weir. We'll have to put off our trip back to Skagway until later. You're welcome to come along for the ride, or hang out in town until I'm done. It's shouldn't take too long."

"I'd love to see the operation there, Ray if you don't mind me tagging along," Conrad replied. "I remember my first trip to Haines, back in 1974 or '75. I caught a couple of coho in the river."

"That was before the state built the weir in 1976, then. The silver salmon are fun to catch and decent eating, but there's nothing like a fresh Chilkoot River sockeye."

"Yeah, but you can't catch those with a pole in the river. I'm afraid until my boat arrives in Juneau I'm reduced to eating salmon at the restaurants."

"As soon as we can steal some time away from this damned investigation we'll go fishing. We never did get around to it last summer, and I can guarantee you will go home with salmon when you fish with me—that is if we can manage to find time before the runs end."

The problem proved to be tourists, who in their scramble to get better photographs of the bears gobbling up the spawning salmon, were blocking access to the weir. The seasonal worker, whose job it was to help count the fish refused to go back to work until something was done about the situation. He protested that Ray's second in command, the man in charge while Ray was helping Conrad, was not doing enough to ensure his or the tourists' safety.

"Yesterday a brown bear charged me. I had to jump off the weir into the river because the gawkers were blocking the way," the seasonal technician complained on the drive out.

"How the hell did you even know I was going to be back in town today?" Ray asked.

"My girlfriend is a waitress at the Bonanza in Skagway."

"Oh yeah, we had dinner there, and I'm sure I did say something about going to Haines today," Ray remembered.

"News travels fast in the north, it seems," Conrad observed.

"Yeah, and rumors too. If I can't remember what I did on a a particular day, I can ask almost anyone in Haines and they'll tell me!" Ray joked.

The roadside leading along the Chilkoot River was crowded with cars, campers, motorhomes, and tour company vehicles. Several tourists had waded into the river only a few yards away from a sow and her two cubs to take photographs of the trio feeding on the spawning fish. Ray shooed them back to a safe distance away. He agreed with the weir technician that something more needed to be done to keep the tourists out of the area in front of the path to the weir.

"The markings and signs aren't enough. On busy days we're going to need someone out here to keep order. The bears aren't hostile, they just need to put on weight for the winter. They see people as an irritant, not as potential food, but just like humans, bears are unpredictable. A good telephoto lens is the only safe or sane way to get close-ups."

On the drive back to town Ray assured the technician that he would speak to his second in charge about the situation.

"We don't have the manpower to have an officer out there all the time, but we'll get someone on the busiest tourist days."

The weir technician drove Ray and Conrad to the small boat harbor. By the time they left Haines it was nearly six in the evening, and a northerly had kicked up a short choppy sea. In spite of the warm sun, the cold spray blowing the tops off the waves forced them to don coats and rain gear. Even so both men were cold and wet by the time they docked at the Skagway small boat harbor.

"I don't know about you Conrad, but I'm starving. It's past my usual dinnertime, and I could use a hot meal and a drink or two."

"Dinner sounds great, but I'm going to pass on the drinks this time, Ray. I've got a couple of calls to make, and I think I'll turn in early tonight. What do you suggest for tomorrow?"

Conrad was far more interested in talking to Linda than spending another night at the bar. He was reluctant to reveal his new relationship to his partner just yet. He knew Ray would think of that development as more than a little odd. Beyond that, he was still trying to sort out his feelings. Conrad had never been married, and his relationships with previous girlfriends had rarely lasted more than a few months.

"Suit yourself. Two trips on that fjord in one day does take it out of you if you're not used to it. I think we should drive out to Dyea after breakfast tomorrow and have a little chat with Hiram Hatcher. There's no road into Hatcher's cabin. From Dyea it's a couple miles up a rough trail, but at least we won't get wet."

After dinner at the Golden North Conrad went directly up to his room, while Ray walked up Broadway to the Eagles club bar. Like most of the locals, Ray found it convenient to be a member of the two fraternal organizations in Skagway, the Eagles and Elks. In addition to the well-stocked barrooms, the Elks building housed the town's bowling alley, while the Eagles gold rush era structure incorporated a theatre. During the long winters the clubs provided much needed and appreciated diversion to Skagway's reduced population.

Seated at one end of the long bar, Alfalfa and Miles Jameson were in fine form, regaling the bar patrons with their descriptions of the antics of the tourists they'd entertained earlier that day.

Miles had performed as Soapy Smith for three showings of the "Days Of 98" musical play at the Eagles theatre, a well equipped hall with seating on two levels adjacent to the bar. Alfalfa had spent his day at the faux tent city tourist trap just outside of town on the banks of the Skagway River; a place called "Liarsville," named after newspaper reporters who had taken up residence there for a time during the gold rush. There, with a huge malamute accompanying him, Alfalfa recited Robert Service poems and showed the tourists how to pan for the seeded gold in the specially built troughs.

"Regretfully it seems your overwrought interpretations of the famed bard of the north's verses are becoming an even bigger tourist draw than our fabulous song and dance production, and Soapy's daily demise under the limelights. I concede you are the winner of our little wager. So, as per our agreement, I must buy the next round for one and all," Miles declared.

"I accept your gentlemanly concession my friend, but must confess I can't take all the credit. The cheechakos are generally more interested in my furry companion and the thought of panning a fortune in gold, than the artfulness of my pitch perfect delivery of such refined frontier sentiment," Alfalfa intoned.

"Far more tourists are compelled to pet the pooch than to shake my hand, and—as much as I hate to admit it—the many letters we get from satisfied visitors confirm my worst fears. That is, that we are a species much more likely to be moved by the panting and drooling countenance of man's best friend than by the most elegant and polished poetry or dramatic performance."

"Well I don't suppose the cur would be as happy with these libations as we are, so perhaps a bone or other doggie treat would suffice in his case," Miles suggested, pointing with a flourish to the canine in question, who was lapping up the last crumbs of a bag of pretzels, compliments of the bartender.

"Perhaps, though I have noticed that he is more than willing, even eager to imbibe any dregs of beer that might find their way into his bowl."

"Pray he does not develop a taste for anything stronger," Miles said. "The devil's drink has undone many a talented actor."

"Well hello Ray!" Alfalfa greeted the biologist. "Your timing is excellent, Soapy's doppelgänger himself is buying a round for the house."

"...and welcome it is, after a long, hard day's work," Ray replied.

"What—counting fish, and dozing away the day sitting next to the weir?" Miles laughed.

"I'll have you know I've been laboring diligently at investigating an important matter. The diversion of the love boats to another harbor would be a severe blow to the bank accounts of you both, who rely on tourism for your incomes."

"Don't expect to drink out on that much longer if you don't get to the bottom of this business soon," Alfalfa declared. "Nobody believes Sam Thornton is behind the murder and that threat to the cruise ships. You've got the wrong man locked up."

"That does not imply we don't have the highest degree of confidence in the trooper's investigative abilities, but we're glad to see you're getting some help from your mysterious sidekick," Miles added.

"You mean Conrad Slocum. Technically he's Sherlock and I'm Dr. Watson on this case. He's been up here on assignment before, and he has the fed's resources at his disposal. I don't claim to be anything but a biologist and wildlife advocate, but Slocum's good at what he does. Don't worry, with his help we'll catch the culprit or culprits."

"Does that mean you've got another suspect?" Miles asked.

"All I should really say is that I don't think Sam Thornton has anything to do with this either, and we're chasing down some other leads. The arrest of Sam was Juneau's affair. Neither Slocum or I had anything to do with that," Ray answered.

"Well, I'll certainly drink to finding the villain—and the sooner the better," Miles said, taking a long pull from his beer. "The only killing we want in these parts is Frank Reid and Soapy shooting it out in the theatre.

We prefer melodrama to realism here in Skag-town, and so do the tourists."

"Our false-fronted buildings are truly a metaphor, in that respect," Alfalfa observed, sagely.

"We like to put a fancy face on things, at least," Miles agreed, "but sometimes it's best not to look too closely at the rickety shack behind."

"Well, if it's ugly, brute function you want in architecture, you have only to go fifteen miles down the fjord to Haines. I'm afraid our Main Street is pretty bedraggled," Ray said.

"But at least you have Fort Seward. Those buildings are gems, and thankfully most have been preserved," Miles replied.

"Actually, I was just over there this morning. Now I don't want to start any more rumors than are already flying around, but I will tell you we would like to interview the local Fjord Foundation members."

"Do you think radical environmentalists are behind the murder?" Alfalfa asked.

"Ha-ha! If that was the case I'd be suspect number one. It's common knowledge how I feel about anything that might impact the wildlife up here. It might be that some foundation member could have heard something, or maybe a far more radical person or group has tried to recruit a Fjord Foundation member recently."

"You can ask me any questions you want, Ray. I joined up a couple years ago, though I haven't made it to any meetings yet," Miles said.

"Isn't that kind of like shooting yourself in the foot, Miles?" Alfalfa observed.

"Some might say so, but I've always liked to bite the hand that feeds me!"

"Sometimes you're pretty damned hard to figure, Miles."

"What do you care—I bought the last round, and if you're nice, I might buy the next one too!" Miles declared, clapping Alfalfa on the back.

The local newspaper owner, Hunter Clio, who had been sitting on the barstool next to Miles, interrupted their conversation.

"Ray, I hate to complain, but we've asked for an update on the case from the troopers and the local police, and we've only gotten the runaround so far. That's one reason there are so many rumors. I don't suppose you would be willing to give the press an interview—even off the record?"

"The radio station asked me the same thing, but I can't give you any more information than you already have, I'm sorry to say—at least for now," Ray replied.

"Well how about this then? As you know I'm a long time member of the Fjord Foundation too. So interview me—but of course I'll expect at least a tiny bit of quid pro quo!"

"Here, here! The man makes a compelling argument for transparency on all sides," Miles agreed, then, raising his voice and his empty glass, he called out: "Another round for all if you please, barkeep!"

"I'll see what I can do, Hunter, but perhaps this is not the best place and time. It's becoming evident to me that my judgement may be impaired," Ray replied.

"May I ask who you have interviewed so far?"

"You're like a dog that won't let go of a bone."

"Part of the job, I'm afraid. Newsworthy stories rarely occur during regular business hours, and sources are often hesitant, or even completely uncooperative."

"Well, this much I can tell you. We interviewed Justin Cook in Haines earlier today, and there are several Fjord Foundation members and ex-members including you, Miles, and Hiram Hatcher who we also hope to interview here in Skagway over the next few days."

"Well good luck finding Hiram. He keeps himself pretty scarce during the summer—not a big fan of tourism or crowds, I'm afraid," Miles said.

"So I've heard."

"It shouldn't be too hard to run him down," Alfalfa offered. "I saw him a while back, and he told me he was on his way back to Dyea after shopping in Whitehorse. Now that I think of it, it might have been around the time that dead man was found under the cruise ship dock."

"That's helpful. Conrad and I had planned to head out to Dyea tomorrow to interview him. I'm aware he had a falling out with the Fjord Foundation a while back. He's not a suspect, but someone we obviously need to talk to, because of his anti-tourism stance and past connection with the foundation," Ray explained.

Of course it wasn't exactly the truth, but Ray didn't want to start any more rumors, or make Hiram's life any harder. Ray and Hiram weren't close friends, but Hiram was a staunch supporter of efforts to protect the region's forests and wildlife, and had joined Ray on several occasions in fights against mining and logging companies that wanted to operate in sensitive areas.

"Now, I think I've said probably too much, and you guys know all too well that I flap my mouth when I drink. So regretfully, I'm going to call it a night," Ray announced, downing the last of his beer and rising from his barstool.

CHAPTER 16

Dyea Shangri-La

The Dyea flats, the delta where the Taiya River braided before it entered the fjord was a riot of high summer green. The recent record breaking flood had undercut the banks where exposed tangles of cottonwood and spruce roots clutched gamely to their precarious purchases. The Dyea valley was more fecund and its microclimate somewhat milder than Skagway's. Where once, a hundred years earlier a thriving gold rush city had existed, now only a handful of mostly seasonal dwellers lived in scattered cabins. Few traces of the old gold rush era structures survived.

From Skagway Dyea was just three miles as the raven flies, but a ten mile drive on a narrow gravel road above sheer cliffs that rose nearly vertically from the Nahku and Taiya bays. Shell middens exposed by glacial rebound had revealed thousands of years of utilization by prehistoric residents of the valley to archeological investigators. The local Tlingits, who controlled the Chilkoot Pass before the gold rush of the 1890s had traded extensively with the interior tribes. Even after they lost control of the pass they continued to profit

from their knowledge of the region by working as pack-
ers for the miners, who were forced to haul a ton of
supplies to the top of the steep trail, or be turned back
by the determined and machine gun equipped Canadian
officers stationed at the top of the pass.

It was another sunny morning with the promise
of real heat before noon. Ray and Conrad parked at the
northwestern end of the flats, just beyond a scattering
of small trees that gradually thinned out to a grassy
meadow. Nearby an old jeep and horse trail led to the
slide cemetery, where victims of a gold rush era avalanche were buried. Two teenaged girls on horseback
galloped by as the men walked from the Fish and Game
vehicle to the trail that led up to the cabin Hiram rented. A model airplane operated by a man further out on
the flats buzzed in circles high above them. Ray found
the unmarked trail head at the base of the cliffs. The
path climbed steeply to a bench above the valley. From
there it continued up a gentle gradient through the pine
and spruce forest to George Ripinski's cabin, where Hiram Hatcher had made his home since moving to Dyea
from Haines.

Phone service had not yet arrived in the Dyea
valley. There was no way the men could be sure Hiram
was home, but Ray knew from his conversation at the
Eagles bar the previous night that he was likely to be
there. Ray also knew Hiram didn't own a car, but relied
on hitching a ride with locals. Dyea Road was busy during the summer months, and Hiram never had to wait
long for a lift. Had the two men explored the area fur-

ther, they would have been surprised to find the Murphy's Dodge van some distance away off the old jeep road, where Hiram had hidden it behind a thicket of alder and stunted shore pine.

The original log cabin, built in the early 1900s, measured sixteen by twenty feet. A crudely constructed plywood addition covered with peeling tar paper and wooden battens had been attached to the rear in the 1960s. Just visible through the trees down a short path was an outhouse, and beyond that, a shed. A pile of split spruce and birch stood off to one side of the front porch. More wood was neatly stacked along the side of the building, where the long overhang of the roof gave it some protection from the weather. A splitting maul embedded in one of the log rounds and the sounds of clucking chickens nearby were sure signs that someone occupied the isolated property.

The cabin door, faced with split logs and hung on substantial iron hinges looked strong enough to deter a bear, or stop a rifle bullet. A heavy, welded black iron raven hinged to a bell and screwed to the door served as the home's unique door-knocker.

"As you can see, Hiram's pretty handy with a welding iron. He used to sell his metal fabrications at the Haines fair every summer, now he hawks them to the tourists from the love boats," Ray said as he worked the contraption.

The metal beak made a surprisingly loud and pleasing clang as it hammered the bell.

"It seems like a woodpecker would have been more appropriate."

The door swung outward suddenly, nearly knocking Ray off the stoop.

"Not so," Hiram Hatcher declared. "The raven is the wisest of birds, and he rings the bell to warn of intruders. The Tlingits and Mr. Poe had the greatest respect for the bird, as do I. But what the hell brings you out here, Ray? I doubt you've come so far to make a social call—and you know damn well I'm no poacher."

"Is that any way to greet an old friend, Hiram? Are you going to let us in or do we have to stand out here on the porch and talk?"

"I find I don't have many friends these days, and I like it that way. You never know when so-called friends might turn on you. But sure—come on in. Who's your pal?"

"Agent Slocum is here to investigate that murder at the cruise ship dock, and I'm his official guide and chauffeur. He's got a few questions for you."

"Well, I don't read the news very regularly or listen to much gossip, so I doubt I can help you any. I'm sorry to disappoint after such a strenuous hike, but I can offer some coffee or tea to brace you for your return trip."

Ray extended a hand, but Hiram ignored the gesture, instead turning his attention to Conrad.

"So what are you—FBI, CIA?"

"Neither," Conrad replied. "As soon as congress passes the act I'll be employed by one of the agencies under the Department of Homeland Security umbrella. In the meantime I'm not at liberty to say who signs my paychecks."

"Well, while you're grilling me, we might as well have a cup of joe. I made a fresh pot not too long ago— might need some reheating, though. I find I need a fair amount of caffeine to speed up the wood chopping. I go through about seven cords every winter, and I've only got about half that much split so far."

Hiram had been packing, not splitting wood. He had tickets for the ferry sailing south two days hence. The firewood he and Liam Murphy had so laboriously split would be a welcome boon to the next occupant of the cabin. With housing so short, his landlord would have no problem finding another renter, even so far from town.

Hiram had planned to spend one more day wrapping up his affairs in Skagway. He hadn't expected law enforcement to move so quickly. The visit was a total surprise. He'd have to come up with another plan. In the meantime, all he could do was stall while he thought of some way to get rid of the men.

Hiram placed two metal mugs on the table along with boxes of powdered milk and sugar. The original log section of the cabin was a single open room. A closed door at the back led into the newer addition. The dining area was furnished with a rough spruce board table, and four mismatched chairs. A sagging old couch covered with a horse blanket, and a couple of duct tape patched bean bag chairs served as seating in the living area. Most of the other side of the room was taken up by a plywood counter with open plywood cabinets above and below. A small propane range and refrigerator were the only appliances. Hiram struck a match and lit a burner under the coffee percolator.

"Can you tell us what you were doing and where you were on Friday, August ninth, the date of the murder?" Conrad began.

"Well, of course I saw the Skagway News headlines about that. But I don't know any more about it than what was in the paper. One day is pretty much like another out here, and I don't keep a journal. I don't think that day was any different than normal. I usually get up about five, feed the chickens and check for eggs, then coffee and breakfast. This time of year I pass the time working on my sculptures, splitting wood, or doing maintenance on the cabin."

"What about that evening?" Conrad pressed.

"Like I said, I don't remember specifically, but I generally eat dinner around 6:00, read or work on my sculptures again, and hit the sack about 9:30 or 10:00."

"I don't suppose anyone can verify that."

"That's not very likely, considering where I live. I don't get many visitors—especially that late—unless you count the owls and occasional black bear or lynx," Hiram laughed.

"I'm sorry I don't have much in the way of snacks to go with the coffee. I could rustle up some pilot bread and blueberry preserves if you'd like—picked the berries myself last summer."

"The coffee is just fine, Hiram—thanks," Ray said.

"I'm sorry to contradict you Mr. Hatcher," Conrad said, looking down at his notes. "I've interviewed two people in Skagway who say they saw you in town that day. One told me he'd seen you get into a van with two men and a woman."

Hiram scowled, but quickly recovered.

"You're right. Now, thinking back, I was in town that afternoon. I got a ride to Whitehorse with some tourists for supplies, and we made a couple of stops in Skagway on the way home. I don't keep much track of dates—just the seasons. I'm aware of what people say about me, but I'm not a hermit or antisocial, and I get to town pretty frequently. I just prefer living out here, with all that damned tourist traffic and chaos, but after the crowds are gone Skagway's a nice place with good people."

"Who were the good people who gave you the lift to Whitehorse and back?" Conrad persisted.

"They were tourists I met at the campgrounds who were headed up that way. I offered to split the gas and show them around Whitehorse."

He couldn't deny he'd been with the trio, but he hoped to keep the investigators' attention on himself, not the Murphys.

"What kind of vehicle, and what were their names? Can they verify you were in Dyea the rest of the day?"

"It was an older Dodge van. I didn't got their last names, or if I did I don't remember. The two guys were, uh, Stan and Oliver, and the woman's name was Mae. They dropped me off around three or four in the afternoon. So no, I guess they can't help much with my alibi. Of course you can check with customs and see I'm telling the truth about driving up the road to Canada and back."

Hiram desperately wanted to protect Mary's identity, even at his own expense, but wasn't sure just how much he should equivocate to dissuade the men from focusing on the Murphy siblings, while still not incriminating himself.

"So, do I have this right? You left here in the morning with campers who you don't know well—or at least not well enough to remember their last names, even though you spent most of the day with them. You did some shopping in Whitehorse and Skagway, then returned home that afternoon. After that you were home the rest of the day and evening," Conrad said.

"That's it. I didn't see anyone after they left— just did my usual chores, had dinner, and hit the sack."

Conrad looked at Ray, and nodded.

"Now Hiram, we've been acquainted a few years, and you have a reputation as an honest man—honest sometimes to a fault. So why the hell are you lying to us now?" Ray asked.

"What are you driving at, Ray? I didn't take notes, and like I said, I don't keep a diary. I've told you all I can remember about that day."

"The hell you have! I know when I'm being bull-shitted, and I just can't figure out why you'd tell us you can't even remember the last name of a woman who's been living with you? I don't believe you murdered Jack Dolon, but you damn well know something that you're not willing to tell us!" Ray insisted.

"Oh—so now it's good cop, bad cop, eh? I'm surprised that you're taking the bad cop role, Ray."

"So you'll have us believe that Stan, Oliver, and Mae were just strangers you met who agreed to drive you to Whitehorse and back. We can assume their last names were Laurel, Hardy, and West. I suppose you'll tell us next that you spent the afternoon and evening with the Marx Brothers," Conrad interrupted.

"Seriously Hiram, if you won't cooperate we will get a search warrant, and you could be arrested," Ray warned.

"On what charges! Where's your goddamned probable cause? You've already got someone sitting in jail, so why are you even nosing around my place. Screw you both! You're bluffing. You don't have a fucking reason to be out here."

"It seems to me he doth protest too much—don't you think, Ray?" Conrad said. "It is true that Sam Thornton sits in prison as we speak, but Thornton insists he's innocent, and he has a better alibi than you've been able to provide so far, Mr. Hatcher."

"Look, Hiram. I don't want to see you hassled for a crime I doubt you committed. Maybe you have your reasons for not wanting to talk about your girlfriend, who I can't help notice seems to have moved on. As I look around your place, I don't see any of the usual signs of a woman's touch. I doubt we would find any women's clothing in your bedroom either," Ray reasoned.

"I'd like to see that search warrant, Ray."

"Mr. Hatcher, we didn't come with the intention of arresting you or invading your privacy. For someone who purports to know nothing of Jack Dolon's death you seem quite defensive, which naturally makes us more inquisitive. In any case we'll figure out the identity of Mary and her two companions with or without your assistance," Conrad said.

"Maybe you can help us in another way. We're curious about a boat, which we understand you have some interest in. Are you willing to tell us more about that, Hiram?" Ray asked.

Hiram hesitated, and was obviously taken aback by the sudden change of subject.

"Sure. I'm a sort of co-owner of a boat with George Ripinski. We use it for fishing and crabbing," Hiram answered.

"What kind of boat is it, Hiram—fiberglass, aluminum, wood?" Conrad asked.

"It's a seventeen foot Boston Whaler Montauk—not too new, but I bought a couple of late model Yamaha outboards, which is a big improvement over the old Johnson and Evinrude it came with. We keep it up—ready to go fishing anytime we feel the urge."

Ray exchanged looks with Conrad at the description of the boat. Although Boston Whalers were popular and common in the region, the description of the newer Yamaha outboards made it likely it was the same boat the caretaker at Burro Creek had seen, and the woman he described must have been Hiram's girlfriend.

"Does George ever rent or charter that boat?" Ray asked.

Hiram looked even more uncomfortable, but answered quickly.

"Well, that's been the only bone of contention we've had in our partnership. He does rent it out now and then, and I don't like it much, since I pay half the maintenance if anything breaks. The boat isn't insured, so if someone damages it, I'm just screwed. George bought the boat itself, but I covered most of the cost of the outboards."

"When was the last time he rented it?" Ray asked.

"I don't know. You should ask George. I doubt he rents it out too often. I've never had a problem using it on short notice whenever I've wanted to go fishing or crabbing."

"We'd love to take a look at that Boston Whaler, Hiram. Is it in the Skagway small boat harbor?" Ray asked.

"Actually, I'm not too sure where it is. Last I knew, George had planned to take it down to Haines on a fishing trip. Hey Ray, if you two don't mind, I'm pretty desperate to visit the outhouse—all that coffee, and my guts have been acting up—maybe that porcupine stew I've been eating the last couple of days. Give me a minute to take care of business and I'll be glad to answer more questions if I can. There's more coffee on the stove."

Looking obviously ill at ease, Hiram got up and hurried out the door. Conrad and Ray watched as he walked briskly down the path to the outhouse.

"Hiram seems pretty nervous," Ray observed, "and he's damn sure not telling us all he knows."

"That much is obvious," Conrad said.

"Well, maybe he's hiding something completely unrelated to that murder. But whatever it is, he's sure uncomfortable talking about his girlfriend—the mysterious Mae."

"...or maybe he's not just figuratively full of crap." Conrad joked. "It's also possible he's not the killer, but knows who is. He might not have offed Dolon himself, but he could have provided the boat to whoever did. His whining about his partner renting the boat, seems fabricated to me. Maybe he's short on cash and rented the boat himself, and he doesn't want George to find out. In any case, I'd like to ask him a few more questions before we decide whether we should get an arrest warrant, or just advise him to stick around until our investigation is over. In the meantime, let me know when you see him coming back—I want to get a quick peek at the bedroom."

"Don't worry, Conrad. I won't ask to see your search warrant," Ray said, facetiously.

The bedroom interior, like the exterior, had never been finished. The walls were exposed studs and bare plywood. One cobwebbed, untrimmed window let a small amount of forest filtered light in above an old, rusty metal frame double bed. There was a low table beside the bed with a twin mantle Coleman lantern for reading, and a dilapidated four drawer bureau against the opposite wall. A few items of clothing hung from a wooden pole in an open closet. A large backpack leaned against the back wall of the closet, and a rifle stood propped in the corner. No women's clothing were in the closet or the bureau.

"I'm getting the feeling that our gracious host has decided he's had his fill of surprise visitors," Conrad said, when he had completed his scan of the bedroom.

"Funny, I was thinking the same thing," Ray agreed.

The two men rushed down the trail to the outhouse. It was empty.

"Looks like that rabbit has run," Ray said.

"Well he can't be very far away—there's only one road out of here," Conrad observed.

"I wouldn't be so sure of that. Hiram probably knows this country better than any man other than possibly that old poacher Craig Martes. He could get up to the pass from here, and over the mountains to Canada. I could probably track him, but we're not outfitted to follow him far in these woods—but it's your call if you want to try."

"No, let's let him enjoy his little hike. We can alert the Canadian Mounties to keep an eye out for him. Someone might see him on the Chilkoot Trail, or if he decides to stop in for supplies at Carcross or somewhere else between here and Whitehorse," Conrad replied. "In the meantime I suppose Mr. Hatcher's behavior would warrant a more thorough search of the property—even without a judge's signature."

"As long is you take responsibility, I'm game."

They looked through the interior of the house, finding nothing of interest. The storage shed beyond the outhouse was secured with a padlock through a hasp. Conrad tore the hasp away from the trim with a single blow of the splitting maul. The shed measured roughly twelve by sixteen feet. Most of the rear section of the single room was stacked nearly to the ceiling with the accumulated refuse of the last several residents, going back at least fifty years.

"It looks like a collection of junk that nobody bothered to take to the dump when they moved out. I suppose some of this might be worth something to a collector or museum," Ray said, holding up a dusty National Geographic.

The issue, dated June, 1985, with a striking green-eyed Afghan girl on the cover, brought back a flood of memories from Conrad's expatriate years in Afghanistan in the early 1970s.

"If it's just junk, why bother to lock it up so well?" Conrad asked, returning to the present. "I don't think it was just to keep the wood rats out."

"Maybe Hiram doesn't want anyone to see his masterpieces until they're finished, or he's afraid someone will steal his welding gear," Ray speculated.

Two large metal creations—a leaping porpoise, a pair of murrelets in flight, and some smaller sculptures, obviously works in progress, occupied the front portion of the shed.

Footprints on the dusty floor led to an old, rat-gnawed mattress in back. Underneath the mattress a rectangular opening had been cut out of the floorboards and covered with a piece of plywood. A ladder led down to a cellar area about seven feet deep and slightly smaller than the footprint of the shed.

"This must be the reason Hiram keeps the shed padlocked," Ray commented.

"Maybe. The cellar is obviously older than the shed. The building was built over the hole, or moved over after it was built," Conrad speculated. "It looks like the entrance to an old mineshaft."

"Why would someone go to so much work to hide a mineshaft by covering it with a building?" Ray wondered.

"Now there's a mystery for some historical sleuth I suppose, but I'm more interested in what this place is being used for now."

"Damn—look at this!" Ray said, as his flashlight beam danced around the dark space. "There's a tunnel here—it's got to be an old mine."

Old pickaxes, pry bars and other tools were piled in a corner, as though the mining activity had stopped suddenly, or the miners had simply dropped their tools at the end of a day's work and never returned.

"We're going to need more than just a flashlight. I'll grab that Coleman lamp from the cabin," Conrad said.

The tunnel, strongly cribbed and supported with rough beams and timbers, proceeded at a gentle downward slope, ending in a low rectangular room twice the size of the space under the shed. A few tattered rug remnants covered the dirt floor, and rough shelving lined one wall. Boards supported by wooden crates had served at one time as seating. Old eating utensils suggested the space had once been a break room for the miners. A dark, moth-eaten blanket hung on the opposite wall. Conrad lifted one corner, and felt a faint current of air.

"Another entrance, I'll bet."

This passage was much smaller. The two men had to crouch low to follow it. The shaft was longer than the first, steeper, and curved gradually as it ascended. At the surface Conrad pushed aside a mat of brush blocking the exit. The opening emerged under a rocky ledge, and was well disguised by a jumble of boulders and tangle of shore pine and alder, the result of an old slide or avalanche. No obvious path led down from the entrance, but Ray quickly picked out a route that was most likely the one used by whoever had originally dug the tunnel.

"We've definitely missed something, Ray. I don't think our ever more enigmatic Mr. Hatcher was doing any prospecting, or working on an archeology dig."

The two men retraced their tracks back down the mine shaft. A careful search of the larger room revealed more recent and ominous contents. A box of dynamite sticks lay on a shelf next to a brochure of the summer's train and cruise ship schedules. Another shelf held cut up magazine pages and a pair of scissors.

"I think we can safely assume Hiram was not planning on using that dynamite for mining," Conrad remarked.

"We may have our man, if we can find him," Ray said. "We'd better get back to town and make some calls. Maybe we can get a helicopter or a tracking dog. We can ask the police to set up a road block on Dyea Road, and alert American and Canadian Customs."

"Sure, Ray. No hurry though. Mr. Hatcher can't do much harm to the tour ships or railroad while he's bushwhacking through some of the roughest country on the planet."

"True enough. If Hiram's heading to Skagway instead of the forest he's made it to the road by now. He might get lucky and catch a ride to town even before we get back to our car. Still, my bet is that he's headed to Canada."

"So you really think he's capable of that?"

"There are about four men I know who you could drop into the wilderness with nothing but a pocket knife, and they could survive indefinitely off the land. Hiram is one of those. The Chilkoot trail is just a stroll for him. There's a lot of unpopulated country on the other side of the pass where he could hide. Plenty of game, fish in the rivers and lakes, and quite a few forgotten old ruins from the gold rush days where he can hole up for days or weeks if he wants. I'll be surprised if we find him any time soon, but I suppose we have to at least make a show of it. I have to admit my heart isn't in it, though. I still can't believe Hiram killed Jack Dolon, or blew up the tracks," Ray explained.

"Why is that?" Conrad asked.

"Mostly the Tlingit knife. Why the hell would Hiram have that, and how would he have gotten hold of it? It just doesn't add up."

"That does seem incongruous. Maybe Hatcher hoped to make it look like the Indians are behind this. We definitely haven't gotten to bottom of it yet," Conrad replied.

The two men hiked back down from Hiram's cabin to the Dyea flats.

"What the Hell!" Ray exclaimed, when they arrived at the Fish and Game vehicle.

Both passenger side tires of the Explorer were flat. They had been deliberately punctured through the sidewalls.

"It looks like Hiram doesn't want us to make it back to Skagway any time soon."

"...a fine way to treat a friend," Ray remarked.

"He didn't seem all that friendly to me."

Maybe we can put the spare on the front, put it in four-wheel drive, and at least make it back to the main road," Ray suggested.

"I've got a better idea," Conrad announced.

He waved over the two girls on horseback they had seen earlier, who, after a spirited gallop on the flats were cooling down their steeds, and approaching them at a leisurely walking pace.

One of the girls, Brenda, knew the biologist's teenaged son. After Ray explained their predicament, the girls agreed to take the men back to Skagway. Brenda and her friend, Susan had both graduated from high school that spring. Susan's parents owned one of the Broadway gift shops where she worked summers. Brenda planned to pursue a career in acting, and had landed her first paid role in the Days Of 98 show at the Eagles theatre as a dancer and singer. During the summer months, whenever they had time off together, the two friends liked to ride their horses out on the flats and on the back roads of the Dyea valley.

While the Brenda and Susan put away their horses, Ray and Conrad removed the two flat tires from the Fish and Game vehicle. The girls gave Ray, Conrad, and their tires a dusty ride back to Skagway in the back of Brenda's pickup.

After dropping off the tires at one of Skagway's two service stations they went their separate ways—Conrad to his room to report the latest results of their investigation to his boss in Seattle, while Ray agreed to check in with the Skagway chief of police, Dan Segrestein and sergeant Tenax in Juneau.

"I was just about to send out a search party for you, Ray," the Skagway chief said.

"Trooper Tenax called me twice today saying he needed to talk to you and agent Slocum ASAP. I figured I'd start at the Red Onion and work my way up the Broadway watering holes. Anyway, you'd better use my phone. All Tenax would tell me is that it has to do with the Dolon case, and you or agent Slocum would fill me in."

Back at his hotel room Conrad thought more about their encounter with Hiram Hatcher. Although he obviously had some reason for giving them the slip and delaying the two investigators, Conrad didn't think they had solved the case. He had a strong feeling that he was missing something crucial. He started to dial his supervisor, then put down the phone, deciding to wait until he had more information. Perhaps Hiram would be found soon. Besides, washing away the Dyea Road dust and calling Linda Daise were his first priorities. He had just gotten out of the shower when Ray, obviously excited, showed up at his hotel room.

"You won't believe the latest, Conrad!"

"Hatcher's passed out at Moe's, so we don't need a helicopter and tracking dogs to find him?"

"Ha ha! If only it was that easy. Sergeant Tenax says the troopers in Juneau have proof Jim Lothar is our man, and Jim's on his way to Kuiu Island."

"What kind of proof? What about Hatcher?"

"It's kind of a long story, but in a nutshell, it seems a witness has stepped up with evidence that ties Lothar to the murder. Tenax told me to forget about Hatcher—at least until we have Lothar in custody. My marching orders are to get my ass down to Kuiu Island on the double. I don't suppose you'd be up for another trip down the fjord tomorrow morning? We'll check in with Tenax, spend the night in Juneau, then head on to Kuiu the next morning."

"I'd be happy to tag along, but why don't the troopers just send someone from Juneau down there to arrest Lothar?"

"I didn't ask, but I'm guessing they're short on manpower, as usual. It's seems like half the troopers take their vacations in August, or else play sick so they can go fishing. I can't say I blame them, but I don't have that option. This is my busy season, and I really should be overseeing the fish counts at Chilkat and Chilkoot weirs—not that I don't enjoy your company."

Conrad looked forward to spending another night with Linda Daise in Juneau, but not going back to Kuiu Island. That place would always be associated in his mind with the grim vengeance he had taken for the murder of his son, Marshall, a year earlier. Technically, he didn't have to answer to trooper Tenax, but even after the discoveries in Dyea he still considered Jim

Lothar to be as likely a suspect as Hiram Hatcher. He also felt obligated to back up his partner in the investigation. If Lothar really was agent Dolon's killer, he might not be easily persuaded to come along peacefully.

"We'd better leave early. We'll have to pick up enough supplies for several days."

"With you it's always early, Ray."

"As they say, the early bird gets the worm—or at least the favorable tide in this case."

After a trip to Skagway's grocery store, and stowing the results of their shopping spree aboard the Fish and Game launch, they had a fresh caught halibut and chips dinner at the Golden North.

"We can eat breakfast on the boat on the way down, and pick up a more food in Juneau if we need to," Ray suggested.

They agreed to meet at the small boat harbor at five AM. Both men went back to their rooms; Conrad to the Golden North, and Ray to the Skagway Inn, a few blocks away up Broadway.

CHAPTER 17

Interrupted Idyll

After leaving Conrad and Ray at the cabin Hiram ran down the trail to the Fish and Game vehicle. He punctured two of the tires with his buck knife and hiked quickly back up the trail, and around behind the property to a cliff above the cabin. From his vantage point he watched through a break in the forest until he saw Conrad and Ray leave. Hiram had no intention of going to either Skagway or up through Chilkoot Pass to Canada, but he needed to gather the supplies for the trip he did plan to make. He saw the two investigators break into the shed. He assumed they would find the old mine entrance under the building, and Jim Lothar's explosives, which the the two men would naturally think were his. After the investigators were gone Hiram doubled back to the cabin.

He could not regret that fateful meeting with the Murphy siblings, though it might cost him his freedom, and certainly made it necessary to abandon this place, which had become home. He would miss Dyea and Skagway, and he would miss Mary even more. There was an ache in his chest as he quickly gathered the things he would need to survive in the wild. His backpack was already mostly packed, it only needed a few more items to account for his sudden change in plans. He slung his trusty lever action .45 brush rifle over his shoulder. For additional protection he had a Colt .44 magnum revolver in a holster on his belt.

Hiram's route through the forest led along a brushy bench south to a seasonal stream, this late in summer a dry gulch. His partially deflated Zodiac, outboard motor, oars, and two plastic tanks of gas were well camouflaged under a pile of branches and driftwood among the boulders above the tideline. While he lived in Haines Hiram had used the boat for subsistence fishing and exploring the coves and rivers in the area. Since moving to Dyea he had occasionally used the inflatable dinghy to fish in Nahku Bay, and a few times for transportation to Skagway. There was no place on the river or near the road to safely store the boat, especially during the busy summer season. Now he was glad that he had not sold the inflatable or its outboard motor, and had thought to fill the two fuel tanks the last time he used the boat.

Hiram motored south down the fjord, staying as close as he dared to the rocky shore. At Taiya Point, about four miles before Haines he turned sharply northeast and ran through the narrow entrance of Taiyasanka Harbor, where the Ferebee River drained into a small bay. Carefully navigating through the shallows Hiram motored the inflatable up the river until he was forced to portage by a mass of fallen trees and brush. Soon afterwards the river became too shallow to navigate even with his outboard raised so that the propellor was barely submerged. He partially deflated the Zodiac, hiding it, the motor, and the fuel, by covering all with brush, as he had at Dyea.

Hiram knew the Ferebee well. The river valley and bay were unpopulated. The only human visitors to the small inlet were fisherman and other boaters seeking temporary shelter from rough weather out in the fjord, and the occasional picnickers from Haines. But hardly anyone went up the steep river valley very far. There were unlimited places to hide in the wilderness of the upper river reaches. The greatest danger was from the large number of bears that frequented the valley and bay—bruins only too happy to steal an easy meal from an unwary visitor, or perhaps make a meal of the interloper himself.

In the past Hiram had hiked all the way over the Ferebee glacier, and could if he had to, reach the remote Yukon interior over an exceedingly rugged route. But for the time being he knew he was safe. His pack contained a butane stove, packages of dried food, water treatment tablets, and other camping supplies. He had also packed a waterproof mountaineering tent, a sleeping bag, warm clothing, and an extra boxes of shells for his rifle and revolver. There was plenty of fish and game in the valley, and ripe berries for the picking. The bears would be his only competition for wild edibles.

Hiram's quickly improvised plan was to spend a couple of weeks in the remote valley, then when the search for him had cooled some, to travel down the fjord to Juneau, where he might be able to stowaway on one of the ferries heading south, or perhaps get passage on a private yacht or fishing boat. He reasoned that taking a plane would be too risky. He could lose himself in Seattle or some other large city. Hiram knew that the absolute worst place to hide was in a small community or sparsely populated area, where strangers stood out. The way to escape detection was in the anonymity of a big city, where a man could forge a new identity if he was careful and stayed under the radar. Perhaps, he dared hope, the Murphys might even make it safely to Ecuador or some other South American country, as Lothar had suggested, and he might eventually rejoin Mary there.

As he set up camp a short distance from the river Hiram thought ruefully about the series of decisions that had resulted in his present predicament. After his troubles with the Fjord Foundation he had decided it was time to leave Haines, where he found he was suddenly persona non grata. He had a few acquaintances in nearby Skagway. George Ripinski had offered the Dyea cabin rent free if he was willing to perform some much-needed repairs and maintenance.

In Skagway, with its booming seasonal tourism he also found a ready market for his metal-work sculpture creations, selling on commission through local gift shops. His relationship with George proved advantageous to both. George was well into his seventies but still spry, and a descendant of a prominent gold rush family. Hiram sometimes entertained George at the cabin, and enjoyed listening to George's tales of the gold rush, old time Skagway, and the Yukon.

But living in Skagway made him doubly aware of the damage to the environment the tour ships caused. He avoided the town on the busiest summer days, when thousands of tourists arrived on the love boats, the state ferry, by plane, and by road and rail. Still, his cabin in Dyea offered a quiet refuge away from all that, and the tourist season was mercifully short. He had been content to live his placid life in the protected little valley.

Living in Dyea had suited him, and in many ways was an improvement over Haines. Hiram earned enough money from the sale of his sculptures and the odd jobs he did for George Ripinski and a couple of George's friends to pay for his necessities, with money to spare. When he wanted a bit more excitement the bars of Skagway or Whitehorse were lively enough for his tastes even in the dead of winter.

Before he left Haines Hiram had a sort of girlfriend, Allison, a determinedly single woman a few years older than him, who sometimes fed him dinner and after a couple of glasses of wine, usually invited him to her bedroom, but rarely to stay the night. She was extremely protective of her independence, and refused to let the relationship develop into anything more serious. Hiram was okay with that. His one try at marriage had ended badly after two years. He was glad no children had resulted from the relationship, though he still hoped someday to have a family.

Skagway was only a fifteen mile boat or plane trip to Haines, where Allison at least cared nothing about his abrupt ejection from the Fjord Foundation. She joked that like W.C. Fields, she would never be a member of any organization that would have her as a member. Allison dismissed his distress. She said it was more the foundation's loss than his. But after he moved to Dyea she lost interest in the relationship, such as it was. He suspected she'd found a more convenient stand-in for her dalliances. He hadn't been back to Haines in months.

He had found no replacement for Allison—not until the Dyea flood, the calamity that had led to his latest difficulties, but also to him finding the woman of his dreams, Mary Murphy. It was as if that huge release of ice and water had set free his own long dammed up emotions.

Ruefully he reflected that the absence of a woman in his life had been the main reason for his poor judgement of late. It was his misfortune that through the Murphy siblings he had become involved with Jim Lothar. Still, he did not regret his time with Mary, and he could not help hoping that they would find some way to reunite, though he realized the odds were against it.

He had hoped to escape his problems by moving to Skagway, but there were supporters of the Fjord Foundation even here—a burgh where nearly everyone owed their livelihoods to tourism, and where almost everyone accepted the industry as a sort of necessary inconvenience during the summer season. A few of the regular dues paying members of the Foundation were year round residents of Skagway. Hiram knew who they were, and avoided them as much as he could, but in such a small town it wasn't always possible. He wondered how much they knew of the reasons for his expulsion, but he had no desire to have anything more to do with the organization.

Now, miles away down Lynn Canal at his camp on the Ferebee River, Hiram knew that once again he would have to find another place to live. For all its limitations he'd grown fond of life in Dyea and Skagway. He didn't look forward to leaving this wild land, and returning to a faster paced anxiety-inducing city existence, but it was too late for regrets. With the perfect hindsight that often comes upon reflection after the fact he could see the series of decisions that had led him to this place and state of affairs. Hiram loved the outdoors, the wilder the better, and he took some comfort in the fact that he was once again, if only for a short time, where he really felt comfortable. But he knew it was only a temporary respite, and unless he stayed hidden he would pay a steep price for his association with the Murphys and Jim Lothar.

CHAPTER 18

On The Run

The Sea finds out everything you did wrong.—Old Norwegian Adage

After dealing with Dolon's body and saying goodbye to Hiram Hatcher the Murphys motored from the Skagway harbor across the fjord to Burro Creek. Early the next morning, a short time before agent Dolon's body was found under the cruise ship dock, they had an awkward encounter with the caretaker, before continuing south to Haines. At Haines every flight to Juneau was booked. They made reservations for the next morning and spent an uncomfortable night camping at a cove in Chilkat State Park, south of the town. A mechanical issue grounded that plane for the day, and once again all flights south were full. They managed to book three seats on a four seater commuter plane for the following day.

"I can't stand another night of these mosquitos and black flies. I'm covered with welts and I need a shower," Mary complained.

"Yeah, I think I'm probably anemic from so many bites," Liam agreed.

"You don't smell so good either, Liam. I agree we should get a room. We haven't seen any cops or hovering helicopters, so I don't think they're on to us yet."

They booked a room at the Captain's Choice motel, just a few blocks from the boat harbor where they had berthed the Boston Whaler. After they took much needed showers the Murphys spent most of the day exploring Haines and the adjacent Fort William Seward grounds. The old fort with all its stately buildings, painted a uniform white, had been sold to a group of WWII veterans after the war, and still retained much of its historic appearance.

That evening they had dinner at the Bamboo Restaurant, and drinks at the Pioneer bar. The friendly and loquacious bartender, who introduced himself as Anthony 'Tony' Acanthurus, proudly pointed out the salt water tank behind the bar containing his prized Blue Tangs. He explained that he normally worked on the Alaska State ferries, but was helping out his sister, the owner of the bar, while the regular bartender was out commercial fishing.

"She takes good care of my pet fish while he catches the wild ones, and I return the favor when I'm not working on the ferry. If I'm not bartending I sometimes bring my mandolin and play a few old Italian and Greek songs."

"You don't seem to have an accent. How did you end up moving from Italy to Alaska?" Mary asked.

"I didn't. My sister and I were born here. Dad's family home in Italy was destroyed in the war. He and mom heard about this place from one of the soldiers who had been stationed here. They fell in love with Haines and bought the bar. It's got quite a history. The usual gold rush stuff, similar to the Red Onion in Skagway. Early in its past a working girl owned the building, though she eventually married and became more or less respectable."

A group of people sat down at the other end of the bar, and Anthony went over to serve them.

"Maybe you're right," Simon told his sister. "It does seem the most interesting people have alliterative names. Anthony Acanthurus—or was it Acanthus? Tony and his Tangs—hey, that would make a good band name, and speaking of bands, I see from the poster on the door that The Lumberjacks are coming over from Skagway to play here tonight. Maybe we should hang out and join the fun. I remember their drummer was quite taken with you, Mary."

Simon was right, Mary reflected. The drummer, Joe Tipoplo had pursued her. She had gone out to dinner with him one evening, gotten drunk, and let things go too far. She liked Joe, but having sex with him had been a mistake. After she met Hiram Hatcher she had not dated Joe again. She wondered despondently if Hiram was still in Skagway, or had already left. She couldn't imagine how they would ever reunite.

As if on cue the the members of The Lumberjacks came through the back entrance of the bar carrying their instruments. Mary could not escape an uncomfortable conversation with Joe, who was disappointed that she had not gone out with him again since their one assignation.

"Hi Mary! It's a nice surprise to see you over here. I can't help thinking you've been avoiding me."

"That's one of the things I like about you, Joe. You're very direct. But even though you're a great drummer, your timing was off."

"What do you mean?"

"I've got a boyfriend. Maybe if we had met earlier it would have worked out. As it is, I'd like to be friends, but that's all."

"I heard a rumor you were living with Hiram Hatcher, so I guess that's true. I see you're here with your brothers. Where's Hiram?"

"He had chores at the cabin, so my brothers and I came over without him."

"How'd you get here—on the shuttle? I didn't see you on the ferry."

"No, we borrowed Hiram's boat. My brothers hope to catch a king salmon, but so far they haven't had any luck."

"Well, I'd better start setting up my drums. We start at nine, and I want to get something to eat before we play. I hope you and your brothers will stick around. We've got some new songs in our set list tonight. It'll be fun!"

"Great—I'm looking forward to hearing you guys, but please don't dedicate Proud Mary to me again —I've never liked that song!"

"Okay, Modest Mary," Joe laughed. "Anyway we've got a better Mary song for you tonight. That's one of the surprises."

"Oh, and what's that?"

"I'm not telling. But it's not 'Mary, Mary' by the Monkees. You'll just have to stick around and find out," the drummer replied.

"I don't think it was such a good idea to tell Joe that we came here on Hiram's boat," Simon reproached his sister, after the drummer left to finish moving his kit into the bar.

"I suppose I could have said we flew over or took the shuttle, but I'm not as quick with lies as you are, Simon."

"Thanks, for the compliment, sis—comes from being a novelist, I guess."

"You mean a would-be novelist. You may be a writer, but you've yet to finish that novel you keep telling Liam and I about. How many years have you been working on that thing?"

"The novel is all done, in my head at least. I just have to find the time to get it on paper, or at least in the word processor, and that's not likely to happen while we're on the run. You'd better go tell Liam that we're supposed to be here in Haines trying to catch a salmon, in case Joe or anyone else asks how the fishing is going."

The Pioneer had no stage. The visiting bands made do, setting up in the adjacent game room. In the main room bar tables and chairs were relocated to make space for a small dance floor. The Murphy's had retained their three barstools at the far end of the bar by the side entrance, and were seated directly in front of the band.

The first surprise Joe had promised occurred half way through the opening set, when Skagway saxophonist, Harry Beardsley joined the band, adding Bobby Keys riffs to a Rolling Stones medley between gulps of Rainier beer. Joe's drumming, inspired in part by the presence of Mary, seemed even more energetic and accurate than usual. The Lumberjacks were in better than average form, perhaps because they hadn't had enough time between setting up their gear and their first set to imbibe their usual amount of alcohol. During their break, while the other band members headed to the bar to rectify that, Joe came over again to speak with Mary.

"How'd we do, Mary?"

"I've only heard you twice, both times at the Red Onion, but I think you sound even better tonight," she said.

"Yeah, I feel pretty good, but our second set is usually our best—after we're warmed up and before we've drunk too much—and we've still got a couple more surprises coming, so don't go away."

"I didn't hear that Mary song you promised."

"It's in the middle of the next set—just stick around. By the way, are you and your brothers staying in Haines again tomorrow?"

Mary thought quickly before answering. She judged it best not to let anyone know of their plan to fly out in the morning. Joe might tell someone, and rumors spread fast in the little towns.

"We haven't decided yet. Maybe we'll stay another day. My brothers still hope to catch that prize king salmon."

"Well, if you don't feel like spending your day sitting in a boat, I've got the band's RV tomorrow, and we could drive up the road if you like. The other guys are sitting in as guest DJs at the radio station. I haven't been up the highway since we were here a few years ago. We could pack a lunch and go all the way to the pass."

"You don't give up easily, do you Joe?"

"Hey—just friends, remember. Friends spend time together, don't they?"

"I'll think about it, Joe. Thanks for the invitation."

"The guys are giving me that look. I'd better get back on my drums."

The band's second set was even livelier. The barroom had filled to capacity and beyond. All the barstools and tables were taken, and many people found space to stand where they could. There was a line of patrons waiting to order drinks at the bar. The bartender, his bar-back, and two waitresses had all they could do to keep up with the orders. Mary's brothers were several drinks ahead of her. Both had found willing dance partners and were happily gyrating on the crowded little dance floor. Mary had accepted one dance offer reluctantly. Usually she enjoyed dancing, but she was not in the mood tonight, and didn't feel much like drinking either.

Once again Harry Beardsley joined the Lumberjacks on saxophone. After several songs they started a slow blues. The side door to the bar opened. A man entered dressed in a black pope's pallium, dark glasses, and an outrageously flamboyant scarlet tiara. His Fender guitar had a wireless connection to an amplifier on stage. He strutted across the floor and joined the band. The sax player grabbed the microphone and announced:

"Here he is—all the way from Memphis by way of Skagway—the Monk of Mojo; the Cardinal of Cool; the Bishop of the Blues; and the Pope of Profundity! The one and only, 'Father Elmore Hooker!'"

Elmore let loose with a furious fusillade of blues licks, before grabbing the microphone and singing:

I'm begging you baby
I'm on my knees
Won't ya listen honey
Can't you hear my pleas
I'm here to confess
My awful sin
I'm tellin' ya woman
It won't happen again

Elmore's voice rose to a higher pitch, and the band picked up the tempo.

You were out of town, and I went down to Moe's
I had a drink or two, maybe more, who knows
Then a little lady, about five foot three
Sat down on the barstool, right next to me
She bought me a whiskey, whispered in my ear
I got something to tell you, that you gotta hear
You're the Bishop of Blues, that's what they say
From Memphis to Chicago, even up Skag-way
But I'm gonna convert you, you ain't fooling me son
'Cause I'm Mother Superior, the real blues nun
If ya wanna rock the blues, and make it real
Get down on your knees, and we'll do the deal
So we left the bar, and went to her pad
But come to find out, her habits were bad
She was the devil herself, in a nun's disguise
She fooled me once, and she fooled me twice
But now I know, I won't get fooled again
If she comes a -knockin', I won't let her in
I'll do my penance, with no complaint
I'll whip it good, 'till I'm a real blues saint

At this point Elmore reached beneath his robe and brandished a short riding quirt, with which he lashed his guitar into a feedback-laden howl. The bar patrons screamed their approval. As he flailed at his guitar strings Alfalfa pushed his way onto the bandstand. The big man squatted down and Elmore climbed on his shoulders, alternately swatting Alfalfa and his guitar as the burly man parted the crowd like Moses parting the Red Sea. He carried Elmore around the floor while Harry followed behind playing his horn, like a modern day blues Pied Piper, to the delight of the now ecstatic audience. After circling the perimeter of the room the trio exited, to the resounding applause of the bar patrons.

"...talk about a hard act to follow!" Joe announced, after the hubbub had died down some.

Although Mary had enjoyed the performance as much as anyone, the music and alcohol had not alleviated her anxieties. What if someone had seen Jim Lothar walking back from the Skagway small boat harbor, and reported him to the police? Mary didn't like or trust the smooth-talking man. If he was somehow connected to the crime, she had no doubt he would blame the death of Jack Dolon on Liam. The Lumberjacks were scheduled to play again the following night in Haines. She wanted to avoid any more encounters with Joe, whose innocent questions were unsettling.

After playing two fast tempo rockers, Jeff, one of the singer-guitarists, made an announcement.

"Our drummer, Joe would like to dedicate this next song to a very special Mary. It's one of the few slow songs we play, so snuggle up!"

Terry, the other guitarist played the opening riffs to "The Wind Cries Mary," by Jimi Hendrix. It was obvious the band had put some effort into the song, as the rendition was true to the original. Joe, who normally sang only backing vocals took the lead on the second verse.

A broom is wearily sweeping up the broken pieces of yesterday's life. Somewhere a queen is weeping. Somewhere a king has no wife. And the wind it cries, Mary.

On the band's second break Joe once again came over to the bar to talk with Mary Murphy.

"Thanks, that was great, Joe, much better than Proud Mary, and it was nice to hear you sing lead. You should do that more often."

"Nope. I know my job, and singing drummers are usually a pain in the ass. It's hard to get the microphone set up right, and hard for me to do as good a job on the drums, usually. Have you thought about tomorrow?"

"I'm sorry Joe, it looks like we're heading back to Skagway in the morning. My brothers have had enough of fishing without catching anything."

During the first set, when they had gone outside briefly to share a joint from the small stash they'd brought along for their trip south, Mary had told her brothers about Joe's invitation to a drive up the road the next day.

"Our made up story didn't help, it just made things more complicated. We need to catch that plane in the morning," she reminded Simon and Liam.

"Why can't you just tell him you don't want to hang out? He knows you have a boyfriend," Liam said.

"I don't want to hurt his feelings. He's a nice guy."

Mary had not told either of her brothers that she had slept with Joe, or they might have understood better why he was being so persistent. At Mary's insistence they went back to their motel before the band finished their last set.

"We have to get up early to board that plane, and I don't want to have to talk to Joe again tonight," she explained.

The next morning the Murphy siblings had breakfast at the Bamboo Room before taking a taxi to the airport. As they pulled into the airport parking lot they saw a state trooper car and another vehicle with official government plates parked together outside the small airport terminal building.

"We've got to go back to the motel!" Mary exclaimed, tapping the taxi driver on the shoulder. "I've forgotten my purse!"

"Sure, but won't you miss your flight?" the driver responded.

"It's okay, we'll call from the motel and book another one," she said.

The taxi driver dropped them and their luggage off at the motel, and collected his fare.

"We can't hang around here any longer. We'll have to continue south in the boat. They'll start searching town when we don't show up for our flight," Mary said.

"I doubt they were even looking for us. They were probably waiting to arrest somebody getting off of a plane from Juneau or Skagway," Simon argued. "Don't you think if the cops were after someone leaving from Haines they would have been parked at the highway or in the parking lot, not next to the terminal?"

"It's not worth the risk. That other car had federal license plates. Why would the feds be involved if it's just local criminals?"

"I don't mind another day or two on the water. At least I got a good night's sleep and a couple of hot meals, and it's a nice morning. We should be able to make it to Auk Bay by this evening," Liam said.

"Okay, then. We've got enough food packed for lunch and snacks today, and enough fuel to make it to Juneau. Let's get going," Simon agreed.

The Murphy siblings had accumulated years of boating experience fishing with their father in the San Juan Islands, and they carried charts of their route. The boat was not suited for rough weather conditions in open waters, but there were plenty of protected bays and coves along the way. The shallow draft vessel could even be beached if conditions became extreme.

The weather continued mild most of the day, but wind and rough water forced the three to pull into St. James Bay about forty-five miles south of Haines later that afternoon. They set up camp for the night, hoping that conditions would improve the next morning.

CHAPTER 19

Tebenkof Bay

The Stuckrath family's sailboat, *Lethe*, an especially fine example of a rare Cape George Cutter 31, bobbed gently at anchor in Thetis Bay, a well protected arm of Tebenkof Bay on the west side of Kuiu Island. Their inflatable dinghy with its small outboard motor was tied to a tree safely beyond the driftwood strewn tide line. With much effort David, Karen, and Cindy Stuckrath had hacked out a rough trail through the thick underbrush leading to a small hollow under a cliff—a site that David's archeologist friend Larry Nemous had asked them to investigate, after Ray Standers found the old Spanish coin there. After days of tedious digging and sifting in the cramped and muddy space—more a grotto than a cave—they were dirty and disappointed. All they had to show for their hours of toil were a few animal bones, shells, and bat guano. The bones would be sent in for dating, and might possibly be old, but there was nothing else of interest.

"I vote we call it a day," David said.

"I vote we give up on this miserable place for good," came the reply from his daughter.

"You're right, Cindy. I don't see any reason to keep at it here. We've already dug deeper than Larry asked us to, and it's obvious others have disturbed the site before us."

Although there was no cell phone service on the island, or most places in Southeast Alaska for that matter, David and Larry communicated by radio nearly every evening. The archeologist's camp was a few miles further south at another bay, Port Malmsbury, where he worked with three graduate student assistants. After dinner David reported that the cave held nothing of interest. The archeologist agreed that they should try a different location. He suggested another group of caves nearby. David reflected it would mean more labor cutting another path through the undergrowth, but even that sounded better than crouching for hours in dark dampness with nothing to show for their efforts.

"Say David, before you start on a new site, why don't you and your family come down to the main camp for the day tomorrow and take a little break. We can go over the topo map together, and you can help us finish the last of the steaks—they won't keep. A couple of my new student assistants aren't much older than your daughter, and she might enjoy their company too. You and Karen can help me defend the booze supply from the troops," Larry laughed.

The next morning they cruised leisurely down the coast in their dinghy. Cindy snapped photos of the scenery and wildlife with her new Nikon, a high school graduation gift from her parents, while David steered a safe distance from the rocky shore. Cindy, who was considering a photojournalism major in college, was eager to add more Alaskan wildlife images to her portfolio.

Karen Stuckrath sat contentedly in the bow, enjoying the perfect summer morning. She had resisted coming to Alaska with David and Cindy at first, but in the end Karen had agreed to this adventure, not wanting to miss the chance to spend time with her daughter. Her feelings about David were still confused and ambivalent, but he was the best of sailing companions. She knew Cindy was disappointed her parents were not sharing the forward berth as in years before. David had taken the starboard quarter berth, somewhat awkwardly explaining he needed to be close to the exit in case he had to pee during the night, and to check on the anchor when the tide changed. Karen did not argue. She was appreciative of David's gesture.

The day was warm, calm and clear. A black bear sow and her two cubs cooperated by posing on a pocket beach, while David cut the motor and let the boat drift within a stone's throw of the boulder and driftwood strewn shore so Cindy could get the perfect camera angle. Besides the photos of the excavations, which Larry Nemous was paying her to document, she had several rolls of otter, whale, and bird negatives waiting to be developed, and hoped to add the more elusive Pacific Marten before they returned to Washington.

They had lunch at the the professor's camp. Afterwards Cindy and the three graduate students paddled kayaks down to one of the nearby Port Malmesbury excavation sites, while David, Karen, and Larry examined a map for other potential sites in Tebenkof Bay.

"I'm sorry I had you spend so much time there. I should have had you explore one of the other caves first, I suppose."

"Sorry you should be Larry! We spent some miserable days in that rathole. At the very least you owe me a bottle of the finest bourbon you can find in Sitka the next supply run you make," David joked.

"So it is written, and so it shall be!" Larry declared.

"At least we won't have to move our boat—those caves aren't far from where we were working. It shouldn't take us long to cut a trail to the other sites."

"Well, it wasn't time entirely wasted. Now that we know that site isn't worth excavating further, we've saved a future expedition some sweat."

"It was worth looking at again, if only because of that remarkable old Spanish coin Ray Standers found there," Karen agreed.

"I'm taking our boat over to Sitka with one of my students tomorrow. It's not just beef and booze we're low on. We'll spend the night and come back the next day. Rest assured you'll have your bottle when we get back, although the selection there isn't always the best," Larry said.

"We weren't sure how much alcohol we could take into Canada, and we're down to the dregs of the vodka and four or five beers, so most any swill is welcome." David declared.

"One more thing, speaking of the Canadian border. Did they let you bring a rifle through?"

"No. We didn't even try. We didn't want to take the chance of getting turned back, or being delayed. We brought some bear spray, and when we told them where we were headed, customs was okay with that."

"Well, I think you need to be armed for the safety of your family. A few days ago a bear came right into our camp. One of my students forgot to clean out a skillet he'd cooked bacon in. We managed to scare the animal away by making a lot of racket, but I was glad to have a gun at hand. Another of my students carries a sidearm, and comes from a family of hunters. I brought along my shotgun, a box of slugs, and a forty-five Winchester. I don't need them both, and I'd feel a lot better if you would take one of the guns while you're here. Luckily there's no brown bears on the island, and either of those would be quite effective against a black bear."

"I won't argue with you. We've seen several pretty close, including a mother and her two cubs on the way here. Since we're in so much brush, I'll take the shorter of the two."

"That would be the Winchester." Larry went into his tent and retrieved the rifle and a box of shells.

"I doubt you'll need it, since you're mostly eating your meals on your boat, but I'll rest easier knowing you're armed when you're on land."

"Nice rifle," David said. "My daughter has one just like it. Cindy was one of only two girls on the shooting team when we lived in Juneau. She won a couple of trophies. Karen can shoot too. In fact both Karen and Cindy are better shots than my son was, or myself. If any bears come near I'll hand the rifle over to the women!" David said.

CHAPTER 20

Thetis Bay Blues

"What do you suggest now?" Jim Lothar asked.

Craig Martes and Jim Lothar had run all day and most of the night before on Craig's fishing boat. They were tired and irritable. They had arrived at Thetis Bay while the Stuckrath's were visiting the archeology camp, and were disgruntled to find a sailboat in the bay near where Craig had planned to anchor.

"No one seems to be aboard, and I don't see a dinghy. They're probably just tourists exploring the bay," Craig suggested.

"Well I wish they would have picked another goddamned place to anchor," Jim complained.

The two men motored Craig's inflatable to the beach. They were even more perturbed to discover that a trail had been cleared back to the cave where Craig and Frank Dermit had found the sixteenth century wheel lock gun and helmet, and that someone, perhaps the owners of the sailboat, had been excavating the cave floor. Martes stood by as Lothar, in a rage, pulled up the carefully placed stakes, and destroyed days of painstaking work the Stuckrath's had put into labeling the features of the dig.

"A hell of a lot of good that does us, Jim. When they come up here again they'll have a pretty good idea who mucked up this place, and they'll probably report us and make some trouble."

Jim didn't respond, but gave Craig a hostile glare that convinced the older man his opinion was not welcome. They didn't speak again until they were back on Craigs's boat.

"Well, if there was anything else worth looking for, they obviously found it. I don't suppose we could convince them to share the booty, seeing as you were there first," Jim mused.

He gazed disconsolately at the Stuckrath's sailboat floating serenely at anchor while he sat in the wheelhouse drinking beer.

"That's a stupid idea. I could see before you tore everything up that they were carefully excavating that cave, not just digging randomly. Archeologists get out to Kuiu Island now and then. But Frank Dermit said there were more caves around here, and I'm pretty sure I can find them," Craig offered, hopefully.

"Yeah, but what if those people in that boat aren't the only ones, and there's a whole gang of archeologists coming back to study this area. Maybe they just left for supplies or something. We need to work fast, and I'd feel a hell of a lot better if we could get rid whoever is in that sailboat," Jim grumbled.

"I don't see how," Craig replied.

"It's definitely a problem. If we threaten them they'll most likely report us, and that's not going to end well for me. I'm on parole, and I'm not even supposed to leave Juneau. If the troopers find me down here I'll go back to the slammer to finish out my full sentence at the very least."

"Well, I suppose I could get a bear or deer while we're here. I hear the moose have made a comeback too. At least the trip wouldn't be a complete waste of fuel and time," Craig suggested. He was always ready for a hunt, in season or out.

"Is that all you think about—shooting animals?"

"It's made a good living for me so far, and I've spent less time in the big house than you," Craig shot back.

"Ah, don't get so excited. I'm sorry I ruffled your feathers. I'm just disappointed. Let's have another drink and see what we can figure out."

"It looks like you already have a head start—at least on the drinking," Craig observed.

Lothar dug another can of beer out of the cooler and opened it.

"If there are more caves we should at least take a look at them. We've come all this way. Fuck whoever is on that sailboat. Maybe they're just visiting, and someone else excavated that cave. Maybe the archeologists are done for the season, or won't be back for days. We might get lucky like you and Frank Dermit. But it's your boat, and your call."

"Sure. I'm the one who invited you on this crazy snipe hunt. I'm happy to stay a couple more days if you're game. But if nothing turns up soon, I'll make the best of it and see if I can bag a little more meat for my freezer, and maybe a hide or two I can sell."

After Jim finished his beer the two men packed up the dinghy and motored along the shore until they found a good place to land, where it appeared the brush was not quite as dense and the beach went inland far enough to drag the dinghy above the high tide line. The men spent hours slashing a rough path up to one of the other caves the prospector had told Craig about.

"That's a good afternoon's work as far as I'm concerned," Jim said. "We can get a fresh start in the morning. We should have brought more to eat. I'm starved."

In addition to their rifles, a pair of long handled pruners, a machete, and a two small camp shovels, they had packed water and a few snacks, but hadn't planned for a long outing.

"Don't you want to at least take a quick look?" Craig asked.

"Okay, I can go another half hour or so, but that's it. If there is anything here it can wait until to-morrow."

After they cleared away the brush in front of the entrance the late afternoon sunlight reached nearly to the back wall of the shallow cave. The two men dug at random. Once Craig yelped when he unearthed bones, but they proved to be bear, probably an animal that had retreated into the cave to die of injuries or old age.

At last, weary and dejected, the men returned to Craig Martes' boat. Craig set out some of his homemade venison jerky and heated up canned beans. He and Jim wolfed them down between bites of pilot bread and gulps of beer.

"Say Craig, I noticed you have some diving gear on board," Jim observed.

"Yep, and I always keep two oxygen tanks filled. It comes in handy. Once it saved my ass when I got my anchor line tangled in the prop and had to dive down and free it. Another time a friend dropped his favorite rifle in the small boat harbor and paid me a hundred bucks to get it back. Scuba gear is good insurance on the water."

"I've done a little diving myself. It's been a while, but I learned how when I was crewing a couple of summers on a gill netter. That diving gear gives me an idea."

"I can see where you're heading with this Jim, but it's not something I want any part of."

"Okay, fine with me. Just let me borrow your gear if you're too squeamish."

"Why risk it, Jim? Let's just check out one of the other caves tomorrow. As long as those people don't bother us, why should we care if they're here? We should at least wait and see what they're up to. If they're tourists they probably won't stay much longer this late in the summer," Craig argued.

The Stuckrath family returned that evening. Craig and Jim watched their dinghy approach the sailboat. Even in the dim light the two men could see there were two women and a man aboard.

"See—like I figured—just some tourists. Whoever was excavating that cave must have either finished, or gone to Sitka or Juneau for supplies. Those folks won't bother us, and we don't need to mess with them," Craig said. "Anyway it's past my bed time. I'm turning in. We should get back at it first thing tomorrow."

Jim sat up a while longer. When finally he did go to to bed he did not fall immediately to sleep. He regretted making the trip to Kuiu Island with Craig. He should have stuck it out in Juneau a while longer, he reflected. Sabastos Melas might have changed his mind by now, and he could have made some quick cash. Although a long shot, the Murphys might actually follow through with the plan to extort money from the railroad. If so, and that scheme worked out as planned, there was no need for him to take part in this wild goose chase. What if the Murphy's were already in the Caribbean? Enough time had passed. His share of the money might already be waiting for him there. He had no doubt they were the kind of people who would honor their agreement if they were successful.

On the other hand, he and Craig Martes had invested so much time and effort in getting to Kuiu Island maybe they should stay at it a while longer, Jim thought. He decided he was willing to spend another day or two, but if they didn't discover anything of value he would insist on giving up the hunt and heading back to Juneau. In the meantime he didn't like the idea of anyone observing their activities. He would have to do something to encourage the people on the sailboat to leave if they weren't gone by tomorrow evening.

The next morning the two men were up early. They spent a frustrating day in the cave they had found the previous afternoon, but their energetic digging turned up nothing of interest. When they returned to Craig's fishing boat that afternoon the sailboat still had not moved. After Craig went to bed Jim remained awake, waiting until the lights in the sailboat were extinguished and he could proceed with his plan.

CHAPTER 21

One Too Many Boats

By the time the Stuckrath family got back to their anchorage from their visit to the archeologist's camp it was nearly eleven o'clock, and about as dark as it got that far north in August. Even so, the newcomer, an older but obviously well maintained fishing boat was plainly visible about a quarter of a mile away, anchored near the entrance to the smaller eastern arm of Thetis Bay.

The next morning David was surprised to see the fishing boat hadn't moved. He had assumed the vessel was spending the night on its way to Sitka and would be away early. Tebenkof Bay and its offshoots were convenient rest stops on the long routes from Juneau, Wrangell, or Petersburg to Sitka, but most didn't linger long. As he drank his coffee and observed with his binoculars through his cabin porthole he saw two men get into the inflatable dinghy tied along side their fishing vessel and motor away. They landed at one of the beaches Larry had suggested the Stuckraths use as a good location from which to start a trail to the additional caves he wanted them to investigate. After dragging their dinghy above the high tide line, the two men disappeared into the forest.

The sight of the men, who paid no attention to his boat, in itself a little odd, gave him an uneasy feeling. He wondered what business anyone could have ashore here, and could only conclude from the rifle barrels he could see resting on the pontoon of the inflatable that they were hunters. Otherwise, no one in their right mind would attempt to penetrate the thick underbrush and savage, thorny devil's club that blocked access to much of the island's interior. On the other hand, David rationalized, it was not really such an uncanny coincidence to find the men here. It was a logical spot for hunters to land, and Thetis Bay was a good anchorage.

After breakfast David and Cindy loaded their inflatable with the tools they needed for trailblazing, and food and water to sustain them for the day. They motored to shore, landing at another small beach some distance away from where the strangers had landed. Although the spot the strangers had chosen was a logical point of departure for cutting a trail to the closest cave Larry had suggested, David decided it would be best to stay away from the hunters, and investigate one of the other sites while the men were in the area.

Karen elected to stay on their sailboat. She preferred preparing the meals and keeping their small vessel well organized and clean to the hard, sweaty work of hacking out a trail through the underbrush, though she liked helping with the excavation of the caves once they were reasonably accessible.

The brush was thick and their progress slow. A little short of the noon hour Cindy and David found a convenient place to pause for lunch. They scrambled up to a rocky promontory that rose above the dense boskage.

"We sure haven't made much progress for a half day's work. I can still see our boat from here," Cindy noted.

While she began removing their lunch from her backpack her father studied the topographic map the archeologist had given them.

"True, but according to Larry's notes here, we don't have much further to go up this ridge to find the cave."

"I see Chatham Strait isn't far either. That looks like a nice protected cove, maybe even closer to the cave than where we are now. Maybe we should move our boat," Cindy observed, looking west.

They had stopped on the slopes of a ridge above a narrow valley that ran west from Thetis Bay. On either side of the valley the thickly forested slopes rose to fifteen hundred feet. David estimated they were about three hundred and fifty feet above a small lake. From their vantage point they could see the lake was fed by a stream that plunged down from the heights of the opposite ridge. A second creek drained the lake to the protected cove to the west.

"According to this map, that cove you're looking at is called Gedney Harbor," David said, between bites of his sandwich.

"That name sounds familiar."

"It should. Somewhere near there was where the man who killed Marshall wounded a cougar, and got what was coming to him."

"Then we're near sacred ground," his daughter said, solemnly. "I wonder if we could find the actual spot where it happened. We're so close. That's partly why I wanted to come to Kuiu Island so badly—I mean besides the adventure and sailing with you and mom— to see the spot. I'd love to photograph it. I'd like to get copies of the photos they took of the cougar too."

At their home the top of Cindy's bureau and the wall behind it were dedicated to the memory of her brother. She had Marshall's athletic awards from high school and college, a collection of his favorite books, music, and the posters that had been on his bedroom walls. Her closet held some of his clothing, including his high school letterman's jacket, which she sometimes wore, though it was several sizes too big for her. A scrap book held photos of Marshall, his obituary, and articles from the Juneau newspaper about his arrest, trial, and death in prison.

David found his daughter's interest in the details of Marshall's killer and the circumstances of his death somewhat obsessive and morbid, but supposed it was her unique way of dealing with her loss. Cindy had been fascinated with photography from the day she got her first camera as a Christmas gift when she was just eight. David didn't fully understand that for Cindy only photographs could prove the reality of anything. The mind could play tricks, invent, and forget, but the camera did not lie.

"The only person I'm aware of who knows exactly where the cougar and Marshall's killer died is Ray Standers, the Fish and Game officer from Haines. You'll remember from the reports in the Juneau newspaper last year that he and another investigator went to Gedney Harbor and found the remains. The other investigator is dead. Larry told us about him—the federal agent they found under the Skagway cruise ship dock with a knife in his chest."

"Maybe when we go up to Skagway I can call Ray and get directions," she replied.

It was frustrating to be so close, but with no way to locate the exact place in the dense forest.

"I don't know. We won't have much time. We're only staying a couple of days on our way back south after our Skagway visit. Just long enough to finish up our reports and hand them and your film rolls of our excavations over to Larry."

David understood that everyone deals with grief and loss in their own way. His wife, Karen had pulled into herself, and their marriage had fallen apart. He had spent the first months after their son's death alone among the fjords of Southeast Alaska on his sailboat, *Lethe*, wandering with no purpose or destination. Both he and Karen had found solace in alcohol for a time. His daughter seemed obsessed with the fate of the cougar, and of Grant Tadlock, Marshall's killer, whose name the family had agreed never to speak aloud.

That afternoon they found one of the caves the archeologist had asked them to explore, but it was too late in the day to start an excavation.

"At least we won't have to do any bushwhacking or trailblazing tomorrow," David said. "We should try to get an early start."

"Sure dad—you know me—always the early riser."

"Well, not too early, but early for you, I mean," David joked as he followed his daughter down the rough trail they had blazed earlier.

"Hey—don't leave me for the bears!"

Cindy, being the better shot, was carrying the rifle, and had disappeared from his sight around a switchback.

"Ahhh—shit!" Cindy yelled.

She had slipped off the promontory they had earlier lunched on, and fallen into the thicket below.

"Are you okay?" David called.

His heart raced as he ran headlong down slope.

"No worries, dad—just a few scratches. I'm fine, and so is Larry's rifle."

Cindy had picked herself up, and was eyeing a glint of metal nestled below her in the tangle of brush.

"Hey—I found gold—well, maybe copper anyway—good luck!"

"Good luck that you're not hurt. That was quite a fall," David said. He was suddenly overcome with relief. "Can I see it?"

"You're shaking, dad," his daughter said as she handed the shiny object to David.

David wasn't only shaking, he was quietly sobbing with relief.

"It's all right dad. I know how you must feel. I'm not going to take chances and get myself killed hiking in the woods, or swimming in the cove, which I know worries you and mom too. But I've got to live. I can't be afraid to do anything out of fear that I'll end up dead like Marshall."

"I know, I know, but just the thought that... I was afraid you might be hurt—I just panicked."

"It's okay dad. I promise no more running or jumping the rest of the way home."

"A spent shell casing—I guess someone was hunting and took a shot from up here," David said.

He handed the shell back to Cindy.

"It's a good spot for it, with a great view of anything down below in the valley."

"I'll keep it. Maybe it really is good luck," she repeated, and put the shell in her pocket.

She had tumbled nearly twenty feet before the yielding branches of willow and alder had checked the speed of her fall.

"I was lucky to fall into this brush that I'm always cursing, instead of on the rocks," she said, noting the adjacent pile of jagged boulders.

"That cartridge might be lucky for you, but chances are it wasn't such a lucky break for the animal someone was shooting at," David said, as they resumed their hike back to Thetis Bay.

"Hey—I've got an idea. When we gat back to the boat you can use your rechargeable drill to make two holes, and I can make a necklace with fishing line," Cindy suggested.

"Sure, maybe your new amulet will bring us good fortune at the next cave."

David and Cindy hadn't heard any gunshots while they were in the forest. The fishing boat was still anchored in the same place. Larry Nemous had informed David that the bear hunting season did not start until the first of September, but deer hunting season was underway. Larry had also noted there was a fair amount of poaching that went on, due to the remoteness of Kuiu Island, and the lack of a permanent human population.

"They would have to be pretty poor or unlucky hunters not to get a shot at a bear or deer here," David said as they motored the inflatable dinghy back to their sailboat.

"Maybe they're hikers, and the guns we saw are just for protection," Cindy suggested.

David didn't think that was very likely, but he kept his thoughts to himself.

Although Jim Lothar tried to be as quiet as possible Craig was a light sleeper.

"I know what you're up to, and I still think it's a bad idea," Craig said sleepily from his bunk. He could hear Jim rummaging in the storage locker.

"Relax, Craig. If I'm not back in an hour or so you can assume I drowned and do whatever the hell you want."

"That diving gear cost me plenty. Are you sure you remember how to work it?"

"If you're so damned concerned, why don't you do the job, smart-ass," Jim retorted.

"You're a crazy bastard, but suit yourself. Try not to bang up my tank. There's a good diving flashlight in there too."

Jim struggled into the tight dry suit and managed to attach the diving apparatus without Craig's help. Craig heard the splash as Jim entered the water. Less than an hour later he heard him climb back into the boat.

"How did it go?" Craig asked.

"Let's just say I don't think that bunch is going to hang around too much past high tide tomorrow," Jim replied.

"What do you mean?"

"The tide is still coming in. That sailboat must draw five or six feet with its full keel. The tide will set them onto the beach. They'll be stuck there until the next high tide tomorrow, which is a foot higher, so it should float them off. In the meantime they'll be busy making sure the water doesn't push them further up the beach as it comes in. They'll have to tie some lines over to a tree or put out a kedging anchor, and maybe even use their dingy to pull them out as the tide comes up."

"What if the boat sinks, or someone drowns? At the very least I bet they'll get in that dinghy and come ask us for help," Craig argued.

"Oh, I doubt that. I arranged things so they'll get the idea they're not welcome here, and get the hell out as soon as they're floating free again."

"Yeah, and they'll go straight to the cops when they leave—not your smartest move, Jim."

"...and tell them what? That they think someone cut their anchor line? Nobody will believe that, and in any case, with no harm done I don't think the cops will be in a hurry to come all the way out here to investigate some tourist's paranoid fantasy. You worry too damn much, Craig. Anyway I don't think we should hang around here much longer. If we don't find anything by tomorrow evening we would be wise to leave before we have any more company. Now, if you don't mind I'd like to grab a couple of hours sleep while I can."

David awoke suddenly and looked at the battery powered alarm clock he kept next to his berth. It was nearly two AM. He thought or had dreamt that he had heard the sound of something moving on deck, and the motion of the boat didn't feel right. He had the sensation that they were in shallow water, though they had been careful to anchor in an area that averaged over thirty feet in depth at the lowest tide.

David threw open the companionway hatch and mounted the ladder to the cockpit. The shore was much closer. The depth meter read only eight feet. Their boat drew over five feet—way too shallow, especially considering the tidal extremes. The anchor, which had held for many days must have somehow lost its purchase.

David walked quickly to the bow. The anchor chain was hanging straight down, and a length of the anchoring line was lying in a jumble on the foredeck!

He pushed the foot control on the electric anchor winch. The rode came aboard without resistance; first the fifty feet of galvanized chain, followed by about twenty feet of rope. The rope had been neatly cut.

"What's going on, dad?" Cindy asked, sleepily.

Karen stood behind her at the bottom of the companionway.

"We've lost our anchor, and we're way too close to shore."

David started the engine and motored slowly away, keeping a careful eye on the depth meter.

"We're lucky it's near slack tide, and I woke up. We would have been aground at low tide. We probably would have floated again at high tide, but it would have been damned uncomfortable laying on our side in the mud for hours. We'll have to rig our backup anchor. It'll take me a few minutes. I'm going to use all chain rode this time, so I'll have to drag that extra chain out of the hold. Cindy can keep an eye on the depth meter and the shore, while you run the engine to keep us in place, Karen."

A half hour later they were safely anchored again. They all went back to their bunks, but David slept little the rest of the night.

"Why do you think our anchor line broke, dad?" Cindy asked as they breakfasted the next morning.

"I don't know for sure. I guess it could have been a sharp rock or maybe some metal down there that wore through it. That's the reason I usually like to use all chain anchor rode. I should have changed that earlier. I just got lazy with all those shallow anchorages we got used to down in the San Juan Islands, and we didn't have any problems on the trip up here. Now we're out a nice Bruce anchor."

He was absolutely sure the line had been purposely cut, and he was equally sure who did it, but he didn't want to frighten Karen and Cindy. The rest of the day he made excuses not to return to the excavation work at the cave site, fiddling with low priority maintenance chores on their boat. He tried to think of a pretext to leave Thetis Bay that would not alarm his family, but while they ate dinner on board David decided to reveal his suspicions.

"But why would anyone do such a thing?" Karen wondered.

"There's obviously some reason they don't want us around, but I'm not about to go over and ask why. Maybe they are poachers. A coil of the anchor line was on our deck, and the end was neatly cut, not worn away or frayed; that much is plain, and there's only one other boat here."

Cindy and Karen followed David's gaze to the fishing boat anchored ominously close by in the calm water.

"How could they even do that?" Karen asked.

"You'll remember that most fisherman up here carry diving gear, in case they need to untangle their net, or get under the boat for some reason. It would be easy to follow our chain down to the end where the rope is tied on, and cut it. Our line didn't wear through —it's a clean cut," David insisted.

"Fucking bastards! Why the hell should we leave!" Cindy exclaimed.

"Calm down Cindy, and be reasonable. Do you really want to confront those two? Most of the time caution is the better part of valor," David said.

"David's right. We'll tell Larry what's going on and he can get the authorities to deal with it. Anyway, we can't really prove they did it," Karen said.

"Oh, I'm sure they did, and I'm pissed off that we'll have to buy a new anchor, but I'm more upset that they were willing to put our boat and lives at risk. Men like that might not stop at that, so it's best we get going."

As they motored past the other boat David could see two men lounging on the deck. They were laughing as they watched the Stuckrath's boat pass by. Suddenly one of the men stood up and pointed at their boat with alarm.

At that instant there were two terrific blasts from inside the boat in quick succession.

The barrel of the archeologist's Winchester protruded from one of the sailboat portholes. Inside Cindy imagined squeezing off two more easy shots.

"Cindy! What the hell do you think you're doing?" David screamed.

"Just a couple of warning shots," she replied.

Cindy continued to sight down the barrel of the Winchester at the fishing boat.

"But they'll have some patching to do on their inflatable."

"What if they decide to start firing back?"

"Then I'll have to put holes in them too. I could hardly miss at this range."

Craig and Jim had dived for the the deck as the shots rang out. After a few minutes Craig cautiously crawled out onto the deck and raised his head above the bulwarks. The sailboat was turning west on its way out of Thetis Bay.

"Shit—the fuckers holed our inflatable!" Craig yelled. "Get your ass out here and help me get it aboard before the damn thing sinks, Jim!"

The dinghy had been hit by both shots. Air was rapidly escaping from the two holes the bullets had torn in the fabric of the top of the pontoon, and the two exit holes underneath.

Cindy's parents were appalled, but she refused to apologize. Ever since her brother's death Cindy had vowed that neither she or any other member of her family would ever be bullied or terrorized if she could do any-thing about it. She had been fully prepared to follow up with far more damaging fire.

CHAPTER 22

Juneau

Shortly after five AM, well before the first love boat was due to arrive, Ray steered the Fish & Game launch out of the Skagway small boat harbor into Lynn Canal fjord. As they sipped coffee from their thermoses and droned steadily southwards, Ray told Conrad what he had learned after they had parted the night before about the latest developments in the Dolon murder case.

"Sergeant Tenax called and told me he has a witness who will swear he overheard Jim Lothar say he was going to get Jack Dolon, at a party in Juneau. Later on I got another call from Tenax, with some weird news. The troopers arrested a local part-time miner and full-time drunk named Frank Dermit in Sitka. He was trying to fence a sixteenth century helmet that he said he found on Kuiu Island at a local pawn shop. Apparently that was too much even for the pawn shop owner's scruples, and he reported it. While they were grilling Dermit Craig Martes's name came up. It seems Martes also found some sort of valuable artifact."

"It sounds like Tenax is working late after school. He must be thinking of running for office," Conrad remarked.

"No, that's just his usual behavior when he's on a big case. The troopers call him 'Tenacious Tenax' for good reason."

"I'm glad you're getting some help from Juneau, because I haven't heard a damn thing useful from my end."

Conrad wasn't surprised at the lack of communication from Seattle, even though former supervisor, now director Richard Head and agent Jack Dolon had been close friends. Although his superior had more than a professional interest in solving the case, his promotion and the reorganization and redirection of agency's mission since the events of September 11 was occupying most of his time and energy. Conrad found it ironic that the director was forced to rely on an agent he genuinely disliked to apprehend the killer of his friend.

Conrad also knew the FBI had two agents in Southeast Alaska investigating the case, but so far he had not met them or had any communications from the team. Although Conrad was officially in charge of the Dolon investigation, he was forced to rely on the state troopers for most of his leads and information. It was an odd position to be in, but as he had learned years earlier, Alaska did things its own way, and he was an outsider here.

Their trip from Skagway to Juneau was uneventful. The two men were able to relax and enjoy the sights and sounds of the vast wilderness of sea, mountains, forests, and glaciers that enveloped them. They were motes in this mighty land that made all human activity seem inconsequential and futile, Conrad mused. Not for the first time he wished he had been able to spend even a day with his son, Marshall in these surroundings. For all the grief that David Stuckrath must feel, he could not help but envy the time they had spent sailing these fjords together before Marshall's death.

The day was clear and warm. They continued down Favorite Channel, until they were safely berthed in Auk Bay that afternoon.

In his Juneau office sergeant Tenax had more information for them. Jim Lothar had been seen in the Haines harbor boarding Craig Martes' boat. A fisherman on an adjacent boat, who disliked Martes, had overheard the two men talking about Kuiu Island. He reported to the Haines police what he heard—something about digging in a cave. The fisherman was of Tlingit ancestry. He knew some of the caves contained tribal remains, and that it was illegal to dig without permission in the region.

Sergeant Tenax provided Ray and Conrad with arrest warrants for Jim Lothar and Craig Martes. It wasn't hard for the sergeant to convince the judge to sign the warrants. It was the same judge who had sentenced Lothar a year earlier for smuggling and illegal drug violations. Agent Dolon had been the arresting officer when Jim Lothar was apprehended. The sergeant suggested that revenge for the arrest was Lothar's motive for killing the man. The troopers had also gathered enough evidence to charge Martes with poaching, and illegal sales and exportation of wild animal parts.

"While you're at Kuiu Island you'll have some familiar company, Ray" the sergeant added.

"An archeologist, Larry Nemous, and some of his students are working on a dig in the Port Malmsbury area. Apparently the Stuckrath family, who you'll remember used to live in Juneau, are helping him out, working nearby in Tebenkof Bay. You'll recall that Jack Dolon went with you to retrieve the bodies of Grant Tadlock and the cougar that killed him. That was a strange affair, and I never felt like we got to the bottom of the whole thing."

The chair groaned in protest as Tenax shifted his massive body.

"I wonder how that archeologist persuaded the family to come back to Alaska."

"Maybe they wanted to see the place where the boy's murderer got what was coming to him," Conrad offered.

Sergeant Tenax, whose intuition was often reliable, felt he had been justified in having Ray Standers interview Conrad Slocum the year before as a person of interest in judge Daise's drowning. He still felt that Slocum knew more about the deaths of Daise and Tadlock than he had revealed.

Ray Standers had discovered that Conrad was an old friend of Karen and David Stuckrath, going back to the 1970s when they had all lived for a time in Kabul,

Afghanistan. But Ray had not told the sergeant of the relationship.

Conrad's tone of voice and matter of fact statement reminded sergeant Tenax that the investigations of both men's deaths, though officially closed had never set well with him. Fortunately for Conrad, neither Ray or the sergeant knew Conrad was Marshall Stuckrath's biological father.

"Larry Nemous and David Stuckrath are old buddies," Ray explained. "They went to college together. I remember Nemous came up to Haines with David in his sailboat a few years back. Nemous gave a presentation at the library. But what the hell does Craig Martes have to do with Dolon's murder?"

"I doubt Martes has any connection to Dolon's death. Craig Martes and Frank Dermit had made plans to go back to Kuiu Island and dig more before they had a falling out. It seems Martes has replaced Dermit with Jim Lothar. Several people saw them together in Haines buying supplies. They were also seen leaving the harbor on Martes's fishing boat. We know they've partnered together before on smuggling deals. I'm sure we can also nail them for the desecration of whatever Tlingit burial site they're planning to rob."

"Do I have this right? You think Jim Lothar killed Jack Dolon because he was the arresting officer who put Lothar in prison last year? Maybe, but I don't think that was his main reason. He had an even better motive—to keep Dolon from breaking up the lucrative deal he had going with Sebastos Melas on the *Opal Princess*," Conrad contended.

"Well at any rate, he had motivation enough to get rid of Dolon one way or another," Tenax replied.

"So did the purser, Melas, and so did Hiram Hatcher perhaps, but we can cross Sam Thornton off the suspect list. I've know Sam for years, and I have a hard time believing he would stab someone to death over a woman—especially with such a unique knife that he had to know would lead investigators right to him. I think we can forget all about Sam, which leaves Hiram Hatcher or Jim Lothar as the most likely culprits," Ray argued.

"Passion can make fools of us all. It's also true that Sam Thornton is on record as hating the cruise ship industry, and he's a dues paying member of the Fjord Foundation," the sergeant temporized. "You recall he's had several run-ins over the years with the cruise industry, which he insists is polluting the waters here, and killing whales."

"Yeah, there was that time Sam and a couple of other fisherman blockaded a love boat and tried to keep them from docking in Haines. The captain got pissed off and just about ran them down—destroyed Sam's net and sent him a bill for hiring a diver to cut it out of the prop. As far as I know Sam never paid it," Ray chuckled.

"Do you still think Sam should stay in the slammer, even though we agreed that he should be let out in a few days? That hardly seems fair or necessary."

"I suppose it's possible that Sam and Hiram could even be working together. I've learned that when it comes to murder, just about any motive is possible. But I don't think we have two suspects, I think we have several," Conrad pronounced.

"Maybe four, if you still include Sam Thornton, which I agree is a stretch," sergeant Tenax said.

"Sam Thornton, Hiram Hatcher, Sabastos Melas, and Jim Lothar all benefitted from Dolon's demise. Sam is the least likely suspect. That still leaves three, and my gut feeling is there's someone else we're overlooking—maybe someone working with Melas on one of the cruise ships," Conrad speculated.

Conrad reflected that although he had an iron-clad alibi, having been in Hawaii when the agent was murdered, he too benefitted from Jack Dolon's death. Agent Dolon had discovered Conrad's complicity in the brutal mauling and death of Marshall Stuckrath's killer, Grant Tadlock a year earlier on Kuiu Island, and Dolon had sent the evidence to their boss, Richard Head.

"I hope you won't miss my company too much if I sleep elsewhere tonight, Ray" Conrad remarked, as their taxi pulled up to the Best Western hotel near the Juneau airport.

"Actually, I figured you might enjoy the down time with Ms. Daise, esquire more than hanging out with this grizzled codger, so I made plans to meet a couple of my old seasonal employees for dinner and drinks at the airport bar."

"I guess it's common knowledge, then."

"...around the water coolers and coffee makers at the trooper office and courthouse, I'm sure. Tenax was concerned you might have a conflict of interest, until I reminded him I've been friends with Sam Thornton, and fought along side of him for salmon protections against the mining and logging corporations for over twenty years, and you only know Sam from one meeting in Spruce Cove a year ago."

Ray and Conrad agreed to meet at the harbor in the morning to continue their voyage south to Kuiu Island.

CHAPTER 23

Conrad In Love

Conrad gave the cabbie directions to Linda Daise's house. On the phone Linda had told him she was running late, but to let himself in with the spare key that she kept under a flower pot on the porch.

After her father died, her mother had left Juneau to live in the family's vacation home in Washington, to be closer to her two sons and Linda, who was practicing law in Seattle at the time. There had been some discussion of selling the Juneau house, but none of them had been able to find the time or will to dispose of their father's belongings, and do the necessary work to put the house on the market. As it turned out Linda was lucky they had held on to it. Rentals were scarce and expensive in Juneau, especially so conveniently close to her law office.

It was a comfortable home, built shortly after the first world war, in the then popular west coast craftsman style. Judge Daise and his family had lived there for most of Linda's life, and had modernized and remodeled the place tastefully, retaining the old charm of the architectural details, while improving the comfort and efficiency.

Conrad grabbed a beer from the refrigerator and went upstairs to the second floor, where a large open landing had served the Daise family as a combination library and guest room. Its generous bow window looked out over the roofs of old Juneau to the Douglas Island Bridge, Douglas Island, and the boat harbors below. Before he had finished his drink he heard the door open, and Linda call to him.

"I'll let you choose the restaurant, but it's definitely my turn to buy," Conrad said, after they finally disengaged from their long embrace.

"Do we have to go out? It was a rough day in court, and I've had enough of the public. I can't seem to go anywhere in Juneau without seeing someone I feel obligated to talk to. I'd like nothing more than to spend the entire evening here, with you. After all, who knows when I'll see you again?"

"That sounds fine to me, but I'm starved—any good takeout restaurants close by?"

"Obviously you were pretty focused on finding something to drink, and didn't check out my refrigerator very well. Sam Thornton gave me about five pounds of some of the best smoked salmon I've ever tasted. I've got the makings for a nice salad and either rice or potatoes to go with it, and I hope a decent bottle of wine."

"Great—better than restaurant fare, I'm sure! How is Sam doing anyway?" Conrad asked.

Linda poured two glasses of wine, and began pulling food from the refrigerator.

"He's doing all right—no thanks to you, Ray, and sergeant Tenax. Is it really necessary to keep him locked up any longer?"

"So far I'd have to say it was an idea that seemed good in theory, but hasn't resulted in any new leads. Ray didn't like the idea from the first, and has always maintained Sam Thornton is innocent."

"Of course Sam was a good sport about things when we told him why. He doesn't care about any recompense for the extra time in prison. He even agreed it was a good plan, and that the real killer might get careless. But what do you honestly think? I have to admit he had motive. He despised Jack Dolon, and not just because Dolon was after his girlfriend."

"Oh? That's news to me. What other reason did he have to dislike the man, or is that confidential lawyer client information?"

"No, it wasn't maybe common knowledge, but plenty of people knew the two of them had other issues. One of their disagreements started last year, and relates to the death of the Stuckrath boy."

Linda was busy cutting thin slices of the succulent salmon and arranging them on the plate with crackers and cheese, and did not look up or she might have wondered at the expression on Conrad's face. With an effort he controlled his agitation and intense curiosity.

"I'd already left Juneau for my Seattle job, and you I gather were sailing away into the sunset. I got the story from my one of my law partners, Theo Phrastus. A tourist boater who happened to be in Spruce Cove at the time Mr. Stuckrath held his mock trial, or whatever you want to call it of my father, accused Sam of assault. Of course you were there for that too, right? Apparently Sam helped Stuckrath by forcing everyone, including the tourist, to stay in the room and participate."

"That's true, but I hadn't heard that David or Sam were charged with anything over the affair."

"It didn't get that far. The tourist, it seems, was angling for a big out of court settlement. He was trying to get Sam and David Stuckrath to pay for his trauma by threatening to bring a civil suit. It went nowhere. Apparently his wife talked him out of it."

"That sounds like John Treadwell. A wealthy, arrogant asshole if I ever met one. Wow—you're right—this has got to be the best smoked salmon I've had in a long while, maybe ever!" Conrad said, after his first bite.

"I'm glad you like it. I wouldn't want you to faint from hunger tonight before I've had my way with you."

"No chance of that, as long as you don't mind my salmon breath."

"I doubt that will bother either of us," Linda said, and if we're lucky, we'll survive to spawn again, unlike these fish, whose first time is their last."

"It's a cruel world for some—especially those low on the food chain," Conrad agreed. "But you haven't told me what Jack Dolon had to do with any of this."

"Oh, right. My mind is wandering. Maybe it's the wine—or the company. For some reason Dolon had agreed to testify against David Stuckrath for Treadwell, and Sam found out. Sam and David are close friends, as you probably gathered."

"What the hell? Jack Dolon wasn't even there. He was miles away en route to capturing the smugglers, and had nothing to do with anything that happened in Spruce Cove, as far as I know."

"That's what Sam said too, but Dolon insisted he had evidence that backed up the tourist's story. That's all I've learned, except that when Dolon started chasing after Sam's girlfriend, it only added fuel to the fire. But I suppose I shouldn't be telling you this—you might decide Sam is guilty after all."

"No, I agree with Ray. I don't think Sam Thornton is involved in either Dolon's death or the threat to the cruise ships."

They finished their meal, opened a second bottle of wine, and moved to the living room couch to cuddle. One thing led to another, and before the bottle was empty they were in Linda's bed in her old room upstairs.

CHAPTER 24

Detours

The Murphy siblings spent the night camped in St. James Bay, somewhat more than half way between Haines and Juneau. They were up early the next morning, anticipating an easy run to the Auk Bay marina, less than thirty miles south. As they were loading up the boat they heard the incongruous but unmistakable sound of bagpipes coming from the forest.

"What the hell?" Liam exclaimed.

"I know you're supposed to make a lot of noise to keep the bears away. I'd bet bagpipes are more effective than whistles or bells," Simon speculated.

"...but a lot more awkward to pack." Mary said.

The sound grew progressively louder until a gray bearded man emerged from the forest edge. He removed the chanter from his mouth and greeted the Murphys.

"Hello, I'm Robert McLeod—unofficial caretaker of St. James Bay. I saw your campfire last night. I thought perhaps you might stay a bit longer, but I see I was wrong. What's the hurry? It's going to be a beautiful day."

"We're on our way to Juneau, but it got a bit rough yesterday afternoon. We hadn't planned on stopping here at all," Simon answered.

"Obviously you're not from the region. You must always be prepared for the unexpected in these parts. But no matter. If go you must, at least let me send you off with a good breakfast. My cabin isn't far from here."

"That's very kind of you, Mr. McLeod," Mary said, "but we really should be going."

"What difference is an hour or two more going to make? I haven't been to town in a while. I'll trade you a hearty meal of Scotch oatmeal and pancakes and eggs for the latest news, and then you can be on your way."

"That sounds like a great trade to me," Liam said. He was famished. The three had not eaten since lunch the previous day.

Their stomachs overruling their caution, the Murphys followed McLeod back to his cabin. As the three gobbled down the ample breakfast he told them about his upbringing in Scotland, where he learned to love the outdoors in the highlands of his homeland before moving to the United States, and eventually, after a stint working on the pipeline, to St. James Bay.

"Since I discovered this place I've never wanted to live anywhere else," he said. "The animals are my friends. I never carry a gun. The bears know me, and go about their business without bothering me or my cabin."

"Maybe it's the bagpipes that keep them away," Simon suggested.

"You could be right at that. The rain and humidity play hell with the reeds, and the pipes don't always play true. Now, I've rambled on for quite a while, and I think I've kept my end of the bargain. So what's the latest news from the so-called civilized world?"

The Murphys told him what they knew of the local gossip and news, the ongoing clean up from the Dyea flood, and the Alaska governor's race.

"So, it looks like old Murkowski's got that one sewed up. What's this I hear about someone getting stabbed and left under the tour ship dock up in Skagway a few days ago?"

The Murphy siblings exchanged looks before Simon answered.

"How did you hear about that?"

"Well, it was kind of strange. A couple of days ago a U.S Customs and Immigration speed boat came limping in with engine trouble. I went down to see if I could help out. The two guys aboard were none to friendly at first, but after I figured out they had a dead mouse plugging up the intake from their fuel tank they loosened up some. They told me they were headed up to Haines and Skagway to investigate a murder and a threat to the cruise ships and railroad. When I tried to get more details they clammed up again. They offered me cash for working on their boat, but I told them I didn't need their money. I'm happy to help out anyone if I can. Anyway, I've found it's best to stay on the good side of the authorities."

"That's news to us. We heard a rumor that a dead man was found under the cruise ship pier, but there hadn't been anything in the news when we left Haines," Simon explained.

He thought it prudent not to reveal they'd been in Skagway, or knew any details about the murder.

"Did the officers say who they were?" Mary asked.

"One of them showed me FBI ID. I don't remember his name, though. They were an unlikely looking pair—sort of a Mutt and Jeff. One was thin as a reed and probably six four or more, and the other one was about as big around as he was tall."

After thanking McLeod for his hospitality the Murphys headed across the fjord, ducking behind Lincoln and Shelter Islands to Auk Bay marina near the Alaska State Ferry terminal in north Juneau.

"We were right not to get on that plane in Haines. I bet those agents the bagpipe man helped were the ones driving that car with the government plates. But how the hell could they already be on to us?" Simon wondered.

At the Auk Bay marina they discussed their next move.

"If it is us they are after, we shouldn't spend much time here. We'd better just fuel up, grab some groceries, and keep going south in the boat," Mary said.

"Mary's right. The airport's just too risky," Liam agreed.

"You're just paranoid. There's no reason they would suspect us," Simon argued. "That's why Lothar stuck that knife in the body. They'll be looking for the owner of that knife for a while yet; that fisherman Lothar stole it from."

Simon had no way of knowing that Sam Thornton was in prison, or that the investigators no longer considered him the most likely suspect.

"Maybe so, but what if someone happened to see Jim Lothar's pickup parked on the pass across from where he derailed the train? Or what if he left fingerprints under the pier or somewhere on the body? If they start investigating Lothar they'll soon enough connect him to Hiram and us," Liam argued.

"That sleazebag will throw us under the bus to save his own skin. I think the caretaker at Burro Creek was suspicious too, and probably has reported us by now. They might be watching the Juneau airport, or even this marina. I still vote we keep going in the boat, after we fuel up and grab a couple of days worth of food," Mary insisted.

"Okay," Simon reluctantly agreed, "but I don't relish the idea of getting into open water in this boat if the weather changes. We're going to have to figure another way to get out of Alaska soon."

They motored out of the Auk Bay marina and around the west side of Douglas Island, hoping to make it to the southern end of Admiralty Island before evening, where there were a variety of secure anchorages to choose from. But their late start and the strong katabatic winds pouring out of Taku Inlet forced them to find shelter earlier in Taku Harbor, just twenty miles south of Juneau.

The next day the winds continued and the Murphys spent a second night in the protected anchorage, using the time to hike and explore the small bay and the ruins of an old cannery. That evening an older couple, also taking a break from the rough seas in Stephens Passage, arrived in a sailboat and tied next to them at the Taku Harbor dock. They invited the trio to dinner and drinks. The Murphys had decided ahead of time to use false names and to pose as Haines residents out on a camping adventure.

"Where are you headed from here?" the man asked as they relaxed over drinks after a salmon dinner. The couple had already revealed they were voyaging to Skagway, with stops at Juneau and Haines en route.

"When this wind lets up some we're going over to Admiralty to do some exploring there," Mary answered.

"I wish I was your age and had your energy," the woman said. "I just don't see how you can enjoy roughing it like you do."

"Well, it does take some getting used to, and I admit it's pretty uncomfortable when it rains, but so far the weather has been good, other than the wind, which I notice has really died down this evening," Simon replied.

"Can you suggest any places we should see in Haines and Skagway? We plan on spending at least a week up there," the man asked.

"Don't miss the Days of 98 show in Skagway, and of course the train ride up White Pass if you have time," Simon answered, all too aware of the irony of recommending the railroad trip.

"The Southeast Alaska State Fair starts next week in Haines. It's a great small town event," Mary suggested. "We plan to make it back north in time for that."

She teared up at the thought of never seeing Alaska or Hiram again. She was forced to pretend a bug had flown into her eye, while Liam distracted the couple with more talk of the attractions of Haines and Skagway.

The next morning the weather was more settled. The Murphys left very early, while the couple in the sailboat still slept. They stayed close to the shore of Admiralty Island, ready to dash in if the weather worsened They saw several fishing boats, two cruise ships and the Alaska ferry heading north out in the middle of the fjord, and a sailboat nearer the eastern side, but otherwise encountered no boat traffic on their trip down the west side of Stephens Passage. The weather was pleasantly warm, and they were happy not to have to endure the rougher conditions of the previous two days.

That afternoon they beached the boat in Snug Cove, a protected anchorage at the south end of Admiralty Island. They planned to get an early start the next day in order to cross the exposed waters where Stephens Passage and Frederick Sound merged, before the the frequent afternoon winds kicked up heavier seas. They hoped to continue on to the small fishing town of Petersburg. But the following morning the big Yamaha outboard refused to start.

"I think it must be the fuel pump. It's getting spark," Liam said, after tinkering with the engine.

"Shit, now what?" Mary exclaimed.

"I don't think we should attempt crossing Frederick Sound with the trolling motor. We'll make three knots or less depending on the current, and if quits we'll be screwed," Liam said.

"I sure as hell don't want to row across!" Simon declared.

"You mean paddle," Mary said. "You forget we lost one of our oars overboard in that rough patch of water before we got into St. James Bay."

"We'll be pretty exposed for about twenty miles. If the weather holds, no problem, just slow, maybe eight or ten hours out in the open water, but if it gets gnarly the little kicker won't handle it. But I've got a better idea. There's a lodge about fifteen miles from here in Prybus Bay. Maybe they can help us out. We can stay close to the shore, and if we leave now we'll have some help from the current," Liam said, pointing to a spot on the chart of the area.

The staff at the lodge were friendly and helpful. Their boat mechanic confirmed the fuel pump was the problem, and offered to order one from Juneau, to be delivered on the next float plane due to arrive in two days with supplies for the lodge.

"We have enough cash to cover the part, but how can we ever repay you for your help?" Mary asked the manager.

"Well, it just so happens we're a little short staffed at the moment, and we need to do some work on the dock. If you don't mind a little manual labor you can have a room, meals, and your fuel pump for free."

The Murphy siblings eagerly accepted the offer, and enjoyed three days of regular meals, showers, and comfortable beds for the first time since leaving Haines.

"Are you sure you don't want to stay the rest of the season? You can see it's fun place to work, and you're just the sort of people we need," the manager said as he and several other employees saw them off.

"Sorry, we've got a schedule to keep," Mary said.

"Well, think about next year then. Have a safe trip!"

Gossamer tendrils of fog slowly dissipated as they picked up speed and headed out of Prybus Bay into Frederick Sound.

"Cut the engine!" Simon suddenly yelled, after they were well out into the sound.

Liam throttled the outboard back to an idle, then switched it off.

"Whales, over there!" Simon exclaimed, pointing to the south.

A group of humpback whales had gathered to feed on the great schools of herring at the intersection of Stephens Passage and Frederick Sound. The Murphys drifted, marveling at the sight of the huge animals broaching and spouting only yards away from them.

"Does that look like a Fish and Game boat to you," Liam said after several minutes, handing the binoculars over to Simon.

"Sure, but so what. I bet they patrol these waters a lot," Simon answered. He passed the binoculars over to Mary.

"It looks like they're coming straight towards us. There's no other boats around, and we don't have any fishing poles out. I guess we must be too close to the whales," Mary said.

"Do you think they're close enough to see our registration numbers?" Simon worried.

The Fish and Game boat had picked up speed and was definitely headed their way.

"I'm not waiting around any longer to find out what they want," Liam declared.

The Yamaha, now with a brand new fuel pump and a tune up compliments of the mechanic at the Prybus lodge, started instantly. Liam slammed the throttle forward. They quickly accelerated to the boat's maximum speed.

"They're breaking off," Mary observed.

"Do you think they'll report us to Petersburg?" Mary wondered.

"Maybe," Simon replied. "But we've got enough fuel to skip Petersburg and head straight down to Wrangell, though it will be a long day on the water."

"Maybe Fish and Game wasn't after us in particular, but just wanted to caution us about the whales, or check our fishing licenses," Mary said, hopefully.

CHAPTER 25

A Suspicious Encounter

Early the next morning, after spending the night with Linda Daise at her home in Juneau, Conrad reluctantly said goodbye, assuring her he would be back in a few days. She drove him to the Auk Bay harbor to meet Ray Standers. Ray and Conrad took the outer route around Douglas Island, avoiding the narrow passage between the island and the city of Juneau. South of Juneau, in the wide expanse of water where the Gastineau Channel, Stephens Passage, and Frederick Sound came together they ate their lunch, sandwiches Conrad had prepared earlier while Ray piloted the boat. They arrived at the area in the southern reaches of Stephens Passage where Humpbacks gathered each summer to feed on the schools of herring.

Conrad was dazed by the drone of the engine and hypnotized by the magnificent panorama of water, mountain, and glacier that, no matter how often he passed through the region, never failed to astound him. He recalled the events almost exactly a year earlier, when he had sailed through the same waters in his own boat, intent on vengeance for the death of his son.

"Martes and Lothar are two days ahead of us, and Kuiu Island has a lot of anchorages, but from what Frank Dermit told the Sitka police, they found those sixteenth century relics in a cave somewhere in Tebenkof Bay, so it shouldn't be too hard to find them," Ray said.

Conrad, with an effort, forced himself back into the present.

Ray reached for his binoculars, focused them, and handed them over to Conrad.

"If you look to the south of us, where you can see a patch of white water and a bunch of seagulls hovering, it looks like some Humpbacks might be bubble feeding. They're directly in our path, so we'll take a little detour. I don't want to disturb them. They need all the calories they can get before they head south to breed. They don't eat in warm waters. As we swing by I'll turn the engine off and coast, and we might get a better look."

Conrad took the binoculars and saw that Ray was right. He had observed the whales feeding in the same area the year before on his trip north from Seattle in his sailboat, *Tisiphone*. Like the whales he too had returned, but for reasons that were certainly incomprehensible to the huge creatures.

"I know you haven't had a chance to see Jack Dolon's reports," Conrad said taking advantage of the break from the engine noise.

"The Agency is pretty uptight about sharing information—pretty stupid in this case. My supervisor apparently didn't see fit to show those to your boss. I read Jack Dolon's notes, and I think the more we both know, the quicker we'll figure this out. Jack had been undercover on the *Opal Princess*, and thought he had enough on Sabastos Melas to arrest him and a couple of his accomplices. He was only waiting for the okay before someone decided to take him off the case for good."

"From what you've told me, Jack was a smart and experienced agent. Wouldn't he have been aware of any potential danger, and prepared to deal with it?"

"Whoever killed him must have caught him completely by surprise. Maybe the killer or killers aren't on our persons of interest list at all," Conrad speculated.

"Something else bugs me," Ray continued. "That supposed accidental derailment that happened up in the pass. The rumor going around Skagway is that it was no accident at all, and a small explosion was the cause. It has to be related to that note the killer left on the body."

"It does seem odd the railroad didn't report the incident, if that's what really happened. But I understand minor derailments with no injuries probably happen more often than they want the public to know. But if that derailment is related, the company may be communicating secretly with whoever planted that warning note on Dolon's body."

"That's exactly what I thought too, and where there's smoke there's usually fire. The person I talked to said he got his information from a friend who works for the railroad, who was told to keep his mouth shut. Of course we were at Moe's, and we'd both had a few drinks—so I don't know how much to make of it."

"Some folks seem to thrive on conspiracy theories, but still, it's at least an interesting coincidence," Conrad mused. "If the derailment was sabotage, then I suppose we should be looking for Hiram, not wasting our time chasing after Jim Lothar."

They drifted slowly closer to the giant mammals with the tide and current, and listened to the sounds of the whales surfacing and exhaling air and water from their blowholes, the screeches of the seabirds circling and diving above the pod, and the waves lapping against the side of the boat. Conrad loved Hawaii's soft ambiance and comfortable climate, but he also felt a strong connection to Southeast Alaska, and a kinship with the cetaceans. These same whales, like Conrad also had a Hawaiian connection. Once they had accumulated enough calories and fattened up, some, perhaps most of them, would migrate to the seas surrounding the Hawaiian island chain. The past winter Conrad had seen Humpback whales breaching off the Big Island of Hawaii—very likely many of these same individuals.

"Hey, we've got company," Conrad said, handing the binoculars back to Ray.

"If I'm not mistaken it's a Boston Whaler, and what looks like a big Yamaha hanging off the stern. If that's the same boat that was at Burro Creek, I wonder what it's doing down this far south?" Ray observed.

"How many people do you see on board, Ray? It looked like three to me."

"Yep, I count three, and I think one is a woman."

"We should check them out. It's pretty likely the same boat the caretaker at Burro Creek shooed away," Conrad said.

"Absolutely. It is well within my purview as a biologist and enforcement officer to warn them not to venture too close to the whales," Ray said, restarting the Fish and Game launch's engine.

Ray motored toward the other boat, while Conrad watched through the binoculars. They got close enough for Conrad to make out the faces of the three Murphy siblings before the Boston Whaler suddenly accelerated and moved rapidly away to the southeast down Frederick Sound.

"We'll never catch up with them in this crate," Ray said. "What do you make of it?"

"They weren't interested in socializing, and one of the three is certainly a woman. It's definitely the Boston Whaler Hiram Hatcher and George Ripinski own, and it must be the same trio that was at Burro Creek. They obviously don't want anything to do with Fish and Game."

"Very curious, but they probably don't have fishing licenses, or have illegal catch on board. That's not my problem today. We'd better get back on track. We've still got a long way to go to Tebenkof Bay."

Ray turned the boat and resumed their original route, southwest down Stephens Passage. The biologist made another course correction to avoid the area where the whales were feeding, only bringing the launch up to cruising speed when they were well away from the animals.

Conrad didn't question Ray's decision to break off, but the presence of the Boston Whaler so far south of its home port, and crewed by the same three who had been camping in Burro Creek seemed suspicious. The Boston Whaler, though a capable boat for local fishing adventures and day trips, was not the sort of vessel most would chose for such a long, exposed voyage. He regretted that they had not thought to ask the Skagway police chief to locate the van Hiram Hatcher had been seen in, and identify its owner and occupants.

Three hours later they neared the entrance to Chatham Strait. Some twenty-five miles in the distance the small native village of Kake was visible to the east.

"Have you ever been to Kake?" Ray asked.

"No, but I was once told it means dog in Tlingit," Conrad replied.

"Well, you were misinformed, it actually means something like 'mouth of dawn' or 'daylight.' It's a very old settlement. The Tlingit have lived in the area for thousands of years. I wish we had the time to get over there. It's an interesting place. It has the world's tallest totem pole."

"When I get a couple of days off to get my boat in the water I hope to make it to a lot of places I haven't seen yet."

"You sound like you plan on spending some time up here," Ray prompted.

"It looks that way. My office wants to keep a presence in Southeast Alaska, and with Jack Dolon gone, they've offered me the job."

"I'm sure you'll make the best of it. It doesn't exactly seem like a hardship posting for you!"

"It's definitely not the worst place I've been assigned to," Conrad replied, thinking of Linda Daise, and smiling.

"You said earlier your sailboat was shipped from Hawaii to Juneau. That must have cost you a small fortune."

"Actually, it didn't cost me a cent—all expenses were covered by the tax payers."

"Well, that makes me feel better. My taxes actually went to a good cause, for once!" Ray quipped. "Maybe if we ever get this damned case solved, you'll take me out for a sail."

"...and hopefully I'll have time to take you up on that fishing trip you promised me last year."

Conrad, normally reticent to speak about his personal affairs, found himself in an expansive mood. He loved being on the water in one of his favorite places in the world on such a perfect day, and Ray was good company.

"My line of work does have a few perks. Besides—I was in a good position to bargain, with poor Jack out of the game."

"I was thinking of how we met last year—when you were a person of interest yourself in judge Daise's sad demise."

"Oh, and why is that, Ray?"

The biologist sensed Conrad's sudden wariness. He made a slight course correction, jogging the boat more to the west, and simultaneously attempted to steer the conversation out of potentially perilous waters.

"Of course I was just doing my job, and I never seriously believed you had anything to do with that," Ray dissembled. "...otherwise I certainly wouldn't be out on a boat by myself with you, right?"

"I hardly think you would have been incautious enough to stand up under a low hanging boom running downwind in such a sea state. In any case, if I wanted to get rid of you, I would have done that last year, don't you think?"

In spite of Conrad's light tone, Ray felt the hairs on the back of his neck stand up, and it wasn't due to any sudden breeze or drop in temperature.

CHAPTER 26

Goodbye Alaska

The Murphys bypassed Petersburg and motored down Wrangell Narrows to Sumner Strait. The weather continued mild, and they stopped only once for a brief lunch break, but it still took over twelve hours to make it to the small fishing town of Wrangell. While monitoring the VHF radio southeast of Wrangell Narrows, they had a good laugh listening as the Coast Guard hailed the *Rhapsody Of The Seas* to inform the cruise ship that they were flying the American flag upside down.

That evening over pizza and beers at the Marine Bar the Murphy siblings discussed their options. They had bought more charts in Juneau, and Liam had studied them carefully.

"We'll have to stop in Ketchikan for fuel, but that's a long day, especially if the winds pick up and we have to stay close to shore running down Ernest Sound and Clarence Strait. We could overnight at Meyers Chuck, and at Ketchikan, and again at Foggy Bay before we get into Canadian waters," Liam suggested.

"But what then? I agree it's too risky to fly out of Ketchikan, but won't we have to report to customs in Prince Rupert?" Mary asked.

"Not if they don't see us. We can take the short-cut zigzag route through Venn Passage to Rupert. That area is busy with of all kinds of pleasure and fishing boat traffic this time of year. We probably won't be noticed, especially if we can somehow get Canadian registration numbers and stickers on our boat. We can fly out of the Prince Rupert airport to Vancouver, then take an international flight from there to St. Kitts," Simon explained.

"Actually, the airport at Rupert is on an island, and you have to take a ferry to get there—not many flights a day, and it's a port of entry with a customs station. Too risky. The Terrace airport is bigger and has more flights to Vancouver. We should ditch the boat somewhere around Prince Rupert, and take a bus to Terrace," Liam advised.

"I hate the idea of just abandoning the boat. It's not fair to Hiram or his partner, George," Mary complained.

"Hiram won't care. It's the least of his worries. When we get that money, we'll have more than enough to pay back George Ripinski and Hiram too, if he's not in jail," Simon insisted.

"You mean if we're not all in jail," Mary demurred.

That night they splurged on a motel room in Wrangell. The next day they camped overnight in the forest near the tiny port hamlet of Meyers Chuck. After a quick but wet run down Clarence Strait, bucking a steep chop, the Murphys arrived in Ketchikan the following day where they once again got a room for the night.

"That's about it for my credit card," Mary announced.

"I've still got plenty of room on mine for buying our airplane tickets," Simon replied. "How much cash do we have left?"

"Six hundred, and change," Mary said.

"What happened to the fourteen hundred dollars in travelers checks and cash we started out with?"

"Maybe if you and Liam hadn't had so many drinks in Haines and Wrangell we'd have more, and we lost nearly three hundred dollars on that flight out of Haines we didn't take. The rest was fuel, food, and hotel rooms," Mary explained.

"We'll have to be more careful the rest of the trip," Liam said. "What if there's a problem withdrawing money at St. Kitts, or one of the flights is delayed?"

Simon walked the Ketchikan docks and noted where several Canadian boats were berthed. That night he returned to a Canadian registered skiff he'd seen during his earlier exploration. Using a razor blade, Simon carefully scraped off the 2002 stickers on each side of the bow. The next day at Foggy Bay, south of Ketchikan and just north of the Canadian border, he used stencils and a can of spray paint to mimic Canadian markings, and attached the stickers he had stolen with adhesive caulk.

The following morning they navigated Venn Passage without incident, following the detailed chart and range markers through the shallow passage. After scouting out the shoreline of Prince Rupert they found a secluded spot to beach the boat not far from downtown. They repacked their backpacks with only what they needed to travel by air, and left their camping gear with the boat.

From downtown Prince Rupert a bus took the trio to Terrace. There they bought tickets on a morning flight to Vancouver, connecting to a flight via Los Angeles and Miami to St. Kitts in the Caribbean. Jim Lothar had assured them the extorted money would be waiting for them there.

CHAPTER 27

Kuiu Island

After a long day's run Ray and Conrad dropped anchor in Port Malmesbury. Larry Numous greeted them on the shore and helped the men drag their dinghy up the beach to a safe spot out of reach of the tides. Ray introduced Conrad to the archeologist, who immediately expressed his misgivings about the presence of the two men in Thetis Bay.

"I'm glad to see you! I don't like the situation at all. The Stuckraths have been working for weeks over in Thetis Bay. Another boat anchored near them a couple of days ago. David thinks the two men on that boat might be illegally digging up one of the caves we had intended to excavate. He's also convinced they cut his anchor line while his family was asleep. Luckily he woke up before they grounded. For now the Stuckraths are here with my crew helping out, but I really need them to work at the other sites, and I can't do that until we get rid of those interlopers. Even now they may have ruined the stratigraphy, or stolen artifacts."

"Take it easy, Larry, we'll deal with it first thing tomorrow, but right now we're tired and hungry from a long day on the water—damned headwind and bumpy seas the last part," Ray replied.

The numerous inlets and bays of the Port Malmsbury region where the archeologist had set up his main camp offered good protection from the wind and waves. The water was nearly calm at their anchorage, a stark contrast to Chatham Strait fjord, which funneled and magnified the prevailing winds.

"I'm sorry Ray, I'm not being a very good host. You're late for dinner, but there's lots of leftovers. How does salmon and homemade biscuits sound?"

"I could just about eat a whole salmon by myself, I think," Ray said.

Over dinner and beers the archeologist described the location of the sites they had been given permission to excavate. Conrad was disappointed to find that the Stuckraths were camped with the graduate students several miles away on the eastern arm of the bay, where they were investigating one of the other Port Malmesbury sites.

"Altogether we've got at least a dozen potential caves and other sites that are worth looking into in Tebenkof and Malmesbury inlets. Unfortunately most of the reasonably accessible and promising locations have been looted over the years. On the other hand, Kuiu Island is off the beaten track even for Southeast Alaska. Some areas are so rugged and unvisited there is reason to be optimistic."

"How do the Tlingit clans feel about you being here?" Conrad asked.

"Everything we do is thoroughly vetted with the tribe, the state, and the feds. In addition one of our graduate students is a Tlingit from Kake, whose ancestors probably migrated there from the historical Tebenkof settlements after a smallpox epidemic. Besides working on his masters degree at the University of Washington, he's writing up an independent report for Sealaska, the native corporation in Juneau."

"I've read some about those devastating epidemics. It seems they started with the early Spanish and Russian explorers and trappers," Conrad said.

"There aren't many records, but the Spanish explorers certainly infected the natives here as early as the 1770s. There was a major outbreak in the 1830s that was probably responsible for the abandonment of the Kuiu Island communities."

"I've read that the Tlingits and Tsimshians were hit especially hard, but many of the Aleuts were vaccinated by the Russians and had much lower fatality rates," Ray added.

"That's true. Vaccinations using infected tissue from milder forms of small pox cases had been used in Europe and Asia with some success since the early 1700s. In 1796 Edward Jenner invented a vaccine using cowpox virus that was far safer. The Russians brought vaccine to Alaska in 1808 and again later on. The Aleuts were much more receptive to receiving the vaccines than many of the other tribes. Some Tlingit settlements suffered up to seventy-five percent fatalities, or were wiped out entirely," the archeologist elaborated.

"What do you think of the possibility that Drake was here?" Conrad asked.

"I wouldn't have given that much credence before I saw the old Spanish coin Ray found; after all, Spanish explorers and settlers had been in the Americas for over seventy years before the Drake expedition, and it's feasible that some items could have made their way to this area through trade or shipwrecks. But so many objects—on the same island?"

"Well, you've got yourself a hell of a mystery, and I'd rather be working your side of the street than chasing down those two scalawags in Thetis Bay, but duty calls. We should get an early start tomorrow, and it's getting late," Ray said.

"If the Stuckrath's want to go with us, one of us should get over to their camp and let them know," Conrad suggested. "They should feel safe enough with us around. We've got arrest warrants for both men, and we plan to take them back to Juneau, in cuffs if necessary, tomorrow."

"It's only about twenty minutes to their camp in the Zodiac. I'll run over and ask them. I hope they'll feel secure enough to get back to work, with you here to deal with those two men. In any case I'm always up early, and I'll see you off in the morning," Larry said.

The archeologist buzzed away to inform the Stuckrath family that help was at hand, while Conrad and Ray motored back in their dinghy to spend the night on board the Fish & Game launch.

The next morning Ray & Conrad took the dinghy back to the archeologist camp, where they were greeted by the Stuckrath family, who were relieved to learn that the unwanted visitors would be arrested. Ray and Conrad promised they would radio back as soon as they had the two men, Jim Lothar and Craig Martes, in custody.

David and Cindy had known Conrad since the 1970s, and were acquainted with Ray from their time in Juneau. They were especially surprised and pleased to see Conrad again. The occasion was bittersweet for Conrad, who was once again reminded of the loss of their son, Marshall.

Larry saw Conrad and Ray off with a breakfast cooked outdoors on the portable propane stove. They motored the Fish and Game launch north from Port Malmesbury to Thetis Bay, a southwestern extension of Tebenkof Bay. The fishing boat David Stuckrath had described had not moved.

Ray was well acquainted with the owner of the boat, Craig Martes, and had a long history with the outdoorsman, who made his living as a hunting guide, and had a reputation as a notorious poacher. Their adversarial relationship was tempered with a certain amount of mutual respect and humor. On a superficial level at least, both men regarded their interactions as a sort of cat and mouse game. Ray respected Craig's great knowledge of the region and its wild inhabitants. Craig was a throwback to an earlier, more self-sufficient era when his hunting and trapping activities would not have been an issue. In turn the poacher had learned the hard way that Ray could be a formidable foe when he broke the law. A few years earlier Craig had lost one of his favorite hunting rifles, paid a hefty fine, and spent several days in prison as a result of an investigation led by the biologist.

Ray maneuvered the launch close to Craig's fishing boat. After placing fenders between the two vessels, the two men tied the vessels securely together.

"They must be out searching for plunder," Conrad observed.

No one was aboard the fishing boat, and Craig's dinghy was gone.

"No doubt," Ray replied. "Do you want to wait for them here, or try to find them?"

"We'll have a better case if we can catch them in the act. Besides, I could use a hike," Conrad suggested.

The two men launched the inflatable dingy and motored over to the small beach the archeologist had described to them.

"Funny, I don't see their dinghy," Conrad wondered.

"They must have hidden it back in the woods," Ray said.

Keeping as quiet as possible, they followed the trail that David and Cindy had blazed, hoping to arrest the men in the act of violating the site.

CHAPTER 28

Finders, Keepers

"I say we give this one up and try the other cave," Jim Lothar said, dejectedly.

He and Craig Martes had been digging in the cramped and muddy grotto for two hours.

"My back is killing me," Craig complained, "but Frank Dermit said this was the least disturbed of the caves he'd explored."

"I'm beginning to think your buddy was pulling your leg. But okay, I'm good for another half hour, then let's call it a morning. I'm more than ready for lunch and a beer. I think I'll try the far corner again—I only just scraped the top earlier."

Lothar moved one of the bright propane lanterns to the back wall of the shallow cave, and began digging.

"Hey—I've got something!" He exclaimed after a few minutes of half-hearted work.

"By god you're right!" Craig agreed.

Together they began with renewed enthusiasm to clear away the dirt, revealing a nearly complete human skeleton. But it wasn't the skeleton that excited the two men. Nestled among the bones were a dagger, helmet, spear point, metal buttons, belt buckle, and remnants of clothing of an obviously great age. Newly energized, the men continued to plow up the area, in their excitement shoveling the bones and anything without obvious value into a pile. When it was evident there was nothing else to be found, they gathered up the metal items and put them into their backpacks.

"I bet this stuff is the same age and even more valuable than that rusted old gun of yours," Lothar remarked.

"You might be right. That helmet looks a lot like the one Frank found, but it's even nicer. He said his was English, from the 1500s, most likely from Drake's expedition. If I had to make a guess, I'd say this was a member of that expedition. This spear point isn't European. It's copper, most likely one a Tlingit got in trade with the Aleuts up on the Copper River. Since we found it under the ribs, it's probably what killed the poor devil."

"That's pretty good sleuthing, Craig—makes sense."

"The Tlingits have a story about a group of sailors that came here generations before the Russians and Spaniards," Craig continued. "The story goes that these strangers had two boats, a big one and a little one, and that their ancestors attacked the small one, sunk it, and killed most of the men. They attacked the bigger boat, but were repelled by men who wore shiny metal armor and had noisy weapons that shot fire and smoke, and could kill from a great distance."

"I can't believe the local natives wouldn't have taken every piece of metal they could find to use for themselves. So you're probably right. This guy got speared, but managed to get away. He hid in this cave until he died. Tough way to go," Jim Lothar speculated.

The two men struggled back over their roughly cleared forest trail, and through the last of the thickets to the beach, where Craig's newly patched inflatable was hidden behind driftwood safely above the high tide line.

"The damn troopers wasted no time getting here. They must have already been nearby, maybe in Port Alexander or Kake," Craig Martes observed.

From the beach they could see the Fish and Game launch tied to Craig's boat.

"You shouldn't have cut that sailboat's anchor line. They must have reported us. We're lucky they didn't shoot us, instead of the dinghy."

"Ah—they were just trying to give us a good scare, but I admit it did rile me some. In any case we're screwed now," Lothar replied.

"Don't panic. I don't think they're on board," Craig said, handing Jim the binoculars.

"You're right. I don't see anybody on either boat. Wait—there's their inflatable, down the beach. I guess they didn't see ours—good thing we hid it."

Jim pointed down the shoreline and gave the binoculars back to Craig.

"Frank told me there's more caves down that way, but nothing in them. I imagine that's where they are, which will hopefully give us a little time to get out of here," Craig said.

"Not enough. If they're close they'll see or hear us," Jim argued.

"We could cut 'em loose and make a run for it. I doubt that Fish & Game tub is any faster than my boat. On the other hand, all they have to do is call for help from Sitka or Juneau," Craig mused.

"They won't be able to call anyone if we deep six their radio."

"Now that's not a bad idea," Craig agreed. "That would at least give us a good head start, and I know of a couple pretty good hidey-holes we could hunker down in until it's safe to fence this stuff. I doubt finding us is too high a priority for the troopers anyway."

Craig was unaware that his partner was the object of a manhunt by the state troopers, the intelligence agency Conrad worked for, and the FBI.

The two men put their tools and findings from the cave into Craig's dinghy, drug it down to the water, and sped back to Craig's boat.

"I was thinking—besides tossing their radio in the drink—if we can hold 'em up some, and get the booty to that buyer of yours before the troopers find us, they won't have anything to charge us with. Nobody saw us digging in that cave."

"What do you have in mind, Craig?" Jim asked.

"Maybe a little modification on their fuel line might take 'em a while to sort out," Craig suggested.

They both stepped over to the Fish and Game launch. While Craig was disconnecting the fuel line Jim had an even better idea. He dug in the Fish and Game boat's tool box and found a hacksaw. It was only few seconds work to cut through the engine's rubber cooling water intake hose. He opened the through hull valve and cold sea water arched in a thick stream.

"What the hell are you doing?" Craig yelled.

"This will give us all the time we need, and more! We'd better get going though; this tub won't float too long."

The bilge was rapidly filling.

"You crazy fucker! Messing with the engine is one thing, sinking a government boat is another. You gotta close that valve! We only need to get a few hours head start anyway. I don't want any part of this shit!"

Craig made an effort to reach the valve. The two men grappled, sliding in the slippery bilge until Craig lost his footing and fell heavily against the engine.

"I think I broke my ankle, Jim," he said, panting. "I can't stand. Help me up."

"I don't think so Craig. I'm in a bit of a hurry. Now they'll have to run you to the hospital in Sitka before they come after me, if you don't drown first."

Lothar turned and climbed rapidly up to the deck as his partner screamed at him.

"Jim, don't leave me here! I swear, I can't walk!"

"Then I guess you'd better crawl, but you'd best get moving quick before that water gets much deeper," Lothar replied, and stepped over to Craig's fishing boat.

Craig crawled slowly and painfully along the bilge towards the ladder that led up to the deck. The water was rising rapidly, and he began to shake uncontrollably from the cold and pain. He reached the ladder and pulled himself upright, putting all his weight on his good leg. He heard his boat's engine cough to life, followed by the grinding of the electric winch as Jim retrieved the anchor. Through the open hatch he watched Jim cast off the lines that held the two boats together. He heard the familiar clunk of the transmission shifting from neutral to forward. The engine revved, and he could only watch helplessly as his boat quit Thetis Bay and motored out into Chatham Strait. Craig was alone on the drifting and rapidly sinking Fish and Game launch.

"Looks like they've given us the slip," Ray said.

He and Conrad had heard the fishing boat engine start up, and quickly raced back to the beach, arriving in time to see the vessel just as it rounded the headlands at the mouth of the bay and disappeared from their sight. They could see the Fish and Game launch, low in the water, drifting slowly towards the shore.

"Help! Somebody help me!" Craig called out.

He had managed to pull himself up onto the deck, which was now awash.

Ray and Conrad quickly got the inflatable into the water and motored towards the sinking boat as fast as the small outboard could push them. By the time they arrived the launch had floated into the muddy bottomed shallows of the bay. It settled with a flurry of bubbles. Only a couple of feet of the cabin top remained visible above the water.

Craig Martes was rapidly losing control of his arms and legs as hypothermia began to set in. He had just enough strength and coordination to thrash his way through the water and grab hold of the cabin top, but he was unable to pull himself completely out of the cold water. Arriving seconds later, Conrad and Ray rolled him into the inflatable dinghy.

"We need to get him warmed up before he loses consciousness. Hopefully he'll hang in there until we can get help," Ray said.

While Conrad steered along the shoreline of Kuiu Island to the archeologist's camp a few miles south, Ray covered Craig up as best he could with a tarp and some rain gear they had brought along in case of a change in weather.

Jim Lothar, already well north of Tebenkof Bay in Craig's fishing boat, smiled in satisfaction as he observed the Fish and Game inflatable heading south through Craig's best Steiner binoculars.

That should keep them busy for a while, Jim thought, then turned his full attention to navigating up Chatham Strait as fast as Craig's fishing boat could travel. He planned to rendezvous with the *Opal Princess*, fence the items to Sabastos Melas, and either convince the purser to help him stowaway on the ship, or if he refused, to sneak across the border into Canada. He reflected that he'd had enough of Juneau anyway. One way or another if he stayed he would end up back in prison, and he was willing to gamble everything on the chance for freedom.

He also hoped that his arrangement with the Murphys would work out. With any luck they should be well on their way to the Caribbean. Between that money and what he should make from the relics, he could set himself up somewhere very well—maybe in South America as he had suggested to the siblings, or perhaps Thailand, where the weather was great and living easy if you had some cash.

But first he had to make it to Skagway. Jim reasoned that the authorities would assume he was bound for Juneau. But instead of turning east and going up Stephens Passage, he would go north along the west side of Admiralty Island, bypassing Juneau and continuing up Lynn Canal fjord to Skagway. It was over 200 miles, but If he ran all night would arrive in plenty of time to meet the *Opal Princess* while it was docked in Skagway.

"C-c-c-careful, I'm pretty sure my ankle's broken," Craig said, weakly through chattering teeth.

Conrad and Ray could see the man was correct. His right foot was twisted at an abnormal angle.

"Don't worry about that. Just hang in there, and we'll get you warm and reasonably comfortable as soon as we can. What the hell were you thinking anyway—sinking a government boat?" Ray asked.

"Th-th-that was Jim's idea. I tried to stop him, but he fought me. Then the f-f-fucker abandoned me—the dirty bastard! I sh-sh-hould have known better than to partner with that asshole—damn him to hell!"

"Just what were you two doing out here anyway?"

"...maybe b-b-best I don't say until I talk to a lawyer."

"Your call, but it might be better to come clean. The court might offer you a better deal if you're willing to cooperate. Jim Lothar's the big fish we're really out to snag," Ray said.

"Well, I'll th-th-think about it," Craig replied.

Under the layers of tarp and rain gear he was beginning to warm up. His ankle throbbed painfully, but his cagey sense of self-preservation had not abandoned him.

After they arrived at the archeologist's camp Larry Nemous radioed Sitka for help. A helicopter for the injured man arrived an hour later. Ray and Conrad described their predicament to the archeologist, and he agreed to send two of his crew in their larger and more burdensome Zodiac to see if they could re-float the Fish and Game launch. Larry also provided them with a gasoline powered pump that he normally used to clear water from the often flooded sites they were excavating.

After an hour of pumping the Fish & Game boat floated free, but the damage was done. The bilge was inches deep in muck, and most of the contents of the cabin were ruined. The engine turned over, but refused to start.

Fortunately Conrad kept his satellite phone in a waterproof container, which they found floating in the cabin. With it Ray Standers was able to call sergeant Tenax in Juneau and apprise him of their situation.

"Did that old rascal Craig Martes spill the beans? Does he know anything about Dolon's death or the ransom note?" Tenax asked.

"He wouldn't talk at first, except to blame Lothar for scuttling the launch, but we told him things would go easier on him if he helped us out. He's madder than hell at Lothar for abandoning him, so I wouldn't be surprised if he cooperates once he's comfortable again. Martes swears they found some valuable relics with an old human skeleton. Craig thinks they date from the 1500s, and Lothar plans to sell them to someone he knows on one of the cruise ships. He says Lothar is headed to Juneau or Skagway to meet the ship, but unfortunately Craig couldn't tell us which cruise ship it is," Ray explained.

"...but nothing about that threatening note, or Dolon?" Sergeant Tenax persisted.

"Martes didn't seem to know anything about that. He did say Lothar told him that if their trip to Kuiu Island didn't pan out, he had other ways of making some cash. But when Craig pressed him, Lothar said it was none of his business."

"There's no news on my end about Hiram Hatcher either. He's still missing. I'll have my men focus on watching for Jim Lothar here in Juneau. But you two need to get up to Skagway. We can monitor cruise ship arrivals here, but we don't have the resources to track Lothar out there on the water. Hopefully you can get your boat running again. If not, I'll try to see if the Coast Guard can spare a helicopter to fly you out," the sergeant said, and ended the call.

"I guess we might as well enjoy our last evening on Kuiu Island. Summer days don't get any nicer here, and fortunately that soaking didn't hurt our booze supply any," Ray declared, after his call with sergeant ended.

"What to you plan to do about the boat?" Conrad asked.

"That's the state of Alaska's problem now. Tenax wants me to stick with you on this case, and get my ass back up to where the action is. I imagine they'll send a crew down to salvage this crate sooner or later. If I'm really lucky they'll scrap it and I'll get a better boat."

"In the meantime, we'd better push it out a little farther so it won't ground every low tide, and put a second anchor out," Conrad suggested.

After ensuring the boat was securely anchored the two men loaded any salvageable items they could find onto the inflatable and motored back to Larry Nemous' camp in Port Malmesbury.

That evening the archeologists, the Stuckrath family, and Conrad and Ray sat around the campfire after dinner, drinking and talking about the eventful day.

"Say, I've been thinking," David said, during a lull in the conversation. "We had planned to spend a couple more days in Thetis Bay at most, then head up to Skagway for some R & R. Cindy has a good friend who lives there, and her parents invited her to stay with them. It occurred to me that since you two need to get up to Skagway too, we might leave tomorrow instead, and come back to Kuiu on our way south to Bellingham to finish up."

"That's a great idea, if it's no inconvenience," Conrad was quick to say.

"It's a long two day run, but the two of us could take the night watches," Ray suggested.

They all agreed it was a good plan, and decided to set out first thing in the morning.

Ray used Conrad's satellite phone again to inform sergeant Tenax.

"As it turns out, we've got a ride back to Skagway tomorrow on a friend's boat. It's a sailboat, so it will take us two days to make it up there. In the meantime this phone's battery is getting low, but you can contact us if you need to," Ray said.

"I doubt I could get the helicopter any sooner, since they won't consider your situation an emergency. But this works out pretty well. With you two in Skagway, and my men covering the Juneau docks we should be able to nab Jim Lothar red-handed."

CHAPTER 29

Skagway Bound

A local resident and police officer saw the cougar near Skagway City Hall at Seventh and Spring early in the morning of Aug. 24. The other report of a cougar sighting came on July 29. The cougar was seen by the city dumpster.—
The Skagway News

It was a perfect day for the start of their voyage north. By midday, with favorable tide and a gentle southwest breeze, the Cape George Cutter, *Lethe*, was making better than seven knots up Chatham Strait. Even so, it would take them two days to navigate the nearly two hundred miles to Skagway. Conrad, David, and Karen sat together in the cockpit, munching snacks and drinking beer while the auto-helm steered the boat up the center of the channel. David made small adjustments to the sails periodically, striving to get the most out of the favorable breeze.

The small cockpit was crowded with more than two or three people, so Cindy and Ray had moved to the foredeck. Cindy had donned her bikini and was working on her tan. She had unfastened her top, and lay on her stomach, enjoying the warmth of the sun on her back, and the pleasant gurgle and swoosh of the boat cutting through the water.

Ray, as a biologist and close observer of nature could appreciate and admire the appearance of any healthy animal, including his own species. Though he made an effort to hide his observation of her, he was only inches away on the small deck of the thirty-one foot sailboat, and his dark glasses did not completely disguise his eye movements.

"Are you enjoying the view, Ray?"

Cindy wasn't really irritated. She knew both men and women liked to look at her, and she didn't expect that any heterosexual man would ignore her mostly unclothed body completely at such close quarters.

"I've always been a great connoisseur of nature's beauty—be it mineral, plant, or animal," Ray replied, somewhat embarrassed.

"Maybe you should borrow my camera and take a picture," she teased.

"I don't think any photograph could do you, this incredible place, or this lovely day justice."

"You're a real charmer, but sadly, a married man."

Cindy was too content to be upset with his gentle ogling, and she genuinely liked the man.

"Yes, and happily married at that, but a wise, if somewhat vulgar friend of mine once said that it doesn't matter where you get your appetite, as long as you eat at home," Ray quipped.

"I hadn't heard that one. Is that how men justify going to strip clubs?"

"Have you seen the movie, 'The Adventures Of Baron Munchausen?'" Ray asked.

"Of course, it's one of our family favorites."

"You will remember the baron became younger and younger each time he encountered the beautiful Uma Thurman. I think perhaps you're having that effect on me."

"You're not so old—not as old as the baron was, anyway. Aren't you and dad about the same age? I don't think of dad as old."

"We're only a few months apart, actually. Besides your lovely form, I was also admiring that amazing tattoo of the cougar on your back. Why that one? Most young women I know get butterflies, flowers, hearts, or maybe their zodiac sign."

"I'm surprised you haven't guessed. Dad told me you discovered the body of the man that murdered my brother, and that man was killed by a cougar last summer—maybe the only cougar ever seen on Kuiu Island."

"Oh, right—I really should have figured that out. That wasn't the only one ever seen in Southeast Alaska, though. They come down from the interior now and then, usually around the time the salmon are spawning. There was one spotted up in Skagway that was reported to my office late last month. I suspect it's still hanging around the area, but will probably head back up the pass when the salmon runs end. At least in Skagway a cougar doesn't have to compete with the large bear populations in the Haines area or on Kuiu Island."

"Aren't there any bears in Skagway?" Cindy asked. She rose up on her elbows, forgetting for a moment her bikini top was unfastened.

"Seems to me we've got a 'bare' issue right here in Chatham Strait."

"Very funny Ray," Cindy said, refastening her top.

"To answer your question; there are a few black bears in the Skagway and Dyea valleys, but very rarely any browns. You'll remember from your time in Alaska that Haines has a huge problem, because of it's far bigger salmon runs, and much more favorable environment. The browns are thick on both the Chilkat and the Chilkoot rivers, and no mountain lion would stand a chance of competing there. Kuiu only has black bears— maybe the most per square mile of any place in the world. An experienced and careful cougar might survive there, but to my knowledge there's never been an established population of the cats on the island."

"Ever since I found out how Marshall's killer died, the cougar has become my favorite animal. I'm just sorry the cougar died too. When dad and I were making a trail to the cave we've been excavating I found this. I wonder if it could have come from the rifle that killed it."

She showed Ray the bullet casing that hung from the length of fishing line around her neck.

"We were close and had a good view of the place where dad says the man and cougar were found. Maybe it's from the hunter that shot that poor creature."

"I can tell you it's not from the rifle that killed that cat. I know you're pretty savvy about firearms, and you can see this is a .308 shell casing. That cougar was killed with a 30-06. The fisherman with Grant Tadlock said that Tadlock shot the animal with a Remington 30-06, and the lab confirmed his story."

"I want to forget that man's name!" Cindy declared, suddenly angry. "I hate the way people remember the names of killers, but not their victims. I'll never say his name out loud—ever!"

"Okay Cindy, I get it. You found that shell casing near where that son of a bitch died, right?"

"No, not that near. It would have been a pretty long shot, but I'm sure I could have made it—but I would have aimed at the man, not the cougar!"

"Yes, I remember you won some shooting trophies in Juneau. But shooting a man isn't the same as shooting at a target, or even a wild animal."

"I've hunted too. I'm no vegetarian, and I like wild game better than store bought. Deer or man, it's the same thing. Stay calm, and wait for the right shot," Cindy contradicted.

Ray shook his head. In the course of over twenty-five years with Fish and Game he'd only drawn his sidearm on the human animal twice, fortunately without having to use it. He wasn't sure he could shoot a man if it came down to it, and hoped he never had to find out. He found Cindy's attitude understandable, but disturbing. He would have found it even more unsettling had he known that she had shot up Craig Martes's dinghy in Thetis Cove the day before he and Conrad arrived on Kuiu Island, but neither Craig or the Stuckrath family had seen fit to bring up the incident.

"We were up on a knoll above the place where dad said the cougar and man were found," Cindy continued. "Dad told me with Jack Dolon dead now, you're the only person who knows exactly where it happened."

"Maybe so, but other people have seen photos of the place. I took a lot of pictures of the scene itself, and some on the way there. I made copies of those, kept some for my files, and sent the rest to headquarters in Juneau. The cougar was shot by Tadlock—I mean your brother's killer—near Gedney Harbor, not far from the area you describe. I think anyone with some patience and willing to do a little bushwhacking could probably find the exact spot where he and the cougar died."

"I'd like to see those photos."

"I don't know, Cindy—some are pretty gruesome."

"What—you think I'm some delicate young thing who can't handle it? I've been into photography since I was a little girl, and I'm studying to be a photojournalist. I guess if I can't stomach the sight, I've got no business in that line of work."

"I can see you're serious—and no, I don't think you're just some empty-headed girl. You're David and Karen's daughter, after all."

"So, unless there is some law that says I can't view those photos, I want to see them, and I'd also like to visit the place where the cougar died. I wish we would have had the time to do it before we left on this trip."

"You're going back to Kuiu on your way home, aren't you—after your Skagway visit?"

"Only for a few days on our way south. We'll wind things up with Larry, then we've got to get back in time for my classes."

"I would love to show you the place, and your mom and dad too, if they want to see where the cougar nailed the asshole that shot him and killed your brother, but I'm afraid I'll be busy with the fish count in Haines. The best I can do is to give you the location and directions from Gedney Harbor, and you should be able to find it on your own."

While Ray and Cindy talked, Karen went down into the cabin to get more snacks and drinks. David left Conrad at the helm, and followed her down the companionway ladder. Karen extracted beers from the cooler and David removed a floor board to get at the bottle of bourbon Larry had given him that he had stashed in the bilge for safe keeping. His hand brushed a plastic freezer bag further back in the dark space.

"I can't believe you brought this without telling me, Karen! If customs had found it when we checked in we would have been in real trouble. They might have turned us around, and banned us from ever entering Canada again, by water or land!" David exclaimed.

"Not me! You must have put it there and forgotten about it," Karen retorted. "Maybe you're getting forgetful in your old age!"

"I sure as hell didn't do it, damn it!" David said, as he climbed the companionway stairs with the bag containing the gun in hand.

"For Christ's sake, Cindy, if you wanted bear protection a .32 pistol is little better than a pellet gun! Bear spray is far more effective, and legal if you declare it! What the hell were you thinking?"

"I didn't bring it for bear protection," Cindy fired back.

"Have you already forgotten someone cut our anchor line in the middle of the night? You insisted mom and I learn how to shoot, and encouraged me to join the team in high school, remember? I swore after Marshall was killed I would never travel unarmed if I could help it!"

"I guess I'd rather you focused more on shooting with your camera—pun intended," David said, cooling off some. "Really, it wasn't good judgement, Cindy, nor was shooting that inflatable."

David put the pistol, a 1917 Colt model that his grandfather had acquired as an officer in World War I, back into the hiding place.

"I just feel safer knowing it's there. I know that sounds stupid, but that's the way I feel."

"We'll have to have it mailed home by a licensed dealer. If we lie about it going home and customs finds it, we'll be in for it. At the very least it's a hefty fine, and they'll confiscate grandpa's gun."

Conrad and Ray listened to their exchange without commenting. Conrad sympathized with Cindy. He knew David had experienced a kind of catharsis by forcing judge Daise to endure a sort of citizen's court over his decision to sentence Cindy's brother, Marshall to prison for a small amount of illegal powder. Later Conrad had made sure the judge did not rise again when he fell from his sailboat, *Tisiphone*. Conrad had hunted and wounded the killer of Marshall Stuckrath, Grant Tadlock, then stood by while a cougar savaged the man. But Cindy and her mother had experienced nothing but loss and emptiness. Conrad was not surprised that Cindy felt the need to be armed, and he knew she was also taking martial arts training.

Ray was more ambivalent. He agreed with David that it was foolish to take firearms across the border, and a .32 was nearly worthless in bear country, but he recalled that at her age he had exercised poor judgement on more than one occasion. In any case he was not about to get involved in a family dispute.

After Marshall's death Cindy had dropped out of Juneau high school. She moved into an apartment with an older boyfriend. Her boyfriend eventually got tired of her moodiness and frequent rages, and kicked her out. When her parents separated and left Juneau Cindy moved in with her father in Bellingham, Washington. By then Cindy was doing better. David urged her to see a therapist, and to his surprise she had agreed. The psychologist suggested she join a martial arts group to help her deal with her pent-up rage. The hard workouts and hand to hand sparing were just what she needed. She began attending school again, and graduated near the top of her Bellingham high school class.

"Unless you want to throw it overboard, we'll just mail the gun back to Washington from Skagway. The hardware store there is a licensed gun dealer," Karen said.

She couldn't stand to hear David and Cindy fight. Since her son's death even the smallest of disagreements between any of them could bring her to tears.

"Sure," Cindy said, reluctantly.

She knew her parents were right, but after her brother's murder, in her mind caused by the stupid and immoral legal system that had exposed him to danger and led to his death in prison, she had little respect for the law. Still, she did not want to get her parents in trouble. In any case they had the rifle the archeologist had loaned them on board, at least until they were finished with their work on Kuiu Island.

All that day and night they sailed north, trading watches every two hours. The self steering mechanism did most of the work, only needing periodic adjustments to keep them on the best course. They arrived in Skagway without incident and took up a berth in the small boat harbor.

CHAPTER 30

A Skagway Melodrama

The Stuckrath family was familiar with Skagway from previous excursions north from Juneau in their sailboat and on the state ferry. Sports teams and other school groups from Haines and Skagway also made frequent trips to Juneau. Cindy, who had for a time been active in her high school theatre program, had become friends with several thespian students from other regional Alaskan towns before the Stuckrath family abandoned Juneau, after Marshall's death. Although Cindy had dropped out of high school for part of her junior year in Juneau, she had maintained friendships with several students, especially Brenda Melpomene.

Brenda had dreams of becoming a Broadway Star. Her part as a dancer and chorus singer in the Days Of '98 show was her first professional role, and she was excited that Cindy was coming to see her that evening. While David and Karen shopped for groceries and other necessities, and Conrad and Ray continued their investigation, Cindy joined her friend in the ruins of the once grand Pullen House Hotel, where they shared a bottle of cheap, sweet wine, which Brenda's older brother had reluctantly bought for the occasion, on condition they didn't reveal his name if they were caught.

"Greg only bought it 'cause he's got the hots for you," Brenda said.

"He is pretty cute, just not my type," Cindy replied.

"What is your type these days, anyway? That guy you lived with in Juneau was a real asshole," Brenda said, taking a long swig from the bottle, and handing it to her friend.

"I don't think I know yet. I'm planning to do more research in college, though," Cindy joked.

"Greg is really possessive. He's afraid that I'll find someone else when I leave home for college—and just between the two of us—he's got a good reason to be worried!"

"Is he jealous of your acting too?"

"Yeah, he comes to every show he can, and hangs around afterward."

"Well now you're a real pro, Brenda—a paid actor!"

"The pay isn't so great, and it gets pretty boring doing the same show several times a day, but you're right—it's a start. Most of the time I love it, even though I'm probably the weakest actor in the cast."

"You're being too modest. I know they hire mostly college actors from out of town, especially Mormons from Utah, and I bet you're as talented as any of them."

"I'm the youngest one in the cast, and I can hold my own, but there's a couple of girls that are way better trained dancers and singers. Miles doesn't have to find me housing, so that saves him money. He hires mostly Mormons because he doesn't want a hung over cast for the morning shows."

"How's that working out for him?" Cindy asked, as she passed the bottle back to her friend.

"Not so well—ha-ha! Most nights they party pretty hard after the last show, except for one of the super straight girls who none of us really like. The morning shows can be pretty sloppy. Miles gets bent out of shape and yells at us, but it's too late in the season for him to fire anyone and rehearse a replacement. You'll get to see a good show. Our evening shows are usually the best."

"Do you party every night too?"

"Well, you know how mom and dad are. If I want them to pay for college and private lessons, I've got to behave myself. Anyway, even though it's kind of funny when things don't go perfectly on stage, I like it best when everyone is on. At least no one has barfed on stage yet, like what happened at a morning show last year!" Brenda laughed.

"I'm so excited you're going to be in Bellingham this fall with me! The university has a great drama department, and I'll get to see all your shows! We can hang out, and you can meet my boyfriend—if we're still together then."

"If you're still together?"

"He wasn't too happy with me being gone for most of the summer. We had a fight, but we made up before I left. He's a good guy—smart, great sense of humor most of the time, and he's got a fabulous body—he windsurfs and he's on the rowing team. But he's starting to get too possessive. It's funny how guys get like that, even when you make it clear you're not interested in any kind of long term commitment."

"The photos of him you sent are great. If you decide to break up maybe you could send him my way!"

"Speaking of photos, I guess I'm a pro now too! I'm getting paid to document the archeology sites we're excavating on Kuiu Island. I got a really nice camera and lenses for graduation. I'll try to get there early tonight and get a seat down in front of the stage, or maybe on the balcony, so I can get some shots for your portfolio."

"Oh, that would be awesome! I'll talk to Miles Jameson, our producer and director. If you agree to give him permission to use some of your photos for promotion, I'm sure he'll reserve good seats for you and your parents."

While Cindy and Brenda enjoyed their illicit drink in the ruins of the old house, Conrad and Ray talked with Skagway chief of police, Dan Segrestein about recent developments in the Jack Dolon murder investigation, and the terrorist threat to the railroad and cruise ships.

"I think the other gumshoes may have got the jump on you," Dan said.

"I was told the FBI had been brought in, but I've yet to meet them," Conrad replied. "I assume that's who you're referring to."

"Yep. They were quite a pair, those two. Mutt and Jeff. The short one is doughy and pudgy—I can't see how he could have passed the physical. The other guy is about six four, and can't weigh more than one fifty. What a duo!" Dan said shaking his head.

"I'm guessing they were chosen for other reasons than physical fitness."

"Definitely. The short guy was mostly interested in getting access to the library computer, and the skinny fellow had a warrant to look into Hiram Hatcher's bank accounts."

"So they've decided Hiram is the culprit—not Jim Lothar?" Ray asked.

"Either him or the trio that was staying with him out in Dyea. They asked a lot of questions about Hiram's girlfriend and her two brothers, who they identified as Mary, Simon, and Liam Murphy, from Orcas Island in Washington."

"There's our Mae West, Stan Laurel, and Oliver Hardy. So I guess sergeant Tenax, Ray, and myself are the three stooges in this theatre of the absurd," Conrad quipped.

"Still, nothing about Jim Lothar? Does that mean we've been on a wild goose chase these last few days, while I should have been in Haines keeping an eye on the salmon count. Shit, what a waste of time!" Ray said incredulously.

"Hey, you're the one that told me time on the water is never wasted, and that all work and no play is unhealthy," Conrad replied. "I enjoyed our little voyage, seeing the whales again, and reconnecting with my old friends, the Stuckraths. I don't regard our trip as a waste of time at all, though I understand a different time of year would have been better for you, Ray."

Conrad had come to believe the threat to the cruise ships and railroad had been a bluff. He guessed the railroad had paid the ransom, but didn't want it known, and that the death of agent Dolon might not even be related. It seemed to Conrad that Jack Dolon, like the previous undercover investigator on the tour ship, was most likely killed by Sabastos Melas or one of his henchmen. He was now mostly motivated by the desire to find out how Lothar might be involved with the Murphys and Hiram Hatcher.

For Conrad, the case was now an intriguing puzzle to be solved, but not a matter of any particular importance. He was happy to wander around Southeast Alaska at the government's expense, while taking every opportunity to spend time with Linda Daise. He was especially looking forward to taking Linda sailing on his boat, which had recently arrived in Juneau on a barge by way of Seattle from Hawaii.

"So Mutt and Jeff haven't located the Murphys or Hatcher yet?" Ray asked.

"Not as far as I know. We found the Murphy's van abandoned in Dyea, and our best guess is that Hiram is hiding somewhere up north. We've asked the

Mounties to keep an eye out for him," the police chief replied.

"The caretaker at Burro Creek, Earl Kharon came in a few days ago and reported a suspicious trio had been camping out there. The description fit the Murphy siblings. He told us they were headed south in a boat that Hiram and George Ripinski own together."

"Yeah, we talked to Earl too. We saw that boat, a Boston Whaler, with two men and a woman aboard in Stephens Passage on our way to Kuiu Island. It had to have been the Murphys," Ray said.

"Coincidences seem to occur all the time here in the north," chief Sergestein observed. "Even though Southeast Alaska is a huge region, not many people live here, and most of them in a handful of towns, so you're constantly running in to people you know under unexpected circumstances."

"What are the FBI agents up to now?" Conrad asked.

"They think the Murphys will meet up with Hiram Hatcher somewhere in Canada. The last I heard, they had worked out some sort of arrangement with the Mounties, and were on their way to Whitehorse. They saw Earl's report too. I think they were under the impression the Murphys would take a plane from Juneau to Canada, where they would rendezvous with Hiram."

"The Murphys were well south of Juneau when we spotted them, and headed up Frederick Sound. I don't think they were going to Canada, unless they intended to cross the border much further south, perhaps at Hyder or Prince Rupert. When they saw us, they took off at high speed towards Petersburg," Ray said.

"Anyway, to continue with the theatre metaphors—it's not over until the fat lady sings. The FBI may have found the identity of the guilty parties, but they haven't arrested anyone yet, so you two still have a chance to be the heroes of the day—unless my officers beat you to it," Segrestein declared.

Miles Jameson agreed to free admission and front row seats to the Days Of '98 show for the Stuckrath family in exchange for the use of Cindy's photos. As the performance progressed Cindy moved around the theatre, taking photographs from various angles. The climax of the show was the shootout between Soapy Smith and Frank Reid, with director and producer Miles Jameson playing Soapy's part, and local newspaper owner Hunter Clio in Reid's role.

"My God—Don't shoot!" Soapy Smith shouted, but the two men fired at point blank range. The audience gasped in unison.

As the deafening reports echoed in the theatre, and the two actors collapsed, a figure burst through the theatre doors, sprinting down the aisle towards the stage. Cindy had moved to the aisle to capture the scene without blocking the audience's view. The man crashed into her. The impact spun her part way around, and nearly knocked her down. She recovered enough to strike the man in the chest with her fist, but he grabbed her and pulled her to him. The audience assumed it was some part of the act, and watched this new development with interest. A split second later two more men, Conrad Slocum and Ray Standers, charged into the hall.

"Let go of the girl Jim. It's all over. Don't make things worse for yourself," Conrad said. His service pistol was in his hand.

"I didn't kill anyone! It was Liam Murphy!"

He held Cindy tightly and backed towards the rear entrance of the theatre.

The dancers, including Cindy's friend Brenda, were assembled in the wings, awaiting their entrance for the finale. Miles Jameson, playing Soapy Smith, had risen and made a move towards Lothar.

"I wouldn't try it, Soapy. This gun doesn't shoot blanks."

Jim Lothar had his 9mm Glock in hand, and waved it at the actor.

The audience suddenly realized this wasn't part of the show. They stood in waves and, except for the oldest ones, some of whom required wheelchairs or walkers, rushed en masse for the exits.

In the chaos Karen Stuckrath moved towards Jim Lothar and her daughter. The Colt .32 Cindy had secreted aboard their sailboat was in her hand. She had placed it in her purse earlier, with the intention of mailing it home from the hardware store, but had not found time to do it before the the show started.

Lothar caught her movement, saw the gun in Karen's hand, and adjusted his aim, but at the same instant Cindy bit deep into his forearm, tasting blood, and simultaneously brought her foot down hard on his instep, a move she'd rehearsed in her martial arts training.

As Cindy broke free of his grip Jim Lothar and Karen Stuckrath, like the actors moments earlier, fired nearly simultaneously, but only Karen's aim was true. Lothar stumbled forward, firing another shot into the floor as Conrad slammed his own pistol down on Jim's injured forearm. The pistol spun away into the aisle where Ray retrieved it. Lothar, now bleeding from his forearm and abdomen, had no strength to resist as Conrad fastened the handcuffs.

"It's over now, Karen. Give me the gun," David gently implored his wife.

Karen appeared to be in shock. She was trembling so badly he was afraid she might accidentally fire again. David had to ask her a second time. She seemed to recover some, and as though sleepwalking, handed him the old pistol.

"Are you hurt, Cindy," David asked. His daughter's face was covered in blood. She looked like a wild animal that had been feeding on its prey.

"I'm feeling better than he is," she said, pointing to Lothar, stretched out on the floor, while Ray Standers applied pressure to his wound.

They waited for the EMTs to arrive. Skagway had no resident doctor. Serious cases were flown out to Juneau.

Suddenly, like an avalanche breaking loose, Karen began to cry. She sobbed uncontrollably, as she hadn't even when she'd first received the news of her son's death the year before.

"Although plenty of witnesses saw that the shooting was in defense of your daughter you could still be charged with illegal concealed carry, or even attempted murder. I understand you want to be on your way back south. I'm not going to arrest you, but I have to ask you to remain in Skagway until the troopers or DA say it's okay for you to go, and I'll have to keep the gun for evidence," chief Dan Segrestein instructed Karen, after he interviewed her.

After they left the police station the Stuckrath family, Ray, and Conrad gathered in the privacy of *Lethe's* cabin to wind down. Brenda was understanding when Cindy said she needed to be with her family on their sailboat that night.

"I don't know about the rest of you, but I could use a good shot of that bourbon you've stashed in the bilge," Conrad said, after they made themselves comfortable around the boat's galley table.

"Funny, I was thinking the same thing," David said. "And considering what she's been through, I think we can ignore Cindy's underage status."

David put an ice cube in each cup and poured a generous shot for the five of them.

"How about a toast, to our own Annie Oakley, Karen Stuckrath, the quickest draw in Alaska," Ray said, raising his glass.

"One thing I'm curious about, Karen. How did you manage to load and arm that Colt so quickly?" Conrad asked.

"I didn't have to load it. The magazine was full and in the gun. I just had to pull the slider and shoot," Karen said.

"So you were walking around all day with a loaded gun in your purse?"

"I planned to take it to the gun counter at the hardware store and mail it back home, but we spent so much time shopping and socializing I didn't get around to it," Karen said.

"Sure, but you couldn't have shipped it with a loaded magazine," Ray pointed out.

"My father always told me that there was no point in carrying around an unloaded gun. So I guess I just put the magazine in out of habit. I can't honestly say I had any premonition that I would need it, or felt unsafe in any way. I know it sounds weird and irresponsible, but I didn't give much thought to it at all."

"Well, even though it was illegal and even reckless, it turned out to be prudent," Conrad said.

"How long do you suppose we'll have to stick around here in Skagway?" David asked.

"We really need to get going as soon as possible. We have to spend a few more days on Kuiu Island wrapping things up, and we'd like to get back to Bellingham before Cindy starts school. I suppose she could fly back, but she has to finish up her photography for Larry at the very least."

"If it was me, I would leave tomorrow," Conrad said.

"Speaking as an Alaskan law officer, I certainly have no objections," Ray added. "I thought chief Dan's suggestion was impertinent, frankly."

"Yes, but the chief did say we had to stay," Karen objected.

"I should point out that technically Ray and I both outrank him," Conrad added.

"After all you've been through? They're certainly not going to chase you down. They know damn well that when the media comes out with this story, which I'd bet will be tomorrow, they won't be able to put together a jury in the state that will convict you of anything, Karen. Besides, chief Dan didn't put an order in writing," Ray explained.

"I agree. If the state decides to prosecute you, or if Lothar recovers and wants to bring a civil suit, they'll have to observe the proper legal procedures. So until it's in writing from the court I suggest you stick to your schedule. Summer is getting on, and this great sailing weather won't hold too much longer. If it was me, I'd head south first thing tomorrow," Conrad advised.

"It's been a roller coaster of a day by any measure. Ray and I should get on our way and let you mull things over. If I see that *Lethe* isn't in the harbor tomorrow, you can bet I won't mention it to anyone," Conrad continued.

"Conrad is right. Anyway I've got to get back to counting fish in Haines. I probably won't see you again before you head south, so I'll say goodbye to you now, and bon voyage! I hope we meet again, but I won't blame you if you're in no hurry to return to Alaska any time soon," Ray said.

They exchanged hugs and best wishes. Cindy set the timer on her camera and took group photos of the five standing on the dock next to the Stuckrath's sailboat.

"Do you think they'll wait for permission to leave?" Ray asked, as he and Conrad walked back to town from the boat harbor.

"I'll bet they're out of the harbor before noon. I don't think either David or Karen are in any mood to be taking orders from anyone. Their boat is all provisioned for their trip south, and they've had enough excitement to last them awhile. I'm going down to Juneau myself on the first available plane tomorrow. My boat's there, and I hope to get her ready to sail before the weather turns."

"Are you sure that trip doesn't have something to do with seeing an attorney?" Ray joked.

"True. I might have been on thin legal ice suggesting that the Stuckrath's should ignore chief Dan's instructions, and that we could pull rank on him. Luckily I do know a good lawyer!"

"I've got to get back to Haines as soon as I can. The sockeye run on the Chilkoot is finishing up, and besides getting back to my regular job, I don't want to miss the chance to get my subsistence allowance. Hey—you should come up and join me! I've been promising you a good fishing expedition since we met last summer," Ray said.

"I just might take you up on that if you can wait a couple of days, Ray. I don't feel a pressing need to get back to work now that Jim Lothar is out of commission."

"The Murphy trio and Hiram Hatcher are still on the loose," Ray reminded Conrad. "But that's a job for you feds now that they've left Alaska. I'll be far more useful counting salmon!"

CHAPTER 31

Fishing With Ray

"I was beginning to think we'd never find time for this. Man, it's good to be on the water with nothing to do but fish, drink a little beer, and enjoy the day," Ray said, contentedly.

"It seems to me we're not doing much fishing, but plenty of beer drinking," Conrad observed.

The two men were approaching the Chilkoot River inlet, sailing from Skagway under mainsail and genoa, with a gentle following breeze in Conrad's sailboat, the Ingrid cutter, *Tisiphone*.

The sailboat had been shipped by barge from Hawaii to Seattle, and then to Juneau, and had arrived while Conrad and Ray were en route from Kuiu Island to Skagway with the Stuckrath family. After arresting Jim Lothar in Skagway Conrad had spent a busy three days with Linda Daise in Juneau while he refitted his sailboat with the help of a Juneau rigger. He and Linda planned to rendezvous later with the Stuckrath family at Port Malmesbury on Kuiu Island before the Stuckraths sailed south to Bellingham. The trip to Skagway and

Haines was a sort of shake-down cruise in the meantime.

"Oh, don't you worry about fish—all in good time. I promise you an abundance of some of the best salmon on the planet! Chilkoot blue backs a-plenty are just around the corner, though it's near the end of this year's run, so it's now or never."

Ray pointed to the low spit that guarded the entrance to Taiyasanka Harbor and the Ferebee River Valley. Just beyond was Lutak Inlet and their destination, the mouth of the Chilkoot River, where Ray knew the last of the season's fine, fat sockeye salmon were gathering for their run up the river and across the lake to their spawning grounds.

Ray's net lay in the bottom of Conrad's dinghy, towed from a bridal attached to the stern of the sailboat. The residents of Alaska were entitled to a large number of salmon each year for subsistence. They were allowed to catch the fish with a set net, its dimensions and web size specified by the state. Ray had agreed to share some of his family's allowance with Conrad in exchange for his help, and transportation from Skagway to Haines. The two men had finished their business in Skagway the day before by interviewing several Skagway locals who had encountered the Murphy siblings during their stay in Dyea.

"It's the only way to really catch fish—forget casting with a pole. We let the fish come to us! The hardest work is pulling 'em out of the net," Ray declared.

As they approached Taiyasanka Harbor they saw a boat emerge from the narrow entrance of the small bay. Out of curiosity Ray grabbed the binoculars.

"Shit, that's Hiram Hatcher! I thought he was long gone!"

Conrad turned the boat slightly to intercept. Hatcher's low powered outboard motor was not capable of pushing his inflatable dinghy much faster than Conrad was sailing, and Hiram had no reason to suspect law enforcement officers would be crewing a sailboat, but as the two boats drew closer together Hiram suddenly recognized the two men, and swerved away.

"Hiram! We're not going to arrest you—we just want to talk," Ray yelled through cupped hands.

Hiram motored on another few seconds, then cut his engine, realizing it was pointless to try to outrun the men, who could easily call in the police boat from nearby Haines.

Conrad doused his sails and let *Tisiphone* drift. Hiram pulled alongside and threw a line to the two men.

"Do you want me aboard?" Hiram asked.

"Suit yourself, Hiram. How about a cold beer?" Ray suggested.

"That sounds great! It's been a long time since I've drank anything but river water," Hiram replied.

Conrad gave Hiram a hand up the side of the sailboat, and Ray passed him a beer.

"Since you're not arresting me, you must have caught poor Liam," Hiram said, after taking a large gulp from the beer can.

"You mean Murphy? We have no idea where he or his sister and brother are. Jim Lothar is in custody, but he insists he didn't kill Jack Dolon, Liam Murphy did. We've been hoping to find you. He says you were a witness," Conrad said.

"Yeah, I was there when Dolon died. It happened at my cabin out in Dyea. But it was an accident, and as much Jack Dolon's own fault as Liam's."

"That's not how Lothar put it," Ray countered. "He says Liam Murphy attacked agent Dolon and broke his neck."

"Lothar's a lying fuck. It was an unfortunate accident, and just bad luck. The two were fighting and fell. The knife was Lothar's idea, later, after Dolon was already dead. He figured it would put the blame on Sam Thornton."

"That didn't stick, so to speak. The coroner determined the knife wasn't the cause of death. Lothar's fingerprints were on the dock pilings and gunwale of the boat—though unfortunately the Seattle lab took forever to get us the results. They found yours too, as well as some other unidentified prints. But Lothar had motive, so he's been charged," Conrad explained.

"Lothar didn't kill Dolon, but he derailed the train and came up with the plan to extort money from the railroad."

"So far Lothar maintains he doesn't know anything about that. Do you have any idea where the Murphys are?" Conrad asked.

"That's bullshit too. Lothar gave them the idea of ransoming the railroad, then set everything in motion by dynamiting the rails up on the pass. As for where the Murphys are—I don't know, and wouldn't say if I did."

"Yes, according to Lothar you and Mary Murphy were pretty close," Conrad continued. "If they're found Liam could be charged with murder, or manslaughter at the least. I think it would be in everyone's best interest if you would tell the court what you know when the time comes. In any case you've been subpoenaed, though of course no one has been able to serve you."

"It seems I've got no choice. I might have a friend I can rent a room from in Juneau until the trial's over, unless they want to lock me up—then I'll get free room and board. But it doesn't make me happy to think I'll be helping that asshole stay out of jail."

"Even if he isn't charged with Dolon's murder, he'll do some time for the other charges—maybe even in a federal prison. He sunk a Fish and Game boat and left his partner to drown on it, and robbed a Tlingit burial site and tried to fence what he found. It might give you some pleasure to know Jim Lothar is in the hospital with a pretty serious bullet wound to his gut, though he's unfortunately expected to recover," Ray said.

"Somebody shot him? Too bad he didn't aim higher!" Hiram exclaimed.

"Actually, it was a woman. He took her daughter hostage when we closed in on him at the Eagles theatre. They were both armed, but the girl's mother was quicker. Lothar's lawyer is trying to get the woman prosecuted for attempted murder, illegal concealed carry, and a few other charges, but I doubt any jury will convict her if it even goes to trial," Conrad explained.

"I'll be damned! Maybe there is some justice in this world after all!"

"I hate to interrupt this interesting and lively discussion, but the salmon won't wait for us all day. How do you feel about a little fishing, Hiram?" Ray asked.

"Sure—I've got nothing better to do, it seems. I don't suppose I could have another beer?"

Soon the three were busy setting out the net. One end was tied to the sailboat, which Conrad had securely anchored. The men whooped like boys when they saw the salmon hitting the net as fast as they could pay it out from the dinghy. As the savvy biologist had predicted, the hardest part was picking the heavy "blue backs" out of the gill net, which in spite of the flotation corks along the head-rope, was sinking from the weight of sixty plump, oleaginous sockeye. The Chillkoot river was famous for the size and oil content of its salmon, among the largest sockeye in the world.

"Well, it might not be quite as good as last year, but a hell of a lot better than the 1990s. In 1995 we only counted seven thousand sockeyes, but last year the weir count was back up to over seventy-six thousand, more like normal—at least for modern times. This year looks pretty good so far—certainly no record return, but decent," Ray said.

"That's how many you counted, but what's the estimate of the total run?" Conrad asked.

"Figuring that out is the tough part, and depends on a lot of factors, especially the harvest rate. Last year we estimated the total run at close to one hundred fifty thousand fish, but the harvest rate was almost fifty per cent. That's considered a healthy number these days, but until the 1920s over a million salmon returned to the Chilkoot and Chilkat rivers most years."

After they had the salmon on board and retrieved Ray's gill net the men motored over to the Haines harbor, where Ray's wife and son met them and helped unload the catch. Conrad and Hiram said goodbye to the biologist, and sailed south with ten fat sockeye Ray had insisted they keep for themselves, packed on ice in two coolers. Late that evening, after a pleasant six hour sail down the long fjord, they dropped anchor in Echo Cove north of Juneau, joining three commercial fishing boats anchored nearby in the bay.

"How about a nightcap before we hit the sack?" Conrad suggested.

"You'll get no argument from me on that score," Hiram agreed.

"Sorry I've got no ice—unless you want some out of the coolers," Conrad said, as he poured generous shots of whiskey into coffee mugs.

"I prefer mine without a fishy aftertaste—neat is just perfect."

The two men had not talked about Hiram's involvement in the investigation during the sail south. By an unspoken agreement they chose to enjoy the journey and the gentle late summer weather, though Conrad did describe some of his adventures with Ray at Kuiu Island, and relayed the latest news and gossip related to the case. For his part Hiram was not anxious to discuss his legal situation until he talked to a lawyer. He liked and trusted Ray Standers, but this officer was a stranger, whose offhand, even casual manner might just be ruse to get him to divulge more about the Murphys.

"When Ray and I went out to Dyea to question you, had you already decided to disappear?" Conrad asked.

"I had a few more things to take care of in town. I'd planned to leave the following day or the day after. I was worried that you or Ray might wander around and find my inflatable before I could get away. Sorry about the tires. Of course I'll repay Fish and Game for two new ones."

"Ray thought you might head up into the Yukon."

"I did think about that option, but I figured I'd be better off hiding in the Ferebee Valley and heading south when things cooled down. I like camping and living off the land, but I don't relish the idea of spending a winter freezing my ass off—and they say the Mounties always get their man," Hiram replied.

"I read somewhere that Thomas Ferebee was the bombardier on the Enola Gay when they dropped the first atomic bomb. I wonder if he was related to the

Navy surgeon, Nelson Ferebee the river was named after?" Conrad mused.

"I don't know the answer to that, but I can tell you this whole affair has really blown my life apart," Hiram said.

"Hey, it looks like we've got company," Conrad exclaimed. "He must have a good nose for whiskey."

A man was motoring over from one of the fishing boats anchored in the cove.

"It's Sam Thornton," Hiram said.

Conrad and Hiram greeted the fisherman and helped tie his boat to a deck cleat.

"I recognized your sailboat, Conrad. There's not many wood blow boats as fine-looking as yours in these parts," Sam said.

"Welcome aboard. You're just in time. I'm pouring good whiskey, and the beer is cold."

"Thank you. I don't drink when I'm fishing, or even carry any booze on the boat, but the latest commercial fishing opening closed today, so I won't be breaking my rule."

Sam seated himself at the small cabin table across from Hiram while Conrad poured.

"I never expected to see you again, Hiram. I didn't think they'd ever find you," Sam said.

"Just good timing and luck on our part. He almost bumped into us coming out of Taiyasanka Harbor, and volunteered to help Ray Standers with his subsistence fishing," Conrad explained.

"So you're not under arrest, then?"

"Not technically, I guess. Or at least not yet," Hiram answered.

"...that true, Conrad?"

"That's correct. Mr. Hatcher has agreed to be a witness at Jim Lothar's trial, whenever that happens. As you're probably aware, the defense is doing their best to delay things—trying to get a change of venue to Anchorage," Conrad said.

"I suppose I should be pissed off at you, Slocum, but I'll accept this fine whiskey in lieu of a private or public apology," Sam said.

"Linda Daise is an exceptional woman, and a great lawyer. I figure anyone lucky enough to be sharing a bed with her has got to be a man of exceptional parts too, though I've known a fair number of otherwise intelligent women who have a weakness for scumbags and scoundrels."

Sam was still bitter about his ex-girlfriend's affair with Jim Lothar, and overjoyed that the man would be going to prison as soon as he recovered enough to be moved from the hospital.

"Ray insisted you were innocent all along, but of course you know we convinced the court to have you held a few days in the hopes our real suspects would surface. I don't mind apologizing to you for that, and I'm sure Ray will too when he sees you. Thanks for being a good sport about it."

"If it helped to get that bastard Lothar behind bars, I'd willingly spend a month in the slammer—but not during fishing season. That's the only part that put me out a little."

"So you and Linda Daise are a couple? Well, congratulations, Conrad! A few years ago, when I was still a member in good standing, the Fjord Foundation retained her as a legal advisor for a time. She's a keeper!" Hiram agreed.

"I am indeed a lucky man. Before Linda Daise and I got together I'd planned to apply for a posting elsewhere once this case was resolved. I'm not a big fan of winters this far north. But now it looks like I'll be getting my workouts shoveling Linda's driveway in Juneau for a few months. Is anybody up for a refill?"

Conrad poured again, opened three cans of beer, and retrieved a bag of smoked salmon from the galley's ice chest.

"Hey, that looks like some of my salmon," Sam said.

"Indeed it is, compliments of Linda—and perhaps the best I've ever tasted."

"It should be good, I've been perfecting the recipe, which I got from my grandmother, for thirty years now."

"I absolutely concur," Hiram said after his first bite. "As much as I hate to admit, it's even better than mine. I don't suppose you'd share the recipe, Sam?"

"No problem. It's not a trade secret, the preparation just takes a bit more time and effort than most people seem to have the patience for. Speaking of lovely women, I heard you had found someone to relieve your monkish existence out at Dyea, Hiram," Sam remarked.

"She's gone now. I'll probably never see her again," Hiram answered, gloomily.

"Oh—too bad. ...you have a fight?" Sam asked.

"Something like that," Hiram replied.

"Sorry to pry, Hiram. It's really none of my business, of course, but it seems like we might have that in common."

Sam felt awkward. Although he didn't consider himself to be a close friend, he and Hiram had known each other for years, and he hadn't thought his question was out of line. Sam had always found that a drinking session was one of the few times when most men were comfortable speaking about their personal lives and emotions. Maybe it was the presence of Conrad that made Hiram reticent, Sam thought.

Hiram wondered if Mary really had abandoned him, and if she was safe somewhere. He chafed at the thought that he would be wasting weeks or even months in Juneau, when he really wanted to get down to Oregon, where he hoped a letter from Mary awaited him in his post office box. In the meantime it was best to let everyone, especially Conrad think he and Mary had broken up.

"It seems that Mary Murphy and her brothers are somehow involved in Dolon's death; at least according to Jim Lothar," Conrad explained.

"Yeah, Linda told me Lothar pinned it on them. Lothar's always been a rotten bastard, and I know he'd turn on his own mother to save his precious ass," Sam said.

"He and Grant Tadlock were two of kind, though at least Jim is a decent fisherman and reliable crew on the water. The whole caper was probably Jim's idea. He's a bundle of contradictions, and unpredictable. He's a good worker, and a better talker, and always trying to come up with schemes to make a quick buck on the side, legal or not. I don't know anything about the Murphys and can't guess how they got involved with him."

"It does seem that some of what Lothar says is true. At the very least the Murphys colluded in extorting money from the railroad. We've been able to trace the Murphy siblings to the Caribbean, where the ransom money was wired and someone matching one of their descriptions withdrew it. They might still be in the region, or not."

Conrad looked directly at Hiram while he spoke. He did not reveal that he had been assigned to track down the trio, and would be flying south soon on that errand.

"I'll tell you two exactly what I'm going to tell the court when the time comes for me to testify. I'm sure they'll dredge up my past and find out all about my activism and arrests in Oregon years ago. It won't be hard to prove I'm a radical environmentalist, and that I don't like the tour ships. Fingerprints on the boat or piers will show I was there when Dolon's dead body was tied up, and in fact, I'm the one that tied the knots. But is it a crime to tie up a corpse? Mary Murphy didn't want any part of it. I begged her to come with me, and leave her brothers. But those three are tight. We had a fight about it and she dumped me."

"Were you promised any money? Was Mary just going along with the extortion scheme because of her brothers?" Conrad asked.

Conrad suspected Hiram Hatcher was dissimulating to protect his former girlfriend, but he doubted he would need Hiram's help to locate the trio. He had decades of experience as an intelligence agent, and the full resources of his employer to call upon.

"Like I said, it was all Lothar's idea. I wasn't promised anything, but I agreed to help them get rid of the corpse. I didn't want that on my property, obviously. Once Lothar derailed the train, Liam and Simon felt like they were involved and really had no choice but to follow through. Lothar convinced them they could get away with it. Mary and her brothers think the railroad owes them for taking their property. But Mary didn't want anything to do with the extortion plan. She hates Jim Lothar."

Hiram went on to explain how their ancestor, Jesse Murphy was rewarded for killing Soapy Smith in 1898, and how his descendants eventually lost their beloved farm on Orcas Island.

It was nearly midnight when Sam finally went back to his boat. Conrad's main berth in the bow was filled with extra sails, so he set Hiram up in one of the midship berths. While at sea he always used the starboard quarter berth, which was closest to the companionway. After going on deck one last time to check that his anchor was holding he lay awake for a time thinking about what Hiram had said about the Murphy sibling's plight, but soon enough the gentle motion of the boat lulled him to sleep.

Hiram had difficulty falling asleep at first. Beyond the frustration of facing months in Juneau waiting to testify at Jim Lothar's trial was the unfinished business he had to deal with in Skagway. More lies and dissembling. After a while, he knew, it became difficult to remember the details of the stories you told. He dreaded having to explain why he had left the cabin so abruptly. He would also have to repay George for the loss of his boat, so that meant trying to find some sort of work in Juneau.

He had no idea where the Murphys might have left the Boston Whaler, but thanks to Conrad, he at least knew they had made it safely as far as the Caribbean.

Why had Conrad told him that? Perhaps the agent hoped Hiram would attempt to contact Mary, and Hiram would lead him to her.

He imagined his movements would be closely monitored in Juneau. Even if she had written him at the Oregon post office box, it might be months before he could check. Sleep came at last, but it was fitful and accompanied by unsettling dreams.

CHAPTER 32

Kuiu Island Again

Two days after the capture of Jim Lothar Skagway chief of police Dan Segrestein went down to the boat harbor to inform Karen Stuckrath, who he had advised to remain in Skagway, that she was free to leave. Lothar was expected to fully recover from the wound, and the state had no interest in prosecuting a mother for the defense of her child. He was surprised to find the *Lethe* was not in the harbor. The harbormaster informed him the family had left the morning after the events at the Eagles hall theatre.

"I'll be damned," the chief told the harbormaster. "I never expected they would leave without my okay. Well, it doesn't matter anyway. A trial would have been a waste of the state's time and money. The rumor is the attorney general ordered the DA to back off if he wanted to keep his job."

The Stuckraths were in a hurry to get back to Kuiu Island, where they would complete their work, and give the archeologist Cindy's film negatives of their excavations before sailing back to Bellingham. Taking turns at the tiller David, Karen, and Cindy sailed all day and night as they had on the trip north. They made good time down Lynn Canal and Chatham Strait to the archeologist's camp at Port Malmesbury.

The *Lethe* could sleep five people with reasonable comfort; one in the starboard quarter berth, two more on the benches on each side of the galley table, and two in the forward v-berth. Cindy was pleased to note that her father and mother, who had berthed together out of necessity on their trip north with five people aboard, continued to use the forward berth during their voyage to Kuiu Island.

As on their previous voyage, they rotated the watches every two hours, day and night. Cindy especially loved the solitude of her night watches. There was little to do but enjoy the sights and sounds of the magnificent fjord and its surroundings. The electronic self-steering mechanism held the course, and only small corrections had to be made periodically. When they made five knots or better they sailed. If their speed fell below that they ran the small diesel engine to keep to their schedule.

As long as they stayed well out in the strait there were few obstacles to avoid. There was very little boating traffic, only the occasional flotsam to watch for. The half submerged logs or deadheads were dangerous and hard to see in the half darkness of the nighttime watches. During one of her daytime shifts Cindy observed the Alaska ferry making its way north from Juneau to

Haines and Skagway. She saw several fishing boats and a cruise ship at the intersection of Icy Straits and Chatham Strait. The fishing boats were most likely coming from the tiny hamlet of Excursion Inlet, or nearby Gustavus, a small town of about six hundred located near the entrance of Glacier Bay, entirely surrounded by Glacier Bay National Park. The cruise ship was certainly headed to the park, where tourists could gape and snap photos of the glacier calving icebergs into the bay.

The day before they planned to leave Port Malmesbury the Stuckraths were pleased to see Conrad's cutter, *Tisiphone* sail into the bay and drop anchor near their own boat. Conrad and Linda planned to spend a few days cruising the fjords and enjoying the last of the mild summer weather.

That evening, while the group sat around the campfire at the archeology camp, Conrad described how Ray had spotted Jim Lothar on the dock, heading back towards the town while he and Ray were interviewing the captain of the *Opal Princess*. They had chased Lothar on foot down Broadway, dodging through the throngs of tourists, until the desperate man finally dashed through the doors of the Eagles theatre.

"His pickup was parked just a couple of blocks away. He hoped to lose us or at least slow us down in the crowd and make his getaway. Of course there's nowhere to hide in Skagway. Customs would have stopped him at the border if he went up the pass, or we would have cornered him in Dyea if he went that way," Conrad explained.

"True, but it might have taken some time to catch him. He could have blasted through the border without stopping. There are plenty of side roads and old mining claim trails once you get further up the road," David observed.

"Well I'm glad you got your man, and especially grateful that Cindy was not injured, thanks to quick-draw Karen. Do you know what items Lothar was trying to fence on that cruise ship?" Larry Nemous wondered.

"I thought you'd be especially curious about that," Conrad replied. "So I brought along photos and descriptions of the relics."

Conrad reached over to his day pack and extracted a manila envelope.

"Wow! Take a look at these, David. You're the historian, but if I'm not mistaken these are from the sixteenth century," Larry exclaimed.

"You're right. I would say English, from the mid 1500s. At least two hundred years earlier than the Spanish and Russian explorations of this region."

"From what that old rascal Craig Martes told us while he was waiting for the helicopter to take him to the Sitka clinic, your family apparently just missed finding these," the archeologist said. "Now the stratigraphy is completely trashed. Still, I'll take my crew up there anyway before we're done this season. At the very least it sounds like we could learn something from the clothing and bones that Martes told us they left behind when they looted the site."

"So what do you two make of all this, anyway? The wheel lock gun Frank Dermit found; the old Spanish coin Ray picked up; and the loot Martes and Lothar stole—all seemingly from the sixteenth century," Conrad asked.

"There's a writer in B.C., Sam Bawlf, who has plans to publish a book next year attempting to prove that Francis Drake sailed around the south end of Kuiu Island, and may have even anchored right here in Port Malmesbury. He maintains that Drake's voyage around the world between 1577 and 1580 had the secret goal of finding the fabled passage between the Atlantic and Pacific oceans, the mythical Strait of Anian. Bawlf and a couple of park service researchers visited here last year. Bawlf had heard from an old prospector who said he had discovered a brass plate in a cave here in 1954, and sent a rubbing to the Smithsonian. Apparently the inscription was in latin. He was told the plate was probably a hoax. Since then it's been lost, according to Bawlf," the archeologist replied.

"Most historians believe that Drake probably got no farther north than Northern California, or perhaps Oregon, although plenty of Canadians think he made it at least as far north as British Columbia. The tallest mountain on Vancouver Island is named after Drake's ship, the *Golden Hinde*, and some believe Drake attempted to found a colony in the Comox area, which he named Nova Albion. This new evidence might change some minds. I can't imagine how these relics got this far north through trade, though I suppose it is possible, as the Tlingit were great voyagers, who traveled long distances in their big war canoes. Some even made it as far south as California," David explained.

"So there are at least a couple of possibilities," Conrad concluded. "If the relics really are from the Drake expedition, at least one of Drake's men was captured by or traded to Tlingit warriors down south and brought back here as a slave, then perhaps killed when he tried to escape; or Drake did make it up here, as Bawlf says, and one or more of his men died right here on Kuiu Island."

"We may never figure it out. Drake's logs of his voyage were taken and suppressed by Queen Elizabeth after he returned to England, and were later lost in a fire. It's possible the finds aren't even English. We won't know for sure until the experts have a chance to see them. The Spanish had already been in the Americas for over seventy years by the time of the Drake voyage. In the 1540s Juan Cabrillo voyaged up the coast of California, and maybe even as far as the Columbia River. So it's at least conceivable the relics did arrive up here through trade. Hopefully an analysis of the bones and clothing will tell us more," David continued.

"I wish you luck with solving the puzzle," Conrad said. "I've got my own to figure out—by myself now that Ray's gone back to work in Haines."

"I thought capturing Jim Lothar and locating Hiram Hatcher would end your investigation. Is there more to it?" Larry asked.

"I can tell you Jim and Hiram were not the only suspects. Hiram's girlfriend and her two brothers were part of a plot to extort money from the railroad, and they were successful. They've left the country, and I've been assigned to track them down."

"Which begs the question—other than the joys of a sailing voyage to this pristine island and the pleasure of our esteemed company—there must be even more compelling reasons for you and Linda to be favoring us with a visit," the archeologist said.

"I promised Linda a cruise on *Tisiphone*," Conrad replied, giving her an affectionate hug. "But there is indeed something else. Ray asked me to show Cindy the place where the cougar and Marshall's killer died. Ray wanted to himself, but he's back at work on the Chilkat River weir. So Cindi, if you or anyone else want to go along, I'll take you there in the morning. Linda and I plan to leave on the tide later tomorrow. We're going to spend a night soaking in the hot springs at Tenekee, and hopefully even make it up to Glacier Bay, before we both have to get back to Juneau."

"I would rather not go," Karen said. "I don't have any interest in seeing that place.

"I should stay and help out Larry, and make sure everything is ship-shape for the voyage back to Bellingham. We'd planned to leave tomorrow, but we can put it off one more day," David replied.

"I've agreed to represent Hiram Hatcher if he is charged with any crimes," Linda said, changing the subject.

She could see the idea of visiting the site of Grant Tadlock and the cougar's death was uncomfortable for both Karen and David Stuckrath, but important to their daughter.

"What are they charging him with?" David asked.

"Probably multiple charges," Linda explained. "He might be charged with not reporting Dolon's death, conspiracy to extort money from the railroad, and a couple of other things. I'm hoping that in return for his testimony at Jim Lothar's trial and information he can give them about the Murphys, the state will let him plead to something minor. I doubt they'll let him off completely."

"The complication is that so far he refuses to say anything about the Murphys, other than that Jack Dolon's death was accidental. He won't say where they've gone, if he knows," Conrad added.

"Is he in prison?" Karen Stuckrath asked.

"Actually, he's housesitting for me while Conrad and I take some time off. He's not under arrest, but he has been advised to stay in Juneau. Ive got lots of room, so I told him he could stay there as long as he wanted. He's pretty handy. When Conrad and I left he was working on replacing my leaky kitchen faucet."

"I'm surprised they haven't charged him yet, considering his involvement," David said.

"The DA owed my partner a favor, but more importantly they've got a detective keeping a close eye on Hiram. If he's locked up there's no chance of him contacting the Murphys. They're hoping he might while he's free. I doubt he'll try. He's pretty determined to protect Mary Murphy, even at the cost of going to prison himself," Linda added.

"How did you find out they have a detective watching him?" Karen wondered.

"Oh, I've got my sources," Linda said, grinning at Conrad.

"Just whose side are you on, anyway, Conrad?" Larry asked.

"I'm sworn to uphold the constitution and to follow the orders of my superiors," Conrad replied. "But I'm maybe not the best person for this job. Perhaps I've grown a bit too fond of Hiram, and by extension, too sympathetic to the Murphy siblings."

"Can you plead a conflict of interest?" David asked.

"Not a chance, but on occasion I have been accused being a somewhat faineant individual, with a deplorable lack of work ethic. When accused of that, I'm usually too lazy to protest," he said, grinning.

The others laughed at his witticism, but not even Linda knew just how conflicted he really was. Conrad was determined to find the Murphys, but he had no intention of keeping anyone else, including the state troopers, FBI, or his own intelligence agency apprised of all his intentions or actions. He was motivated mostly by curiosity, not by any desire to bring the trio to justice. Conrad had his own opinions about what constituted justice, as he had demonstrated the year before in Clarence Strait and on Kuiu Island.

"Still, I wish you didn't have to go so soon and so far. Why can't someone else track down the Murphys? I'm sure there's more pressing work for you here. There's no end of criminal activity in Southeast Alaska, and way too many unsolved murders and disappearances," Linda protested.

"Yes, but I'm the one assigned to this investigation. I'm already on thin ice over going AWOL last year. I have reason to hope the search won't take too long, though I'm not at liberty to elaborate," Conrad equivocated.

"Don't you ever get tired of having to keep so many secrets?" Linda asked.

Karen looked briefly startled by Linda's question, and changed the subject abruptly.

"I hate to be the party-pooper, but it's getting late. I've had plenty to drink, and I'm ready for bed."

"Me too. I'd like to get an early start up to Gedney Harbor with Cindy," Conrad quickly agreed.

The group made plans to get together for breakfast in the morning. Then Conrad would take Cindy to the place where Grant Tadlock had met his end at the fangs and claws of the cougar the previous year. The Stuckrath family, Conrad, and Linda motored their two dinghies across the nearly calm waters to their boats, anchored a few hundred yards away from the camp.

CHAPTER 33

Cindy And Conrad

Early the next morning Conrad Slocum and Cindy Stuckrath left the archeology camp in *Tisiphone's* dinghy. They made their way up the coast of Kuiu Island to Gedney Harbor, a small bay just a few miles north of the archeologist's main camp in Port Malmesbury by water, but separated by nearly impenetrable forest and brush by land. The mood was somber. Both were lost in their own thoughts and memories of the circumstances of Marshall Stuckrath's death, and the fate of his killer. In any case the noise of the outboard motor was not conducive to conversation.

When they arrived at their destination Conrad secured his dinghy to the small floating dock. No other boats were at the dock, or anchored in the bay. Cindy shouldered a small pack that contained her camera and lenses, a bottle of water, and some trail mix. Conrad had also packed water and snacks, as well as a machete in case they encountered stinging Devils Club along the way. In addition he carried his .308 rifle, service pistol, and bear spray for protection. They hiked up a faint but passible game trail Ray Standers had described.

After thirty minutes the trail, such as it was, seemed to end at a rocky outcrop.

"This is where Ray said they found blood. The troopers later determined it was from your brother's killer" Conrad said.

"Jack Dolon, the officer who was killed and left under the Skagway dock, went with Ray to investigate the man's death after his crew-mate reported it. They thought perhaps he fell and injured himself, or maybe this was where the cougar first attacked him."

"Wasn't his rifle found here too?" Cindy asked. She had taken out her camera and was taking photos of the outcrop from various angles.

"Yes, down in the brush below here, where he must have dropped it when he was injured."

"I'm glad the cougar lived long enough to kill him."

Cindy's comments made Conrad uncomfortable. He knew Ray had told her some details about Grant Tadlock and the cougar's deaths. *Had Ray told her that Tadlock had been shot too?*

Supervisor Richard Head and agent Jack Dolon both knew that Conrad had wounded Tadlock before the cougar mauled the man to death. Ray had gone with agent Dolon to retrieve the bodies of the man and the cat, so he too must know Tadlock had been shot, though he had never brought it up with Conrad in their time together. That alone made Conrad uneasy. Conrad would have been even more mystified by the biologist's reticence, had he known that Ray had not told anyone that visiting campers he had spoken with in Tebenkof Bay while investigating the death of Grant Tadlock had seen Conrad's sailboat anchored in Thetis Bay, and heard two shots.

"According to Ray's directions, the place where the cougar attacked your brother's killer is just over there," Conrad said, pointing to a stand of mature forest just a few yards away.

The clearing under the ancient spruce trees was just as Conrad remembered it from a year earlier, when he had encouraged the wounded mountain lion to finish off Grant Tadlock after he had felled him with a shot from his .308 rifle. The bullet had hit Tadlock in the leg while he stood on the ledge. Though severely wounded Tadlock had managed to drag himself from there to the clearing.

The scene was still vivid in his memory. He recalled staring into the cougar's eyes, who somehow sensed it was Grant Tadlock, not Conrad who had shot him. The cougar had then turned and badly mauled Tadlock. As Tadlock attempted to crawl to safety, begging Conrad to kill the animal, Conrad had urged the mortally wounded cat on. Just before the cougar attacked Tadlock for the final time, Conrad told the doomed man he was there to see that he paid the ultimate price for murdering, his son, Marshall Stuckrath. Like Cindy, he felt a mystical connection to the animal, though he had not gone so far as to get its likeness tattooed on his body. Unlike Cindy, he had been present to see his revenge realized, and needed no physical marks to remind him of the event.

In the clearing they both searched in vain for any sign of the previous year's violence. Despite this Cindy took many photos.

"Can you take some pictures of me holding your rifle, Conrad?" She asked.

"Of course. I know you can handle a firearm—but why?"

"Just humor me, Conrad. I want to imagine what it would have been like to have been here in this place with the means to kill either the cougar, the man, or both, and not interfere."

Conrad took her camera, and handed her his rifle.

"You know I can shoot. I imagine that as an intelligence agent, or whatever the hell you are you've had some experience with cameras," Cindy said.

There was no trace of sarcasm in her voice, but Conrad was aware she was driving at something.

"Yes, I'm a reasonably competent photographer, though I doubt my compositional skills are as good as yours. In my line of work I rarely have time to wait for the perfect lighting or angle."

After examining the rifle closely Cindy walked across the clearing to a slightly more open area, where the sun's rays, diffused by the branches of the towering evergreens managed to illuminate a few square feet of the spongy, needle-compacted forest floor.

"So this is the place," Cindy said.

She held the rifle with one hand, reached under her jacket with the other, and brought out the necklace with the .308 shell casing that she had worn since her father had drilled holes just large enough for the fishing line to pass through. Hung on the same line as the spent shell casing was a small locket that contained a miniature graduation photo of her brother.

"I found this .308 shell between here and Thetis Bay, where our boat was anchored. It would have been a long shot, but someone could have hit that man (She still refused to utter Grant Tadlock's name.) while he was exposed on the outcrop. There was no cougar blood there, only that man's. It wasn't an easy shot, but doable with a rifle like this," she said, sighting along the barrel of Conrad's .308. "I know I could have made the shot."

Conrad remembered climbing as fast as he could through the thickets to a rise between Thetis Bay and Gedney Harbor, and focusing on Grant Tadlock standing perhaps two hundred fifty yards below him. His aim had been low, and the bullet had shattered Tadlock's leg, crippling but not killing him.

"Whoever shot Marshall's murderer must have had a rough hike to this place, and he must have been in a hurry. He probably knew he'd hit the man, but he would have been cautious. The man might be only slightly wounded, and he might have a pistol. I bet he was surprised to see the cougar. Take my picture now," Cindy said, lifting the .308 to her shoulder.

Cindy had uncannily aimed Conrad's rifle at exactly the spot where Conrad remembered the cougar had sunk his teeth into Tadlock's neck, killing the man. He took several photos as Cindy slightly adjusted her pose.

"Have you ever thought about becoming a detective, instead of a photojournalist, Cindy?"

His question was not entirely fatuous.

"Maybe I should become an intelligence agent, like you, if that's what you really are. I could work for the same people you do. Oh—One more thing before we leave, Conrad. I want you to stand just where I was, so I can get a couple of shots of you holding the rifle, if you don't mind."

Conrad complied with her wish, though it made him more than a little uncomfortable.

"You seem convinced that someone else was here," Conrad remarked.

"Conrad, I may be young and naive, but I'm not stupid. I know you had an affair with mom, and I know you are Marshall's biological father. I think you made sure Marshall's killer got what he deserved, and I'm glad you did. So don't worry. I'd be the last person to tell anyone."

"Is this something Ray told you, or did you figure it out on your own?"

There was no point in denying it. He would not insult her intelligence.

"It came to me a few days ago, while I was talking to Ray, before we left Skagway. I'd shown Ray the .308 shell on my necklace when we were sailing from Kuiu to Skagway. He'd asked where I found it, and I told him. He seemed pretty disconcerted by that. I knew you always carried a .308 on your sailboat, and I remembered you had sailed out of Chatham Strait on your way to Hawaii when you left Alaska last summer. Then I thought about an old photograph we have of you, mom, dad and some other people from your time in Afghanistan in the 1970s. You were all in your twenties, and I remembered how much Marshall looked like you at that age."

"I had always hoped to spend some time with Marshall. It was a selfish wish, of course. I had no hand in raising him. He was David's son more than mine."

"I'm not sure dad knew until Marshall got older and the resemblance to you was obvious, though it wouldn't have lessened his love for Marshall. Dad would have done anything to keep our family together, and he still would if mom would take him back again. Maybe she will after this trip."

"Do you hate me for it, Cindy?"

"How could I? You're my brother's father. I think mom still loves you in some way. Maybe it's possible to be in love with more than one person at the same time. The four of us have something important in common, besides past history and friendship. We all grieve over the loss of Marshall. You are family. The older I get the more I realize life is complicated."

"Well Cindy, you're eighteen now, technically an adult as far as the law is concerned, but I can't say I was as mature or aware as you seem to be at that age."

In spite of her assurances Conrad was uneasy. He wasn't worried that she would voice her suspicions. In any case his supervisor, Richard Head already knew about his dalliance with Karen Stuckrath so many years earlier, and that he had shot Grant Tadlock. That evidence, sent to Richard Head a year ago by Jack Dolon was safely stored somewhere, and ensured that Conrad would always be at the Agency's beck and call. It was part of the price of his vengeance.

More worrisome to Conrad was that his superior probably knew or at least suspected he'd been the cause of judge Daise's death too. That could be a real problem, now that he had found love with Linda Daise. He imagined his boss must be gloating gleefully over the irony of Conrad's situation. Evasion, Equivocation, dissemblance, deceit, dissimulation; English had so many words for describing the countless ways people lied. Now it seemed he was enmeshed in a sticky web of his own deceptions. It occurred to Conrad that the only sure way to freedom was to get rid of Richard Head, but it was only a fleeting thought.

"I've seen what I wanted to see. I'm ready to go," Cindy said.

"Sure, Cindy. Linda and I should leave this afternoon, and I know you need to head south soon to make it back to Bellingham in time for school."

"Thank you, Conrad. I had to see this place."

"I promised Ray I would take you here, and I try to keep my promises."

"It can't be easy for you—coming here again. He was your son."

Cindy was softly crying.

"I don't care what the law is, you did the right thing—killing that man."

Conrad took her gently in his arms, as he wished he could David and Karen. His father had died when he was young, and his mother and grandmother, who had raised him were also gone. The Stuckrath family, now reduced since last year to just three, were the only family he had left.

CHAPTER 34

Down, Not Out

The doctor stood next to the hospital bed where Jim Lothar lay recovering from his surgery. Machines monitored his vital signs and controlled the amounts of drugs and fluids flowing into his veins.

"I see you're awake now. How are you feeling Mr. Lothar?"

"I felt a lot better before I was shot. Will I live, doc?"

"Ha-ha! I'm glad to see you still have a sense of humor. That's always a good sign in a patient. Yes, I assure you that you will recover. The bullet lodged in your sacrum. I managed to remove it and repair most of the tissue damage caused by the path of the projectile through your abdomen."

"Most of the damage?"

"Yes, most, but not all. There was some irreparable nerve injury. I'm sorry to say you will experience some problems with bladder control for a few weeks to months. That situation will likely improve, but unfortunately a certain amount of loss of sensation in the penis may be permanent, and getting and maintaining an erection will be challenging."

"Permanent? Can't those nerves be repaired somehow?" Jim Lothar was stunned.

"Unfortunately, no. You must make the best of it. You are very fortunate to be alive. Had the bullet entered at a slightly different angle it almost certainly would have killed you."

"I'm not sure I wouldn't rather be dead."

"You're a relatively young man. You face a difficult future, but your body will heal. In the meantime you are under our care here at Forelle Hospital. We will do our very best for you, as we would with any patient. Starting tomorrow you will need to get up and walk at least twice each day. As soon as you have an appetite you should eat something. If your pain becomes too great you need only press the call button. I'll be in again tomorrow to check your progress."

Outside the hospital room Sergeant Tenax waited with a state appointed lawyer and one of the guards assigned to watch the prisoner until he recovered enough to be moved to a cell at the Lime River penitentiary.

"Do you really have to speak with the patient now? He's barely out of surgery and needs time to rest and recover. In a day or two he'll be up to it," the doctor said.

"We'll just be a few minutes. His lawyer will make sure I don't get the thumbscrews or cattle prod out," the sergeant said.

It wasn't the first time he and the doctor had been in the same circumstances, and both knew the limits of their authority, but the state trooper was willing to push things to that limit to get the information he wanted.

"Frankly, I don't see the urgency. He won't be going anywhere for a while."

"Just the same, I would like to ask the patient a few questions before we go," Sergeant Tenax insisted.

"Okay, you have ten minutes," the doctor replied, crisply. "Mr. Lothar has had a shock, both physically and emotionally and needs to rest. You will have plenty of time once he is stronger."

"Thanks, I promise I'll keep it short."

"You could make this a lot easier on yourself, Jim," sergeant Tenax said, without prequel.

Lothar needed no introduction to either men. Sergeant Tenax had led the investigation that resulted in his arrest and conviction the year before, and the same lawyer had represented him at his trial.

"How's that?" Lothar replied.

"We know you derailed the train in White Pass, and we know you and the Murphy siblings are behind the extortion threats. Things will go a lot better for you if you tell us where the Murphys are. The DA might be willing to offer you a better deal."

"As your council I advise you to say nothing until we've had time to speak in private," the lawyer countered.

"Sergeant Tenax does not speak for the DA, and the authorities most probably will find the Murphys without your help. It's an empty promise. Except for the damage you did to the Fish and Game boat, the state's case against you is weak."

"Look," the sergeant said, ignoring the lawyer's comments, "we have more than enough evidence right now to convict you of several felonies, even without a charge of domestic terrorism, besides which you will have to serve out the remainder of your previous sentence for violating parole. So far we haven't been able to locate the Murphys. Your help and cooperation could save us hundreds of man hours. The state would definitely take that into consideration."

"Isn't your ten minutes up?" Lothar said.

The dull pain in has abdomen had sharpened. He longed to sleep again. He reached over and pushed the call button.

"Just one more thing. Your partner in crime, Craig Martes is limping around with a cast on his ankle. I'm afraid he's not too happy with you, Jim. He's agreed to testify against you in exchange for pleading guilty to reduced charges. I think he'll make a pretty convincing witness at your trial," Tenax replied.

"Fuck Martes!"

A nurse entered the room. She was a middle-aged no-nonsense woman, with thirty years of experience. She saw immediately that her patient was in pain, and stressed by the presence of the two men.

"The patient is not up to having visitors so soon after surgery," she declared, imperiously.

"Okay, nurse, we were just leaving. We'll talk again when you're up to it, Jim. Call me anytime. Things aren't has hopeless as the sergeant wants you to believe," the lawyer said, in parting.

The two men left the room.

"Stay alert. Lothar's out of it now, but once he's recovered some he might try to give us the slip before we have permission to move him over to Lime River," the sergeant advised the guard.

"For Christ's sake Joe. Do you always have to be such a hard-ass? The poor guy just about died, and it's obvious he's in a lot of pain. He's not going anywhere," the lawyer said.

"Is that so? You also told me I didn't have to worry about him being a good citizen and staying out of trouble while he was on parole. I'm afraid you've got a client who's a habitual criminal and can't be trusted. If it was up to me they'd stick him in a cell and throw away the key," the sergeant contended.

"If it was up to you half the state of Alaska would be behind bars."

"Well, it's common knowledge that only Washington D.C. is more corrupt, and the crookedest city in our crooked state is Juneau. If I chose names at random from the phone book, I'd bet at least half would turn out to be involved in some sort of criminal activity."

"Well, I might agree with you there, especially if you include the state legislature. As the song goes, 'everybody does what nobody will allow.'"

"What song is that?"

"Oh, you wouldn't know it. A Stan Ridgeway tune. I understand your taste runs more to line dancing hits, like 'Elvira.'"

"Now that's a damn good song!"

"I'd love to talk more about your appalling lack of taste in music, but I've got a hearing in less than an hour to prepare for. I assume I can trust you not to badger my client in my absence."

Sergeant Tenax gave the man a dismissive wave. Though the lawyer enjoyed razzing the trooper, he did not underestimate the officer's competence. Most of the cases Joe Tenax investigated ended with a conviction, in spite of the defense council's best efforts on behalf of his clients.

In turn the sergeant realized the public defender had a tough job, and his jibes were mostly the result of frustration with his low batting average in the courtroom.

Sergeant Tenax lingered outside of Lothar's hospital room and spoke briefly with the officer assigned to guard the prisoner and monitor who came to visit him, reminding him again to stay alert.

The daytime officer was an especially attentive guard, but his night shift replacement, an older, corpulent retired city policeman with a drinking problem, was not. The night shift guard was supposed to look in on the prisoner every hour, but after Lothar was asleep he spent most of his time in the break room lounge, where he could watch television, snack, and drink coffee and soft drinks spiked with the flask of vodka he brought along. The guard had developed a regular routine. He checked on the prisoner at midnight to make sure he was asleep, and didn't normally return to look in again until just before his shift ended.

Ten days after his surgery the doctor informed Jim Lothar he would be released from the hospital the following day. He would go from there directly to a cell in Lime River to await his trial. It was that night or never, Lothar knew. His lawyer had informed him there would be no possibility of getting out on bail.

Just before midnight the guard looked in as usual, and Lothar pretended to sleep. After the guard left he quickly dressed. The troopers had confiscated his wallet, keys, and shoes. He would have to do something about that, but first he had to get away from the hospital.

It was only about two miles from the hospital to the Juneau harbor, but Lothar had only hospital slippers, and had to avoid walking along the highway shoulder. By the time he got to his destination his slippers were shredded and his feet were bloody.

On previous summers, off and on since his high school years he had commercial fished with several different Juneau fisherman. He knew where one of them left his spare boat keys. He located the boat, found the keys, and motored out of the harbor. Luckily the fuel tanks were nearly full, and the owner was out of town. The boat wasn't reported missing for six days. By that time, motoring day and night, and sleeping little, Lothar had arrived in Seattle, where he abandoned the boat at one of the busy marinas.

Jim Lothar spent several days in Seattle. For years he had utilized a bank account and a safe deposit box there, where he kept a forged passport, travelers checks, and some cash. Before buying plane tickets he exchanged emails with Simon Murphy. They agreed to meet in Panama to withdraw their extorted funds, which Simon had deposited in a bank there by a circuitous route after withdrawing them from the original St. Kitts bank.

CHAPTER 35

Panama City

While he was tracing the movements of the Murphy family Conrad called Linda Daise often. This was not typical. He had never before been in a relationship where he felt the need to stay in touch on a regular basis. It was a new and strange sensation. Though Conrad had dated several women over the years, none of the affairs had lasted longer than a few months. Due to the nature of his job, his frequent foreign postings, and his usual reticence, he had never stayed in touch consistently with former girlfriends. His secretive and unforthcoming behavior had been the main cause of the failure of most of his relationships. With Linda it was different. Conrad felt a building anxiety when he went more than a few days without speaking with her. That evening he called Linda when he judged she would be home from work.

"It's so good to hear your voice! Where are you now, or can you say?"

"I'm at the airport in Panama City," Conrad replied. "How are things in Juneau?"

"Not great. Jim Lothar broke out of the hospital a few days ago. Hiram is gone too. He left me a note thanking me for everything and promising to pay me for the time I spent working on a defense strategy as soon as he was able. As long as Jim Lothar was here Hiram had his testimony to trade for a better deal on the charges against him, but with Lothar gone I'm expecting an indictment and warrant for his arrest any day."

This was old news to Conrad. His supervisor had called the day Lothar broke out of the hospital with that information, and two days later to inform him that Hiram Hatcher had taken a flight from Juneau to Seattle, where they had lost track of him.

"I can understand why Hiram left. He didn't want to stick around and end up doing time. So it sounds like you've lost your client, and handyman."

"Well, at least he replaced the kitchen faucet, and took care of that constantly running toilet. We've had a lot of snow, and he even shoveled out my driveway and sidewalk the day he left. But I'm afraid Hiram's only made it worse for himself. When he and Jim are caught the state won't be so keen on making a deal for his testimony in Jim Lothar's case."

"You mean if they're caught. Both of those guys are pretty good at evading the authorities."

"I try to avoid becoming too friendly with my clients, but I really like Hiram. I can't help hoping he escapes and starts a new life somewhere."

"Then I suppose that puts us on opposite sides, Linda. I've been assigned to track him down too, since

I'm already on the hunt for their partners in crime, the Murphys."

"I'm sure you're very good at your job, but I still hope Hiram isn't caught."

"That's not likely, and he'll eventually lead me to Mary Murphy, I'm sorry to say."

Conrad was sorry. Sorry that Hiram had gotten involved, and sorry that the task of arresting Jim Lothar and Hiram Hatcher would keep him away from Linda even longer.

Conrad was sure that Hiram was communicating with Mary Murphy. He would be headed to wherever she was. His best guess was somewhere in Mexico, Central, or South America. He had traced the Murphys to a hotel in St. Kitts. The Agency had a woman undercover at the bank where the extorted railroad money was deposited. The day before Conrad arrived in St. Kitts a man resembling Simon Murphy, going by the name of Sirin Quilty, though now somewhat disguised with shorter hair and a beard, had transferred the funds by a circuitous route to a bank in Panama City.

Jim Lothar had been caught on a LAX airport security camera booking a flight to Mexico City. Conrad reasoned that Panama City, an important center for international banking, and with daily flights to many South American cities, was a logical place for Simon, now apparently traveling alone, and Jim Lothar to meet and withdraw their extorted funds.

"I hope you'll be careful. Are you working by yourself, or is someone helping you?"

"I'm in no danger, Linda. In any case I can call for backup just about anywhere I go in the world."

Conrad would not admit, even to Linda, that he had a perverse urge to let the Murphy trio and Hiram get away with their audacious scheme. He too had gotten to know Hiram better while he stayed at Linda's house in Juneau. He liked the man, and had no desire to see him lose his freedom. Jim Lothar was another matter, though. He would have to be found and dealt with. By leaving his partner, Craig Martes injured and at risk of drowning on a sinking boat, and taking Cindy Stuckrath hostage he had shown that he would not hesitate to resort to violence as a means to his ends.

"I think Hiram is telling the truth about Jack Dolon's death being an accident. Beyond that, I trust my intuition. I don't yet know the full story of the Murphy's motivations, or how much of the plan to extort money from the railroad was Lothar's idea, but I'll get that when I find them. Right now I'm motivated more by curiosity than anything else—and of course I am getting a bonus and generous per diem for the travel outside my normal region," Conrad joked. "We can plan a real vacation this winter! I'd like to take you to Hawaii."

"If I keep losing clients I'll have plenty of time off, but not much money for travel. Maybe I should just fly down and join you now."

Linda was half serious. She had judged that Hiram's case would take up most of her time for six months or longer, and she had only two other less demanding cases in her queue. Until Hiram was brought back to Juneau, she had time on her hands.

"I'm afraid it wouldn't be much of a vacation for you; unless your idea of a good time is standing around on a hot sidewalk for hours waiting for someone to walk into a bank."

After their phone call ended Conrad went to the car rental agency. While he waited in line to get his keys and paperwork he noticed a man on a bench nearby reading a paper. Although the man now wore sunglasses and a Panama hat, he was sure it was the same man he had seen twice before; the first time while waiting in line at the Seattle airport, and again at the Miami airport. He assumed that Richard Head had assigned another agent to tail him. That didn't bother him as much as the arrogance of the man, who wasn't making much of an effort to conceal the fact.

Conrad drove the rental car from the airport to a parking lot in downtown Panama City. With the help of the agent in St. Kitts he had traced the money to a local bank, but he didn't know if Simon and Jim had already withdrawn or moved the funds again. The Panamanian banks would not give up that information without a court order, which could take weeks to get. Conrad reasoned that Lothar had contacted the Murphys, and was either en route or already in Panama City, where they would rendezvous. He hoped they had not already left the city.

Conrad's timing was fortunate. Jim Lothar and Simon Murphy had made arrangements to meet at the bank the following afternoon.

"Where are you calling from, Jim?" Simon asked.

"I'm in Mexico City. I've got a flight out tomorrow morning. I can meet you at your room or downtown," Lothar replied.

"Downtown is fine. What time?"

"My flight gets in at ten. I'll get a cab."

They decided to meet at a restaurant conveniently located across the street from the bank.

"How the hell did you manage to break out of jail in Juneau?" Simon asked, as they sat with their drinks at the al fresco dining area in front of the restaurant.

From their table they could watch for police or plainclothes officers at the bank's entrance. They had agreed to observe the bank for awhile before going inside.

"I didn't. I broke out of the hospital the night before they planned to move me to the big house. They're bound to trace me sooner or later, so I need to stay on the move. The law is probably looking for two men and a woman too, so it's good you came here without your brother or sister," Lothar said.

"I thought of that. That's why I came to Panama alone, and cut my hair and grew the beard."

"...also a wise move. Where are Mary and Liam?"

"I'd rather not say. The fewer people know, the better."

"Sure, that makes sense. I might blab when they put me on the rack," Lothar joked.

Simon didn't like the idea of Jim Lothar knowing their ultimate destination. He couldn't be trusted. In Vancouver, Canada, while waiting for their flight Mary had sent a postcard to Hiram's post office box in Oregon, giving him the number of Simon's new cell phone. Hiram called and told the Murphys that Jim had fingered Liam as agent Jack Dolon's killer. Mary and Liam had flown on to Ecuador, where Simon would join them after moving their money to a bank in Guayaquil. Simon wasn't sure how long they would remain in Ecuador, but the less Lothar knew of their plans the better, he thought.

In any case Simon wanted nothing more to do with Lothar once they had their money. Because only Simon had the account number at the Panama bank he had considered taking all the funds and disappearing. Taking Lothar's share would be just punishment for his perfidy. But after more thought, he had concluded that such a man would not rest until he tracked them down. He decided not to reveal that Hiram had told them of Lothar's betrayal. Once the man had his share of the extorted money, they would never see him again, Simon hoped.

"I should probably go in the bank alone, and the less time I spend there, the better. It takes a while to close an account, and might also draw attention, so I suggest we leave a couple thousand in, and keep the account open for now," Simon said.

"I plan to keep a little cash for my traveling expenses, but I'm going to transfer most of our share to another bank. I could withdraw your entire half, or have it transferred to a different bank if you like."

"I could do the same if you gave me your information," Lothar replied.

"That won't work. They'll ask for photo ID, and we don't look anything alike. You don't trust me? I could have taken all the money in St. Kitts and run with it. So much for fucking honor among thieves. You can sit right here and watch me go into the bank and come back out. There's no other exit," Simon argued.

"Fine, then. I want ten grand in cash, and the rest transferred to this account number."

Lothar copied a number from a card in his wallet to a napkin and handed it to Simon.

The transaction went smoothly. The clerk made no attempt at small talk, and didn't raise an eyebrow when presented with the details of moving nearly a million dollars into two accounts in different countries, and the withdrawal of several thousand dollars in cash. It was obvious the bank personnel were used to dealing with large amounts of money, and asking no questions. Afterwards they walked a short distance to a small park where Simon gave Jim his deposit receipt and cash.

"Well I suppose this means the end of our very pleasant and lucrative relationship. I would have loved to have said goodbye to your brother and lovely sister," Lothar said.

"I don't think either of them would have enjoyed seeing you again, especially since you ratted Liam out."

"What are you talking about?"

Lothar was surprised that Simon knew. He thought he had been dealing privately with the prosecution and trooper Tenax.

"Don't fuck with me, Jim. We got the news from Hiram, whose lawyer is Linda Daise, so we know it's true. It seems you didn't think to mention the fact that it was an accident."

"Accident or not, if you kill a cop you're screwed. There's no way I'm taking a fall for Liam. Besides, that's water under the bridge. Liam's safely away now, and all three of you are free to enjoy your financial windfall, thanks to my plan and expertise."

"You would see it that way, I suppose. Hiram also told us about how you double-crossed your other partner, Craig Martes, and how you tried to take a hostage in Skagway before that woman shot you. I'd have to be an idiot to ever have anything to do with you again. So goodbye and good riddance!"

"Yeah?—well fuck you too, and your whole god-damned family!"

Jim Lothar's arm shot out, and and he slapped Simon hard on the cheek. But Simon, though smaller and lighter had grown up sparring with his even bigger and tougher brother, and never backed down from an insult. What he lacked in power he made up for in experience, quickness, and situational awareness. Also in his favor was the fact that Lothar was out of shape from so much time in the hospital, and had not completely healed from his surgery.

In an exchange of blows that lasted only a few seconds Simon evaded most of Jim's punches and bested him with a well placed jab to the abdomen squarely on top of Jim's surgical incision. Jim fell to his knees, nearly blinded by the sudden pain, while his weakened bladder let loose a stream of urine.

Simon, noticing that several people in the park had observed the altercation, began to walk quickly away. Just before he turned the corner at the end of the block he slowed and looked back. A tall, well dressed man was running towards the scene. As Simon watched the stranger bent over Lothar. Simon did not linger longer. They had obviously been followed. He caught a taxi in front of a nearby hotel, directing the driver to take him to the airport. He knew there was a flight to Guayaquil in less than two hours.

Conrad had staked out the bank since it opened that morning. His plan had been to watch for the two men and continue to shadow them to the airport, or wherever they were headed after their dealings at the bank. By following Simon he could locate Mary and Liam Murphy.

It seemed likely the two men were bound for the airport. They would want to get out of Panama as quickly as possible once they had their money. He was sure there would be an opportunity to arrest Jim Lothar at the airport while he waited for his flight. He did not intend to arrest Simon until he located and interviewed all three of the siblings. If need be, he could call for backup from the Agency office in Panama City. But his plans changed as soon as the two men began fighting. He sprinted down the sidewalk to the small park.

"It looks as though your bad karma has finally caught up to you Jim. I bet that hurts like hell," Conrad said, leaning down over the stricken man.

"Fuck...you," Lothar barely managed to retort. Every breath brought excruciating pain.

"I'm getting pretty tired of following you around, Jim. On the other hand you've already escaped from one hospital, so in spite of your obvious distress I'm hesitant to take you to the emergency room. But one way or the other you're headed back to Alaska to stand trial."

Jim didn't have the will to resist as Conrad fastened the handcuffs. Several people nearby watched, but no one interfered.

"Can you walk?"

"Why the hell should I?" Lothar replied. The pain was easing a little.

"Because if you can't walk I'll have to call in the local police to help me, and they'll be a lot rougher with you."

With help from Conrad Jim managed to stand.

"Where is Simon Murphy headed?" Conrad asked.

"What's in it for me if I tell you?"

"I can't help noticing you've wet yourself. I imagine it will be pretty uncomfortable while you wait at the station for me to make the necessary arrangements to get you back up north. If you help me out, we can stop at your hotel room on the way there, and you can change."

"You've got a deal, then. I don't know for sure where the Murphy's are, as Simon wouldn't tell me when I asked, but I'd bet money he's headed to Ecuador."

Besides the opportunity to clean up and change into dry clothing, Lothar hoped that a stop at his hotel room might give him an opportunity to escape, or to somehow convince the agent not to take him back to Alaska.

"Why are you so sure the Murphy's are headed to Ecuador?"

"I suggested that and a couple of other South American countries. Liam and Simon seemed especially keen about Ecuador."

"I agree it would seem to be a good choice in their situation. Were you headed there too?"

"I hadn't decided for sure. I was thinking of Thailand, or somewhere in Asia."

Jim wanted to mislead Conrad in case he somehow found a way to escape. Although he had not bought tickets as yet, he intended to fly to Medellin, Columbia, where he had directed Simon to transfer the bulk of his money. He was somewhat familiar with the country from two trips he had made a decade earlier, when he had smuggled cocaine into Juneau. Unfortunately most of the profits from that venture had gone up his own nose and been squandered in partying.

They walked slowly to Lothar's hotel, only a few blocks away. The pain in his abdomen gradually faded to a dull ache. Reassuringly, there was no bleeding from the celiotomy.

After Lothar had washed up and changed into clean clothing Conrad moved to put the handcuffs back on.

"Wait! I've got a better idea. Let's just split the money and you can say you couldn't find me, or that I escaped," Lothar said.

"Attempting to bribe an officer is only going to get you more time in the slammer, Jim," Conrad replied, snapping the handcuffs on his wrists.

"Actually, I'd call it blackmail. I might be a thief and a smuggler, but I've never murdered anyone, unlike you."

It was a desperate move, and he knew it was risky. The agent might decide it was safer to snuff him. If this gambit didn't work he would have to cause a scene and try to attract the local police, in hopes that would buy him some time. Perhaps he might be able to bribe the local officers. As long as he wasn't actually en route to Alaska Lothar figured he had some chance of escaping.

"Blackmail, how do you figure?" Conrad asked.

As far as Conrad knew, now that agent Dolon was dead, only three people; his supervisor, Richard Head, and Karen and Cindy Stuckrath knew for sure that he had shot Grant Tadlock the year before. He was aware that Ray Standers at least suspected he had something to do with Tadlock's death, and he also knew that Charlie Jackson, the fisherman Grant Tadlock had traveled with to Kuiu Island, must have heard the second shot, but probably assumed it was also from Tadlock's rifle.

Suddenly Conrad remembered Linda Daises's surprising revelation that Jim Lothar seemed to know about the events at Spruce Cove, and had been willing to testify against Sam Thornton for his part in forcing Henry Daise to endure a sort of kangaroo court that David Stuckrath had subjected the judge to there.

"You should be more careful when you're drowning people in the fjords. You never know who might be watching."

Conrad was shaken. There had been no other boats anywhere near him when judge Daise was knocked into the water by his mainsail boom, and there were no other settlements in that part of Clarence Strait, which was as wild as any place in Alaska.

"It's true Craig Martes and I had a falling out at Kuiu Island recently, but we've been doing business together for years. Last summer he told me about watching a sailboat's strange maneuvers in Clarence Strait. I guess it's lucky for you he didn't tell the law about everything he saw from up on Steamer Knoll on Etolin Island. Of course he always carries his nice Steiner binoculars when he's out in the forest. Craig wondered why the hell someone would sail a boat over a drowning man, instead of throwing him a life preserver—not very sporting, but I'm sure you had your reasons. Craig didn't report it because he wanted no part of whatever happened, and he had his own reasons to celebrate judge Daises' untimely demise. Still, now that you're shacking up with the judge's daughter, it could become pretty awkward for you if she was to find out."

Conrad had known and accepted the reality that the price of his vengeance for the death of his son would be the loss of any chance for a relationship with Linda Daise. Though balance had been temporarily restored, and his rage had been assuaged, he had tempted the fates whose instrument he imagined he was by becoming involved with Linda.

He seemed to be faced with two stark choices; he could kill this man, or find some excuse to break up with Linda. Prisoners sometimes died trying to escape, and as long as there were no witnesses, that would be safest route. Conrad had killed several men and one woman in the line of duty, as well as engineering the deaths of Grant Tadlock and judge Daise for their parts in the murder of his son. He didn't like Jim Lothar, but killing him would inevitably result in more complications, and could only be a last resort. The man's offer to split the money was tempting, but not because of the money itself. It offered another possible way out of the deadlock.

"It's not that simple, Jim," Conrad replied.

"I don't see any problem. It's a straightforward exchange."

"While you were in the bathroom I called my contact here. Another agent is on his way to the airport to meet us. He'll see that you get back to Juneau, while I track down the Murphys."

"That is awkward, but perhaps I could escape on our way to the airport, or even from this hotel," Jim suggested.

It seemed to Jim that his gamble was succeeding. The agent was at least considering his idea, and he was still alive.

"What guarantee do I have that you won't talk to Linda even if I do let you escape?"

"I guess some level of trust is involved. How do I know you won't just take my money and kill me anyway?" Jim replied.

"You don't seem the trustworthy type, Jim."

"But compared to you, when it comes to deceit, I'm a rank amateur."

"We seem to be at an impasse. I don't want your money, which in any case I could not spend without drawing attention to myself. My activities are closely monitored by the agency I work for. On the other hand, I would have to come up with a pretty good explanation if you were to expire suddenly here in Panama. No—I'm going to have to refuse your exchange and hope that you reconsider your threat from the relative security of the Juneau prison. If Linda does somehow hear from you, even that cell may not guarantee your safety."

There was a cold-blooded ruthlessness in Conrad's response that reminded Lothar that, for all his years of criminal activity, he was the one in the room who had never killed a man.

CHAPTER 36

Flight Risk

Agent Juan Cortez was reluctant to take the assignment of escorting Conrad Slocum's prisoner to the United States. His wife, Maria was nine months pregnant and he worried he would not be home for the event. But he had no choice in the matter. He was the only person available for the task. Agent Slocum had been ordered to continue his search for the Murphy siblings, and other officers were busy with more important matters. The first leg of their flight was to Mexico City. There they would transfer to another airline for the flight to Los Angeles, where another agent would take over, and Juan could head back to Panama, hopefully in time for the birth of his first child.

Juan had only been with the Agency a few months. He had been recruited from the University of Panama language department. He spoke Spanish, Portuguese, English, and several Central American indigenous languages. The promise of higher pay and benefits, his wife's pregnancy, and the fact that he had not managed to get tenure at the college were all factors in his decision to take the job offer. He had been assured that the position would not normally put him in harm's way. He would mostly be employed in translating documents and processing intelligence gathered by agents in the field.

The flight to Mexico went without incident. Although agent Slocum had warned Juan to stay alert, as his his prisoner had already escaped custody once, Jim Lothar was subdued, cooperative, and seemed depressed. The prisoner spent most of the flight dozing. They had a two hour layover at the Mexico City airport.

"Is everything okay at home?" Lothar asked, after Juan hung up from a conversation with his wife.

"Maria's contractions are only thirty minutes apart. She is headed to the hospital."

"How sad, to miss the birth of your child. Why not put me on the plane and go back home. You told me someone else will take over in Los Angeles anyway. I can hardly escape once I'm on the flight. I can tell you I won't be bailing out without a parachute!"

"You know I can't do that, Mr. Lothar. I need to keep my job even more than I need to see my baby's birth."

"Okay, just an idea. We have a little time to kill until our next flight. I'm sick of reading the same old airplane magazine articles. Would you mind taking me over to that shop so I can pick up a book for the next flight?"

"Why not—I could use a snack myself."

The two walked from the waiting area to a small gift shop. The clerk, who was intently watching a soccer match on a small television blaring from behind the counter, glanced at them briefly before turning back to his game. He did not notice that one of the men was handcuffed. The book section, mostly pulp novels and magazines in both Spanish and English, was in the back of the store. As Jim perused the shelves Juan's phone rang again. He spoke rapidly and excitedly in Spanish. His wife had started labor, and there was a complication. The baby was not head down. A cesarian birth would be necessary.

While Juan Cortez was immersed in his stressful phone call, Jim Lothar saw his chance. He quickly raised his arms over the shorter man's head, and began to strangle the agent. The old Darby chain style handcuffs that Juan had been provided with had just enough length and movement for Jim to exert lethal pressure on the officer's neck. Agent Cortez struggled desperately, but was soon unconscious. Jim found the the handcuff key in Juan's pocket, and freed himself from the restraints. Hi switched off Juan's cell phone, relieved the agent of his wallet and sidearm, and found his own wallet and passport in an inner pocket of the officer's jacket. He noted the agent was still unconscious, but breathing. He stopped briefly at the counter, and bought a candy bar. The clerk was still preoccupied with the soccer game, and assumed the other man had left while he was distracted.

On his way out of the airport Lothar removed the battery from the officer's cell phone and, after taking the cash from the Juan's wallet, threw it and the phone into a trash can. He quickly located a taxi with an operator who spoke passable English, and instructed the driver to take him to a bus stop. Assuming that a search for him would soon be underway at the airport, Lothar boarded a bus to Veracruz, where he planned to catch a flight to Columbia and withdraw his money from the Medellin bank.

Reluctantly Conrad answered is cell phone. It was the director, Richard Head.

"It seems you managed to fumble the ball a few yards from the end zone, Conrad. Lothar's on the loose again, thanks to you delegating your responsibility."

"As I recall my priority was to locate the Murphy siblings," Conrad replied testily.

"Yes, but since you had Lothar in hand, you could have delivered him to Los Angeles yourself, losing only a day. I suppose our man in Panama City bears some responsibility for sending a newly hired translator, who had only minimal training for such an assignment. Fortunately he is still alive, though it will take some time for him to recover from the injury to his neck."

"Well, what the hell do you want me to do now, Dick?"

"Fortunately you had the foresight to send us the bank account number Lothar had written on that card in his wallet. It's a bank in Medellin, Columbia. I'm sure that's where he's headed. We've got two men on that, so go ahead with your search for the Murphys. If you do manage to find them, don't delegate your responsibility this time. You are to escort them personally all the way back to Juneau."

"Understood."

"Do you have some idea where they might be?"

"Jim Lothar didn't seem to know, or wouldn't say" Conrad lied. "Obviously, judging by the altercation I saw, they had some sort of falling out, but he didn't want to talk about that either."

"Lothar didn't say why they were fighting?"

"All he would tell me was that it was a private matter. I plan to do some sniffing around at the hotels and the airport here. The Murphys have a lot of options. I don't think they'll stay here. I think they'll go to another country where there are more places to disappear. One of the bigger Mexican cities would be a logical choice."

Ecuador

Like her brothers, Mary Murphy had always wanted to visit South America, but she had never expected to find herself living there. Bahía de Caráquez was a seaside tourist destination and shrimp harvesting town of about twenty thousand people, ninety minutes by road from the much larger coastal city of Manta. It's pleasant climate reminded her of Southern California, or the dry side of the Big Island of Hawaii, which she had visited twice. She sat under the shade of a palm tree in the courtyard of the Puerto Amistad, a shoreside restaurant and marina, siping a margarita and shooing away the occasional cockroach from the remains of her lunch. The weather was warm and settled after a several days of wind and rain. Her brothers had booked a fishing charter for the day. Mary looked forward to having some privacy and time to herself.

The last weeks had been stressful and eventful, and she was glad for the respite. Surprisingly Jim Lothar had been as good as his word. Simon had no trouble retrieving their extorted money, and did as Lothar had advised, moving it from bank to bank as they hopped from island to island through the Caribbean. Ultimately, after weeks of traveling, they landed in Ecuador. After a quick tour of the country the Murphy siblings had taken out a six month lease on a house in Bahia. They had not been challenged anywhere along the way. The locals were friendly, the weather pleasant, and living expenses were far cheaper than back home.

Liam and Simon liked the place even more than their sister. They wanted to buy property, and persuade their mother and father to join them in South America. Their ill-gotten money would purchase a much nicer house and more good farmland in Ecuador than it could in the states. But Mary had so far vetoed the idea. How would they explain their sudden financial windfall to their parents?

"We could tell them we won it in the lottery," Liam suggested.

"What if they ask us why we don't just buy another farm on Orcas or one of the other San Juan islands?" she replied.

"We'll tell them all about this place—how the climate is better, and you get so much more for your money. They could even grow bananas!" Simon insisted.

"What if they're still unwilling to move? After all, they've got old friends and some of our family there," Mary pointed out.

"In that case, we still have enough money to help them out, but we will have to settle for a more modest place of our own."

Ultimately the Murphys decided to put off making a decision. Anyway, they temporized, it was not safe to contact anyone they knew yet. Using the local library's computer—their rental had a phone, but no internet—Simon read the news reports of Jim Lothar's arrest. Although their names were not mentioned in the news articles, he knew from Mary's earlier conversation with Hiram that Lothar had implicated them, or at least Liam. When Simon rejoined Mary and Liam in Ecuador after his stop in Panama City, he told them about Jim Lothar's escape from the Juneau hospital, and his altercation with him in Panama City.

Simon also told his siblings about the man he had seen running towards Jim Lothar after their fight. Simon assumed the man must have been a law enforcement officer, perhaps an FBI agent. He had not been close enough to recognize Conrad Slocum, or stayed to see him arrest Lothar, but Simon assumed their accomplice had been apprehended and was either waiting in some Panamanian prison to be extradited back to Alaska, or was already sitting in a Juneau jail cell.

The Murphys reasoned that investigators found out too late about the railroad shakedown to stop the money transfer, or to give authorities enough advance warning to catch them while they traveled. Perhaps Jim Lothar was keeping what he knew about their movements secret as a bargaining chip, hoping to exchange that information for lesser charges. It was also possible that he had refused to divulge the location of his share of the extorted funds, and planned to withdraw the money after he served his prison time.

Mary was relieved that her brothers had agreed with her about not contacting their parents. She doubted they would believe any story they could concoct about the source of their new wealth. They would sense something was amiss, if only because they had been out of touch with their children for so long. Eventually, Mary hoped, they would find some safe way to invite their parents for a visit. That would be the time to try to convince them to at least consider a move. Regardless, Mary doubted that she and her brothers would ever be able to return to the United States. One big reason for their choice of Ecuador was the ease of becoming a permanent resident here. Just a small investment in real estate or a business was all that was required. Additionally, the US dollar was the national currency.

Mary was surprised that she was not more content. She hated to admit it, but she missed Hiram desperately. Telling herself there were many fish in the sea didn't help. As she finished her drink she was aware of the handsome bartender's admiring glances. His parents were expatriate Canadians about the same age as her mother and father, who had bought the restaurant and its small marina after visiting the town while on vacation to Ecuador and the Galapagos Islands. They made additional income selling fishing and sightseeing charters like the one her brothers had booked, and by aiding foreign sailors with the sometimes confusing customs and immigration forms. Both their son and daughter, who were somewhat younger than Mary and her brothers, worked in the restaurant and marina—the daughter during breaks from college, and the son whenever he ran short on funds.

Mary finished her margarita and was considering another when a tall man entered the restaurant. He looked vaguely familiar, but she couldn't remember where or when she had seen him. He hesitated briefly, glanced quickly around the room, and walked over to her table.

"Hi Mary. Do you mind if I join you?"

Without waiting for her reply he sat down.

"Are we acquainted? How do you know me?" Mary replied, defensively.

The man was obviously American, and most likely a law enforcement officer, perhaps the man Simon had seen running towards Jim Lothar after the scuffle in Panama City, she judged. He wasn't dressed like the average tourist, but more formally, in a collared shirt, khaki slacks, and leather walking shoes—instead of the more usual t-shirt, shorts, and flip-flops. Mary's heart raced. There was no way to warn her brothers.

"I certainly feel that I know you and your brothers pretty well. I've spent a lot of time the last several weeks learning about your family, and following your interesting route from Alaska to Ecuador. I feel like we're acquainted, though we've never been properly introduced."

"Are you here to arrest me?"

The man smiled slightly at her question, and paused before answering.

"Frankly I'm undecided, although that is what's expected of me, and I do have warrants for the three of you. My employer has contacts here who can ensure that the Ecuadorian government will not oppose your extradition. Of course that's assuming I tell my office that I've located the meandering Murphys," Conrad answered.

"Before I decide on a course of action I would like an honest description of what really happened in Dyea and Skagway in August. I have reason to suspect Jim Lothar's version of events may not be accurate."

The bartender, observing Mary's discomfort, approached their table.

"Is everything okay, Mary?" He asked.

"Oh, thanks for asking, Ted, we were just going to ask you for a menu—my friend doesn't have it memorized like I do. Oh, and I'd like another margarita, please."

"Sure thing Mary. Would you like a drink while you wait, sir?"

The bartender was suspicious. Something didn't feel right to him. Mary seemed agitated, and she certainly didn't seem very pleased to see this supposed friend.

"I'd like to order lunch, and I could use a beer—a lager is fine. My name's Conrad. I'm an old associate of Mary's parents."

"So you must be on vacation, then?" The bartender pressed.

"Yes, of sorts. I'm a sailor, Ted. I'd like to rent a boat and sail to the Galapagos Islands."

"Oh, you'll love it out there! If you decide not to try to rent a boat yourself we've got a great charter service. It's less expensive, and the captain really knows the islands. We have permits to visit a couple of places independent boaters aren't allowed to land. As you might have heard, access to most of the islands is pretty strictly limited by the government. I'll get those drinks and be right back."

Ted, who spent money faster than he could make it, got a percentage of every charter that was sold on his shift.

"That was pretty smooth," Mary said.

"I'm more practiced at deception than you and your brothers. It comes with the job, and age."

"You know a lot about my family—but what do I know about you? Maybe you're just trying to blackmail us. How much money do you want to keep quiet and leave us alone?"

"My, on the offensive so quickly! I won't make the mistake thinking you are naive, though I know you don't have a criminal record, or as far as I can tell, any previous history of nefarious dealings."

"I'm not sure if you mean that as a compliment, but I've always tried to stay on the right side of the law, and I have a pretty strong survival instinct."

"I'm not here to take any of your money, even if it wasn't lawfully acquired. My real name is Conrad Slocum. I drove up from Guayaquil yesterday—a scenic and interesting trip that I was in too much of a hurry to appreciate properly. I could show you my ID and elaborate more, but perhaps we should put that off until after my lunch. Our bartender, who I can see is quite infatuated with you, is about to bring our drinks."

"I'll be back in a few minutes with your lunch, sir. Mary, do you want anything else to eat? There's banana cream pie," Ted asked, hopefully.

Mary declined dessert, and the bartender left them alone again. When they had finished with Conrad's lunch and their drinks Conrad picked up the check. As he paid the bartender made one last pitch for the Galapagos charter.

"I'll certainly give it some thought. I'll decide after I've talked to Mary's brothers," Conrad equivocated.

"Perhaps you could do my a favor in the meantime, Ted," Conrad continued.

As he spoke he added a fifty dollar bill to his already generous tip.

"Sure—any friend of the Murphys is a friend of mine!" the waiter replied, eagerly.

"I would like you to call me, discreetly, at this number if another American man shows up asking about Mary or her brothers."

"Are they in some kind of trouble?"

"No, but there is someone who Mary would rather not see again, who apparently hasn't got the message, if you follow me."

"Of course. I get it," Ted said, blushing slightly. "Some guys won't take no for an answer."

"Yes, that's the gist of it. Thanks, Ted."

"What was that all about?" Mary asked as they left the restaurant.

"I'm not the only person interested in finding the migrant Murphys."

They walked away from the restaurant, and turned onto busy Bolivar Street. The avenue was crowded with bicycle taxis and and motorcycles. The town of Bahia de Caraquez was a popular tourist attraction, especially with Ecuadorians from Quito and Guayaquil. Most of the restaurants, hotels, and bars were located along Avenue de Noviembre, the boulevard that circled the town adjacent to the white sand beaches.

"Your friend Ted is quite the determined salesman, yet I get the feeling he hasn't been successful at winning you over, Mary."

"Not for lack of trying," Mary laughed.

"He's handsome, seems nice enough, but not tempted?"

"Is prying into people's personal lives part of the job too, or perhaps it's not money you want from me," Mary retorted.

"I assure you I'm not interested in your other assets either, though I'd be less than honest if I didn't acknowledge at least a passing appreciation. It does seem the climate here has been good for you," Conrad said, giving her an exaggerated ogle.

She laughed again in spite of herself, then stopped and pointed to a typical two story stucco house just off Bolivar Street.

"That's our place. We're just leasing, but we've been looking around, hoping to buy property eventually. Maybe across the bridge in San Vicente, where it's quieter and houses are cheaper, or some farm land somewhere inland. If we do that, we can become permanent residents. But I suppose now that you've found us, we'll be going back to Alaska, and free room and board at Lime River prison compliments of the state."

The house and yard were enclosed by a concrete and metal fence typical of most of the nicer homes in the city. Mary led Conrad through a gate into the backyard, a private oasis filled with palms, ferns, and flowering plants. A small cabana with an attached tool shed occupied one corner of the yard. Nearby was a tiled table shaded by a canvas canopy. While Conrad admired the space Mary retrieved two beers from the kitchen.

"Okay, here we are. What is it you want to know exactly?" Mary asked, seating herself across from Conrad at the table.

"Everything. How did you get hooked up with Jim Lothar? How did Jack Dolon really die? What was your part in the train derailment, and the extortion plot? Most importantly—to me anyway—why? Why did you take such a risk?"

Conrad had heard Jim Lothar's version of events, and Hiram Hatcher's story. But Lothar had plenty of reason to lie, and Hiram, Conrad knew, would say anything to protect Mary.

"Well, I suppose I've got nothing to lose by telling you what I know at this point. First; Dolon's death was an accident. He attacked Liam, they fought, and when they fell Dolon died from a broken neck. Liam feels terrible about it, but it wasn't his fault. It was just bad luck."

"Okay, that agrees with what Hiram said at least —go on."

"You talked to Hiram? Is he in jail?"

"No one, including me, seems to know where Hiram is. He hadn't yet been charged with anything, but agreed to stick around Juneau. I'm sure he's on his way to find you now. He was to be called as a witness to the circumstances of Dolon's death. He would have testified at Jim Lothar's trial, but he left Juneau shortly after Lothar escaped from the hospital. I tracked him as far as Panama City, where he and Simon were withdrawing your hard earned money. I assume Simon told you about his dustup with him. They may charge Hiram for not reporting Jack Dolon's death and for his part in posing the body under the cruise ship dock. Now, how about telling me how this whole thing started."

Mary was relieved that Hiram was still free, but she wondered what Conrad's intentions were.

Why hadn't he arrested her? Why should he care what motivated them to commit a serious crime? It's as though he's acting as judge and jury as well as an international cop, or whatever he is. Maybe I should ask to see his ID? But how would I know if that was fake, like my own passport?

She took a long drink and began, starting with Jesse Murphy's murder of Soapy Smith in 1898, and the railroad's part in rewarding their great grandfather for killing the legendary bunco man, and ending with her family's efforts to save the Orcas Island property.

CHAPTER 38

Soapy's Revenge

"That's quite a tale," Conrad replied, when Mary had finished. "I guess you could say you and your brothers helped Soapy get his revenge, though it took a few generations."

"Have you decided to arrest us—now that you have my confession?"

"I didn't record you. You could still deny it. I'd like to talk to your brothers too. When do you expect them back from their fishing trip?"

Conrad had watched the Murphy brothers go aboard the charter vessel earlier. The fishing charter schedule was posted on a sandwich board outside the marina. He wanted to see if Mary would tell the truth about when they were returning, and if she did it would go some way to convincing him she was being truthful with him.

"The charter boat gets back around five o'clock normally, but sometimes they can run a little late," Mary replied.

"Do you mind if I hang around until they arrive?"

"Do I have a choice?"

"I suppose not, when you put it that way," Conrad replied.

"Why the hell are you so damned polite anyway?"

"It's not always a pleasant job—why make it any worse? I often find I can catch more bees with honey than lemons."

"Bees? I guess criminals are a sort of social pest."

"Bees are very beneficial insects, though they will sting with enough provocation. Do you think of yourself as a criminal?" Conrad asked.

Mary paused before replying.

"I suppose I've never thought about it that way. What we did was certainly against the law, so we're lawbreakers by definition. But I don't think we harmed anyone. The railroad has made huge profits in Skagway for over a hundred years, and most of that goes to a few stockholders and fat cats at the top. I consider that a legal sort of thievery. My great grandfather screwed up, but our offer to buy back the property was more than generous, and was rejected out of sheer greed. The house still sits empty. The apples weren't harvested and rotted on the ground. It's just another asset in some asshole's financial ledger."

"Well, legally you're not a criminal until you're convicted of a crime, and you certainly can't be tried if you can't be found."

Mary was taken aback by how casually this man seemed to be toying with her and her brother's fates.

Was it all just a game for him? He had eyed her playfully earlier. Was that really just a ploy to disarm her, or was he waiting for her to offer herself in return for their freedom? She knew the world sometimes worked that way, and men could often have their heads turned by a pretty woman. She decided to test the idea.

"I could use another beer–how about you, Conrad?"

"Why not. We still have three more hours before your brothers get back."

"Okay, two more on the way. Give me a minute though, I've got to get into something cooler. It's going to be another hot afternoon."

"You're not going to run out the back door, are you?"

"Where would I go? You found us here even after all our efforts to cover our tracks. Besides, I can't help but hope you decide not to take us back to Alaska. It's a little warmer than I like this afternoon, but my brothers and I like the weather here much better than up north."

Mary went to her bedroom and picked out her most revealing bikini top and a pair of very short cut-off jeans. She put on the shorts and went into the kitchen topless. She was sure Conrad could see her through the dining room French doors as she walked to the kitchen. After she got the beers from the refrigerator, she sat them on the dining table while she put on her top. Conrad smiled as he watched her through the glass panes, but he did not rise from his seat and start for the house as she half hoped yet half dreaded he might.

"Thank you, Mary," he said as she sat the cold beers on the table. "That was a lovely display, and I'm very pleased to have been positioned perfectly to observe it—and thanks for the beer too."

"I thought maybe you've been traveling alone so long you might be tempted, and I do find you quite a bit more attractive than Ted, the bartender, but I see I misjudged you."

"Look Mary, I don't blame you for trying the gambit. Who knows, it might have worked a few months ago, but I have a girlfriend in Juneau, and she's more than enough woman for me. You invite an exchange I can't accept. I would feel bad taking advantage of your desperation. Anyway, I would be a poor substitute for Hiram."

Mary looked down at her beer and blushed slightly.

"No reason to be embarrassed. You played your best card, and it was at least a queen, if not an ace. It's a fine afternoon, and I'm enjoying your company. I'd like to hear what you plan to do with all that money, and how you imagine your future here if I decide against taking you back to Alaska."

Mary was relieved Conrad had refused her ambivalent offer. Besides, she thought, he might have enjoyed her favors and arrested her anyway. It truly had been a dubious and desperate idea, yet somehow the act of allowing him to view her dishabille, though it hadn't resulted in a physical seduction, had brought them closer, almost as though they had become co-conspirators, or intimates. Although he had declined her offer, Mary's attempted seduction had not been in vain.

She told Conrad of their plan to buy a farm and eventually bring their parents to Ecuador to start a new life, and teared up when she spoke more about the loss of the family property on Orcas Island.

As Mary talked Conrad thought of how he could convince his superior that his search for the Murphy's had led to a dead end; and beyond that, how he could somehow feed his office information that would prevent any other agent from following up and discovering their whereabouts.

Someone was definitely tailing him. He hadn't seen the man again, but he felt sure he hadn't evaded him. The two FBI agents might also still be involved. Conrad had no idea if his office was exchanging intelligence with them, or if they had been taken off the case. He understood that Hiram Hatcher had been the focus of their investigation, and he might yet lead them to the Murphys.

All too soon, for Conrad was enjoying his tete-a-tete with Mary, they heard the gate open. Liam and Simon were surprised to find their sister seated with the stranger, and were suspicious and alarmed.

"Who's your friend, Mary?" Liam asked.

"Are we friends now Conrad?"

Mary and Conrad exchanged a look that seemed to the brothers to indicate they were at least well acquainted.

"My name is Conrad Slocum. I've been looking for you for quite some time—glad to finally meet you."

He stood, offering his hand; a tall, lean, fit man, who might pass for forty, though he was a decade older.

Simon took his hand, then Liam. Liam tried the hard, dominant grip that some tough men like to employ. Conrad returned a quick, matching pulse that took Liam by surprise, and he quickly let go. As Liam stepped back he noticed a bulge under the man's shirt, and correctly assumed that Conrad carried a pistol in a belly band holster.

"Please, sit down, and let's talk," Conrad said. "I've heard your sister's version of events. I know that Jim Lothar suggested the plan, and that Hiram was only involved because of Mary. I was assigned the task of tracking you down, arresting the three of you, and bringing you back to Alaska for prosecution. Jim Lothar is on the loose once again. He escaped in Mexico City."

"Do you plan to arrest us on your own? Let's see your ID. Where's your backup?" Liam said. He still stood, menacingly glowering at Conrad.

"We have other agents in this country, and the Ecuadorian government is very cooperative. Quid pro quo, we sometimes do them small favors. The legality doesn't figure into it. The government here simply looks away while my organization goes about its business. Yes, normally I would have a partner in this situation—

if I had come prepared to make an arrest today. That's not the case. Sit down Liam, and listen to what I have to say."

The way Conrad spoke those last words, the memory of that quick, forceful handshake, and the knowledge that the agent was armed convinced Liam it would be fruitless to pick a fight. He sensed this was no mere barroom brawler, and he was suddenly not so sure of his ability to best the man if it came to blows. In any case, if not this agent, someone else would come for them. Liam sat down.

"Let me start by saying I have decided not to arrest you, and I have not reported your whereabouts to any law enforcement agency."

Simon gave his sister a knowing look. Her bikini top left almost nothing to the imagination. He grinned at her and shook his head.

"Knock it off, Simon! It's not what you think, you jerk!" Mary said.

"Rest assured your sister's honor remains inviolate. It is a warm day, and in fact I find myself overdressed for the occasion, as well as thirsty. Do you have any more beer, Mary?" Conrad asked. "How about a round for us all."

"Your sister is indeed quite fetching, but I assure you she has not compromised herself for the sake of your freedom," Conrad said after Mary left to get the drinks.

"I've learned a lot about your family since I began the search for you, and Mary has been filling in the gaps in my knowledge."

When Mary returned with the beers she had replaced the bikini top with a much less revealing Sea Shepherd t-shirt. She had been an active advocate and volunteer for the organization, which had their headquarters on San Juan Island, just a few miles from the Murphy family home on neighboring Orcas Island.

"That's the last of the brews. If you want to keep drinking we'll have to switch to something stronger or go buy some more."

"Besides protecting your privacy, I have another problem—Hiram Hatcher," Conrad continued.

"He desperately wants to find you, or at least Mary."

"I don't understand. We've committed a serious crime, and though you haven't said who you work for, you say you were sent to arrest us. Why do you want to help us?" Simon wondered.

"I'm not sure I can explain my reasons in a way you would find believable. I could say that I'm a natural born iconoclast, and that I sympathize with your motivation; or that no one was really harmed, and the railroad's bottom line won't be affected by losing that amount of money; or even that I just don't want to see you all locked up for a crime of passion—love of the home you lost. All of that is true, but I have other more personal reasons as well."

Conrad's sense of morality owed much to his understanding of ancient conceptions of balance, personified by the the furies and other demigods of Greek mythology. He believed that the Murphy siblings were justified in seeking redress for their loss, legally or otherwise. Additionally, since finding love with Linda Daise Conrad was especially sympathetic to the plight of Mary and Hiram. He knew that life was love and loss. Love was often fleeting, and loss final.

"I think the lyrics of that old song explain my motivation as well as anything. 'The world will always welcome lovers, as time goes by.' So I guess I'm just a sentimental fool who would like to see Mary and Hiram reunited."

"You must want something in exchange," Simon insisted. "A share of the money?"

"No, I've got enough for my needs. My job pays well, and has its perks. There is something I would like, though. While Mary and I were talking she told me how your family originally came by the property on Orcas Island, and how you lost it, and was about to show me some documents before you arrived. I would like to see those. I have a friend who is an authority on Alaskan history. He would be very interested in seeing your family papers, and I hope you will allow me to photograph them."

"Can we trust your historian friend?" Simon asked.

"That's beside the point. He doesn't know about you yet, but sooner or later your names will come out in the news, as Jim Lothar will certainly incriminate you at his trial—when and if he's found. It doesn't matter what my historian friend or anyone else learns about you, as long as they don't know where to find you."

"I don't see why not," Mary said. "After all, we were originally going to release the information to the press, before we got involved with Jim."

"It's okay by me," Liam agreed.

"You're a strange one Mr. Slocum. An officer of the law with a penchant for history, who doesn't seem to be very loyal to his employer," Simon replied.

"I'm an intelligence agent. Gathering information is my job and my passion. That's certainly no odder than an aspiring writer and lover of Nabokov who plots extortion as a hobby."

"As soon as I saw your nom de guerre on the passenger list, 'Sirin Quilty,' I knew I had you. You're lucky one of the ticketing officers wasn't more familiar with Nabokov."

"You've got me there," Simon replied, laughing. "I'll go dig those papers out. If you want to take photos, the light's better out here."

CHAPTER 39

Jesse's Confession

Simon returned from the house with a thin, brown leather attache case. He first showed Conrad the faded deed Jesse Murphy had been given to the acreage on Orcas Island, signed in Skagway and dated 1898. Then he carefully extracted a hand written document that Jesse had dictated to his daughter before he died.

"Grandma wrote in a very elegant cursive, so the original is easy to read, and she also made a typed copy," Simon explained. "She told us she wrote it down as near as she could to how he related it to her."

I'm not long for this world, and I mean to set the record straight before I go. I ain't too proud of what I done, but I was young, and I suppose foolish. Anyways I weren't no friend of Soapy's, and I just done what others were too scared to do.

Everyone knows or thinks they know about how Soapy died, killed by Frank Reid. Frank weren't no angel neither. He killed a man down in Oregon, and everyone in Skagway knew he was a crooked bartender.

I'll allow Soapy may have even been the better man, but me and Frank, and a lot of other people in town could see the railroad was the future, and Soapy's bunco days were done. Hell, I think Soapy knew it too. Rumor was he planned to make as much money as he could that summer, then head back to his family and take up the life of a respectable gentleman. I think that's why he bought that schooner, "Janus" from captain Bright on July 8, the very day he died. That's how he planned to make his getaway. But as it turned out, that's how I made mine.

I will go to meet my maker soon. I ain't never been much of a church-goer. I ain't even sure if there is a heaven nor hell, but I'm damn sure that if there is, it's not like any of them preacher-men describe. Maybe Soapy's down there playing the bunco games still, or maybe he's just bones in that Skagway graveyard. It don't matter one way or the other. I'll grant a lot of folks don't care about the facts either, but I'll tell 'em anyhow.

How it's been told is that Frank Reid and Soapy had a shoot-out on the Skagway dock, and they both died of their wounds—Soapy quick and clean, and Frank in a lingerin', painful sort of way. But Frank didn't kill Soapy, I did, and if there's a judgement in the hereafter I guess I'll pay for it. Soapy was a-layin' there bleedin' and I grabbed his own rifle out of his hands and shot him straight through the heart as he lay there defenseless. I told a few people the truth, but the railroad men and their lawyers hushed that up, and hustled me out of town.

The railroad folks lied; the doctors lied; the lawyers lied; and the press lied. But a few of us knowed the truth. Captain Bright lied too—said Soapy never paid him for the schooner. The railroad people paid him and his crew to get me the hell out of Skagway, and they gave me this here property on Orcas Island to disappear and keep my mouth shut.

It was a terrible voyage. It seemed like even old Neptune was out to punish us for our deeds. I've never seen storms and seas like that again, though I've fished on the ocean many a year since. But we finally made it down here to Washington, and the rest my family knows.

As I lay here with nothing left to loose, I'll swear on any book you want me too that I'm telling the truth, so help me God.

"Grandma knew Jesse had tried years earlier to get the press to publish his story, but the newspapers he contacted weren't interested, or didn't believe him. Grandma didn't know what to do with his confession and the deed, so she just locked them up in the safe. We found the papers when we were helping mom and dad move," Mary said.

"That's remarkable. Why didn't you try to go public with this? You surely would have gotten a better reception than your great grandfather did, and there are more media options now than during his time."

"We couldn't agree on what to do, so when Jim Lothar came up with his plan, I took it upon myself to go with that," Simon explained.

"Mary is the only one that really objected," Liam confessed. "I got sucked in too."

"I'm sure the museums, historians and Soapy's descendants would love to see these documents, but they will have to have the originals. Now that you've got the money to do what you want, they're of no use to you except as family mementos, and copies might serve as well. These papers should be in the Skagway museum," Conrad said, after he had photographed the documents.

"We thought of that too, but they seem too valuable to send by mail. They might be lost or stolen. Anyway the postmark would give away our location," Mary replied.

"That won't be a problem if I take the papers back with me. One of the perks of my job is that my luggage is never searched by customs or immigration. In any case these papers won't be of much interest to law enforcement."

"That seems less risky, and reasonable if you're willing," Simon replied.

"Then you're absolutely not going to arrest us, or turn us over to some other officer?" Liam asked, incredulously.

"No, but I hope you won't make a habit of extortion. Some other investigator might figure out where you are. I know two FBI men were on your trail, and it's always possible that someone else from my agency may have been assigned to find you without my knowledge."

"That must be the two FBI men the bagpiper at St. James Bay told us about," Simon said.

"When I left Alaska those two were looking for Hiram in Canada, but I haven't been privy to their movements since then. I'll do my best to throw the investigators off your scent, but if were you, I would stay alert. It takes money and manpower to continue investigating a case like yours, and you're a pretty low priority compared to some of our others. I do expect interest will fade quickly as more pressing matters demand our time and resources."

"I guess that's somewhat reassuring," Mary said.

"What about your boyfriend? Has Hiram contacted you recently?"

"He called from Seattle while we were in the Caribbean, but we haven't heard from him since then. I told him we were bound for Ecuador. I'm worried he's been caught, or something happened to him."

Conrad noticed Simon smiled and glanced at his brother, who covered his mouth and suppressed a cough.

"I would know if the law had caught up with him. My guess is he is just being very cautious. The kind of man who can survive in the wilderness of the Ferebee Valley is certainly capable of finding his way here. He's probably traveling by land, perhaps by bus and train. I don't think he'll risk flying. One thing I do know is that wily papillon has not lost the scent of his bonny Irish butterfly, and I suspect he'll eventually find you, Mary," Conrad reassured her.

When evening came they continued their conversation indoors. It was nearly midnight before Conrad left the house and walked back to his hotel, a few blocks away across from the restaurant and marina.

CHAPTER 40

Complications

As Conrad drew near the Bahia Hotel he felt his cell phone vibrate.

"Conrad? It's Ted—the bartender."

"Yes, it's me. What's up?"

"A man left the bar a few minutes ago who was asking about Mary and her brothers. I thought I should let you know."

"What did you tell him? Did he say who he was?"

"He told me he was looking for two men and a woman. He had their names right, and said he was an old friend of the family. I thought it pretty strange that two American friends of the Murphys would show up here the same day, so I played dumb. But I'm not an idiot. Are they in some kind of trouble?"

"Look, Ted. I don't have time to explain, but Mary and her brothers are in danger. Can you describe the man? Did he say anything else?"

As he spoke Conrad crossed the street and walked over to the small parking lot behind the Puerto Amistad marina and restaurant.

"He told me he was staying across the street at the Bahia Hotel—same place you are! He gave me his phone number and said to call him if I happened to see them. Frankly, he made me nervous. I don't think he believed me. He was a big man—not as tall as you, but he had the look of a bodybuilder or wrestler. He wore dark glasses and a Panama hat."

"Okay, thanks Ted. You were right to call me. This man is no friend of theirs, but don't worry, I'm sure I can convince him he'd be better off leaving them alone."

Conrad pocketed his phone. He edged quietly around the luxuriant hedge-like mix of native tropical shrubs and trees that screened the back of the building from the outdoor eating area and street. A man stood next to a mud-caked Yamaha TW200 motorcycle with well worn saddle bags and a Mexican license plate. Conrad recognized Hiram Hatcher.

"That bike would certainly be one of my top choices for a long road trip through Central America," Conrad said.

"Yeah, it never failed me, and I really put it through hell. They haven't changed anything since they first started making these back in 1987. I picked this one up in Mexico City for $500 bucks. It's a 1989, but it only had a couple thousand miles on it," Hiram replied.

"That must have been quite a ride. I hope to hear the tale before I leave. But I imagine you are in a hurry to reunite with Mary. How did you find her? She told me she hadn't heard from you for weeks."

"She hasn't. Her brothers and I want it to be a surprise. I lost my cell phone, but bought a new one in Mexico. Mary and her brothers were sharing the same phone, but Simon had it in Panama, and he answered when I called. He told me Mary and Liam had leased a house here in Bahia."

"How did you get around the Darian Gap with your motorcycle?"

It wasn't easy to arrange, but I finally got myself and the bike on a charter boat for a reasonable fee, thanks to a chance meeting with some American sailors."

As they talked a man appeared, walking towards the parking lot along the short sidewalk that led from the restaurant entrance. He was wearing sunglasses and a Panama hat. As he drew closer he pulled a pistol from a chest holster and aimed it at Hiram.

"I don't think you need the gun. The two of us should be able to handle him. Did my boss send you, or are you working for the FBI?" Conrad asked the man.

"Ha! You government guys can't find your dicks in the dark without help. That's why certain other interested parties hired me. I'll handle things from here. I hear Lothar's on the loose, thanks to your incompetence. I'm not going to let you screw up with Hatcher or the Murphy clan."

"So you're a bounty hunter. How much is your employer paying you? I imagine the Murphys would be willing to beat that."

"I'm no bounty hunter. I work for Securitas, and we don't negotiate with criminals."

Conrad knew the huge Stockholm based firm had bought the Pinkerton Agency in 1999. Obviously the railroad or one of their primary stockholders or officials had hired the company. The man shifted his aim, and Conrad backed away slowly.

"Pinkerton man, eh? I've worked with a couple of your colleagues—generally pretty competent, I've found. But how do you propose to get four people back to the states by yourself?"

"That's not your concern. But since you asked, I have access to sufficient funds to ensure I'll have help from the locals when I need it."

Conrad guessed that although the detective had followed Hiram this far, he hadn't yet located the Murphys. He decided to feign cooperation, and try to get back to the Murphy's house to warn the siblings ahead of the man.

"It sounds like you've got things in hand," Conrad said. "You must know you're on pretty thin legal ice without my help, but have it your way."

"Hold it right there," the man said, as Conrad started to walk away.

"Put your sidearm down on the ground nice and easy. I don't relish the idea of you following me."

"Now why would I do that? We both want the same thing—to get the Murphys and Hatcher back to the states, and to return the money to the railroad. You're making my job easier. This frees me to try to locate Jim Lothar."

"Securitas already has a better man on that, and your services are no longer needed or welcome. We know Hiram has been living with you and your hot-shot lawyer girlfriend in Juneau. You're more than compromised. Your loyalties are suspect. If you really want to help me out, tell me where the Murphys are holed up."

"I've had no communication from my office instructing me to share intelligence with Securitas agents."

"Nor am I obliged in any way to you. Regardless, I'm telling you for the last time—put your sidearm on the ground, and walk away from here."

This time Conrad complied.

"Now, Mr Hatcher, it's time for you to take me to meet your girlfriend and her brothers."

"I can't seem to recall where they live just now," Hiram said.

"Maybe this will jog your memory."

The detective slammed the butt of his pistol against the side of Hiram's head. Hiram fell hard against the motorcycle, knocking it over. Conrad lunged forward, and tackled the agent. The detective lost his grip on his pistol as they fell together.

The Securitas officer was tremendously strong. Although he fought with all his skill, the heavier man pulled free and hit Conrad with a blow that sent him reeling. Conrad realized he was up against a more powerful foe, and only guile, luck, or Hiram's help would give him the upper hand. Hiram was upright, but still leaned against the overturned motorcycle. Conrad moved backwards to gain time while he desperately parried the detective's blows as the man came on.

Hiram had been momentarily dazed, but quickly recovered. When he got to his feet he could see that Conrad was struggling to fend off the ferocious punches of the bulkier man. He drew his six inch hunting knife from the sheath strapped to his leg.

The detective connected with a jab to Conrad's cheek, and followed it up immediately with a second, harder punch to his solar plexus that doubled him over. While Conrad recovered the detective bent down to retrieve his gun. Hiram rushed over and plunged the knife to the hilt into the officer's back. The man made an effort to turn and face this new threat, before crumpling to the ground. Blood flowed from the wound. The Securitas detective crawled forward slowly for several feet, then twitched briefly and was still.

"Are you all right, Conrad?" Hiram asked.

"I'm doing better than he is, at least," Conrad replied. "Is he dead?"

"If he isn't he's pretty good at playing possum," Hiram replied.

Conrad quickly went through the man's pockets, taking his wallet, cell phone, and the keys to his hotel room and rental car. The wallet contained the man's ID, two credit cards and nearly a thousand dollars in cash.

"He wasn't lying about working for Securitas," Conrad said. "I know a little something about Pinkerton history. Henry Julian was the name of a Pinkerton agent who chased a suspect to Peru, then kidnapped him and brought him back to the states. It's an appropriate alias for our unfortunate shamus. How's your head feeling, Hiram?"

I could use a couple of aspirin, but I'll live. What do you suggest now?"

"We need to make it look like he was robbed. Help me move him," Conrad insisted.

Together the two men drug the corpse down to the beach. Conrad threw the bounty hunter's gun into the sea, and they rolled the body into the water.

"That's the best we can do. They'll discover the body tomorrow, but without identification the police will just have a gringo John Doe on their hands. We're lucky it's so late and no one seems to be around."

"What about the bartender?" Hiram asked.

"Did you talk to him much?"

"I got here so late I decided not to call Mary until tomorrow morning. I had a snack and a beer at the bar. I asked the bartender about a place to stay tonight. He suggested the hotel across the street, but no one was in the lobby, and the sign at the counter said no vacancy. I was getting ready to go look for another hotel when you showed up."

"You're sure that's all the information you gave him?"

"We just made small talk. I said my name was Herbert Wells. I'm learning to be pretty wary. I told him I was a tourist from Seattle. I didn't say anything about being on a motorcycle or having any friends here."

"Still, the local police will check out the restaurant and hotel, and find the blood in this parking lot. I've got a flight out of Guayaquil tomorrow, so I'll say goodbye and good luck for now. It's almost two AM," Conrad continued, looking at his watch.

"I suggest you get over to the Murphy's house and wake them up—never mind the time. Not only will Mary be ecstatic to see you, but you need to tell them to be on their guard, and make sure your stories agree if you're questioned."

"I don't know how to thank you and Linda. I feel bad about leaving Juneau like that, but I just couldn't stay any longer."

"I get it. But I'm the one that owes you now. I have no doubt that Mr. Julian would not have hesitated to do whatever he thought necessary to get rid of me. My employer's relationship with Securitas has always been problematic. Let's get going before some random drunk or early riser sees us. I have Simon's phone number, give me yours and I'll be in touch tomorrow."

Hiram put on his helmet and backpack, picked up his motorcycle, and rode away. Conrad walked back to his hotel. The lobby was empty. He looked forward to getting a couple of hours of sleep, but before going to bed he searched the detective's room.

The man certainly traveled light. His small suitcase contained only essential clothing and toiletries, but buried under the clothing he found a business card and another cell phone.

The phone was an ordinary flip open model, and unencrypted. Conrad read a series of text exchanges between the detective and his employer. In all the texts between them Hiram Hatcher was referred to as the "fox," and the Murphy siblings as "crows." The last text from Henry Julian to the number had been sent the day before.

"Suspect Fox and crows may be in Ecuador will update soon"

Conrad keyed in a message to the same number and hit send.

"Fox and crow on bus to Bolivia following more later."

CHAPTER 41

Paul Sherman

Paul Sherman, the man who had originally recruited Conrad Slocum in 1973 when he was an expatriate draft dodger in Kabul, Afghanistan sat across from Conrad in the cabin of his sailboat, docked at the Juneau marina. Paul had aged some since the last time he had seen him several years earlier, Conrad noted, but he was still a, trim, movie star handsome man, who did not look or move like a man in his mid seventies. Paul had risen through the ranks, and for the last fifteen years had held the top position in the Agency. He reported directly to the Secretary of State, and had advised the last three presidents.

"What a beautiful boat, Conrad. I wish I had time to go sailing with you," Paul remarked.

"Why not? You're the boss, after all," Conrad replied.

"Ironically, in our line work, the higher your position, the less freedom you seem to have. I've got a plane to catch this afternoon, and an appointment with a senator tomorrow."

"That's a shame. It's a beautiful day. It doesn't get any nicer in Juneau in May."

"Well perhaps we can make it happen the next time I'm out this way. I miss this place. Washington D.C. is claustrophobic. As you know I grew up in the Northwest too, and I still own that little cabin over in Eastern Oregon, but I haven't been there in years."

Paul Sherman had never married, and had no children. Early in his career he had decided it would be unfair to have a family. Paul had begun his career with the Agency during the Cold War, and had served as an intelligence agent in more than twenty countries. Although his nominal home base had been the Capitol, he was often gone for months at a time. He liked to travel, and spent as much time as he could away from his desk.

"By the way, I appreciate you taking the time to stop and check in on my place now and then. I think I still owe you for that maintenance work you did a couple of years ago."

"I think that debt is more than cancelled by the rent free vacation I got. That week on the John Day River was almost as nice as my time in Hawaii."

"I don't have to tell you that is an awkward subject, and your recent failure to round up the persons responsible for the death of agent Dolon and the extortion plot has not helped your standing in the Agency."

"I imagine not. Maybe it's time for me to try another line of work."

"I'm not letting you off that easily, Conrad. Jack Dolon was a wolf, and you are a catamount. We have need of both. The wolf is most effective working in a pack, and the cougar hunts alone. The fact is, only a half a dozen of our agents are fluent in Pushtu, and none of them have the experience in Central Asia that you do. Ironically, in spite of your recent less than stellar efforts, I've come here not to censure you, but to give you another promotion, albeit one that comes with more responsibility, and perhaps a greater element of personal danger."

"I was just promoted last year. It seems that in spite of my recalcitrance I flourish."

"As you know since 9-11 our budget has burgeoned. We are recruiting and hiring at a rate I haven't seen since the Cold War. Some of the promotions I'm doling out are well earned and overdue, some are favors to a few especially loyal employees who have helped me on my rise through the ranks, and a couple are purely personal in nature. You fall into the last category."

"I'm thankful in advance, but you've done enough for me already. I can't see why I deserve any special attention," Conrad demurred.

"In fact your position might not be completely secure in spite of my efforts to protect you. I've had all the evidence Richard Head and the late Jack Dolon found that implicated you in the death of Grant Tadlock destroyed, but I can't purge it from Richard's memory. Jim Lothar, who is still at large, could also be a threat. I've done all I can, but others in the Agency may know of the DNA evidence that proves you are Marshall Stuckrath's father."

"I'm profoundly in your debt. I'm guessing this has something to do with Dick's promotion, and my move to Juneau."

"Yes. Richard and I came to an understanding. That was only an interim promotion, in return for him giving up all the incriminating evidence he had gathered about you. But there's more. I'm transferring him to the Texas headquarters."

"That's a real relief. I don't how I can ever repay you for that."

"You can't. Even though you don't get along with Richard, the Agency needs him. He's an adequate if not outstanding supervisor, but far more important is his connection to the senator, who has been instrumental in getting our remarkable budget increase. Besides, I can't have our agents neutralizing each other, and I suspect that if Richard is not kept busy with other matters things could get out of hand. I'm not going to mince words with you, Conrad. I know what you're capable of doing if threatened. I know because we're alike in that way."

"I don't know what to say, except thank you, Paul."

"There are, regrettably for you, strings attached. You will accept a promotion to Richard Head's present position as head of the Northwest region. This is not negotiable. I'm sorry about the timing. I know you're living with Linda Daise. I hope you understand that after I retire, which I hope to do while I'm still in decent health, I won't be in a position to protect you anymore.

I know love trumps everything, but it can sometimes lead to serious lapses of judgement, and disaster."

Conrad could think of no response to Paul's demand. It wasn't the first time Paul had gone to bat for him. There was no way he could refuse.

"Look, it won't be all that bad. You'll have more paid leave and freedom than in your present position. With the bigger budget you can delegate much of the tedious desk work to your expanded staff. You won't even have to come to the office every day. I understand Ms. Daise practiced law for a time in Seattle. Maybe she would be willing to do that again."

"I'm afraid she's a real Alaskan girl, and her position in Juneau is way better than when she was just an underling in that big Seattle firm, taking all the cases the other lawyers didn't want. But I understand, and it's not your problem. I guess we'll work it out somehow. How soon do I need to be in Seattle?"

"Richard Head starts at his Texas office the first Monday in August. You'll need at least a week before he leaves to get oriented."

"That leaves me half the summer in Juneau, unless we find out where Lothar is, and I have to bring him in."

"Yes, you are still in charge of that investigation—at least until Lothar, Hatcher, and the Murphy's are found, or until you take over Richard's position. Then you'll have to give the assignment to someone else. You'll be concerned with far more important matters."

"...more important than extortion and a terrorist threat to the tourist industry?"

"You'll get all the details when you take over Richard's job, but here's the situation, in brief. In the past you have worked with the expatriate Afghan communities in the bay area and Seattle. Several emigres we recruited from among them have consistently contributed valuable intelligence. Their hatred for the Taliban and its methods has made them especially dedicated and effective agents for nearly two decades. Recently we lost two of our best."

"Lost—as in quit, or killed?"

"While you were enjoying your Caribbean and South American tour two agents died the same week under suspicious circumstances."

"So killed, then."

"That's our assumption. One was the victim of a hit and run accident while jogging. The driver has not been identified or located. The other, I am sad to tell you is a woman you know from your time in Kabul, Reshtina Butler. She was strangled a few days later in her Bellingham home. The local police think she was the target of a burglary, but her husband doesn't think so, and neither do Richard or I.

"That's terrible news. I haven't seen either Dennis or Reshtina for several years.. The last I knew Dennis ran a small construction company, and their daughter was a schoolteacher in Bellingham. We never talked about it, but I assume Dennis knew his wife was one of our agents. I occasionally saw Reshtina at the Seattle office, and even worked with her on a case a few years back. She was an exceptional woman."

Conrad thought back to his time in Afghanistan, and that eventful summer of 1973. Reshtina had married Dennis Butler, a Peace Corps Volunteer, to escape a horrific future in a forced marriage. Both Paul and Conrad had helped her escape the country and her fiancé.

"I can guess what you're probably thinking. The man Reshtina was supposed to marry, Sartor, was and continues to be a supporter of the Taliban. He has provided money and arms regularly to them in the past, and we assume he still does. Could he be behind Reshtina's murder, after all these years? I suppose that's possible. Vengeance is a powerful motive, as you well know," Paul said, locking eyes with Conrad. "But that does not explain why the other agent was killed."

"You will inherit this investigation when you take over from Richard at the Seattle headquarters. I'm hoping you'll be more motivated to resolve this case than the one you've been working on the last few months."

After Conrad dropped Paul Sherman off at the Juneau airport he drove back to Linda Daise's house. Linda was still at work. He did not look forward to telling her he would be moving back to Seattle later that summer. He poured himself a double shot of Irish whiskey, although it was hours before his normal pre-dinner libation.

1579

Captain Francis Drake sailed from England in December of 1577 with five ships and one hundred sixty-four men, but only Drake's flagship, the *Golden Hind* and its compliment of about eighty men continued on past the Straits of Magellan. Drake sailed up the coast of South America, engaging or evading the Spanish on his way north at the wily captain's pleasure. Near the equator, off the coast of Ecuador he captured the *Cacafuego*, a Spanish ship loaded with silver, gold, and other treasure. The ship was so heavy with booty that Drake replaced some of the *Golden Hind's* ballast with twenty-six tons of silver bars from the prize.

Drake continued his voyage north, exploring and mapping the western shores of California and the Pacific Northwest. Before finally turning southwest to cross the Pacific in the harsh winter of 1579, Drake and his crew ventured among the maze of islands, inlets, straits, and fjords of British Columbia and Southeast Alaska. They sailed up the wide southern entrance of Chatham Strait in 1579, which Drake concluded was the opening to the fabled Northwest Passage, the Strait of Anian.

It was an exceptionally cold year, near the start of the Grindelwald Fluctuation, a period of below normal temperatures and rapid growth of glaciation in North America and Europe. There were icebergs in the strait, many large enough to sink their ship. The men battled the ice and frost that coated the decks and rigging, froze fingers, and made the vessel dangerously top-heavy. They could go no further safely in the flagship. They took refuge in Port Malmesbury on Kuiu Island, which Drake named "Discovery Bay." Captain Drake's crew then put together their pinnace, a small sailboat which had been specially designed and constructed to be stowed aboard the flagship in pieces for reassembly as needed.

While Drake and the bulk of his crew repaired worn sails and rigging on the Golden Hind, and hunted for game in the forest, he directed several of his men to take the pinnace further up the strait to determine if it continued on as he hoped, or ended, and how far it was ice free and navigable. The pinnace was far more maneuverable than the flagship, and was capable of dodging the icebergs that floated in the channel. It also drew much less water than the nine feet of the *Golden Hind*, allowing it to sail closer to land.

The pinnace was equipped with a small cannon mounted at the bow, and its crew were well supplied with a variety of firearms, including harquebuses, and snap lock and matchlock pistols and muskets. The captain of the pinnace was from a wealthy family, and carried an expensive German made wheel lock or "puffer" pistol. In addition the crew could don leather and chain mail armor for protection, and each had a sword and dagger for hand to hand combat.

But though well armed and seasoned fighters, the small crew of the pinnace was vastly outnumbered by the dozens of Tlingit warriors who attacked them while they were anchored their first night out, only a few miles distant in Thetis Cove. Drake's men fought furiously, using the canon and their muskets effectively to keep the natives at a distance. They weighed anchor and set sail in an attempt to return to the protection of the flagship's big cannons, but an errant spark from one of the harquebuses started a fire in the rigging which rapidly spread to the sails and engulfed the pinnace in flames.

Most of the crew jumped into the water where they drowned or were killed by the Tlingit warriors. Just two men, the captain of the pinnace and his armorer managed to launch the pinnace's dinghy and row to shore. Two young Tlingit warriors who had come late to the scene in a smaller canoe were the only ones to see them. They gave chase and quickly overtook the Englishmen, who were slowed by the weight of their armor and weapons.

The natives were quicker, but the Englishmen were more experienced fighters. Back to back they held off the two attackers with agile use of their swords until the armorer slipped and fell. One of the Tlingit warriors quickly dispatched the armorer with a spear through the neck, while the captain of the pinnace disabled his assailant with a sword thrust into the man's abdomen. Then, seeing there was nothing he could do for his fellow crewman, he ran for the protection of the forest. But the warrior who had killed the armorer withdrew his spear from his victim, and threw it at the fleeing Englishman. The pinnace captain fell, the copper spearhead and several inches of the shaft buried in his side.

The captain of the pinnace was mortally wounded, but still had fight left in him. He lay unmoving on the ground until the Tlingit warrior came close, then suddenly lunged with his sword. The warrior backed away, parrying the Englishman's thrusts, thinking he could tire out the wounded man. But the captain was an expert swordsman, and his skill eventually prevailed. Even in his wounded state, and hampered by the spear embedded in his side, the desperate captain fought like the wounded animal he was, finally killing his attacker with quick jab following a feint, in a classic sword fighting move he had perfected many years and bouts earlier.

Panting and bleeding, the Englishman watched from the shore as the pinnace sank in the shallows until only the flaming top of the mast was visible. That flickering glow illuminated canoes packed with Tlingit warriors whooping with the joy of victory as they circled the wreck. The Englishman moved to the cover of the forest, where he used his knife to cut the spear shaft shorter. He realized he was finished, but he had no desire to die at the hands of the Indians. He knew they would torture him to death as vengeance for the loss of their fellows, or keep him as a slave if he survived.

Finally, weak with loss of blood and exhausted from his efforts, he found a shallow cave, and lay down to die. Later torrential rains flooded the cave with mud and debris, covering the explorer until his remains were discovered over four centuries later by Jim Lothar and Craig Martes.

While the crew attended to maintenance on the *Golden Hind* the Tlingit natives, at first friendly and interested in trading with the strangers, began to harass the Englishmen, stealing what they could, and attacking foraging crew members. Drake and his crew heard the reports of the cannon and small arms as the crew of the pinnace fought the Tlingit warriors a few miles away, but by the time he gathered his men together and sailed into Thetis Bay the battle was lost, the pinnace destroyed, and its crew dead or lost.

After the *Golden Hind* sunk one of the Tlingit canoes with a well placed cannon shot, the natives quickly dispersed and paddled away. Drake's men retrieved the body of the armorer from the beach. They would bury him at sea later as custom demanded, rather than leave him to the natives. Captain Drake assumed all the rest of the men, including the wounded captain of the pinnace, had drowned or been killed.

Drake gave up the idea of following the wide strait northeast to see if it ended, or was truly the fabled northwest passage that so many cartographers had drawn on their maps of the world. He needed to get south to a warmer and more secure harbor to prepare the *Golden Hind* for the voyage across the Pacific, and back home to England.

Unlike Magellan, who died before his bedraggled wreck of a flagship limped home captained by his second in command, Drake would return to England in glory—a hero with a hold full of pirated Spanish treasure for himself and his queen, Elizabeth.

<u>N O T E S   A N D   A C K N O W L E D G E M E N T S</u>

The rise and fall of Jefferson "Soapy" Smith is one of the great stories of the Old West. By far the most authoritative and complete biography of Soapy is "Alias Soapy Smith" by his great grandson, Jeff Smith. It is an absolute must read for anyone interested in the life of the famous bunco man, and the history of Skagway.

Not much is known about the enigmatic Jesse Murphy, who was without a doubt the actual killer of Soapy Smith. Jeff Smith and this author are hopeful that more information about him will surface in the future. Until that time he remains an intriguing character, and it is fun to speculate, as I have in this novel, about what sort of reward he was offered for his service to the Citizen's Committee.

Jeff Smith also maintains a fascinating and informative website.

<u>https://www.soapysmith.net</u>

Sir Francis Drakes's circumnavigation of the globe from 1577-1580 is shrouded in mystery. Since Drake's log of the voyage has been lost, and he and his crew were sworn to secrecy by Queen Elizabeth, information about the voyage is sparse and not always reliable.

"The Secret Voyage of Sir Francis Drake" by Samuel Bawlf reads like a great seafaring mystery novel. Every chapter contains fascinating research and revelations about Drake's remarkable voyage. I find many of Bawlf's arguments and conclusions compelling, or at least plausible.

Although my postscript is fictional, it was inspired by Bawlf's conclusion that Drake sailed up Chatham Strait and dropped anchor in one of the southern Kuiu Island bays.
https://www.goodreads.com/book/show/2615089-the-secret-voyage-of-sir-francis-drake-1577-1580

Chapter 2.

The Dyea flood of July.23, 2002 was referenced from a 2018 BLM study.

https://www.blm.gov/documents/national-office/blm-library/report/field-investigation-glacial-lake-outburst-potential

Chapter 29.

The story of the two cougar sightings was reported on the front page of the September 13, 2002 issue of The Skagway News. Vol. XXV No. 17

ABOUT THE AUTHOR

Author, playwright, and musician Michael Rostron was born and raised in Oregon, and spent over twenty-five years in Alaska. He now lives in Northwest Washington State, just a few miles from the Canadian border. His website can be found at mikerostron.com